To Robin, for the months of literally backbreaking work tightening the plot until it was seaworthy, making Merrick even smarter, and keeping me focused on each character's motivations.

To Peter DeBrule, who started this whole thing by trying to cheer me up in 1989 with a proposed chain story about two guys who walk into a tavern, whom I named Royce and Hadrian.

And to the members of the fantasy blogging community, who took the time to look at a new author from a small press and wrote such great reviews. I am eternally grateful for your contributions in turning my dreams into reality.

Books in the Riyria Revelations

CONTENTS

CONTENTS

THE
SOUND

W i l

T R E N T

Lanksteer

Lingard

Dunmore

Niswalden River

Ervanon
G h e n t
Sheridan

Glamrendor   Dalfgren

Lake
Windermere

Melengar
Galilin Medford

Avempartha

Winds Abby

Windham
Chadwick

Amber
Heights

Sean Upland

The Lost Lands

Roe

Glouston

A V R Y N

Galewyr River

Elan Valley

W a r r i c

Colnora

A l b u r n

Aquesta

Caren
Rochelle

Ratibor

Bernum River

R h e n y d d

Kilnar

Vilan Hill

Vernes

G a l e a

M a r a n o n

Manzar

SHARON
SEA

D E L G O S

Vandon

T i e r r e

Dagastan
Bay

Tur Del Fur

DACCA

derlands

ERIVAN
elvenlands

Eastern coastline drawn
from ancient imperial text

N
W ——— E
S

BARAN
Archipeligo

GOBLIN
SEA

lls

non

• Rolandue
Wesbaden

CALIS

Gur Em

Mandalin •

Dur Guron

• Dagastan

GHAZEL
SEA

Elan

THE
EMERALD
STORM

Chapter 1

ASSASSIN

Merrick Marius fitted a bolt into the small crossbow before slipping the weapon beneath the folds of his cloak. Smoke-thin clouds drifted across the sliver of moon, leaving him and Central Square shrouded in darkness. Looking for movement he searched the filthy streets lined with ramshackle buildings, but found none. At this hour, the city was deserted.

Ratibor may be a pit, he thought, *but at least it is easy to work in.*

Conditions had improved with the Nationalists' recent victory. The Imperial guards were gone, and with them went the regular patrols. The town lacked even an experienced sheriff, as the new mayor refused to hire seasoned men or members of the military to administer so-called "law and order." She opted instead to make do with grocery clerks, shoemakers, and dairy farmers. Merrick found her actions ill-advised, but expected such mistakes from an inexperienced noble. Not that he was complaining—he appreciated the help.

Despite this shortcoming, he admired Arista Essendon's accomplishments. In Melengar, her brother, King Alric, reigned, and as an unwed princess, she possessed no real power. Then she came here and masterminded a revolt, and the surviving peasants rewarded her with the keys to the city. She was a foreigner and a royal, yet they thanked her for taking rule over them. *Brilliant.* He could not have done better himself.

A slight smile formed at the edge of Merrick's lips as he watched her from the street. A candle still burned on the second-floor of City Hall, even at this late hour. Her figure moved hazily behind the curtains as she left her desk.

It will not be long now, he thought.

Merrick shifted his grip on the weapon. Only a foot and a half long, with a bow span even shorter, it lacked the penetration strength of a traditional crossbow. Still, it would be enough. His target wore no armor, and he was not relying on the force of the bolt. Venden pox coated the serrated steel tip. A deplorable poison for assassination; it neither killed quickly nor paralyzed the victim. The concoction would certainly kill, but only after what he considered an unprofessional span of time. He had never used it before, and only recently learned of its most important trait—venden pox was invulnerable to magic. Merrick had it on good authority that the most powerful spells and incantations were useless against its venom. Given his target, this would prove essential.

Another figure entered Arista's room, and she sat abruptly. Merrick thought she had just received some interesting news and he was about to cross the street to listen at the window when the tavern door behind him opened. A pair of patrons exited, and by the sway of their steps and the volume of their voices they had obviously drained more than one mug that night.

"Nestor, who's that leaning against the post?" one said, pointing in Merrick's direction. A plump man with a strawberry nose whose shape matched its color squinted in the dim light and staggered forward.

"How should I know?" said the other. The thin man's mustache still glistened with beer foam.

"What's he doing here at this time 'a night?"

"Again, how should I know, you git?"

"Well, ask him."

The tall man stepped forward. "Whatcha doin', mister? Holding up the post so the porch doesn't fall down?" Nestor snorted a laugh and doubled over with his hands on his knees.

"Actually," Merrick told them, his tone so serious it was almost grave, "I'm waiting to appoint the position of Town Fool to the person who asks me the stupidest question. Congratulations. You win."

The thin man slapped his friend on the shoulder. "See, I've been telling you all night how funny I am, and you haven't laughed once. Now I'm getting a new job...probably pays better than yours."

"Oh, yeah, you're quite the entertainer," his friend assured him as they staggered off into the night. "You should audition at the theater. They're gonna be doing *The Crown Conspiracy* for the mayor. The day I see you on a stage—now *that* will be funny."

Merrick's mood turned sour. He had seen that play several years ago. While the two thieves depicted in it used different names, he knew they portrayed the exploits of Royce Melborn and Hadrian Blackwater. Royce was once Merrick's best friend, back when the two of them were assassins for the Diamond. That friendship ended seventeen years ago on that warm summer night when Royce murdered Jade.

Although he had not been present, Merrick had imagined the scene countless times. That was before Royce had his white dagger, back when he used a pair of curved, black-handled kharolls. Merrick knew Royce's technique well enough to picture him silently slicing through Jade with both blades at once. Merrick did not care that someone had set up Royce, or that he did not know his victim's identity when it happened. All Merrick knew was that the woman he loved was dead and his best friend had killed her.

Nearly two decades had passed, and still Jade and Royce haunted him. He could not think of one without the other, and he could not bear to forget. Love and hate welded together forever, intertwined in a knot too tight to untie.

Loud noises and shouts from Arista's room pulled Merrick back to the present. He checked his weapon, then crossed the street.

"Your Highness?" the soldier asked, entering the mayoral office.

Her hair a tangled mess and eyes wreathed in shadow, Princess Arista looked up from her cluttered desk. She took a moment to assess her visitor. The man in mismatched armor displayed an expression of unabated annoyance.

This is not going to go well, she thought.

"You sent for me?" he asked with only partially restrained irritation.

"Yes, Renquist," she said, her mind catching up with his face. She had hardly slept in two days and was having difficulty concentrating. "I asked you here to—"

"Princess, you can't be summoning me like this. I have an army to run and a war to win. I don't have time to chat."

"Chat? I wouldn't call you here if it wasn't important."

Renquist rolled his eyes.

"I need you to remove the army from the city."

"What?"

"It can't be helped. Your men are causing trouble. I'm getting daily reports of soldiers bullying merchants and destroying property.

There has even been an accusation of rape. You must take your men out of the city where they can be controlled."

"My men risked their lives against the Imperialists; the least this lousy city can do is feed them. Now you want me to take away their beds and the roof over their heads as well?"

"The merchants and farmers refuse to feed them because they can't," Arista explained. "The Empire confiscated the city's reserves when the Imperialists took control. The rains and the war destroyed most of this year's crops. The city doesn't have enough to feed its citizens, much less an army. Fall is here, and cold weather is on its way. These people don't know how they will survive the winter. They can't take care of themselves with a thousand soldiers raiding their shops and farms. We're thankful for your contribution in taking the city, but your continued presence threatens to destroy what you risked your lives to liberate. You must leave."

"If I force them back into camps with inadequate food and leaky canvas shelters, half will desert. As it is, many are talking of going home for the harvest season. I shouldn't have to tell you that if this army disappears, the Empire will take this city back."

Arista shook her head. "When Degan Gaunt was in charge, the Nationalist Army lived under similar conditions for months without it being a problem. The soldiers are becoming complacent here in Ratibor. Perhaps it is time you pressed on to Aquesta."

Renquist stiffened at the suggestion. "Gaunt's capture makes taking Aquesta all the more difficult. I need time to gather information and I'm waiting for reinforcements and supplies from Delgos. Attacking the capital won't be like taking Vernes or Ratibor. The Imperialists will fight to the last man to defend their empress. No. We need to stay here until I'm fully prepared."

"Wait if you must, but not here," she replied firmly.

"What if I refuse?" His eyes narrowed.

Arista put the parchments she was holding on the desk but said nothing.

"My army conquered this city," he told her pointedly. "You hold authority only because *I* allow it. I needn't take orders from you. You are not a princess here, and I am not your serf. My responsibility is to my men, not to this city and certainly not to you."

Arista slowly rose.

"I am the mayor of this city," she said, her voice growing in authority, "appointed by the people. Furthermore, I am steward and acting administrator of all of Rhenydd, again by the consent of the people. You and your army are here by *my* leave."

"You are a princess of Melengar! At least *I* was born in Rhenydd."

"Regardless of your personal feelings toward me, you will respect the authority of this office and do as I say."

"And if I don't?" he asked coldly.

Renquist's reaction did not surprise Arista. He was a career soldier who had served with King Urith, as well as the Imperial army, before joining the rebel Nationalists when Kilnar fell. When Gaunt disappeared, Renquist was appointed commander in chief, a position far higher in rank than he could ever have hoped for. He was finally realizing the power he possessed, and starting to assert himself. She had hoped he would demonstrate the same spirit Emery had shown, but Renquist was not a commoner with the heart of a nobleman. If she did not take action now, Arista would face a military overthrow.

"This city just liberated itself from one tyrant, and I won't allow it to fall under the heel of another. If you refuse to obey me, I'll replace you as commander."

"And how will you do that?"

Arista revealed a faint smile. "Think hard…I'm sure you can figure it out."

Renquist continued to stare at her; then his eyes widened in realization and fear flashed across his face.

"Yes," she told him, "the rumors about me are true. Now take your army out of the city before I feel a need to prove it. You have just one day to remove them. Scouts found a suitable valley to the north. I suggest you camp where the river crosses the road. It is far enough away to prevent further trouble. By heading north, your men will feel they are progressing toward the goal of Aquesta, thus helping morale."

"Don't tell me how to run my army," he snapped, although not as loudly, nor as confidently, as before.

"My apologies," she said, with a bow of her head. "It was only a suggestion. The order to leave the city, however, is not. Good evening to you, sir."

Renquist hesitated, his breath labored, his hands balled into fists.

"I said, good evening, sir."

He muttered a curse and slammed the door as he left.

Exhausted, Arista slumped in her chair.

Why does everything have to be so hard?

Everyone wanted something from her now: food, shelter, assurances that everything would be all right. The citizens looked at her and saw hope, but Arista could see little herself. Plagued by endless problems and surrounded by people, she felt oddly alone.

Arista laid her head on her desk and closed her eyes.

Just a few minutes' catnap, she told herself. *Then I will get up and figure out how to deal with the shortage of grain and look into the reports of the mistreatment of prisoners.*

As mayor a hundred issues had demanded her attention, such as who was entitled to harvest the fields of the farmers lost in battle. With food in short supply and harsh autumn weather threatening, she needed a quick solution. At least these problems saved her from thinking about her own loss. Like everyone in town, Arista remained haunted by the Battle of Ratibor. She bore no visible injury—her pain came from a memory, a face seen at night when her heart ached as if pierced. It would never fully heal. There would always be a wound, a deformity, a noticeable scar for the rest of her life.

When she finally fell asleep, thoughts of Emery, held at bay during her waking hours, invaded her dreams. He appeared, as always, sitting at the foot of the bed, bathed in moonlight. Her breath shortened in anticipation of the kiss as he leaned forward, a smile across his lips. Abruptly he stiffened, and a drop of blood slipped from the corner of his mouth—a crossbow bolt protruding from his chest. She tried to cry out but could not make a sound. The dream had always been the same, but this time Emery spoke. *"There's no time left,"* he told her, his face intent and urgent. *"It's up to you now."*

She struggled to ask what he meant, when—

"Your Highness." She felt a gentle hand jostle her shoulder.

Opening her eyes, Arista saw Orrin Flatly. The city scribe, who had once kept track of the punishment of rebels in the Central Square, had volunteered to be her secretary. His cold efficiency had given her pause but eventually she relented, realizing there was no crime in doing one's job well. Her decision had proved sound and he had turned out to be a loyal, diligent worker. Still, waking to his expressionless face disturbed her.

"What is it?" she asked, wiping her eyes and feeling for the tears that should have been there.

"Someone is here to see you. I explained you were occupied, but he insists. He is very…" Orrin shifted uncomfortably, "hard to ignore."

"Who is he?"

"He refused to give his name, but he said you knew him and claims his business is of utmost importance and he must speak to you immediately."

"Okay." Arista nodded drowsily. "Give me a moment and then send him in."

Orrin left, and in his absence, she smoothed the wrinkles from her dress to ensure her appearance was at least marginally presentable. Having lived the life of a commoner for so long, what Arista deemed acceptable had reached an appallingly low level. Checking her hair in a mirror, she wondered where the Princess of Melengar had gone and if she would ever return.

While she was inspecting herself, the door opened. "How may I help—"

Esrahaddon stood in the doorway, wearing the same flowing robe whose color Arista could never determine. His arms, as always, were lost in its shimmering folds. His beard was longer, and gray streaked his hair, making him appear older than she remembered. She had not seen the wizard since that morning on the bank of the Nidwalden River.

"What are *you* doing here?" she asked, her warm tone icing over.

"I am pleased to see you as well, Your Highness."

After admitting the wizard, Orrin had left the doors open. With a glance from Esrahaddon, they swung shut.

"I see you're getting along better without hands these days," Arista said.

"One adapts to one's needs," he replied, sitting opposite her.

"I didn't extend an invitation for you to sit."

"I didn't ask for one."

Arista's own chair slammed into the back of her legs, causing her to fall into it.

"How are you doing that with no hands or sound?" she asked, disarmed by her own curiosity.

"The lessons are over, or don't you remember declaring that at our last meeting?"

Arista hardened her composure once more. "I remember. I also thought I made it clear I never wanted to see you again."

"Yes, yes, that's all well and good, but I need your help to locate the heir."

"Lost him again, have you?"

Esrahaddon ignored her. "We can find him with a basic location spell."

"I'm not interested in your games. I have a city to run."

"We need to perform the spell immediately. We can do it right here, right now. I have a good idea where he is, but time is short and I can't afford to run off in the wrong direction. So, clear your desk and we can get started."

"I have no intention of doing anything of the sort."

"Arista, you know I can't do this alone. I need your help."

The princess glared at him. "You should have thought of that before you arranged my father's murder. What I should do is order your execution."

"You don't understand. This is important. Thousands of lives are at stake. This is larger than your loss. It is larger than the loss of a hundred kings and a thousand fathers. You are not the only one to suffer. Do you think I enjoyed rotting in a prison for a thousand years? Yes, I used you and your father to escape. I did so out of necessity—because what I protect is more important than any single person. Now stop this foolishness. We are running out of time."

"I am so happy not to be of service to you," she smirked. "I can't bring my father back, and I know I could never kill you, nor would you allow yourself to be imprisoned again. This is truly a gift—the opportunity to repay you for what you took from me."

Esrahaddon sighed and shook his head. "You don't really hate me, Arista. It's guilt that's eating you. It's knowing that you had as much to do with your father's death as I. But the church is to blame. They orchestrated the events so I would escape and hopefully lead them to the heir. They enticed you to Gutaria, knowing I would use you."

"Get out!" Arista got to her feet, her face flushed red. "Orrin! Guards!"

The scribe struggled with the door and it opened a crack, but a slight glance from Esrahaddon slammed it shut again. "Your Highness, I'll get help," Orrin's voice came from behind the door.

"You need to forgive yourself, Arista."

"GET OUT!" she screamed. With the wave of her hand, the office door burst open, nearly coming free from the hinges.

Esrahaddon got up and moved toward the door and added, "You need to realize you didn't kill your father any more than I did."

After he left the room, Arista slammed the door and sat on the floor with her back against it. She wanted to scream, *It wasn't my fault!* Even though she knew that was a lie. In the years since her father's death, she had hid from the truth but she could not hide any longer. As difficult as it was to admit, Esrahaddon was right.

Esrahaddon stepped out of City Hall into the darkness of Ratibor's Central Square. He looked back and sighed. He genuinely liked Arista. He wished he could tell her everything, but the risk was too great. While he was free of Gutaria Prison, he feared the church still listened to his conversations—not every word, as when he was incarcerated, but Mawyndulë had the power to hear from vast distances. As such, Esrahaddon had to assume all conversations were suspect. A single slip, the casual mention of a name, and he could ruin everything.

Time was growing short but at least now there was no doubt that Arista *had* become a cenzar. He had safely planted the seed, and the soil had proved fertile. He had begun to suspect on the morning of the Battle of Ratibor, when Hadrian mentioned that the rain was not *supposed* to stop. He knew Arista had cast the spell instrumental to the Nationalists' victory. Since then, he had heard the rumors concerning the new mayor possessing *unnatural powers*. But it was only when she broke his locking charm with a simple wave of her hand that he knew Arista finally understood the Art.

Aside from Arcadius and himself, no human wizards remained, and the two of them were pitiful representatives of the craft. Arcadius was nothing but an old hack, what they used to refer to as a *faquin*, an elven term for the most inept magician—knowledge without talent. *Faquins* never managed to transition from materials-based alchemy to the kinetic true version of the Art.

Esrahaddon did not consider himself any better. Without his hands, he was as much a magical cripple as a physical invalid. Now, however, with Arista's birth into the world of wizardry, mankind once again possessed a true artist. She was still a novice, a mere infant, but given time, her talent would grow. One day she would become more powerful than any king, emperor, warrior, or priest.

Knowing that she could hold sway over all mankind was more than a little disturbing. During the Old Empire safeguards existed. The Cenzar Council oversaw wielders of the Art and ensured its proper use, but that was gone now. All the other wizards, his brethren and even the lesser mages, were dead. With him effectively castrated, the church thought they had eliminated the cenzar threat from the world. Now a true practitioner of the Art had returned, and he was certain no one understood the danger this simple princess posed.

He needed her and, though she did not know it yet, she needed him. He could explain the Art's source and how they came to use it. They were the guardians, the preservers, and the defenders. They held the secrets that would protect mankind when the *Uli Vermar* ended.

ASSASSIN

When Esrahaddon had learned the truth so long ago he felt relieved it would not be his problem to face, as the day of reckoning was centuries away. How ironic that his imprisonment in the timeless vault of Gutaria had extended his life to this age. What had once been forever in the future was now but months away. He allowed himself a bitter laugh, then walked to the center of the square to sit and think.

His plan was so tenuous, so weak, but all of the pieces were in their proper places. Arista just needed time to master her feelings and then she would come around. Hadrian knew he was the Guardian of the Heir, and worthy of that legacy. Then there was the heir, an unlikely choice to be sure, but one that somehow made perfect sense.

Yes, it will be all right, he concluded. Things always work out in the end. At least that is what Yolric always used to say.

Yolric was the wisest of them all and had been passionate about the world's ability to correct itself. Esrahaddon's greatest fear when the Old Empire fell had been that Yolric might side with Venlin. The fact that the emperor's descendent still lived proved his master had not helped the Patriarch find the emperor's son when the boy was taken into hiding. Esrahaddon allowed himself a grin. He missed old Yolric. His teacher would be dead now; he was ancient even when Esrahaddon was a boy.

Esrahaddon stretched his legs and tried to clear his mind. He needed to rest, but rest had eluded him for centuries. Rest was only enjoyed by men of clear conscience, and he had too much innocent blood on his hands. Too many people had given their lives for him to fail now.

Remembering Yolric opened the door to his past and through it emerged faces of people long dead: his family, his friends, and the woman he had hoped to marry. It seemed his life before the fall was merely a dream, but perhaps this was the dream, a nightmare that he was trapped in. Maybe one day he would wake and find himself back in the palace with Nevrik, Jerish, and his beloved Elinya.

Had she somehow survived the destruction of the city?

He wanted to think so, no matter how unlikely. It pleased him to believe that she had escaped the end, but even that thought gave little comfort.

What if she believed what they said about me afterward? Did she marry someone else, feeling betrayed? Did Elinya die at an old age, hating me? Or was she killed in the civil war?

He needed to stop thinking this way. What he had told Arista was true: the sacrifices they made were insignificant when compared against the goal. He should try to get some sleep. He rose and headed back toward the inn. A cloud covered the moon, snuffing out what little light it cast, as it did Esrahaddon felt a stabbing pain in his back. Crying out in anguish, he fell to his knees. Twisting at the waist, he felt his robe stick to his skin with a growing wetness.

I'm bleeding.

"*Venderia*," he whispered, and instantly his robe glowed. The square lit up, awash in an unearthly light. At the fringe of its radiance he caught a glimpse of a man dressed in a dark cloak. At first he thought it might be Royce. He shared the same callous gait and posture, but this man was taller and broader.

Esrahaddon muttered a curse and four beams supporting the porch directly over the man exploded into splinters. The heavy roof collapsed just as the man stepped out from under it. The force of the crashing timbers merely billowed his cloak.

With sweat coating his face and a stabbing pain in his back, Esrahaddon struggled to rise and confront his attacker, who walked casually toward him. The wizard concentrated, spoke again, and the dirt of the square whirled into a tornado traveling directly toward his attacker. It engulfed the man, who burst into flames. Esrahaddon could feel the heat of the inferno as the pillar surged, bathing the square in a yellow glow. At its center, the figure stood wreathed in blue tongues of flame, but when the fire faded the man continued forward, unharmed.

Reaching the wizard, he looked curiously at Esrahaddon—the way a child might study a strange bug before crushing it. He said nothing, but revealed a silver medallion that hung from a chain he wore around his neck.

"Recognize this?" the man asked. "Word is you made it. I'm afraid the heir won't need it any longer."

Esrahaddon gasped.

"If only you had hands, you might rip it from my neck. Then I'd be in real trouble, wouldn't I?"

The noise of the collapse, and the explosions of light, had woken several people in nearby buildings. Candles were lit in windows and doors opened on to the square.

"The Patriarch bid me to tell you that your services are no longer required." The man in the dark cloak smiled coldly. Without another word, he walked away, disappearing into the maze of dark streets.

Esrahaddon was confused. The bolt or dart he felt lodged in his back did not feel fatal. He could breathe easily, so it had missed his lungs and was nowhere near his heart. He was bleeding but not profusely. The pain was bad, a deep burning, but he could still feel his legs and was certain he could walk.

Why did he leave me alive? Why would—poison!

The wizard concentrated and muttered a chant. It failed. He struggled with his handless arms to weave a stronger spell. It did not help. He could feel the poison now as it spread throughout his back. He was helpless without hands. Whoever the man in the cloak was, he knew exactly what he was doing.

Esrahaddon looked back at City Hall. He could not die—not yet.

THE EMERALD STORM

❧

The noise from the street caught Arista's attention. She still sat against the office door as voices and shouts drifted from the square. What had happened was unclear, but the words "He's dying" brought Arista to her feet.

She found a small crowd gathered on the steps outside. Within their center, an eerie pulsating light glowed as if a bit of the moon had landed in Central Square. Drawing closer, Arista saw the wizard. The light emitted from his robe, growing bright, then ebbing, then brightening again in pace with his slow and labored breath. The pale light revealed a pool of blood. Lying on his back, a bolt beside him, Esrahaddon's face was almost luminous with a ghostly pallor, his lips a dark shade of blue. His disheveled sleeves exposed the fleshy stumps of his wrists.

"What happened here?" she demanded.

"We don't know, Your Highness," someone from the crowd replied. "He's been asking to see you."

"Get Doctor Gerand," she ordered and knelt beside him, gently pulling down his sleeves.

"Too late," Esrahaddon whispered, his eyes locked intently on hers. "Can't help me—poison—Arista, listen—there's no time." His words came hurriedly between struggles to take in air. On his face was a look of determination mixed with desperation, like a drowning man searching for a handhold. "Take my burden—find…" The wizard hesitated, his eyes searching the faces gathered. He motioned for her to draw near.

When she placed her ear close to his mouth, he continued. "Find the heir—take the heir with you—without the heir everything fails." Esrahaddon coughed and fought to breathe. "Find the Horn of Gylindora—Need the heir to find it—buried with Novron in

Percepliquis—" He drew in another breath. "Hurry—at Wintertide the *Uli Vermar* ends—" Another breath. "They will come—without the horn everyone dies." Another breath. "Only you know now— only you can save…Patriarch…is the same…" The next breath never came. The next words were never uttered. The pulsating brilliance of his robe faded, leaving them all in darkness.

Arista watched the foul-smelling, chalk-colored smoke drift as the strand of blond hair smoldered. There was no breeze or draft in her office, yet the smoke traveled unerringly toward the northern wall, where it disappeared against the stone and mortar.

A spell of location required burning a part of a person. Hair was the obvious choice, but fingernails or even skin would work. The day after Esrahaddon's death, she requested delivery of any personal belongings left behind by the missing leader of the Nationalist Army. They sent over an old pair of Degan Gaunt's worn muddy boots, a tattered shirt, and a woolen cloak. The boots were useless, but the shirt and cloak held treasures. Scraping the surface, she found a dozen blond hairs and hundreds of flakes of skin, which she carefully gathered and placed in a velvet pouch. Convincing herself she merely wanted to see if it would work, she cast the spell with no intention of acting on the results. Now she was unsure of what to do next.

To Esrahaddon, the heir had meant everything. Since leaving Gutaria, the wizard had dedicated his life to finding the emperor's descendent even coercing Arista to assist him with a spell cast in Avempartha to identify the heir and his guardian. The guardian she recognized immediately as Hadrian; however, the heir, she had never seen before. The blond-haired image was just a face until after the Battle of Ratibor, when she learned that he was Degan Gaunt, the leader of the Nationalists. There was no doubt that the New Empire was responsible for Gaunt's disappearance, and the smoke's color confirmed he was alive and held somewhere to the north within a few days' travel. She stared at the wall where the smoke disappeared.

"This is crazy," she said aloud to the empty room. *I can't possibly go in search of the heir. The Empire has him and they'll kill me on sight. Besides, I'm needed here. Why should I care about Esrahaddon's obsession.*

If Arista wanted, she could declare herself high queen of Rhenydd and the citizenry would welcome her. She could permanently reign over a kingdom larger than Melengar and be rich as well as beloved. Long after her death, her name would endure in stories and songs— her image immortalized on statues and in books.

She glanced at the neatly folded robe on the corner of her desk delivered after Esrahaddon's burial. The sum of the wizard's entire worldly possessions amounted to just this piece of cloth. He had devoted everything to his quest, and after nine hundred years he died without fulfilling his mission. The question of exactly what that mission was, nagged at her. Loyalty to the descendent of a boy ruler from a millennium ago could not have driven Esrahaddon so fanatically—she was missing something

"They will come."

What did that mean? Who was coming?

"Without the horn everyone dies."

Everyone? Who is everyone? He couldn't mean everyone, everyone—could he? Maybe he was just babbling. People do that when they're dying, don't they?

She remembered his eyes, clear and focused, holding on like… *Emery. There's no time left. It's up to you now."*

"Only you know now—only you can save…" When Esrahaddon spoke those words she did not really listen, but now she could hear nothing else. She could not ignore the fact that the wizard used his last breath to deliver to her the secrets he had carried for a thousand years. She felt that he had presented her with sparkling gems of immeasurable

worth, but without his knowledge, they were nothing more than dull pebbles. While she could not unravel what he was trying to say it was impossible to ignore what had to be done. She had to leave. Once she discovered where Degan was being held, she could send word to Hadrian and leave the rest to him. After all, he was the guardian, and Gaunt was his problem, not hers.

Arista stuffed the only possession she cared for, a pearl-handled hairbrush from Tur Del Fur, into a sack. She wrote a letter of resignation and left it on the desk. Reaching the door, she paused and glanced back. Somehow, it seemed appropriate…almost necessary. She crossed the office and picked up the old wizard's robe. It hung gray and dull in her hands. No one had cleaned it, yet she found no stain of blood. Even more surprising, no hole marked the passage of the bolt. She wondered at this puzzle—even in death the man continued to be a mystery. Slipping the robe over her dress, she was amazed that it fit perfectly—despite the fact that Esrahaddon had been more than a foot taller than herself. Turning her back on her office, she walked out into the night.

The autumn air was cold. Arista pulled the robe tight and lifted the hood. The material was unlike anything she had ever felt before—light, soft, yet wonderfully warm and comforting. It smelled pleasantly of salifan.

She considered taking a horse from the stables. As mayor, no one would begrudge her a mount. But she had resigned. Wherever she was going, it could not be too far, and a long walk suited her. Esrahaddon indicated a need for haste, but it would be imprudent to rush headlong into the unknown. Walking seemed a sensible way to challenge the mysterious and unfamiliar. It would give her time to think. She guessed Esrahaddon would have chosen the same mode of travel. It just felt right.

Arista filled a water skin at the square's well, and packed some food. Farmers, who objected to providing for the soldiers always placed a small tribute on the steps of City Hall. Most she gave to the city's poor, which only resulted in more appearing. She helped herself to a few rounds of cheese, two loaves of bread, and a number of apples, onions, and turnips. Hardly a king's feast, but it would keep her alive.

She slipped the full water bag over her shoulder, adjusted her pack, and headed for the north gate. She was conscious of the sound of her feet on the road and the noises of the night. How dangerous, even foolhardy, leaving Medford had been, even in the company of Royce and Hadrian. Now, just a few weeks later, she set out into the darkness by herself. She knew her path would lead into Imperial territory but traveling alone, she hoped to avoid attention.

"Your Highness!" the north gate guard said with surprise when she approached.

She smiled sweetly. "Can you please open the gate?"

"Of course, my lady, but why? Where are you going?"

"For a walk," she replied.

The guard stared at her incredulously. "Are you certain? I mean…" He looked over her shoulder. "Are you alone?"

She nodded. "I assure you I'll be fine."

The guard hesitated briefly before relenting and drew back the bar. Putting his back against the giant oak doors, he slowly pushed one open.

"You need to be careful, my lady. There is a stranger about."

"A stranger?"

"A fellow came to the gate just a few hours after sunset wanting in—a masked man in a hood. I could see he was up to no good, so I turned him away. Likely as not, he's out there somewhere waiting for me to open at sunrise. Please be careful, Your Highness."

"Thank you, but I'm sure I'll be fine," she said, while slipping past him. Once she was through, the gate closed behind her.

ASSASSIN

Arista stayed to the road, walking as quickly and quietly as she could. Now on her way, she felt exhilarated despite the dangers that lay ahead. Leaving Ratibor without farewells was for the best. They would have insisted she appoint a successor and remain for a time to counsel whoever was selected. While she did not feel enough urgency for a horse, she worried that too long of a delay would be a mistake. Besides, she could not risk an Imperial spy discovering her plan and placing sentries to capture her.

In one way she felt safer on the road than in her office—she was confident no one knew where she was, and this was as comforting as the old wizard's robe. In the days following Esrahaddon's death, she was concerned that she too might be a target. His assassin had escaped capture. The only trace being an unusually small crossbow discovered in an East End Square rain barrel. She felt certain that the killer was an agent of the New Empire sent to eliminate a lingering threat. She was Esrahaddon's apprentice, who had helped defeat the church's attempt to take Melengar, and led the revolt in Ratibor. Surely those in power wanted her dead as well.

Before long, she spotted the flicker of a light not far off the road—a simple campfire burning low.

The man turned away at the gate? Could he be the assassin?

She kept her eyes on the fire while carefully walking past. She soon cleared a hill and the light disappeared behind it. After a few hours, the excitement of the adventure waned and she found herself yawning. With several hours until dawn, she pulled a blanket from her bag and found a soft place to lie.

Is this what each night was like for Esrahaddon?

She never felt so alone. In the past, Hilfred would have been her ever present shadow, but her bodyguard disappeared more than two years ago after suffering burns in her service. Most of all, she missed Royce and Hadrian, a common thief and rogue. To them, she was nothing more than a wealthy patron, but to her, they were nothing less than her closest friends. She imagined Royce disappearing into the trees to search the area as he had at every camp. Even more, she wanted Hadrian there by her side. She pictured him with a lopsided grin making that awful stew of his. He could always make her feel safe. She remembered how he had held her on the hill of Amberton Lee and at the armory after the Battle of Ratibor. Soaked in rain, mud, and Emery's blood, his arms held her up. She had never felt so horrible and no one's embrace had ever felt so good.

"I wish you were here now," she whispered.

Lying on her back, she looked up at the stars scattered like dust over the immense heavens. Seeing them, she felt even more alone. She closed her eyes and drifted off to sleep.

Chapter 2

THE EMPTY CASTLE

A bove Hadrian's head the wooden sign rocked in the morning breeze, displaying a thorny branch and a faded bloom. Weathered and worn, it would require imagination to determine that the flower depicted was a rose. The tavern it announced displayed the same haphazard charm of necessity as the other buildings along Wayward Street. The crooked length of the narrow road was empty. Autumn leaves scattering in the wind and the rocking sign marked the only movement.

The lack of activity surprised Hadrian. At this time of year, Medford's Lower Quarter usually bustled with vendors selling apples, cider, pumpkins, and hardwood. The air should have been scented with wood smoke. Chimney sweeps should be dancing across rooftops as children watched in awe. Instead, the doors of several stores were nailed shut—and to his dismay, even The Rose and Thorn Tavern lay dormant.

Hadrian sighed as he tethered his horse. Skipping breakfast in exchange for an early start had left him eager for a hot meal eaten indoors. He expected the war to take its toll and for Medford to be affected, but he never expected The Rose and Thorn to—

"Hadrian!"

He recognized the voice before he turned and saw Gwen, the lovely Calian native, looking more like an artisan's wife than a madam in her sky-blue day dress. She swept down the steps of Medford House, one of the few open businesses. Prostitutes were always the first to arrive and the last to leave. Hadrian hugged her, lifting her small body. "We were worried about you," she said. "What took you so long?"

"What are you doing back at all?" Royce called as he stepped out on the porch. The lithe and slender thief stood barefoot, wearing only black pants and a loose unbelted tunic.

"Arista sent me to make sure you made it all right and were able to convince Alric to send the army south."

"Took you long enough. I've been back for weeks."

Hadrian shrugged. "Well, Alric's forces laid siege to Colnora right after I arrived. It took me a while to find a way out."

"So, how did—"

"Royce, shouldn't we let Hadrian sit and eat?" Gwen interrupted. "You haven't had breakfast, have you? Let me grab a shawl, and I'll have Dixon fire the stove."

"How long has the tavern been closed?" Hadrian asked as Gwen disappeared back inside.

Royce raised an eyebrow and shook his head. "Not closed. Business has just been slow, so she opens for the midday meal."

"It's like a ghost town around here."

"A lot of people left, expecting an invasion," Royce explained. "Most who stayed were called to serve when the army moved out."

Gwen reappeared with a wrap around her shoulders and led them across the street to The Rose and Thorn. In the shadows of an alley, Hadrian spotted movement. People slept huddled amid piles of trash. Unlike Royce, who easily passed for human, these shabbily dressed creatures bore the unmistakable angled ears, prominent cheekbones, and almond eyes characteristic of elves.

"The army didn't want them," Royce commented, seeing Hadrian's stare. "No one wants them."

Dixon, the bartender and manager, was taking chairs off the tables when Gwen unlocked the doors. A tall, stocky man, he had lost an arm several years ago in the Battle of Medford.

"Hadrian!" he shouted in his booming voice. He stopped work to extend his good hand. "How are you, lad? Gave 'em what for in Ratibor, eh? Where you been?"

"I stayed to sweep up," Hadrian replied with a wink and a smile.

"Denny in yet?" Gwen asked Dixon, stepping past him and rummaging through a drawer behind the bar.

"Nope, just me. I figured, why bother? All of you want breakfast? I can manage if you like."

"Yes," Gwen told him, "and make some extra."

Dixon sighed. "You keep feeding them and they'll just keep hanging around."

She ignored the comment. "Did Harry deliver the ale last night?"

"Yup."

"Three barrels, right?"

As Gwen talked with Dixon, Royce slipped his arm around her waist and gave her a gentle squeeze. The fact that he loved her was no secret, but Royce had never even held Gwen's hand in public before. Seeing him with her, Hadrian saw that his friend looked different. It took him a moment to realize what it was—Royce was smiling.

When Gwen followed Dixon into the pantry to discuss inventory, Royce and Hadrian resumed the task of pulling chairs off tables. Throughout the years, Hadrian had likely sat in each one and drunk from every wooden cup or pewter tankard hanging behind the bar. For more than a decade The Rose and Thorn had been his home, and it felt odd to be *just visiting*.

"So, have you decided what you'll do now?" Royce asked.

"I'm going to find the heir."

Royce paused, holding the chair inches above the floor. "Did you hit your head during the Battle of Ratibor? The heir is dead, remember?"

"Turns out he's not. What's more, I know who he is."

"But the nice priest told us the heir was murdered by Seret Knights forty years ago," Royce countered.

"He was."

"Am I missing something?"

"Twins," Hadrian told him. "One was killed, but the midwife saved the other."

"So, who is this heir?"

"Degan Gaunt."

Royce's eyes widened and a sardonic grin crossed his face. "The leader of the Nationalist Army, who is bent on the New Empire's destruction, is the Imperial heir? How ironic is that, and how unfortunate for you, seeing as how the Imps snatched him up."

Hadrian nodded. "Yeah, it turns out Esrahaddon's been helping him win all those victories in Rhenydd."

"Esrahaddon? How do you know that?"

"I found him in Gaunt's camp right before the Battle of Ratibor. Looks like the old wizard was planning to put Gaunt on the throne by force."

The two finished with the chairs and took seats at a table near the windows. Outside, a lone apple seller wheeled a cart past, presumably on her way to the Gentry Quarter.

"I hope you're not taking Esrahaddon's word about Gaunt being the heir. You can never be sure exactly what he's up to," said Royce.

"No—well, yes—he confirmed the heir was alive, but I discovered his identity through Gaunt's sister."

"So, how do you plan to find Gaunt? Did either of them tell you where he is?"

"No. I'm pretty sure Esrahaddon knows, or has a good idea, but he wouldn't tell me, and I've not seen him since the battle. He did say he would need us for a job soon. I think he'll want help rescuing Gaunt. He hasn't been around here, has he?"

Royce shook his head. "I'm happy to say I haven't seen him. Is that why you're in town?"

"Not really. I'm sure he can find me, wherever I am. After all, he found us in Colnora when he wanted us to come to Dahlgren. I'm on my way to see Myron at the abbey. If anyone knows about the history of the heir, he does. I also had to drop off a letter to Alric."

"A letter?"

"When I was stuck in Colnora during the siege, your old friends helped get me out."

"The Diamond?"

Hadrian nodded. "Price arranged for me to slip away one night in exchange for delivering the letter. He preferred risking my neck rather than one of his boys."

"What did it say? Who was it from?"

Hadrian shrugged. "How would I know?"

"You didn't read it?" he asked incredulously.

"No, it was for Alric."

"Let me see it."

"Can't. I dropped it off at the castle on the way in."

Royce dropped his face into his hands. "Sometimes, I just..." Royce shook his head. "Unbelievable."

"What's wrong?" Gwen asked, joining them.

"Hadrian's an idiot," Royce replied, his voice muffled by his hands.

"I'm sure that's not true."

"Thank you, Gwen. See, at least *she* appreciates me."

"So, Hadrian, tell me about Ratibor. Royce told me about the rebellion. How did it go?" Gwen asked with an excited smile.

"Emery was killed. Do you know who he was?"

Gwen nodded.

"So were a lot of others, but we took the city."

"And Arista?"

"She survived the fight but took the aftermath hard. She's become something of a heroine there. They put her in charge of the whole kingdom."

"She's a remarkable woman," Gwen said. "Don't you think so, Hadrian?" Before he could answer, a loud crash from the kitchen made her sigh. "Excuse me while I help Dixon."

She started to stand but Royce reached his feet first. "Sit," he said, kissing the crown of her head. "I'll help him. You two get caught up."

Gwen looked surprised but simply said, "Thank you."

Royce hurried off, shouting in an unusually good-natured tone, "Dixon! What's taking you so long? You've still got one hand, haven't you?"

Gwen and Hadrian both laughed, mirroring surprised expressions.

"So, what's new around here?" Hadrian asked.

"Not a whole lot. Albert came by last week with a job from a nobleman to place the earrings of a married woman in the bedchambers of a priest, but Royce declined it."

"Really? He loves plant jobs. And a priest? That's just easy money."

She shrugged. "I think with you retired, he's—"

THE EMPTY CASTLE

Outside, an approaching clatter of hooves halted abruptly. A moment later a man with a distinct limp, dressed as a royal courier, entered the tavern. He paused at the doorway, looking puzzled.

"Can I help you?" Gwen asked, as she stood.

"I have a message from His Majesty for the Royal Protectors. I was told they were here."

"I'll take that," Gwen said, stepping forward.

The courier stiffened and shook his head. "It is for the Royal Protectors only."

Gwen halted and Hadrian noticed her annoyed expression.

"You must be new," Hadrian addressed the courier, rising to his feet. "I'm Hadrian Blackwater."

The courier nodded smartly and pulled a waxed scroll from his satchel. He handed over the dispatch and departed. Hadrian sat back down and broke the falcon seal.

"It's a job, isn't it?" Gwen's expression darkened and she stared at the floor.

"It's nothing. Alric just wants to see us," Hadrian said. She looked up, her eyes revealing a troubled mix of emotions Hadrian could not decipher. "Gwen, what's wrong?" he pressed, his voice softening.

At length she replied, almost in a whisper, "Royce asked me to marry him."

Hadrian sat back in his chair. "Seriously?"

She nodded and added hastily, "I guess he thought that since you retired from Riyria, he would, too."

"That's—why, that's wonderful!" Hadrian burst out as he leaped to his feet and hugged her. "Congratulations! He didn't even say anything. We'll be like family! It's about time he got around to this. I would have asked for your hand myself years ago, except I knew if I did I'd wake up dead the next morning."

"When he asked me it was as if—well, as if a wish I never dared ask had come true. So many problems solved, so much pain eased. Honestly, I didn't think he ever would."

Hadrian nodded. "That's only because he's not only an idiot, he's blind as well."

"No. I mean, well—he's Royce."

"Isn't that what I just said? But yeah, he's really not the marrying type, is he? Clearly, you've had tremendous influence on him."

"You have, too," she said, reaching out and taking hold of his hand. "There are times I hear him say things I know come from you. Things like *responsibility* and *regret*, words that were never part of his vocabulary before. I wonder if he even knows where he found them. When I first met you two he was so withdrawn, so guarded."

Hadrian nodded. "He has trust issues."

"But he's learning. His life has been so hard. I know it has, abandoned and betrayed by those who should have loved him. He doesn't talk about it, at least not to me. But I know."

Hadrian shook his head. "Me either. Occasionally something might come up, but he usually avoids mentioning anything about his past. I think he's trying to forget."

"He's built so many defenses, but every year it's as if another wall has fallen. He even summoned the courage to tell me he's part elven. His fortress is dissolving, and I can see him peering out at me. He wants to be free. This is the next step—and I am so proud of him."

"When will the wedding be?"

"We were thinking in a couple of weeks at the monastery, so Myron can preside. But we'll have to postpone, won't we?"

"Why do you say that? Alric just wants to see us, it doesn't mean—"

"He needs the two of you for a job," Gwen interrupted.

"No. He might *want us*, but we're retired. I have other things to do and Royce…well, Royce needs to start a new life—with you."

"You'll go, and you must take Royce with you," her voice was filled with sadness and a sense of regret, emotions so unlike her.

Hadrian smiled. "Listen, I can't think of anything Alric could say that would get me to go, but if he does, I'll do the job on my own—as a wedding present. We don't even have to tell Royce the courier was here."

"No!" she burst out. "He *has* to go. If he doesn't, you'll die."

Hadrian's first impulse was to laugh, but that thought evaporated when he saw her face. Nevertheless, he tried to lighten the strain he found there. "I'm not as easy to kill as all that, you know?" He winked at her.

"I'm from Calis, Hadrian, and I know what I'm talking about." Her gaze drifted off toward the windows, but her eyes were unfocused, as if seeing another place. "I can't be the one responsible for your death. The life we would have after…" She shook her head. "No, he *must* go with you," she repeated firmly.

Hadrian was not convinced but knew there was no reason to argue further. Gwen was not the type for debate. Most women he knew invited discussion and even enjoyed arguments, but not Gwen. There was clarity to her thinking that let you know she had already made her own journey to the inevitable conclusion and was just politely waiting there for you to join her. In her own way, she was much like Royce—except for the polite waiting.

"With you two gone, I'll have time to organize a first-rate wedding," she said, her voice strained as she blinked frequently. "It will take that long just to decide what color dress a former prostitute should wear."

"You know something, Gwen," Hadrian began, as he reached out and took her hand. "I've known a lot of women, but I've met only two I admire. Royce is a very lucky man."

"Royce is a man on the edge," she replied thoughtfully. "He's seen too much cruelty and betrayal. He's never known mercy." She gave his hand a squeeze. "*You* have to do this, Hadrian. You have to be the one to show him mercy. If you can do that, I know it will save him."

Royce and Hadrian entered Essendon Castle's courtyard, once the site of Princess Arista's witchcraft trial. Nothing remained of that unfortunate day except a slightly raised patch of ground where the stake and woodpile had stood. It had been just three years ago, and the weather had been turning cold then too. It was a different time. Amrath Essendon was only recently murdered and the New Empire was little more than an Imperialist dream.

The guards at the gate nodded and smiled at them.

"I hate that," Royce muttered as they passed.

"What?"

"They didn't even think to stop us, and they actually smiled. They know us by sight now—*by sight*. Alric used to have the decency to send word discreetly and receive us unannounced. Now, uniformed soldiers knock on the door in daylight, waving and saying, 'Hello, we have a job for you.'"

"He didn't wave."

"Give it time, he will be—waving and grinning. One day Jeremy will be buying drinks for his soldier buddies at The Rose and Thorn. They'll all be there, the entire sentry squad, laughing, smiling, throwing their arms over our shoulders and asking us to sing *Calide Portmore* with them—'once more, with gusto!' And at some point one particularly sweaty ox will give me a hug and say how *honored* he is to be in our company."

"Jeremy?"

"What? That's his name."

"You know the name of the soldier at the gate?"

Royce scowled. "You see my point? Yes, I know his name and they know ours. We might as well wear uniforms and move into Arista's old room."

They climbed the stone steps to the main entrance, where a soldier quickly opened a door for them and gave a slight bow. "Master Melborn, Master Blackwater."

"Hey, Digby." Hadrian waved as he passed and caught Royce scowling. "Sorry."

"It's a good thing we're both retired. You know, there's a reason there are no famous *living* thieves."

Hadrian's heels echoed on the polished floor of the corridor as they walked. Royce's footsteps made no sound at all. They crossed the west gallery past the suits of armor and the ballroom. The castle appeared as empty as the rest of the city. As they approached the reception hall, Hadrian spotted Mauvin Pickering heading their way. The young noble looked thinner than Hadrian remembered. There was a hollow cast to his cheeks, a shadow beneath his eyes, but his hair was the same wild mess.

"About time," Mauvin greeted them. "Alric just sent me to look for you."

Two years had passed since his brother Fanen's death, and Mauvin still wore black. The haunted look in his eyes would be unnoticeable to most. Only those who had known him before the contest in Dahlgren would see the difference. That was where Sentinel Luis Guy had attacked Hadrian with a force of Seret Knights and Mauvin and Fanen took up arms with him. The brothers had fought masterfully, as was the nature of Pickerings. Yet Mauvin had been unable to save his brother from the killing stroke. Before that day, Mauvin Pickering had been bright, loud, and joyful with a permanent smile and a wink that challenged the world. Now, he stood with his shoulders slumped and his chin dipped.

"You're wearing it again?" Hadrian gestured toward Mauvin's sword.

"They insisted."

"Have you drawn it?"

Mauvin looked at his feet. "Dad says it doesn't matter. If the need arises, he's certain I won't hesitate."

"And what do you think?"

"Mostly I try not to." Mauvin opened the doors to the hall and let them swing wide. He led them past the clerk and the door guards into the reception hall. Tall windows let in the late-morning light, casting bright spears on the parquet floor. The great tapestries still lay rolled in bundles against the wall, stacked in hope of a better day. In their places maps with red lines covered by blue arrows pointing south plastered the walls.

Alone, Alric paced near the windows, his crowned head bowed and his mantle trailing behind him like—*like a king*, Hadrian thought. Alric looked up as they entered and pushed the rim of the royal diadem back with his thumb.

"What took you so long?"

"We ate breakfast, Your Majesty," Royce replied.

"You ate break—never mind." The king held out a rolled parchment. "I'm told you delivered this dispatch to the castle this morning?"

"Not me," Royce said. Unrolling it, he found two parchments and began reading.

"I did," Hadrian admitted. "I just arrived from Ratibor. Your sister has matters well in hand, Your Majesty."

Alric scowled. "Who sent this?"

"I'm not sure," Hadrian replied. "I got it from a man named Price in Colnora."

Royce finished reading and looked up. "I think you're about to lose this war," he said without bothering to add the expected *Your Majesty*.

"Don't be absurd. This is likely a hoax. Ecton is probably behind it. He enjoys seeing me make a fool of myself. Even if it is authentic, it's simply someone making wild claims to extort a bit of gold from the New Empire."

"I don't think so." Royce handed the letter to Hadrian.

King Alric —

Found this on a courier traveling from Calis to Aquesta. Sweepers bumped him in Alburn but he was more than he seemed. Three Diamonds dead. Bucketmen caught him and found this letter addressed to the Regents. The Jewel thought you'd like to know.

Esteemed Regents,

The fall of Ratibor was unexpected and unfortunate but, as you know, not fatal. Thus far, I have delivered Degan Gaunt and eliminated the wizard Esrahaddon. This completes two-thirds of our contract, but the best is yet to come.

The Emerald Storm rests anchored in Aquesta Harbor, ready to sail. When you receive this message, place the payment on board along with the sealed orders I left. Once loaded, the ship will depart, the fortunes of war will shift, and your victory will be assured. With the Nationalists eliminated, Melengar is yours for the taking.

While I have all the time in the world, you, on the other hand, might wish to make haste, lest the flame you call the New Empire is snuffed out.

Merrick Marius

"Merrick?" Hadrian muttered and looked at Royce. "Is this...?"

Royce nodded.

"You know this Marius?" Alric asked.

Again, Royce nodded. "Which is why I know you're in trouble."

"And do you know who sent this?"

"Cosmos DeLur."

"Isn't Cosmos a wealthy merchant in Colnora?"

"He's also the leader of the thieves' guild known as the Black Diamond."

Alric paused to consider this, taking the opportunity to pace once more. "Why would he send this to me?"

"The Diamond wants the Imps out of Colnora. I guess with Gaunt gone, Cosmos thought you could make the best use of this information."

Alric stroked his beard thoughtfully. "So, who is this Merrick fellow? How do you know him?"

"We were friends when I was a member of the Diamond."

"Excellent. Find him and ask what this is all about."

Royce shook his head. "I have no idea where Merrick is, and we're not on good terms anymore. He won't tell me anything."

Alric sighed. "I don't care what kind of terms you're on. Find him, resolve your differences, and get me the information I need."

Royce said nothing and Hadrian hesitantly added. "Merrick had Royce sent to Manzant after he mistakenly killed the woman Merrick loved."

Alric stopped pacing and stared. "Manzant Prison? But no one ever leaves Manzant."

"That was the plan. I was happy to disappoint him." Royce replied.

"Nowadays, Royce and Merrick have an unspoken agreement to stay out of each other's way."

"So how can I find out if this Merrick is just boasting, or if there is a real threat to Melengar?"

"Merrick doesn't boast. If he says he can turn the war in the Empire's favor, he can. I suggest you take this seriously." Royce thought a moment. "If I were you, I'd send someone to deliver this message and then stow away on this ship and see where it leads."

"Fine. Do that, and let me know what you find out."

Royce shook his head. "We're retired. Only a week ago I came here and explained how—"

"Don't be ridiculous! You said to take his threat seriously, which is why I need my best—and that means you."

"Pick someone else," Royce said firmly.

"All right, how much do you want? It's land this time, right? Fine. As it happens, the Baron Milborough of Three Fords was killed in battle a few weeks ago. He doesn't have any sons, so I'll grant you his estate if you succeed. Land, title—all of it."

"I don't want land. I don't want anything. *I'm retired.*"

"By Mar, man!" Alric shouted. "The future of the kingdom may depend on this. I'm the king and—"

Hadrian interrupted. "I'll do it."

"What?" Alric and Royce asked together.

"I said I'll go."

❧

"You can't take this job," Royce told him as they walked back to The Rose and Thorn.

"I have to. If Esrahaddon is dead, Merrick is my only chance to find Gaunt. Do you think he really could have done it?"

"Merrick wouldn't lie to a client about a job."

"But Esrahaddon was a wizard. He's survived a thousand years—I can't imagine he could be murdered by a common killer."

"I just said it was Merrick. He's not common."

As the two walked through an empty Gentry Square, even the bells of Mares Cathedral were silent. Hadrian sighed. "Then I'm on my own in finding the heir now. If I follow the payment to Merrick, I'll be halfway to finding Gaunt."

"Hadrian." Royce placed a hand on his friend's arm, stopping them mid-step. "You're not up to this. You don't know Merrick. Think a minute. If he can kill a wizard, one who could create pillars of fire even without hands, what do you think your chances are? You're a good—no, you're a great fighter—the best I've ever seen, but Merrick is a genius and he's ruthless. You go after him, he'll know, and he'll kill you."

They were across from Lester Furl's old haberdashery in Artisan's Row, the shop that the monk Myron once worked in. The sign of the cavalier hat still hung out front, but the place was empty.

"Listen, I'm not asking you to come. I know you're marrying Gwen. Congratulations on that, by the way. And it's about time, I might add. This isn't your problem. It's mine. It's what I was born to do. What my father trained me for. Protecting Gaunt, and finding a way to put him on the Imperial throne—that's my destiny."

Royce rolled his eyes.

"I know you don't believe that, but I do."

"Gaunt could be dead already, you know? If Merrick killed Esrahaddon, he might have slit Gaunt's throat, too."

"I still have to go. By now, even you must see that."

THE EMPTY CASTLE

When they reached The Rose and Thorn, Gwen was waiting with anxious eyes. She stood on the porch, her arms crossed, clutching her shawl. The autumn wind brushed her skirt and hair. Behind her, within the darkened interior, patrons talked loudly around the bar.

"It's okay," Hadrian reassured her as they approached. "I'm taking the job, but Royce is staying. With luck I'll be back for—"

"Go with him," Gwen told Royce firmly.

"No—really, Gwen," Hadrian said, "it's nothing—"

"You have to go with him."

"What's wrong?" Royce asked. "I thought we were getting married. Don't you want to?"

Gwen closed her eyes, shaken. Then her hands clenched into fists and she straightened. "You *must* go. Hadrian will be killed if you don't—and then you…you…"

Royce took her in his arms on the steps of the tavern and held her as she began to cry.

"You have to go," Gwen said, her voice muffled by Royce's shoulder. "Nothing will be right if you don't. I can't marry you— *I won't* marry you if you don't. Tell me you'll go, please, Royce, please…"

Royce gave Hadrian a puzzled glance and whispered, "Okay."

"Here, I made this for you," Gwen said to Royce, holding out a folded bit of knitted cloth. They were in Gwen's room at the top of the stairs of Medford House and he had just finished packing.

He held it up. "A scarf?"

Gwen smiled. "Since I'm going to be married, I thought I should take up knitting. I hear that's what proper wives do for their husbands."

Royce started to laugh but stopped when he saw her expression. "This is important to you, isn't it? You realize you've always been better than all those ladies in the Merchant Quarter. Having a husband doesn't make them special."

"It's not that. It's just...I know you had a less-than-perfect childhood, and so did I. I want something *better* for our children. I want their lives—our home—to be perfect, or as much as possible for a pair such as us."

"I don't know, I've met dozens of aristocrats who had ideal childhoods and they turned out to be horrors. You, on the other hand, are the best person I've ever met."

She smiled at him. "That's nice, but I highly doubt you would approve of our daughter working here. And would you really want our son living the way you did as a boy? We can raise them right. Just because they grow up in a proper home doesn't mean they will turn out to be *horrors*. You'll be firm, and I'll be loving. You'll spank little Elias when he acts disrespectfully, and I'll kiss his tears and give him cookies."

"Elias? You've named our son already?"

"Would you prefer Sterling? I can't decide between the two. But the girl's name is not negotiable—it's Mercedes. I've always loved that name.

"I'll sell this house and my other holdings. Combined with the money I banked for you, we'll never want for anything. We can live peaceful, happy, simple lives—I mean, if you want to live like that. Do you?"

He looked into her eyes. "Gwen, if it means being with you, I don't care where we are or what I do."

"Then it's settled." Gwen grinned and her eyes brightened. "It's what I've always dreamed of…the two of us in a small cottage somewhere safe and warm, raising a family."

"You make us sound like squirrels."

"Yes, exactly! A family of squirrels tucked in our cozy nest in some tree trunk while the troubles of the world pass us by." Her lower lip quivered.

Royce pulled her close and held her tight as she buried her face in his shoulder. He stroked her head, feeling her hair linger on his fingertips. For all Gwen's strength and courage, he was forever amazed at how fragile she could be. He had never known anyone like her and considered telling Hadrian he had changed his mind. "Gwen—"

"Don't even think it," she told him. "We can't build a new life until you're done with the old one. Hadrian needs you, and I won't be blamed for his death."

"I could never blame you."

"I couldn't bear it if I felt you hated me, Royce. I'd rather be dead than let that happen. Promise me you'll go. Promise me you'll take care of Hadrian. Promise me you won't despair, and that you'll set things right."

Royce let his head lower until it rested on hers. He stood there, smelling the familiar scent of her hair as his own breathing tightened. "All right, but you have to agree to go to the abbey if things get bad like they did before."

"I will," she said. Her arms tightened around him. "I'm so scared," she whispered.

Surprised, Royce said, "You've always told me you were never frightened when I left on missions."

She looked up at him with tears in her eyes and a guilty expression on her face. "I lied."

Chapter 3

THE COURIER

Hadrian stood in the anteroom, waiting in line to deliver the dispatch. The clerk was a short, plump, balding man with ink-stained fingers and a spare quill behind each ear. He sat behind a formidable desk, scribbling on documents and muttering to himself, unconcerned with the growing line of people.

They had ridden to Aquesta, and Hadrian had volunteered to deliver the dispatch while Royce waited at a rendezvous with horses at the ready. Although Hadrian had performed jobs for many of the nobility, few here would know him by sight. Riyria had always conducted business anonymously, working through third parties such as the Viscount Albert Winslow, who fronted the organization and preserved their anonymity. He doubted that Saldur would recognize him, but Luis Guy certainly would. As a result, Hadrian kept a clear map of the nearest exit in his head and a count of the Imperial guards between him and freedom.

The seat of the New Imperial Empire was busy. Members of the palace staff hurried by, entering and exiting through the many doors around him. They ran or walked as briskly as need dictated and dignity allowed. Some turned his way, but only briefly. As he knew from experience, the degree of attention people paid others was inversely proportionate to his or her status. The lord chamberlain and high chancellor passed without a glance, while the serving steward ventured a long look, and a young page stared curiously for nearly a full minute. Although Hadrian was invisible to those at the highest levels, he was becoming uncomfortable.

This is taking too long.

Two dispatch riders reached the front of the line, quickly dropped off their satchels, and left. A city merchant was next and came to file a complaint. This took some time, as the clerk asked numerous questions and meticulously recorded each answer.

Next came the young, plain-looking woman directly ahead of Hadrian. "Tell the chamberlain I wish an audience," she said, stepping forward. She wore no makeup, leaving her face dull. Her hair, pulled back and drawn up in a net, did nothing to accentuate her appearance. She was pear-shaped, a feature made even more evident by her gown, which flared at the hips into a great hoop.

"The lord chamberlain is in a meeting with the regents and cannot be disturbed, Your Ladyship."

The words were proper, but the tone disrespectful. The inflection on *Ladyship* sounded particularly sarcastic. The woman either did not notice or chose to ignore it.

"He's been ducking me for over a week," the woman accused. "Something must be done. I need material for the empress's new dress."

"My records indicate that quite a large sum was spent on a gown for Modina recently. We are at war and have more important appropriations to make."

"That was for her presentation on the balcony. She can't walk around in that. I'm talking about a day dress."

"It was very expensive nonetheless. You don't want to take food from our soldiers' mouths just so the empress can have another pretty outfit, do you?"

"Another? She has two worn hand-me-downs!"

"Which is more than many of her subjects, isn't it?"

"The Empire has spent a fortune remodeling this palace. Surely it won't break the Imperial economy to buy a bit of cloth. She doesn't need silk. Linen will do. I'll have the seamstress—"

"I am quite certain that if the lord chamberlain thought the empress needed another dress, he would provide one. Since he has not, she doesn't need it. Now, *Amilia*," he said brazenly, "if you don't mind, I have work to do."

The woman's shoulders slumped in defeat.

Footsteps echoed from behind them, and the small man's smug expression faltered. Hadrian turned and saw the farm girl he once knew as Thrace walking up, flanked by an armed guard. Her dress was faded and frayed just as Amilia had said, but the young woman stood tall, straight, and unabashed. She motioned to the guard to wait as she moved to the front of the line to face the clerk.

"The Lady Amilia speaks with my authority. Please do as she has requested," Thrace said.

The clerk looked confused. His bright eyes flickered nervously between the two.

Thrace continued, "I am sure you do not wish to refuse an order from your empress, do you?"

The scribe lowered his voice, but his irritation still carried as he addressed Amilia. "If you think I am going to kneel before your trained dog, you're mistaken. She's as insane as rumored. I am not as ignorant as the castle staff, and I'm not going to be toyed with by common trash. Get out of here, both of you. I don't have time for foolishness this morning."

Amilia cringed openly, but Thrace did not waver. "Tell me, Quail, do you think the palace guards share your opinions of me?" She looked back at the soldier. "If I were to call him over and accuse you of…let's see…being a traitor, and then…let me think…order him to execute you right here, what do you think he would do?"

The clerk looked suspiciously at Thrace, as if trying to see behind a mask. "You wouldn't dare," he hissed, his eyes shifting between the two women.

"No? Why not?" Thrace replied. "You just said yourself that I'm insane. There's no telling what I might do, or why. From now on, you will treat the Lady Amilia with respect and obey her orders as if they come from the highest authority. Do you understand?"

The clerk nodded slowly.

As Thrace turned to leave, she caught sight of Hadrian and stopped as if she had run into an invisible wall. Her eyes locked on his and she staggered a step and stood, wavering.

Amilia reached out to support her. "Modina, what's wrong?"

Thrace said nothing. She continued to stare at him—her eyes filling with tears, her lips trembling.

The door to the main office opened.

"I don't want to hear another word about it!" Ethelred thundered as he, Saldur, and Archibald Ballentyne entered the anteroom together. Hadrian looked toward the hall window, estimating the number of steps it would take to reach it.

The old cleric focused on Thrace. "What's going on here?"

"I'm taking Her Eminence back to her room," Amilia replied. "I don't think she's feeling well."

"They were requesting material for a new dress," the clerk announced with an accusing tone.

"Well, obviously she needs one. Why is she still wearing that rag?" Saldur asked.

"The lord chamberlain refuses—"

"What do you need him for?" Saldur scowled. "Just tell the clerk to order what you require. You don't need to pester Bernard with such trivialities."

"Thank you, Your Grace," Amilia said, placing one arm around Thrace's waist and supporting her elbow with the other as she gently led her away. Thrace's eyes never left Hadrian, her head turning over her shoulder as they departed.

Saldur followed her gaze and looked curiously at Hadrian. "You look familiar," he pondered, taking a step forward for a closer look.

"Courier," Hadrian said, his heart racing. He bowed and held up the message like a shield.

"He's probably been here a dozen times, Sauly." Ethelred snatched the folded parchment and eyed it. "This is from Merrick!"

All three lost interest in Hadrian as Ethelred unfolded the letter.

"Your Lordships." Hadrian bowed, then turned and quickly walked away, passing Amilia and Thrace. With each step, he felt her stare upon his back until he turned the corner and disappeared.

"Any problems?" Royce asked when Hadrian met him outside.

"Almost. I saw Thrace," Hadrian said as they walked. "She doesn't look good. She's thin, real thin, and pale. They have her begging for clothes from some sniveling little clerk."

Royce looked back, concerned. "Did she recognize you?"

Hadrian nodded. "But she didn't say anything. She just stared."

"I guess if she was planning to arrest us, she'd have done it by now," Royce said.

"Arrest us? This is Thrace we're talking about, for Maribor's sake."

"They've had her for two years—she's the Empress Modina now."

"Yeah, but…"

"What?"

"I don't know," Hadrian said, remembering the look on Thrace's face. "She doesn't look well. I'm not sure what's going on in the palace, but it's not good. And I promised her father I'd look out for her."

Royce shook his head in frustration. "Can we focus on one rescue at a time? For a man in retirement, you're really busy. Besides, Theron's idea of success was to get his eldest son a cooper's shop. I think he *might* settle for his daughter being crowned empress. Now, let's get rid of these horses and make our way down to the wharf. We need to find the *Emerald Storm*."

Chapter 4

THE RACE

While not as large or as wealthy as Colnora, the Imperial capital of Aquesta was the most powerful city in Avryn. The palace dated back to before the age of Glenmorgan and was originally a governor's residence in the ancient days of the Novronian Empire. Scholars pointed to the gray rock of the castle's foundation with pride, and boasted about how Imperial engineers from Percepliquis had laid it. Here, at Highcourt Fields, great tournaments were held each Wintertide. The best knights from all of Apeladorn arrived to compete in jousting, fencing, and other contests of skill. These weeklong events included an ongoing feast for the nobles and provided healthy revenue for the merchants, who showed their wares along the streets. The city became a carnival of sights and sounds that attracted visitors for hundreds of miles.

Much of Aquesta's economic success came from possessing the largest and busiest saltwater port in Avryn. The docks were awash with all manner of sailing watercraft. Brigs, trawlers, grain ships, merchant vessels, and warships all anchored in its harbor. To the south lay the massive shipyard along with rope, net, and sail manufacturers. The northern end of the bay held the wharf and its fish houses, livestock pens, lumberyards, and tar boilers. All the industries of the sea and seagoing were represented.

"Which one is the *Emerald Storm?*" Hadrian asked, looking at the forest of masts and rigging that lined the docks.

"Let's try asking at the information office." Royce hooked his thumb at a tavern perched on the edge of the dock. The wooden walls were bleached white with salt and the clapboards warped like ocean waves. The door hung askew off leather hinges, and above it, a weathered sign in the shape of a fish announced: The Salty Mackerel.

The tavern had few windows, leaving the interior dim and smoky. Each tiny table had a melted candle, and a weak fire smoldered in a round brick hearth in the center of the room. Men packed the place, dressed in loose trousers, long checkered shirts, and wide-brimmed hats with glossy tops. Many sat with pipes in mouths and feet on tables. Some stood leaning against posts. All heads turned when they entered, and Hadrian realized that they stood out in their tunics and cloaks.

"Hello." Hadrian smiled as he struggled to close the door. The wind whistled through and snuffed out the three candles nearest them. "Sorry, could use some better hinges."

"Iron hinges rust overnight here," the bartender said. The thin, crooked man wiped the counter with one hand while gathering empty mugs in the other. "What do you two want?"

"Looking for the *Emerald Storm,*" Royce spoke up.

Neither took more than a step inside. None of the haggard faces looked friendly, and Hadrian liked the comfort of a nearby exit.

"Whatcha want with it?" another man asked.

"We heard it was a good ship, and we were wondering if there are any openings for sailors."

This brought a riotous round of laughter.

"And where be these sailors who be lookin' fer a job?" another voice bellowed from within the murky haze. "Certainly not two sand crabs like you."

More laughter.

"So, what you're saying is you don't know anything about the *Emerald Storm*. Is that right?" Royce returned in a cutting tone that quieted the room.

"The *Storm* is an Imperial ship, lad," the crooked man told them, "and it's all pressed up. They're only taking seasoned-salts now—if there's any room left a'tall."

"If yer lookin' fer work, the fishery always needs gutters. That's about as close to seafaring work as is likely for you two."

Once more the room filled with boisterous laughter.

Hadrian looked at Royce, who shoved the door open and with a scowl stepped outside. "Thanks for the advice," Hadrian told everyone before following his partner.

They sat on the Mackerel's steps, staring at the line of ships across the street. Spires of wood draped with tethered cloth looked like ladies getting dressed for a ball. Hadrian wondered if that was why they always referred to ships as women.

"What now?" he asked softly.

Royce sat hunched with his chin on his hands. "Thinking," was all he said.

Behind them the door scraped open, and the first thing Hadrian noticed was a wide-brimmed hat with one side pinned up by a lavish blue plume.

The face beneath the hat was familiar, and Royce recognized him immediately. "Wyatt Deminthal."

Wyatt hesitated as he locked eyes with Royce. He stood with one foot still inside. He did not look surprised to see them, but merely questioning the wisdom of advancing, like a child who approached a dog that unexpectedly growled. For a heartbeat no one said a word, then Wyatt gritted his teeth and pulled the door shut behind him.

"I can get you on the *Storm*," he said quickly.

Royce narrowed his eyes. "How?"

"I'm the helmsman. They're short a cook and can always use another topman. She's ready to sail as soon as a shipment from the palace arrives."

"Why?"

Wyatt swallowed, and his hand absently drifted to his throat. "I know you saw me. You're here to collect, but I don't have the money I owe. Setting you up in Medford was nothing personal. We were starving, and Trumbul paid gold. I didn't know they were going to arrest you for the king's murder. I was just hiring you to steal the sword—that's all. A hundred gold tenents is a lot of money. And honestly—well, I've never saved that much in my life and I doubt I ever will."

"So, you think getting us on the *Emerald Storm* is worth a hundred gold?"

Wyatt licked his lips, his eyes darting back and forth between them. "I don't know…is it?"

Royce and Hadrian crossed the busy street, dodging carts, and stepped onto weathered decking suspended by ropes. The boards bobbed and weaved beneath their feet. The two were dressed in loose-fitting duck-trousers, oversized linen shirts, tarpaulin hats with a bit of ribbon, and neckerchiefs tied in some arcane way that Wyatt had fussed with for some time to get right. They both carried large, heavy cloth seabags in which they stowed their old clothes and

Hadrian hid his three swords. Being unarmed left him feeling off-balance and naked.

They snaked through the crowded dock, following Wyatt's directions to the end of the pier. The *Emerald Storm* was a smart-looking, freshly painted ship, with three masts, four decks, and the figurehead of a golden winged woman ornamenting the bow. Her sails were furled and green pennants flew from each mast. A small army of men hoisted bags of flour and barrels of salted pork onto the deck, where the crew stowed the supplies. Shouts came from what appeared to be an officer, who directed the work, and another man, who enforced the orders with a stout rattan cane. Two Imperial soldiers guarded the ramp.

"Do you have business here?" one asked at their approach.

"Yeah," Hadrian replied with an innocent, hopeful tone. "We're looking for work. Heard this ship was short on hands. We were told to speak with Mister Temple."

"What's this here?" asked a short, heavyset man with worn clothes, bushy eyebrows, and a gruff voice worn to gravel from years of yelling in the salt air. "I'm Temple."

"Word is you're looking to put on a cook," Hadrian said, pleasantly.

"We are."

"Well then, this is your lucky day."

"Ah-huh." Temple nodded with a sour look.

"And my friend here is an able—ah—topman."

"Oh, he is, is he?" Temple eyed Royce. "We have openings, but only for *experienced* sailors. Normally, I'd be happy to take on green men, but we can't afford anymore landlubbers on this trip."

"But we are sailors—served on the *Endeavor*."

"Are you now?" The ship's master asked skeptically. "Let me see yer hands."

The Race

The master examined Hadrian's palms looking over the various calluses and rough places while grunting occasionally. "You must have spent most of your time in the galley. You've not done any serious rope work." He examined Royce's hands and raised an eyebrow at him. "Have you *ever* been on a ship 'afore? It's certain you've never handled a sheet or a capstan."

"Royce here is a—you know—" Hadrian pointed up at the ship's rigging. "The guy who goes up there."

The master shook his head and laughed. "If you two are seamen, then I'm the Prince of Percepliquis!"

"Oh, but they are, Mister Temple," a voice declared. Wyatt exited the forecastle and came jogging toward them. A bright, white shirt offset his tawny skin and black hair. "I know these men, old mates of mine. The little one is Royce Melborn, as fine a topman as they come. And the big one is ah…"

"Hadrian," Royce spoke up.

"Right, of course. Hadrian's a fine cook—he is, Mister Temple."

Temple pointed toward Royce. "This one's a topman? Are you joking, Wyatt?"

"No, sir, he's one of the best."

Temple looked unconvinced.

"You can have him prove it to you, sir," Hadrian offered. "You could have him race your best up the ropes."

"You mean up the *shrouds*," Wyatt corrected.

"Yeah."

"You mean *aye*."

Hadrian sighed and gave up.

The master did not notice as he focused on Royce. He sized him up then shouted, "Derning!" His strong, raspy voice carried well against the ocean wind. Immediately, a tall, thin fellow with leathery skin jogged over.

"Aye, sir?" he responded respectfully.

"This fellow says he can beat you in a race to loose the topsail and back. What do you think?"

"I think he's mistaken, sir."

"Well, we'll find out." The master turned back to Royce. "I don't actually expect you to beat Derning. Jacob here is one of the best topmen I've seen, but if you put in a good showing, the two of you will have jobs aboard. If it turns out you're wasting my time, well, you'll be swimming back. Derning, you take starboard. Royce, you have port. We'll begin after I have Lieutenant Bishop's permission to get under way."

Mister Temple moved toward the quarterdeck and Wyatt slid down the stair rail to Royce's side. "Remember what I taught you last night...and what Temple said. You don't need to beat Derning."

Hadrian clapped Royce on the back, grinning. "So, the idea is to just free the sail and get back down alive."

Royce nodded and looked apprehensively up at the towering mast before him.

"Not afraid of heights, I hope." Wyatt grinned.

"All right, gentlemen!" Mister Temple shouted, addressing the crew from his new position on the quarterdeck. "We're having a contest." He explained the details to the crew as Royce and Jacob moved to the base of the mainsail. Royce looked up with a grimace that drew laughter from the rest.

"Seriously, he isn't afraid of heights, is he?" Wyatt asked, looking concerned. "I mean, it looks scary, and well—okay, it is the first few times you go aloft, but it really isn't that hard if you're careful and aren't afraid of heights."

Hadrian grinned at Wyatt, but all he said was, "I think you're going to like this."

An officer appeared on the quarterdeck and stood beside the master. "You may set sail, Mister Temple."

THE RACE

The master turned to the main deck and roared, "Loose the topsail!"

Royce appeared caught by surprise, not realizing this was the order to begin the competition. As a result, Jacob got the jump on him, racing up the ratlines like a monkey. Royce turned but did not begin climbing. Instead, he watched Jacob's ascent for several seconds. The majority of the crew rooted for Jacob, but a few, perhaps those that heard they would win a ship's cook if the stranger won, urged Royce to get climbing and called to him like a dog, "Go on, boy! Climb, you damn fool!" Some laughed, and a few made disparaging comments about his mother.

Royce finally seemed to work something out in his head and leapt to the task. He sprang, clearing the deck by several feet, and began to run, rather than climb, up the ratlines. It appeared as if Royce was defying gravity as he pumped his legs up the netting, showing no more difficulty than if he were running up a staircase. He had nearly caught up to Jacob by the time he reached the futtock shrouds. Here the webbing extended away from the mast, reaching toward the small wooden platform known as the masthead. Both men were forced to hang upside down using the ratlines, and Royce lost momentum without the ability to go no-handed.

Jacob swung around the masthead and jumped to the topmast shroud, where he ascended rapidly once more in monkey form. By the time Royce cleared the masthead, he was well behind Derning. He made up time when he could once again advance without crawling inverted. They reached the yard together and both ran out along the top of the narrow beam like circus performers. Seeing them balance a hundred feet above the deck drew gasps from some of the crew, who gaped in amazement. Royce stopped, pivoting to watch his opponent. Derning threw himself down across the yard, lying on his belly. He reached below for the gaskets to free the buntlines. Royce quickly imitated him, and together they worked their way across the arm. As they did, the sail came free, revealing its bright white face and dark green crown. It spilled down, whipping in the wind. Royce and Jacob lifted themselves back to their feet and moved to the end of the beam. They each grabbed the brace, the rope connected to the far end of the yardarm, and slid to the deck with the cheers of the crew in their ears. The two touched down together.

Mister Temple shouted to restore order over the unruly crew. It did not matter who had won. The skillful display by both men was impressive enough to earn their approval. Even Hadrian found himself clapping, and he noticed Wyatt was staring with his mouth open. Temple nodded at Hadrian and Wyatt.

"Stand by at the capstan!" Lieutenant Bishop shouted, returning order. "Loose the heads'ls, hands aloft, loose the tops'ls fore and aft!"

The crew scattered to their duties. A ring of men surrounded the wooden spoke wheel of the capstan, ready to raise the anchor. Wyatt moved quickly toward the ship's helm while the rest, Jacob included, climbed the shrouds of the three masts.

"An' what are you two waiting for?" Mister Temple asked after Hadrian joined Royce. "You heard the lieutenant—get those sails loosed. Hadrian, take station at the capstan."

As they trotted to their duties, Mister Temple gestured in Royce's direction and remarked to Wyatt, "No wonder he doesn't have rough hands, he doesn't use them!"

The ship's captain appeared on the quarterdeck. He stood beside the lieutenant, his hands clasped behind his back, chest thrust out, and chin set against the salty wind that tugged at the edges of his uniform. Of slightly less than average height, he seemed the opposite of the lieutenant. While Bishop was tall and thin, the captain was plump, with a double chin and long hanging cheeks, which quickly flushed red with the wind. He watched the progress of the crew and then nodded to his first officer.

THE RACE

"Take her out, Mister Bishop."

"Raise anchor!" the lieutenant bellowed. "Wheel hard over!"

Hadrian found a place among those at the capstan and pushed against the wooden spokes, rotating the large spool that lifted the anchor from the bottom of the harbor. With the anchor broken out, the wheel hard over, and the forecastle hands drawing at the headsail sheets, the *Emerald Storm* brought her bow around. As she gained steerage, she moved away from the dock and into the clear of the main channel, and the rigging crew dropped the remaining sails. The great canvases quivered and flapped, snapping in the wind like three violent white beasts.

"Hands to the braces!" Mister Temple barked, and the men took hold of the ropes, pulling the yards around until they caught the wind. The sails plumed full as the sea breeze stretched them taut. Hadrian could feel the deck lurch beneath his feet as the *Emerald Storm* slipped forward through the water, rudder balanced against sail-pressure.

They traveled down the coast, passing farmers and workers who paused briefly to look at the handsome vessel flying by. At the helm, Wyatt spun the wheel, steering steadily out to sea. The men on the braces trimmed the yards so not a sail fluttered, sending the ship dashing through the waves as she raced from shore.

"Course sou'west by south, sir," Wyatt updated Temple, who repeated the statement to the lieutenant, who repeated it to the captain, who in turn nodded his approval.

The men at the capstan dispersed, leaving Hadrian looking around for something to do. Royce descended to the deck beside him, neither one certain of his duty now that the ship was under way. It did not matter much, as the lieutenant, the captain, and Temple were all busy on the quarterdeck. The other hands moved casually now, cleaning up the rigging, finishing the job of stowing the supplies, and generally settling in.

"Why didn't we ever consider sailing as a profession?" Hadrian asked Royce as he moved to the side and faced the wind. He took a deep, satisfying breath and smiled. "This is nice. A lot better than a sweaty, fly-plagued horse—and look at the land go by! How fast do you think we're going?"

"The fact that we're trapped here, with no chance of retreat except into the ocean, doesn't bother you?"

Hadrian glanced over the side at the heaving waves. "Well, not until now. Why do you always have to ruin everything? Couldn't you let me enjoy the moment?"

"You know me, just trying to keep things in perspective."

"Our course is south. Any clue where we might be going?"

Royce shook his head. "It only means we aren't invading Melengar, but we could be headed just about anywhere else." Someone arriving deck side caught his attention. "Who's this now?"

A man in red and black appeared from below and climbed the stair to the quarterdeck. He stood out from the rest of the crew by virtue of his pale skin and silken vestments, which were far too elegant for the setting and whipped about like streamers at a fair. He moved hunched over; his slumped shoulders reminding Hadrian of a crow shuffling along a branch. He sported a mustache and short goatee. His dark hair, combed back, emphasized a dramatically receding hairline.

"Broken-crown crest," Hadrian noted. "Seret."

"Red cassock," Royce added. "Sentinel."

"At least he's not Luis Guy. It'd be pretty hard to hide on a ship this size."

"If it was Guy," Royce smiled wickedly, "we wouldn't need to hide."

Hadrian noticed Royce glance over the side of the ship at the water that foamed and churned as it rushed past.

"If a sentinel is on board," Royce continued, "we can assume there are seret as well. They never travel alone."

"Maybe below."

"Maybe disguised in the crew," Royce cautioned.

To starboard, a sailor dropped his burden on the deck and wiped the sweat from his brow with a rag. Noticing them standing idle, he walked over.

"Yer good," he said to Royce. "No man's beaten Jacob aloft 'afore."

The sailor was tan and thin, with a tattoo of a woman on his forearm and a ring of silver in his ear.

"I didn't beat him. We landed together," Royce corrected.

"Aye, clever that. My name's Grady. What do they call you?"

"Royce, and this is Hadrian."

"Oh, yeah, the cook." Grady looked at the thief, studying him. "Royce, huh? I'm surprised I haven't heard yer name 'afore. With skills like you got, I woulda figured you'd be famous. What ships 'ave you served on?"

"None around these waters," Royce replied.

Grady looked at him curiously. "Where then? The Sound? Dagastan? The Sharon? Try me, I've been around a few places myself."

"Sorry, I'm really bad at remembering names."

Grady's eyebrows rose. "You don't remember the names of the ships you served on?"

"I would prefer not to discuss them."

"Aye, consider the subject closed." He looked at Hadrian. "You were with him then?"

"We've worked together for some time."

Grady nodded. "Just forget I said anything. I won't be getting in the way. You can bank money on Grady's word, too." The man winked, then walked away, glancing back over his shoulder at them a few times as he went off, grinning.

"Seems like a nice sort," Hadrian said. "Strange and confusing, but nice. You think he knows why we're here?"

"Wish he did," Royce replied, watching Grady resume his work. "Then he could tell us. Still, I've found that when hunting Merrick, stranger things have been known to happen. One thing's for certain—this trip is going to be interesting."

Chapter 5

BROKEN SILENCE

It was early, but Nimbus was already waiting outside the closed door of Amilia's office with armloads of parchments. He smiled brightly at her approach. "Morning, Your Ladyship," he greeted, with as much of a bow as he could manage without spilling his burden. "Beautiful day, isn't it?"

Amilia grunted in reply. She was not a morning person, and today's agenda held a meeting with Regent Saldur. If anything was likely to ruin a day, that would. She opened her office door with a key kept on a chain around her neck. The office was a reward for the successful presentation of the empress nearly a month before.

Modina was near death when Saldur first appointed Amilia to the post of Imperial Secretary to the Empress. The young ruler never spoke a word, was dangerously thin, and had an unwavering expression that was never more than a blank stare. Amilia provided her with better living conditions and worked hard to get her to eat. After several months, the girl began to improve. Modina managed to memorize a short speech for the day of her presentation, but abandoned the prepared text and publically singled out Amilia, proclaiming her a hero.

No one was more shocked than Amilia, but Saldur held her responsible. Rather than exploding in anger, he congratulated her. From that day on, his attitude toward Amilia changed—as if she had bought admission into the exclusive club of the deviously ambitious. In his eyes, she was not only capable of manipulating the mentally unbalanced ruler, but willing to do so as well. This raised opinion of her was followed by additional responsibilities and the new title: Chief Secretary to the Grand Imperial Empress.

She took her directions from Saldur, as Modina remained locked in the dark recesses of her madness. One of her new responsibilities was reading and replying to mail addressed to the empress. Saldur gave her the task as soon as he discovered she could read and write. Amilia also received the responsibility of official gatekeeper. She decided who could, and who could not, have an audience with Modina. Normally a position of extreme power, it was all a farce because absolutely no one *ever* saw Modina.

Despite her grandiose new title, her office was a small chamber, nothing but an old desk and a pair of bookshelves. The room was cold, damp, and sparse—but it was hers. She was filled with pride each morning when she sat behind the desk, and pride was something Amilia was unaccustomed to.

"Are those more letters?" Amilia asked.

"Yes, I am afraid so," Nimbus replied. "Where would you like them?"

"Just drop them on the pile with the others. I can see now why Saldur gave me this job."

"It is a very prestigious task," Nimbus assured her. "You are the de facto voice of the Empire as it relates to the people. What you write is taken as the word of the empress, and thus the voice of a god incarnate."

"So, you're saying I am the voice of god now?"

Nimbus smiled thoughtfully. "In a matter of speaking—yes."

"You have a crazy way of seeing things, Nimbus. You really do."

He was always able to cheer her up. His outlandishly colored clothes and silly powdered wig made her smile on even the bleakest of days. Moreover, the odd little courtier had a bizarre manner of finding joy in everything, blind to the inevitable disaster that Amilia knew lurked at every turn.

Nimbus deposited the letters in the bin beside Amilia's desk then fished out a tablet and looked it over briefly before speaking. "You have a meeting this morning with Lady Rashambeau, Baroness Fargal, and the Countess Ridell. They have insisted on speaking to you directly about their failed petitions to have a private audience with Her Supreme Eminence. You also have a dedication to make on behalf of the empress at the new memorial in Capital Square. That's at noon. Also, the material has arrived, but you still need to get specifications to the seamstress for the new dress. And, of course, you have a meeting this afternoon with Regent Saldur."

"Any idea yet what he wants to see me about?"

Nimbus shook his head.

Amilia slumped in her chair. Certainly Saldur's visit had to do with Modina berating the clerk yesterday. She had no idea how to explain the empress's actions. It was the only time since her speech that Modina had uttered a single word.

"Would you like me to help you answer those?" Nimbus asked with a sympathetic smile.

"No, I'll do it. Can't have both of us playing god now can we? Besides, you have your own work. Tell the seamstress to meet me in Modina's chambers in four hours. That should give me time to reduce this pile some. Reschedule the Ladies of the Court meeting to just before noon."

"But you have the dedication at noon."

"Exactly."

"Excellent planning," Nimbus praised. "Is there anything else I can do for you before I get to work?"

Amilia shook her head. Nimbus bowed and left.

The pile beside her got higher each day. She plucked a letter from the top and started working. While not a hard job, the task was repetitious, as she said the same thing in each.

The Office of the Empress regrets to inform you that her most serene and royal Grand Imperial Majesty the Empress Modina Novronian will not be able to receive you due to time constraints caused by important and pressing matters of state.

She had only replied to seven of the letters when there was a soft knock at the office door. A maid hesitantly popped her head inside. It was the new girl. She only started yesterday, but she worked hard and quietly, which Amilia liked. Amilia nodded an invitation, and the maid wordlessly slipped inside with her bucket, mop, and cleaning tools, taking great pains not to bang them against the door.

Amilia recalled her own days as a servant in the castle. As a kitchen worker, she rarely cleaned rooms but occasionally would fill in for a sick chambermaid. She used to loathe working in a room with a noble present. It always made her so self-conscious and frightened. You could never tell what they might do. One minute they might be friendly, the next they were calling for you to be whipped. She never understood how they could be so capricious and cruel.

Amilia watched the girl set about her work. The maid was on her hands and knees scrubbing the floor with a brush, the skirt of her uniform soaked with soapy water. Amilia had a stack of inquiries to attend to, but the maid distracted her. She felt guilty not acknowledging the girl's presence. It felt rude. *I should talk to her.* Even as Amilia thought this, she knew it would be a mistake. This new girl saw her as a noble, the Secretary to the Empress, and would be terrified if Amilia so much as offered a *"good morning."*

Perhaps a few years older than herself, the girl was slender and pretty, although little could be determined, given her attire. She wore a loose-fitting dress with a canvas apron, her figure hidden, a mystery lost beneath the folds. All serving girls adopted the style except the foolish or ambitious. While working in the halls of those who took what they wanted, it was best to avoid notice.

Amilia wondered if the girl was married. Might she have a family in the city that she went home to each night, or like herself, had she left everything, and everyone, to live in the castle? Despite her youth, she likely had several children by now. Pretty peasant girls married young.

Amilia chided herself for watching the maid instead of working, but something kept her attention. The way she moved and how she held her head looked out of place. She watched her dab the brush in the water and stroke the floor, moving it from side to side like a painter. She spread water around, but did little to free the dirt from the surface. Edith Mon would whip her for that. The headmistress was a cruel taskmaster. Amilia had found herself on the wrong end of her belt on a number of occasions for lesser infractions. For that reason alone, Amilia felt sorry for the poor girl. She knew all too well what she faced.

"Are they treating you well here?" Amilia found herself asking, despite her determination to remain silent.

The girl looked up and glanced around the room.

"Yes, you," Amilia assured her.

"Yes, milady," the maid replied, looking up.

She is looking right at me, Amilia thought, stunned. Even with her title, and a rank equivalent to a baroness, Amilia still had a hard time returning the stare of even the lowest nobles, but this girl was looking right at her.

"You can tell me if they aren't, I know what it is like to—" she stopped, realizing the maid would not believe her. "I understand new servants can be picked on and belittled by the others."

"I am getting along fine, milady," she said.

Amilia smiled, trying to set her at ease. "I didn't mean to suggest you weren't. I am very pleased with you. I just know it can be hard sometimes when you start out in a new place. I want you to know that I can help you if you are having trouble."

"Thank you," she said, but Amilia heard the suspicion in her voice.

Having a noble offering to help with bullying peers was probably a shock to the girl. If it had been her, Amilia would think it a trap of some kind, a test perhaps to see if she would speak ill of others. If she admitted to problems, the noble might have her removed from the palace. Under no circumstances would Amilia have admitted anything to a noble, no matter how kindly the woman might have presented herself.

Amilia felt instantly foolish. There was a division between nobles and commoners and, for good or ill, she was now on the other side. The conditioning that separated the two was far too entrenched for her to wipe away. She decided to stop tormenting the poor girl and return to her work. Just then, however, the maid put down the scrub brush and stood.

"You're, Lady Amilia, is that right?"

"Yes," she replied, surprised at the sudden forwardness.

"You're the Secretary to the Empress?"

"How well informed you are. It's good that you are learning your way around. It took me quite some time to figure out—"

"How is she?"

Amilia hesitated. It was very inappropriate to interrupt, and terribly bold to inquire so bluntly of Her Eminence. Amilia was touched, however, by her concern for the welfare of Modina.

Perhaps this girl was unaccustomed to interacting with the gentry. She was likely from some isolated village that never saw a visiting noble. The unnerving way she held Amilia's stare revealed she had no experience with proper social etiquette. Edith Mon would waste no time beating those lessons into her.

"She's fine," she replied. Then as a matter of habit added, "She was ill, and still is, but getting better every day."

"I never see her," the maid went on. "I've seen you, and the chancellor, the regents, and the lord chamberlain, but I never see her in the halls or at the banquet table."

"She guards her privacy. You have to understand, as empress everyone wants time with her."

"I guess she gets around using secret passages?"

"Secret passages?" Amilia chuckled at the imagination of this girl. "No, she doesn't use secret passages."

"But I heard this palace is very old and filled with hidden stairs and corridors that lead to all kinds of secret places."

"I don't know anything about that," Amilia replied. "What got this into your head?"

The maid immediately put a hand over her mouth in embarrassment. Her eyes dropped to the floor in submission. "Forgive me, milady. I didn't mean to be so bold. I'll get back to my work now."

"That's all right," Amilia replied as the maid dunked her brush again. "What's your name, dear?"

"Ella, milady," the maid replied softly, without pausing or looking up.

"Well, Ella, if you have problems or other questions, you have permission to speak to me."

"Thank you, milady. That is very kind of you."

Amilia returned to her own work and left the maid to hers. In a short time, the servant finished and gathered her things to leave.

"Goodbye, Ella," Amilia offered.

The maid smiled at the sound of her name and nodded appreciatively. As she walked out, Amilia glanced at her hands where they gripped the bucket and mop, and was surprised to see long fingernails on each. Ella noticed her glance, shifted her grip to cover her nails, and promptly left the chamber.

Amilia stared after her awhile, wondering how a working girl could manage to grow nails as nice as hers. She put it out of her mind and returned to her letters.

"You realize they are going to get wise," Amilia said, after the seamstress had finished taking Modina's measurements and left the chamber.

The Imperial Secretary moved around the empress's bedroom, straightening up. Modina sat beneath the narrow window, in the only patch of sunshine to enter the room. It was where Amilia found her most often. She would sit there for hours just staring outside, watching clouds and birds. It broke Amilia's heart a little each time she saw her longing for a world barred to her.

The empress showed no response to Amilia's comment. Her lucidity from the day before had vanished. The empress heard her, though. She was quite certain of that now.

"They aren't stupid," she went on as she fluffed a pillow. "After your speech and that incident with the clerk yesterday, I think it's only a matter of time. You would have been wiser to stay in your room and let me handle it."

"He wasn't going to listen to you," the empress spoke.

Amilia dropped the pillow.

Turning as casually as she could, she stole a glance over her shoulder to see Modina still looking out the window with her traditional vague and distant expression. Amilia slowly picked up the pillow and resumed her straightening. Then she ventured, "It might have taken a little time, but I'm certain I could have persuaded him to provide us with the material."

Amilia waited, holding her breath, listening.

Silence.

Just when she was certain it had only been one of her rare outbursts of coherency, Modina spoke again. "He never would have given in to you. You're scared of him, and he knows it."

"And you aren't?"

Again silence. Amilia waited.

"I'm not afraid of anything anymore," the empress finally replied, her voice distant and thin.

"Maybe not afraid, but it would bother you if they took the window away."

"Yes," Modina said simply.

Amilia watched as the empress closed her eyes and turned her face full into the light of the sun.

"If Saldur discovers your masquerade—if he thinks you've been just acting insane and misleading the regents for over a year—it might frighten him into locking you up where you can't do any harm. They could put you in a dark hole somewhere and leave you there."

"I know," Modina said, her eyes still closed and head tilted upward. Immersed in the daylight, she almost appeared to glow. "But I won't let them hurt you."

The words took a moment to register with Amilia. She heard them clearly enough, but their meaning came so unexpectedly that she sat on the bed without realizing. Looking back it was obvious, but not until that moment did she see it. The speech was for Amilia's benefit—to ensure that Ethelred and Saldur could not have her removed or killed. Few people had ever gone out of their way for Amilia. It was unimaginable for Modina—the crazy empress—to risk herself in this way. Such an event was as likely as the wind changing direction to suit her, or the sun asking her permission to shine.

"Thank you," was all she could think to say. For the first time she felt awkward in Modina's presence. "I'm going to go now."

She headed for the door. As her hand touched the latch, Modina spoke again.

"It isn't completely an act, you know."

Waiting inside the regent's office, Amilia realized she had not heard a word in her meeting or during the dedication that morning. Dumbfounded by her conversation with Modina—the mere fact that she even had a conversation—little else registered. Her distraction, however, vanished the instant Saldur arrived.

The regent appeared imposing, as always, in his elegant robe and cape of purple and black. His white hair and lined face lent him a grandfatherly appearance, but his eyes held no warmth.

"Afternoon, Amilia," he said, walking past her and taking a seat at his desk. The regent's office was dramatically opulent. Five times larger than her office, it featured a more elegant decor. A fine, patterned rug covered the polished hardwood, and numerous end tables flanked couches and armchairs around a table and chessboard. The fireplace was an impressively wide hearth of finely chiseled marble. There were decanters of spirits on the shelves, along with thick books. Religiously themed paintings lined the spaces between the bookcases and windows. One illustrated the familiar scene of Maribor anointing Novron. The immense desk, behind which Saldur sat, was a dark mahogany polished to a fine luster and adorned with a bouquet of fresh flowers. The entire office was perfumed with the heady scent of incense, the kind Amilia had only smelled once before in a cathedral.

"Your Grace," Amilia replied, respectfully.

"Sit down, my dear," Saldur said.

Amilia found a chair and mechanically sat. Every muscle in her body was tense. Amilia wished Modina had not spoken to her that morning—then she could honestly plead innocence. Amilia was no good at lying and had no idea how she should respond to Saldur's interrogation in order to bring the least amount of punishment to her and the empress. She was still debating what she might say when Saldur spoke.

"I have some news for you," he said, folding his hands on the surface of the desk and leaning forward. "It will not be public for several weeks, but you need to know now so you can begin preparations. I want you to keep this to yourself until I announce it, do you understand?"

Amilia nodded as if she understood.

"In almost four months, during the Wintertide celebrations, Modina will marry Regent Ethelred. I don't think I need to impress upon you the importance of this. The Patriarch himself is personally coming to perform the ceremony. All eyes will be on this palace… and on the empress."

Amilia said nothing and barely managed another shallow nod.

"It is your charge to ensure that nothing embarrassing occurs. I have been very pleased with your work to date, and as a result I am giving you an opportunity to excel further. I am putting *you* in charge of arranging the ceremony. It will be your responsibility to develop a guest list and prepare invitations. Go to the lord chamberlain for help with that. You will also need to coordinate with the palace cooks for meals. I understand you have a good relationship with the head cook?"

Once more she nodded.

"Wonderful. There should be decorations, entertainment—music certainly, and perhaps a magician or an acrobat. The ceremony will take place here, in the Great Hall. That should make things a bit easier for you. You will also need to have a wedding dress made—one worthy of the empress." Seeing the tension on her face Saldur added, "Relax, Amilia, this time you only need to train her to say two words… *I do.*"

Chapter 6

THE EMERALD STORM

As the ship lurched once more, Hadrian stumbled and nearly hit his head on the overhead beam. It would have been his third time that day. The lower decks of the *Emerald Storm* provided meager headroom and precious little light. An obstacle course of sea chests, ditty bags, crude wooden benches, tables that swung from ropes, and close to one hundred thirty men were all crammed into the berth deck. Hadrian made his way aft, dodging the majority of the starboard watch, most of whom were asleep, swaying in hammocks strung from the same thick wooden crossbeams on which Hadrian had nearly cracked his skull. It was not merely the clutter or the shifting of the ship that made Hadrian stagger; he had been feeling nauseated since sunset.

The *Emerald Storm* had been at sea for nearly fifteen hours, and the enigma of life aboard ship was slowly revealing itself. Hadrian had spent many years in the company of professional soldiers and recognized that each branch of the military held its own jargon, traditions, and idiosyncrasies, but he had never set foot on a ship. He knew he could be certain of only two things: he had a lot of learning to do, and little time to do it.

He had already picked up several important facts, such as where you relieved yourself, which, to his surprise, was at the head of the ship. A precarious experience, as he had to hang out over the sea at the base of the bowsprit. This might be second nature to sailors, and easy for Royce, but it gave Hadrian pause.

Another highly useful bit of information was at least a cursory understanding about the chain of command. It was easy to see that there were officers—noblemen mostly—and skilled tradesmen, who held a higher rank than the general seamen, but Hadrian could also tell there were substrata within these broad classes. There were different ranks of officers and even more subtle levels of seniority, influence, and jurisdiction. He could not expect to penetrate such a complex hierarchy on his first day. All he managed to determine with any clarity was that the boatswain and his mates were the ones charged with making sure the seamen did their jobs. They were quite persuasive with their short rope whips and kept a keen eye on the crew at all times. As such, they were the ones he watched.

The ship's crew divided into two watches. While one worked the ship, the other rested, slept, or ate. Lieutenant Bishop placed Royce on the starboard watch assigned to the maintop. His job was to work the rigging on the main or center mast. This put him under boatswain Bristol Bennet and his three mates. Hadrian had seen their like before. Drunks, vagrants, and thugs, they would never have amounted to much on land, but aboard ship they held power and status. This chance to repay others for their mistreatment made them cruel and quick to punish. Hadrian still waited to discover his watch assignment, but he hoped it would be the same as Royce.

He had been lucky so far. This being the first day out, meals had been little more than placing out fresh foods from the recent stay at port. Fruit, fresh bread, and salted meats were merely handed out with no actual cooking required. Consequently, Hadrian's talents remained untested, but time was running out. He knew how to cook, of course. He had prepared meals for years using little more than a campfire, but that had mainly been for himself and Royce. He didn't know how to cook for an entire ship's crew. Needing to find out exactly what they expected drove him to wander in hopes of finding Wyatt.

"The Princess of Melengar rules there now," Hadrian heard a young lad say.

He didn't look to be much more than sixteen. He was a waif of a boy with thin whiskers, freckles darkened by days in the sun, and curly hair cut in a bowl-like fashion except for a short ponytail he tied with a black cord. He sat with Wyatt, Grady, and a few other men around a swaying table illuminated by a candle melted to the center of a copper plate. They were playing cards and the giant shadows they cast only made Hadrian's approach more disorienting.

"She doesn't rule Ratibor, she's the mayor," Wyatt corrected the boy as he laid a card on the pile before him.

"What's the difference?"

"She was appointed, lad."

"What's that mean?" the boy asked, as he tried to decide which card to play, holding his hand so tight to his chest he could barely see them himself.

"It means she didn't just take over, the people of the city *asked* her to run things."

"But she can still execute people, right?"

"I suppose."

"Sounds like a ruler to me." The boy laid a card with a wide grin, indicating that he thought it was a surprisingly good play.

"Sounds like them people of Ratibor are dumb as dirt," Grady said, gruffly. His expression betrayed his irritation at the boy's discard. "They finally get the yoke off their backs and right away they ask for a new one."

"Grady!" said a man with a white kerchief on his head. "I'm from Ratibor, you oaf!"

"Exactly! Thanks for proving me point, Bernie," Grady replied, slamming his play on the table, so hard several surrounding seamen groaned in their hammocks. Grady laughed at his own joke and the rest at the table chuckled good-naturedly, except Bernie from Ratibor.

"Hadrian!" Wyatt greeted him warmly as the new cook staggered up to them like a drunk. "We were just talking about land affairs. Most of these poor sods haven't been ashore in over a year and we were filling them in on the news about the war."

"Which has been bloody cracking, seeing as how we didn't even know there was one," Grady said, feigning indignation.

"We were just in dock though," Hadrian said. "I would have thought—"

"That don't mean nuttin'," one of the other men said. With next to no hair and few teeth, he appeared to be the oldest at the table, and possibly the entire ship. He had a silver earring that glinted with the candlelight, a tattoo of a mermaid that wrapped around his forearm, and he, too, wore a white kerchief on his head. "Most of this 'ere crew is pressed. The captain would be barmy to let them touch solid ground in a port. He and Mister Bishop would be the only ones left to rig her!"

This brought a round of laughter and garnered irritated growls from those trying to sleep.

"You don't look so good," Wyatt mentioned to Hadrian.

He shook his head miserably. Looking around at the others, he said, "It's been a long time since I've been on a ship. Does the *Storm* always rock so much?"

"Hmm?" Wyatt glanced at him then laughed. "This? This here is nothing. You won't even notice it in a day or so." He watched the next man at the table play his card. "We're still in the sound. Wait until we hit the open sea. You might want to sit. You're sweating."

Hadrian touched his face and felt the moisture. "Funny, I feel chilled, if anything."

"Have a seat," Wyatt said. "Poe, give him your spot."

"Why me?" the young boy asked, insulted.

"Because I said so." Poe's expression showed that was not enough for him to give up one of the limited places. "And because I am a quartermaster and you're a seaman, but even more importantly, because Mister Bishop appointed you cook's mate."

"He did?" Poe asked and blinked, a smile crossing his face.

"Congratulations," Wyatt said. "Now, you might want to make a good impression on your new boss and move your infernal arse!"

The boy promptly stood and pretended to clean the bench with an invisible duster. "After you, sir!" he said, with an exaggerated bow.

"Does he know anything about cooking?" Hadrian asked dubiously, taking the seat.

"Sure, sure!" Poe declared exuberantly. "I know plenty. You just wait. I'll show ya."

"Good, I don't feel up to working with food yet." Hadrian let his head drop into his hands. The old man next to Wyatt tossed down his card and the whole group groaned in agony.

"You bloody bastard, Drew!" Grady barked at him, tossing what remained of his cards onto the pile. The others did the same.

Drew grinned, showing his few yellowed teeth, and collected the tiny pile of silver tenents. "That's it for me, boys. Goodnight."

"Night, Drew, ya lousy Lanksteer!" Grady said, shooing him away as if he were a bug. "We can talk at breakfast, eh?"

"Sure, Grady," Drew said. "Oh, that reminds me, I heard something right funny tonight when I was reefing the tops'l. We're going to be taking on a passenger to help find the horn. How stupid are these landlubbers? It's only the most well-known point on the Sharon! Anyway, remind me at breakfast and I'll tell ya about it. It's a real hoot it is. Night now."

Most of the rest of the men headed off, leaving just Wyatt, Grady, Poe, and Hadrian.

"You should turn in as well," Wyatt told Poe.

"I'm not tired," he protested.

"I didn't ask if you were tired, did I?"

"I want to stay up and celebrate my promotion."

"Off with ya before I report you for disobeying a superior."

Poe scowled and stomped off, looking for his hammock.

"You too, Grady," Wyatt told him.

The old seaman looked at Wyatt suspiciously, then leaned over and quietly asked, "Why you trying to get rid of me, Deminthal?"

"Because I'm tired of looking at that ugly scowl of yours, that's why."

"Codswallop!" he hissed. "You wanna be alone to talk about the you-know-what, don't ya? Both of you are in on it. I can tell, and that Royce fellow, he's in too. How many more you got, Wyatt? Room for another? I'm pretty good in a fight."

"Shut up, Grady," Wyatt told him. "Talk like that can get you hanged."

"Okay, okay," Grady said, holding up his palms. "Just letting you know, that's all." He got up and headed for his own hammock, casting glances back over his shoulder several times until he disappeared into the forest of swinging men.

"What was that all about?" Hadrian asked, hooking a thumb toward Grady's retreating figure.

"I don't know," Wyatt replied. "There's always one sailor on board any ship looking for a mutiny. Grady seems to be the *Emerald Storm's*. Ever since he signed on, he's been thinking there's a conspiracy going on—mostly because he wants there to be, I think. He has issues with authority, Grady does." Wyatt started gathering up the scattered deck of cards into a pile. "So, what's your story?"

"How do you mean?" Hadrian asked.

"Why are you and Royce here? I stuck my neck out getting you on board. I think I have a right to know why."

"We're looking for a safer line of work and thought we'd try sailing," Hadrian offered. Wyatt's face showed he was not buying it. "We're on a job, but I can't tell you more than that."

"Does it have to do with the secret cargo?"

Hadrian blinked. "It's possible. What *is* the secret cargo?"

"Weapons. Steel swords, heavy shields, Imperial-made crossbows, armor—enough to outfit a good-size army. It came aboard at the last minute, hauled up in the middle of the night just before we sailed."

"Interesting," Hadrian mused. "Any idea where we're headed?"

"Nope, but that's not unusual. Captains usually keep that information to themselves, and Captain Seward doesn't even share that with me…and I'm the quartermaster."

"Quartermaster? I thought you were the helmsman."

"I'm guessing you've served in armies, haven't you?"

"A few, and the quartermaster is the supply officer."

"But on the sea, the quartermaster steers the ship, and as I mentioned the captain hasn't even told me where we are going." Wyatt shuffled the cards absently. "So, you don't know where the ship is going, and you weren't aware of the cargo. This job didn't come with much in the way of information, did it?"

"What about you?" Hadrian turned the tables. "What are you doing here?"

"I could say I was working for a living, and for me it would actually make sense, but like you I'm looking for answers."

"To what?"

"To where my daughter is." Wyatt paused a moment, his eyes glancing at the candle. "Allie was taken a week ago. I was out finding work, and while I was gone the Imps grabbed her."

"Grabbed her? Why?"

Wyatt lowered his voice, "Allie is part elven, and the New Empire is not partial to their kind. Under a new law, anyone with even a drop of elf blood is subject to arrest. They've been rounding them up and putting them on ships, but no one can tell me where they've taken them. So, here I am."

"But what makes you think this ship will go to the same place?"

"I take it you haven't ventured down to the waist hold yet?" He paused a second, then added, "That's the bottom of the ship, below the water line. Ship stores are there, as well as livestock like goats, chickens, and cows. Sailors on report get the duty to pump the bilge. It's a miserable job on account of the manure mixing with the seawater that leaks in. It's also where—right now—they have more than a hundred elves chained up in an area half this size."

Hadrian nodded with a grimace at the thought.

"You and Royce gave me a break once because of my daughter. Why was that?"

"That was Royce's call. You need to take that up with him. Although, I wouldn't do that for a while, he's sicker than I am. I've never seen him so miserable, and this sea business is making him irritable."

Wyatt nodded. "My daughter's the same way on water. Pitiful little thing, she's like a cat on a piece of driftwood. It takes her forever to get accustomed to the rocking." He paused a moment, looking at the candle, then said, "I got the impression the two of you might be sympathetic. Maybe, if you finish this job, you might be willing to help me a little—a turn for a turn?"

"I thought you got us aboard to pay off a debt."

Wyatt sighed.

"I don't know—maybe." Hadrian glanced at the mass of men around him and lowered his voice to a whisper. "The job we're on is important, and we can't afford to be distracted, but if the situation presents itself, we might be able to help. Something tells me I won't have much trouble convincing Royce to stick his neck out for this one."

Hadrian felt the nausea rising in his stomach once more. His face must have betrayed his misery.

"Don't worry. Seasickness usually only lasts three days," Wyatt assured him as he put the cards in his breast pocket. "After that, both of you will be fine."

"If we can stay on board that long. I don't know anything about being a ship's cook."

Wyatt smiled. "Don't worry. I've got you covered. Poe will do most of the work. I know he looks young, but he'll surprise you."

"So, how is it that I get an assistant?"

"As ship's cook, you rank as a petty officer. Don't get all excited though. You're still under the boatswains and their mates, but it does grant you the services of Ordinary Seaman Poe. It also exempts you from the watches. That means so long as the ship's meals are on schedule, the rest of your time is your own. What you need to know is that breakfast is promptly at the first bell of the forewatch," Wyatt paused. "That's the first time you'll hear a single bell toll after eight bells is rung just after the sun breaks above the horizon.

"So have Poe light the galley fires shortly after middle watch. He'll know when that is. Tell him to make skillygalee—that's oatmeal gruel. Don't forget biscuits. Biscuits get served at every meal. At eight bells, the men are piped to breakfast. Each mess will send someone to you with a messkid, sorta like a wooden bucket. Your job will be to dish out the food. Have Poe make some tea as well. The men will drink beer and rum at dinner and supper, but not at breakfast, and no one on board will risk drinking straight water."

"Risk?"

"Water sits in barrels for months, or years if a ship is on a long voyage. It gets rancid. Tea and coffee are okay 'cause they're boiled and have a little flavor. Coffee is expensive, though, and reserved for the officers. The crew and the midshipmen eat first. After that, Basil, the officers' cook, will arrive to make meals for the lieutenants and captain. Just stay out of his way.

"For dinner make boiled pork. Have Poe start boiling it right after Basil leaves. The salted meat will throw off a thick layer of fat. Half of that goes to the top captains to grease the rigging, the other half you can keep. You can sell it to tallow merchants at the next port for a bit of coin, but don't give it to the men. It will make you popular if you do, but it can also give them scurvy, and the captain won't like it. Have Poe boil some vegetables and serve them together as a stew, and don't forget the biscuits."

"So, I tell Poe what to make and dish it out, but I don't actually do any cooking?"

Wyatt smiled. "That's the benefit of being a petty officer. Sadly, however, you only get a seaman's rate of pay. For supper, just serve what's left over from dinner, grog, and, of course, biscuits. After that, have Poe clean up and like I said, the rest of the day is open to you. Sound easy?"

"Maybe, if I could stand straight and keep my stomach from doing back-flips."

"Listen to Poe. He'll take good care of you. Now you'd best get back in your hammock. Trust me, it helps. Oh, and just so you know, you would have been wrong."

"About what?" Hadrian asked.

"About thinking sailing was a safer line of work."

The Emerald Storm

It was still dark, when the captain called, "All hands!"

A cold wind had risen, and in the dark hours before dawn a light rain sprayed the deck, adding a wet chill to the seasick misery that had already deprived Hadrian of most of his sleep. During the night, the *Emerald Storm* passed by the Isle of Niel and now approached the Point of Man. The Point was a treacherous headland shoal that marked the end of Avryn Bay and the start of the Sharon Sea. In the dark, it was difficult to see the shoals, but the sound was unmistakable. Somewhere ahead there came the rhythmic, thundering boom of waves crashing against the point.

The below decks emptied as the boatswain and his mates roused all the men from both watches with their starter ropes, driving them up to stations.

"Bring her about!" shouted the captain from his perch on the quarterdeck. The dignified figure of Lieutenant Bishop echoed the order, which Mister Temple repeated.

"Helm-a-lee!" shouted the captain. Once more, the order echoed across the decks. Wyatt spun the ship's great wheel.

"Tacks and sheets!" Lieutenant Bishop barked to the crew.

At the mizzen, main, and foremasts the other lieutenants shouted more orders, which the boatswains reinforced.

Hadrian stood on the main deck in the dark and drizzling rain, unsure of his station or even if he had one. He was a cook after all, but it seemed even a cook was expected to lend a hand on deck when necessary. He still felt ill, but Royce appeared worse. Hadrian watched as Boatswain Bristol, a big burly man, ordered him up the ropes, waving his short whip menacingly. Drained of color, Royce's face and hands stood out pale in the dark, his eyes unfocused and empty. He reluctantly moved up the main mast's ratlines, but he did not display any of the acrobatics of the day before. Instead, he crawled miserably and hesitated partway up. He hovered in the wet rigging as if he might fall. From below, Bristol cursed at him until, at last, he moved upward once more. Hadrian imagined that the higher into the rigging Royce went, the more pronounced the sway of the ship would be. Between that, the slippery wet ropes, and the cold wind-driven rain, he did not envy his friend.

Several men were working the ropes that controlled the direction of the sails, but others, like him, remained idle, waiting in lines, which the boatswains formed. There was a tension evident in the silence of the crew. The booming of the headlands grew louder and closer, sounding like the pounding of a giant's hammer or the heartbeat of a god. They seemed to be flying blindly into the maw of some enormous unseen beast that would swallow them whole. The reality, Hadrian imagined, would not be much different should they come too close to the shoals.

All eyes watched the figure of Captain Seward, anticipating something. The ship was turning, he could tell by the feel of the wind and the direction of the rain. The sails, once full and taut, began to flutter and collapsed as the bow crossed over into the face of the wind.

"Mains'l haul!" the captain suddenly shouted, and the crew cast off the bowlines and braces.

Seeing the movements, Hadrian realized the strategy. They were attempting a windward tack around the dangerous point, which meant the wind would be blowing the ship's hull toward the treacherous rocks even as they struggled to reset the sails to catch the wind from the other side. The danger came from the lack of maneuverability caused by empty sails during the tack. Without the wind driving the ship, the rudder could not push against the water and turn her. If the ship could not come about fully, it would not be able to catch the wind again. If that happened, they would drift into the shoals, which would shatter the timbered hull like an eggshell and cast the cargo and crew into a dark, angry sea.

Hadrian took hold of the rope in his line and, along with several others, pulled the yards round, repositioning the sails to catch the wind as soon as she was able. The rope was slick, and the wind jerked the coil so roughly that it took the whole line to pull the yards safely into position.

There was another deafening boom and a burst of white spray shot skyward as the breakwater exploded over the port bow. The vessel was turning fast now, pulling away from the foam, struggling to get clear. No sooner had the bow cleared the wind then he heard the captain, "Now! Meet her! Hard over!"

His voice was nearly lost as another powerful wave rammed the rocks just beside them, throwing the *Emerald Storm's* bow upward with a rough lurch that staggered them all. On the quarterdeck, Wyatt followed the order, spinning the wheel back, checking the swing before the ship could turn too far and lose her stern into the rocks.

Overhead, Hadrian heard a scream.

Looking up, he saw the figure of a man fall from the mainsail rigging. His body landed a dozen steps away with a sickening thud. All eyes looked at the prone figure lying like a dark stain on the deck, but none dared move from their stations. Hadrian strained to see who it was. The man lay face down, and in the dim light it was difficult to tell anything.

Is that Royce?

Normally he would never have questioned his friend's climbing skills, but with his sickness, the motion of the ship, and his inexperience, it was possible he could have slipped.

"Haul off all!" Mister Temple shouted, ignoring the fallen man. The crew pulled upon the sheets and braces, once more capturing the wind. The sails bloomed full, and Hadrian felt the lurch under his feet as the ship burst forward once more, heaving into the waves, now steering out to the open sea.

"Doctor Levy on deck!" Bishop shouted.

Hadrian rushed over the instant he could, but stopped short upon seeing the tattoo of the mermaid on the dead man's forearm.

"It's Edgar Drew, sir. He's dead, sir!" Bristol shouted to the quarterdeck as he knelt next to the fallen man.

Several sailors gathered around the body, glancing upward at the mainsail shrouds until the boatswain's mates took them to task. Hadrian thought he could see Royce up near the top yard, but in the dark he could not be sure. Still, he must have been close by when Drew fell.

The boatswain broke up the crowd and Hadrian, once more unsure of his duty, stood idle. The first light of dawn arrived, revealing a dull gray sky above a dull gray sea that lurched and rolled like a terrible dark beast.

"Cook!" A voice barked sharply.

Hadrian turned to see a young boy not much older than Poe, but wearing the jacket and braid of an officer. He stood with a firm-set jaw and a posture so stiff he seemed made of wood. His cheeks were flushed red with the cool night air, and rainwater ran off the end of his nose.

"Aye, sir?" Hadrian replied, taking a guess it would be the right response.

"We are securing from all hands. You're free to fire the stove and get the meal ready."

Not knowing anything better to say, Hadrian replied, "Aye, aye." He turned to head for the galley.

"Cook!" the boy-officer snapped, disapprovingly.

Hadrian pivoted as sharply as he could, recalling some of his military training. "Aye, sir?" he responded once more, feeling a bit stupid at his limited vocabulary.

"You neglected to salute me," he said, hotly. "I'm putting you on report. What's your name?"

"Hadrian, sir. Blackwater, sir."

"I'll have the respect of you men even if I must flog you to obtain it! Do you understand? Now, let's see that salute."

Hadrian imitated the salute he had seen others perform by placing his knuckles to his forehead.

"That's better, seaman. Don't let it happen again."

"Aye, aye, sir."

It felt good to get down out of the rain and wind, and Poe met him on the way to the galley. The boy knew his way around the kitchen well, which was no doubt why Wyatt suggested him. They fired up the stove and Hadrian watched Poe go to work cooking the morning oatmeal, adding butter and brown sugar in proper amounts and asking Hadrian to taste test it. Despite its name, the skillygalee was surprisingly good. Hadrian could not say the same about the biscuits, which were rock hard. Poe had not made them. He merely fetched the round stones from the bread room, where boxes of them were stored. Hadrian's years of soldiering had made him familiar with hardtack, as they were known on land. The ubiquitous biscuits lasted forever, but were never very filling. They were so hard that you had to soften them in tea or soup before eating.

With the meal made, stewards from the mess arrived to gather their share and carry them below.

Hadrian entered the berth deck, helping the mess steward carry the last of the servings. "Bloody show off couldn't even make it up the lines," Jacob Derning was saying loudly. The men of the tops, and the petty officers, sat together at the tables as befitted their status on board, while others lay scattered with their copper plates in amid the sacks and chests. Jacob looked like he was holding court at the center table. All eyes were on him as he spoke with grand gestures.

On his head he wore a bright blue kerchief, as did everyone on the foretop crew.

"It's a different story with 'im when the sea's heaving and the lines are wet," Jacob went on. "You don't see him prancing then."

"He looked scared to me," Bristol the boatswain added. "Thought I was gonna have to go up and wallop him good to get him going again."

"Royce was fine," said a thin, gangly fellow with a white kerchief tied over his head and a thick, blond walrus mustache. Hadrian did not know his name, but recognized him as the captain of the maintop. "Just seasick that's all. Once he was aloft, he reefed the tops'l just fine, albeit a bit oddly."

"Make excuses for him all ya want, Dime," Jacob told him, pointing a finger his way, "but he's a queer one he is, and I find it more than a little dodgy that his first day aloft finds his fellow mate falling to his death."

"You suggesting Royce killed Drew?" Dime asked.

"I ain't saying nuttin', just think it is odd is all. O' course you'd know better what went on up there, wouldn't you, Dime?"

"I didn't see it. Bernie was with him on the tops'l yard when he fell. He says Drew just got careless. I've seen it 'afore. Fools like 'im skylarking in the sheets. Bernie says he was trying to walk the yard when the ship lurched 'cause o' that burst from the shoal. He lost his footing. Bernie tried to grab him as he hung onto the yard, but the wet made him slip off."

"Drew walking the yard in a rainstorm?" Jacob laughed. "Not likely."

"And where was Royce during all this?" Bristol asked.

Dime shook his head. "I dunno, didn't see him till later when he turned up at the masthead."

"Bernie was playing cards with him last night, wasn't he? I heard Drew walked away with a big pot."

"Now you're saying Bernie killed him?" A third fellow with a red kerchief asked. Hadrian had never seen him before, but guessed he must be the captain of the mizzenmast, as the tops captains along with the boatswains seemed to dine together at the same table.

"No, but I'm saying the cook was there and he and Royce are mates, aren't they? I think—" Jacob stopped short when he spotted Hadrian. "Bloody good thing you're a better cook than your mate is a topman or Mister Temple's liable to chuck you both in the deep."

Hadrian said nothing. He looked around for Royce, but could not find him, which was not too surprising as he guessed his friend would not want to be anywhere near food.

"Might want to let your mate know I've asked Bristol here to have a word with Mister Beryl about him."

"Beryl?" Bristol responded, puzzled. "I was gonna talk to Wesley."

"Bugger that," Jacob said. "Wesley's useless. He's a bleeding joke, ain't he?"

"I can't go over his head to Beryl," Bristol said, defensively. "Wesley was Watch Officer when it happened."

"Are you barmy? What're you scared of? Think Wesley's gonna have at ya for going to Beryl? All Wesley will do is report you. That's all he ever does. He's a boy and hasn't grown a spine yet in that midshipman's uniform o' his. Only reason he's on the *Storm* is 'cause his daddy is Lord Belstrad."

"We need to serve the midshipmen next," Poe reminded Hadrian, urgently tugging at his sleeve. "They mess in the wardroom aft."

Hadrian dropped off the messkid, hanging it from a hook the way he saw Poe do, and gave Jacob one last glance only to find the fore captain grinning malevolently.

The midshipmen's mess was far smaller and not much more comfortable than the crew's quarters. It was a tiny room aft on the berth deck that creaked loudly as the ship's hull lurched in the waves. Normally, Basil delivered the food he cooked for the officers, but this morning he was kept particularly busy working on the lieutenants' and captain's meal and had asked Poe and Hadrian for help in delivering the food to the midshipmen's mess.

"What are you doing in here?" the biggest midshipman asked abruptly as Hadrian and Poe entered. Hadrian almost answered when he realized the question was not addressed at him. Behind them, coming in late, was the young officer who had put Hadrian on report earlier. "You're supposed to be on watch, Wesley."

"Lieutenant Green relieved me a bit early so I could get some food while it was hot."

"So, you've come to force yourself in on your betters, is that it?" the big man asked, and got a round of laughter from those with him. This had to be Beryl, Hadrian guessed. He was by far the oldest of the midshipmen—by ten years or more. "You're going to be nothing but a nuisance to the rest of us on this voyage, aren't you, boy? Here we thought we could have a quiet meal without you disturbing us. What did you do, whine to Green about how your stomach was hurting because we didn't let you have anything to eat last night?"

"No, I—" Wesley began.

"Shut it! I don't want to hear your sniveling voice. You there, cook!" Beryl snapped. "Don't serve Midshipman Wesley any food, not a biscuit crumb, do you understand?"

Hadrian nodded, guessing that Beryl somehow outranked Wesley despite both of them wearing midshipmen uniforms.

Wesley looked angry, but said nothing and turned away from the table toward his sea chest.

"Oh, yes," Beryl said, rising from the table and walking across the room to Wesley. As he did, Hadrian noticed an old scar down the side of Beryl's face that looked to have nearly taken out his eye. "I've been meaning to go through your stuff to see if you had anything I might like."

Wesley turned, closing his chest abruptly.

"Open it, boy, and let me have a look."

"No, you have no right!"

Beryl's toadies at the table jeered the boy and laughed.

He took a step forward and from his posture, Hadrian knew what was coming even if Wesley was oblivious. The big midshipman struck Wesley hard across the face. The boy fell over his chest onto his back. He rolled to his side, his face red with fury, but never got further than his knees before Beryl struck him again, this time hard enough to spray blood from his nose. Wesley collapsed to the floor again with a wail of pain and lay crumbled in a ball holding his face. The other midshipmen cheered.

Beryl sifted through the contents of Wesley's chest. "All that for nothing? I thought you were a lord's son. This is pathetic." He pulled a white linen shirt out and looked it over. "Well, this isn't too bad, and I could use a new shirt." He slammed the chest shut and returned to his breakfast.

Disgusted, Hadrian started to move to help Wesley but stopped when he saw Poe earnestly shaking his head. The young seaman took hold of Hadrian's arm and nearly dragged him back up to the main deck, where the sun had risen sufficiently enough to cause them to squint.

"Don't involve yourself in the affairs of officers," Poe told him earnestly. "They're just like nobles. Strike one and you'll hang for it. Trust me, I know what I'm talking about. My older brother Ned is the coxswain on the *Immortal*. The horror stories he's told me can turn one's stomach. Blimey, you act like you've never been on a ship 'afore."

Hadrian did not say anything as he followed Poe back toward the galley.

"You haven't, have you?" Poe asked suddenly.

"So, who is this big fella? Is he Beryl?" Hadrian asked, changing the subject.

Poe scowled, then sighed. "Yep, he's the senior midshipman."

"So, Beryl's a noble?"

"Don't know if he is or he ain't. Most are third or fourth sons, the ones not suited for the tournaments or monastic life who volunteer to serve, hoping they can one day manage a captain's rank, rule their own ship, and make some money. Most midshipmen only serve about five years before making lieutenant, but Beryl, he's been a midshipman for something like ten years now, I reckon. I guess it makes a man sorta cranky, being left behind like that. Even if he isn't a true blue-blooded noble, he's still an officer, and on this ship, that means the same thing."

"Royce?" Hadrian whispered.

Royce lay in his hammock near the bow of the ship, his head still covered with the white kerchief—the insignia of the maintop crew. He was shivering and wet, lying in soaked clothes.

"Royce," he repeated. This time, he shook his partner's shoulder.

"Do that again and I'll cut your hand off," he growled, his voice garbled and sickly.

"I brought you some coffee and bread. I put raisins in the bread. You like raisins."

Royce peered out from under his thin blanket with a vicious glare. He eyed the meal and promptly looked away with a grimace.

"Sorry, I just knew you hadn't eaten since yesterday." Hadrian put the tray down away from him. "They gave you extra duty, didn't they? You seemed to be up there longer than anyone else."

"Bristol kept me on station as punishment for being slow yesterday. How long was I up there?"

"Twelve hours at least. Listen, I thought we'd have a look around the forward hold. Wyatt tells me the seret are hiding a special cargo up there. If you can get your stomach under control, maybe you can open a few locks for me?"

Royce shook his head. "Not until this ship stops rolling. I stand up and the world spins. I've got to sleep. How come you're not sick?"

"I am, but not like you. I guess elven blood and water don't mix."

"It might," Royce said, disappearing back under his blanket. "If I don't start feeling better soon, I'll slit my wrists."

Hadrian took his blanket, laid it over the shivering form of Royce, and was about to head back up topside when he paused and asked, "Any idea what happened to Edgar Drew?"

"The guy that fell?"

"Yeah, some of the crew think he might have been murdered."

"I didn't see anything. Spent most of my time hugging the mast. I was pretty sick—still am. Get out of here and let me sleep."

It was late and the port watch was on duty, but most of them slept on deck or in the rigging. Only a handful had to remain alert during the middle watch: three lookouts aloft at the masthead, the quartermaster's mate who manned the wheel in Wyatt's absence, and the Officer of the Watch. Hadrian nearly ran into him as he came up.

"Mister Wesley, sir," Hadrian said, shifting the tray so he could properly perform the salute.

Wesley's face was blotchy, his nose and eyes black and blue. Hadrian knew he was standing an additional watch. On his way to Royce, Hadrian had overheard Lieutenant Bishop questioning the midshipman about a brawl, but since Wesley had refused to divulge the name of his adversary, the young man took his punishment alone.

"Mister Wesley, I thought you might like a bit of hot coffee and something to eat. I'm guessing you haven't had much today."

The officer glared at him a moment, then looked at the tray. Seeing the steam rising from the coffee cup, his mouth opened and abruptly shut. "Who sent you here? Was it Beryl? Is this supposed to be funny?"

"No, sir. I just know you didn't get to eat breakfast, and you've been kept on duty through the rest of the meals today. You must be starved."

"You were ordered not to feed me."

Hadrian shrugged. "I've also been ordered by the captain to see that the crew is fed and fit for duty. You've been up a long time. A man could fall asleep without something to help keep his eyes open."

Wesley looked back down. "That's coffee, isn't it?" the young midshipman asked, astonished. "There's not more than a few pounds on the entire ship, and most of that is reserved for the captain."

"I did a bit of trading this afternoon with the purser and managed to get a couple cups worth."

"Why offer it to me?"

Hadrian looked up at the night sky. "It's cold tonight, and punishment for falling asleep can be severe."

Wesley nodded gravely. "On this ship, a midshipman is flogged."

"Do you think that's Beryl's plan, sir? For standing up to him this morning in front of the other officers, I mean."

"Maybe. Beryl is a tyrant of the worst order, and a libertine who squandered his family's fortune. If it wasn't for my brother, Breckton, I suspect Beryl wouldn't even notice me. Beating me must make it seem to Beryl as if he's better than my brother."

"Your brother is Sir Breckton?"

Wesley nodded. "But the joke is on him. I'm nothing like my brother. If I was, I wouldn't be on this lousy floating piece of wood or allow myself to be bested by a lout like Beryl."

"Take the coffee and bread, sir," Hadrian said. "I can't say I care for Beryl, and if keeping you awake tonight gets under his skin, it will make tomorrow all the better in my book. The orders of the captain are more important than a senior midshipman."

"I'll still have to put you on report for this morning. This kindness won't change that."

"I didn't expect it to, sir."

The midshipman studied Hadrian, his face betraying a new curiosity. "In that case, thank you," he said, taking the food.

Dovin Thranic walked through the waist hold. Dark and cramped, the ship's bottom deck reeked of animal dung and salt water. A good four inches of liquid slime pooled along the centerline gutter, forcing him to walk up the sides, hurdling the futtock rider beams to keep his shoes dry. Tomorrow he would order Lieutenant Bishop to direct the detail of men to work the bilge pump in the evening to ensure he did not need to go through this every night.

His unsettled stomach made the ordeal even more miserable. After several days of sleeping on board the *Emerald Storm* while she was in dock, he thought he had gained his sea legs. The initial wretchedness had subsided, only to return now that the ship was rolling at a different cadence on the open sea. It was not nearly as bad as before, but it was still a nuisance and would not make his work any easier.

Thranic carried no light, but did not need one. The sentry's lanterns at the far end of the hold gave sufficient illumination for him to see. He passed several sentries, seret who stood rigidly at their stations, ignoring his approach.

"They seem quiet tonight. Have they been behaving?" Thranic asked as he approached the cages.

"Yes, sir," the senior guard replied, breaking his statuesque facade only briefly. "Sea sickness. They're all under the weather."

"Yes," Thranic noted, not without a degree of revulsion. He watched them. "They can see me, you know, even in the dark. They have very good eyesight."

Because a response was not required, the seret remained silent.

"I can see recognition on their faces, recognition and fear. This is my first trip to visit them, but already they know me. They can sense the power of Novron within me, and the evil in them instinctually cowers. It is like I am a candle, and the light I give off pushes back their darkness."

Thranic stepped closer to the cages, each so densely packed they were forced to take turns between standing and lying. Those standing pressed their filthy naked bodies against each other for support. Males, females, and children were jammed together tightly, creating a repugnant quivering mass of flesh. He watched with amusement as they whimpered and whined, struggling to move away from his approach.

"See? I am light, and the putrid blackness of their souls retreats before me." Thranic studied their faces, each gaunt and hollow from starvation. "They are disgusting creatures—unnatural abominations that never should have been. Their very existence is an insult. You feel it, don't you? We need to purge the world of the stain they cause. We need to do our best to clear the offense. We need to prove ourselves worthy."

Thranic was no longer looking at the elves. He was staring at his own hands. "Purification is never easy, but always necessary," he muttered, pensively. "Fetch me that tall male with the missing tooth," Thranic ordered. "I'll begin with him."

Following the sentinel's direction, the guards ripped the elf from his cage and bound his elbows behind his back. Using a spare rigging pulley, they hoisted the unfortunate prisoner by his arms to the overhead beam. The effort pulled the elf's limbs from their sockets, causing him to scream in agony. His wails and the wretched look on his face caused even the seret to look away, but Thranic watched stoically, his lips pursed approvingly.

"Swing him," he said. The elf howled anew from the motion.

The sentinel looked at the cages again. Inside, others were weeping. At his glance, one female pushed forward. "Why can't you leave us alone?"

Thranic searched her face with a look of genuine pity. "Maribor demands that the mistake of his brother be erased. I am merely his tool."

"Then why not—why not just kill us and get it over with?" she cried at him, eyes wild. Thranic paused. He stared once more at his hands. He turned them over, examining both sides with a distant expression. He was silent for so long that even the seret turned to face him. Thranic looked back at the female, his eyes blurring and lips trembling. "One must scrub very hard to remove *some* stains. Take her next."

Chapter 7

ROTTEN EGGS

Modina descended the curved stair, feeling the hem of her new gown drag along the stone steps. Since leaving her bedroom, she had passed two young women carrying a pile of linens and a page with an armful of assorted boots, who dropped one the moment he spotted her. They only gave her the briefest of sidelong glances before trotting by. The two girls chatted excitedly to each other, but no one spoke to her.

Since her appearance on the balcony over a month ago, Modina enjoyed an unprecedented degree of freedom within the palace. Now able to wander freely inside the castle keep, she owed much of this to Amilia's constant chipping away at the regent's resolve.

She walked gracefully in her new dress, silent and pensive, the way an empress should. The dress Amilia fashioned for her was brilliant white, yet unlike previous Imperial attempts to clothe her, this one was simple and unadorned. During the fittings, Amilia repeatedly scolded the seamstress each time she attempted to embellish it. Amilia knew Modina would be more comfortable in a plain gown, but she doubted her secretary realized the unexpected effect this garment would produce.

When Modina had first come to the castle, everyone avoided her the way one evades a dog known to bite, but all that had changed. After her speech, those few members of the castle staff she chanced upon looked at her with affectionate admiration and an unspoken understanding, as if acknowledging that they finally comprehended her behavior. Now seeing her in the new gown, admiration became adoration as the white purity gave her an angelic aura. She went from *the mad empress* to the saintly—although troubled—high priestess. They clearly believed her to be the Chosen One of Maribor.

Everyone attributed her recovery to Amilia's healing powers. Modina admitted this to the kingdom during her speech on the balcony, and it was the truth. Amilia had saved her, if *saved* was the right word. She did not feel saved.

Since Dahlgren, she drowned in overwhelming terrors she could not face. Amilia had pulled her to shore, but no one could call her existence living. There was a time when she would have said that life carried hope for a better tomorrow, but for her, hope was a dream blown away on a midsummer's night. The horrors were all that remained, calling to her, threatening to pull her under again. It would be easy to give in, to close her eyes and sink to the bottom once more, but if pretending to live could help Amilia, then she would. Amilia had become a tiny point of light in a sea of darkness, the singular star Modina steered by, and it did not matter where that light led.

Modina took to walking the corridors of the palace each day, mostly out of boredom. She never went anywhere in particular and oftentimes after returning could not recall where she had been. She wanted to feel grass beneath her feet, but her newly found freedom did not extend past the palace walls. She was certain no guard would stop her, but Amilia would pay the price. So instead, Modina spent each afternoon wandering the sequestered halls and chambers like a ghost searching for something long forgotten. She heard that people with missing limbs felt an itching in a phantom leg or arm. Perhaps it was the same for her, as she struggled to scratch at her missing life.

The smell of food indicated she was near the kitchen. Modina did not recall the last time she had eaten, but she was not hungry. Ghosts did not get hungry, at least not for food. She had come to the bottom of the stairs. To the right, cupboards lined a narrow room holding plates, goblets, candles, and utensils. To the left, folded linens were stacked on shelves. Filled with laboring servants and steam, the place was hot and noisy.

Modina spotted the big elkhound sleeping in the corner of the kitchen and immediately recalled that his name was Red. She had not been down this way in a long time, not since Saldur caught her feeding the dog. That was the first day since her father died that she could remember clearly. Before that—nothing—nothing but...*rotten eggs.*

She smelled the rancid stench as she stood at the bottom of the steps. Modina glanced around with greater interest. That awful smell triggered a memory. There was a place, a small room. It was cold and dark, no windows, and it was damp. The floor was dirt, and she remembered that smell. She could almost taste it.

Modina approached a small wooden door. With a shaking hand, she pulled it open. Inside, was a small pantry filled with sacks of flour and grain. This was not the room, but the smell was stronger here.

There was another place—small like this—small, dark, and evil. The thought came at her with the force of a forgotten nightmare. Black, earthy, and cold, a splashing and a ratcheting that echoed ominously, the wails of lost souls crying for mercy and finding none. She was one of them. She had cried aloud in the dark until she could cry no more, and always the smell of dirt penetrated her nostrils and the dampness soaked into her skin. A sudden realization jolted her.

I'm remembering my grave! I am dead. I am a ghost.

She looked at her hands—this was not life. The darkness closed in all around her, growing deeper, swallowing her, smothering her.

"Are you all right, Your Eminence?"

"Ya think she's sick again?"

"Don't be daft. She's just upset. You can see that well enough, can't ya?"

"Poor thing, she's so fragile."

"Remember who you're speaking of. That lass slew Rufus' Bane!"

"*You* remember who *you're* speaking of, *that lass* indeed! By Maribor's beard, she's the empress!"

"Out of my way," Amilia growled, as she shooed the crowd like a yard full of chickens.

She was in no mood to be polite. Fear made her voice harsh, and it lacked the familiar tone of a fellow kitchen worker—it was the voice of an angry noblewoman. The servants scattered. Modina sat on the floor with her back against the wall. She was weeping softly with her hands covering her face.

"What did you do to her?" Amilia snapped accusingly while glaring at the lot of them.

"Nothing!" Leif defended.

Leif, the butcher and assistant cook, was a scrawny little man with thick dark hair covering his arms and chest, but absent from his balding head. Amilia had never cared for him, and the thought that he, or any of them, might have hurt Modina made her blood boil.

"No one was even near her. I swear!"

"That's right," Cora confirmed. The dairymaid was a sweet, simple girl who churned the butter each morning and always added too much salt. "She just sat and started crying."

Amilia knew better than to listen to Leif, but Cora was trustworthy. "All right," she told them. "Leave her be. Back to work, all of you."

They were slow to respond until Amilia gave them a threatening glare.

"Are you all right? What's wrong?" she asked, kneeling beside Modina.

The empress looked up and threw her arms around Amilia's neck as she continued to sob uncontrollably. Amilia held her, stroking her hair. She had no idea what was wrong, but needed to get the empress to her room. If word reached Saldur, or worse, if he wandered in— she tried not to think of it.

"It's okay, it's all right. I've got you. Try to calm down."

"Am I alive?" Modina asked with pleading eyes.

For the briefest of moments, Amilia thought she might be joking, but there were two things wrong with that. First, there was the look in Modina's eyes, and second, the empress *never* joked.

"Of course you are," she reassured. "Now come. Let's get you to bed."

Amilia helped her up. Modina stood like a newborn fawn, weak and unsure. As they left, excited whispering rose. *I'll have to deal with that right away,* she thought.

She guided Modina upstairs to where Gerald, the empress's personal guard, gave them a concerned look as he opened the chamber door.

"Is she all right?" Gerald asked.

"She's tired," Amilia said, closing the door on him.

The empress sat on the edge of her bed, staring at nothing. This was not her familiar blank stare. Amilia could see her thinking hard about something.

"Were you sleepwalking? Did you have a nightmare?"

Modina thought a moment then shook her head. "I remembered something," her voice was faint and airy. "It was something bad."

"Was it about the battle?" This was the first time Amilia brought up the subject. Details of Modina's legendary combat with the beast that destroyed Dahlgren were always vague or clouded by so much dogma and propaganda it was impossible to tell truth from fiction. Like any Imperial citizen, Amilia was curious. The stories claimed Modina slew a powerful dragon with a broken sword. Just looking at the empress, she knew that was not true, but Amilia was certain something terrible had happened.

"No," Modina said softly. "It was afterward. I woke up in a hole, a terrible place. I think it was my grave. I don't like remembering. It's better for both of us if I don't try."

Amilia nodded. Since Modina had begun speaking, most of their conversations had centered on Amilia's life in Tarin Vale. On the few occasions when she asked Modina about her own past, the empress's expression would darken and the light in her eyes would fade. She would not speak anymore after that, sometimes for days. The skeletons in Modina's closet were legion.

"Well, don't think about it then," Amilia told her in a soothing voice. She sat next to Modina on the edge of the bed and ran her fingers through the empress's hair. "Whatever it was, it's over. You're here with me now. It's getting late. Do you think you can sleep?"

The empress nodded, but her eyes remained troubled.

Once she was certain the empress was resting peacefully, Amilia crept out of her room. Ignoring Gerald's questioning looks, she trotted downstairs to the kitchen. If left to themselves, the scullions would start a wave of rumors certain to engulf the entire palace, and she could not afford to have this getting back to Saldur.

Amilia had not visited the kitchens for quite some time. The moist steamy cloud that smelled of onions and grease, once so familiar, was now oppressive. Eight people worked the evening shift. There were several new faces, mostly young boys fresh off the street or girls still smelling of farm manure. All of them worked perfunctorily, as they were engrossed in the conversation that rose above the sound of the boiling kettles and the clatter of pans. That all stopped when she entered.

"Amilia!" Ibis Thinly boomed the moment he saw her. The old sea cook was a huge barrel-chested man with bright blue eyes and a beard that wreathed his chin. Blood and grease stained his apron. He held a towel in one hand and a spoon in the other. Leaving a large pot on the stove, he strode over to her, grinning. "Yer a fine sight for weathering eyes, lass! How's life treating you, and why don't you visit more often?"

She rushed to him. Ignoring his filthy garment and all courtly protocol, she hugged the big man tight.

The water boy dropped both buckets and gasped aloud.

Ibis chuckled. "It's as if they plum forgot you used to work here. Like they think their old Amilia died er sumptin' and the Chief Secretary to the Empress grew outta thin air." He put down the spoon and took her by the hand. "So, how are you, lassie?"

"Really good, actually."

"I hear you got a fancy place up there in the East Wing with all the swells. That's sumptin' to be proud of, that is. Yer moving up in the world. There's no mistaking that. I just hope you don't forget us down here."

"If I do, just burn my dinner and I'll remember who the really important people are."

"Oh, speaking of that!" Ibis quickly used the towel to lift the steaming pot from the stove. "Don't want to be ruining the sauce for the chamberlain's quail."

"How are things here?"

"Same as always." He hoisted the pot onto the stone bench and lifted the lid, freeing a cloud of steam. "Nuttin' changes in the scullery, and you picked a fine time to visit. Edith ain't here. She's upstairs hollering at the new chambermaid."

Amilia rolled her eyes. "They should have dismissed that woman years ago."

"Don't I know it, but I only run the kitchen and don't have no say over what she does. Course, you being a swell an all now, maybe—"

She shook her head. "I don't have any real power. I just take care of Modina."

Ibis used the spoon and tasted the sauce before replacing the lid.

"Well now, I know you didn't come here to jaw with me about Edith Mon. This have sumptin to do with the empress crying down here a bit ago? It wasn't the pea soup I made for her, was it?"

"No," Amilia assured him. "She loves your cooking, but yes, I did sort of want to explain things." She turned to face the rest of the staff and raised her voice, "I just wanted everyone to know the empress is okay. She heard some bad news today and it saddened her is all. But she's fine now."

"Was it about the war?" Nipper asked.

"I bet it had to do with the prisoners in Ratibor," Knob the baker speculated. "The Princess of Melengar done executed them, didn't she? Everyone knows she's a witch and a murderess. She'd think nothing of slaughtering defenseless folk. That's why she was weeping, wasn't it? 'Cause she couldn't save them?"

"The poor dear," the butcher's wife declared. "She cares so much, it's no wonder she's so upset with everything she has to deal with. Thank Maribor she has you taking care of her, Lady Amilia. You're a mercy and then some, you are."

Amilia smiled and turned to Ibis, "Didn't she always used to yell at me about the way I cleaned her husband's knives?"

Ibis chuckled. "She also accused you of taking that pork loin a year ago last spring. Said you ought to be whipped. I guess she forgot about that. They all have, I 'spect. It's the dress, I think. Seeing you in a gown like this, even I have to fight the impulse to bow."

"Don't do that," she told him, "or I'll never come back here."

Ibis grinned. "It's good to see you again."

In her dream, Modina saw the beast coming up behind her father. She tried to scream, but only a muffled moan escaped. She tried to run to him, but her feet were stuck in mud—thick, green, foul-smelling mud. The beast had no trouble moving as it charged down the hill toward him. To her anguished amazement, Theron took no notice of the ground shaking from the monster's massive bulk. It consumed him in a single bite, and Modina collapsed in the dirt. The musty smell filled her nostrils as she struggled to breathe. She could feel the damp earth against her body. In the darkness, the sounds of splashing told her that the beast came for her too. All around, men and women cried and howled in misery and fear. The beast came for them all. Splashing, cranking, splashing, cranking, it was coming to finish the job, coming to swallow her up as well.

It was hungry. Very hungry. It needed to eat.

They all needed to eat, but there was never enough food. What little they had was a putrid gruel that smelled awful—like rotten eggs. She was cold, shivering, and weeping. She had cried so hard and for so long, her eyes no longer teared. There was nothing left to live for...or was there?

Modina woke in her darkened room shivering in a cold sweat.

It was the same dream that haunted her each night and made her fear closing her eyes. She got up and moved toward the moonlight of her window. By the time she reached it, most of the dream was forgotten, but she realized something had been different. Sitting in her usual place, she looked out over the courtyard below. It was late and everyone was gone except the guards on watch. She tried to remember her nightmare, but the only thing she could recall was the smell of rotten eggs.

Chapter 8

THE HORN

After the first few disorienting days, life aboard the *Emerald Storm* settled into a rigid pattern. Every morning began with the scrubbing of the upper deck, although it never had a chance to get dirty from one day to the next. Breakfast followed. The watches changed and the scrubbing continued, this time on the lower decks. At noon, Lieutenant Bishop or one of the other officers fixed their position using the sun and confirmed it with the captain. Afterward, the men drilled on the masts and yards, launching longboats, boarding and repelling, archery, the ballista, and hand-to-hand combat. Not surprisingly, Hadrian won high marks in sword fighting and archery, a display of skill not lost on Grady, who nodded knowingly.

From time to time, the men were drummed to the main deck to witness punishment. So far, there had been four floggings, but Hadrian knew the victims only by name. In the afternoon, the men received their grog, a mixture of rum and sugar water, and in the evening, the master-at-arms went about making certain all fires were out.

THE HORN

Most days were the same as the one before, with only a few exceptions. On Make 'n Mend day, the captain granted the crew extra time in the afternoon to sew up rips in their clothing or indulge in hobbies such as wood carving or scrimshaw. On Washday, they cleaned their clothes. Because using fresh water was forbidden and there was no soap, shirts and pants usually felt better after a day working in the rain than they did after Washday.

By now, everyone knew their responsibilities and could perform them reasonably well. Hadrian and Royce were pleased to discover they were not the only novices aboard. Recently pressed men comprised nearly a quarter of the crew. Many came from as far away as Alburn and Dunmore, and most had never seen the ocean before. The other men's bumbling presence, and Wyatt's assistance, masked Hadrian and Royce's lack of experience. Now, both knew the routine and their tasks well enough to pass on their own.

The *Emerald Storm* continued traveling due south, with the wind on her port quarter laying her over elegantly as she charged the following sea. It was a marvelously warm day. Either they had run so far south that the season had yet to change, or autumn blessed them with one last breath of perfect weather. The master's mate and a yeoman of the hold appeared on deck at the ringing of the first bell to dispense the crew's grog.

About four days into the voyage, Royce finally found his sea legs. His color returned, but even after more than a week, his temper remained sour. Much of the reason came from Jacob Derning's constant accusations about his culpability in Drew's death.

"After I slit his throat, I can just drop the body into the sea," Royce casually told Hadrian. They had collected their grog and the crew lay scattered about the top decks, relaxing in the bright sunshine. Royce and Hadrian were no exception. They found a cozy out-of-the-way space on the waist deck between the longboat and the bulkhead where the sailmaker and his mates had left a pile of excess canvas. It made for a luxurious deck bed from which to watch the clear blue sky with its decorative puffs of clouds.

"I'll dump him at night and he's gone for good. The body won't even wash up on shore, because the sharks will eat it. It's better than having your own personal vat of lye."

"Okay, one more time," Hadrian had become exhausted from the conversation. "You can't kill Jacob Derning. We have no idea what's going on yet. What if he's Merrick's contact? So, until we know something—anything—you can't kill anyone."

Royce scowled and folded his arms across his chest in frustration.

"Let's get back to what we know," Hadrian went on. "We've got a cargo hold full of elves, enough weapons to outfit an army, a sentinel with a company of seret, a Tenkin, and an ex-Diamond. I think Thranic must be part of this. I doubt a sentinel is just taking a pleasure cruise."

"He does stand out like a knife in a man's back, which is why I doubt he's involved."

"Okay, let's put him in the maybe category. That leaves Bernie at the top of the list. What did you say his name was?"

"He went by Ruby when he was in the Diamond, but his real name is Defoe."

"Was he in the guild at the same time as you and Merrick?"

He nodded. "But we never worked with him—hardly even saw him. Defoe was a digger—specialized in robbing crypts mostly, and then he got into looking for buried treasure. Taught himself to read so he could search old books for clues. He found Gable's Corner and the Lyrantian Crypt, apparently buried somewhere out in Vilan Hills. Came back with some nice stuff and all these tall tales about ghosts and goblins. He ended up having some disagreement with the Jewel, and it wasn't long before he went independent. Never heard of him after that."

"But Merrick knew him, right?'

"Yeah."

"Think he recognized you?"

"I don't know. Maybe. He wouldn't let on if he had. He's no fool."

"Any chance he's turned a new leaf and taken up sailing for real?"

"About as likely as me doing it."

Hadrian eyed Royce for a heartbeat. "I put him at the top of the list."

"What about the Tenkin?"

"That's another strange one, he—"

"Land-ho!" The lookout on the foremast shouted while pointing off the port bow. Royce and Hadrian got up and looked in the direction indicated. Hadrian could not make out much just a thin gray line, but he thought he could see twin towers rising in the distance. "Is that..."

"Drumindor," Royce confirmed, glancing over his shoulder before sitting back down with his rum.

"Oh, yeah? We're that far south? Been a while since we've been around here."

"Don't remind me."

"Okay, so the fortress wasn't the best of times, but the city was nice. You have to admit Tur Del Fur is better than Colnora, really. Beautiful climate, brightly painted buildings on an aqua sea, and it's a Republic port. You've got to love an open city."

"Oh? Remember how many times you banged your head?"

Hadrian frowned at him. "You really do hate dwarves, don't you? Honestly, I'm surprised you let Magnus stay at the abbey. All right, so there's a bit too much dwarven architecture there, but it sure is built well. You've got to admit that, and you liked the wine, remember?"

Royce shrugged. "What were you going to say about the Tenkin?"

"Oh, yeah. His name is Staul."

"Doesn't seem like the sailor type."

"No." Hadrian shook his head. "He's a warrior. Most Tenkin men are. Thing is, Tenkins never leave the Gur Em."

"The what?"

"You've never been to Calis, have you? The whole eastern half is a tropical forest, and the thickest part is a jungle they call the Gur Em. This is the first time I've ever seen a Tenkin outside of Calis, which makes me think Staul is an outcast."

"Doesn't sound like the type Merrick would be doing business with."

"So, Defoe remains our number one." Hadrian thought a moment, "Ya think he had anything to do with Drew's death?"

"Maybe," Royce replied, taking a sip of rum. "He was on the main mast that night, but I was too sick to pay attention. I wouldn't put it past Defoe to give him a little push. He'd need a reason, though."

"Drew and Defoe were both at a card game earlier that night. Drew won the pot and if Defoe is a thief..."

Royce shook his head. "Defoe wouldn't kill him over a gambling dispute. Not unless it was really big money. The coppers and silvers they were likely playing for wouldn't qualify. That doesn't mean he didn't kill him; it just wasn't about gambling. Anything else happen at the game?"

"Not really, although Drew did mention he was going to talk to Grady the next morning at breakfast about someone coming aboard to help find a horn. Drew thought it was kinda funny, actually. He seemed to think the horn was easy to find. He was going to go into more detail at breakfast."

"Maybe Drew overheard something Defoe preferred he hadn't. That's a more likely reason. But, a horn?"

They came across Wyatt at the ship's wheel. His plumed hat was off and his white linen shirt fluttered about his tan skin like a personal sail. He had the *Storm* tight-over, playing the pressure of the rudder against the press of the wind. He was staring out at the headland with glassy eyes as they approached, but when he spotted them he abruptly cast his head down at the binnacle and quickly wiped his face with the sleeve of his forearm.

"You all right?" Hadrian asked.

"Y-yeah," Wyatt croaked, then coughed to clear his throat. "Fine." He sniffed and wiped his nose.

"There's a good chance we'll find her," Royce assured him.

"See," Hadrian said, "you've even got Mister Cynical feeling optimistic about your chances. That's gotta count for something."

Wyatt forced a smile.

"Hey, we've got a question for you," Royce said. "Do you have any idea what the *horn* is?"

"Sure, you're looking right at it," Wyatt declared, gesturing toward the point. "That's the Horn of Delgos. As soon as we clear it, the captain will likely order the ship to weather round the point and then tack windward."

Royce frowned. "Let's assume for just a moment that I'm not an experienced sailor, shall we?"

Wyatt chuckled. "We're gonna make a left turn and head east."

"How do you know?"

Wyatt shrugged. "The horn is the farthest spit of land south. If we stay on this course, we'll sail into the open sea. There's nothing out there but whirlpools, Dacca, and sea serpents. If we weather round—er—turn left, we'll sail up the eastern coast of Delgos."

"And what's up that way?"

"Not much. These cliffs you see continue all the way round to Vandon, the only other sea port in Delgos. Besides being the headquarters for the Vandon Spice Company, it is also a haven for pirates, or more accurately *the haven* for pirates. We aren't going there either. The *Storm* is as fine a ship as they come, but the jackals would gather like a pack of wolves and dog her until we surrender, or they sink us."

"How does the spice company manage any trade, surrounded by pirates?"

"Who do you think runs the spice company?"

"Oh."

"Beyond that?" Royce asked.

"Dagastan Bay and the whole coast of Calis, with ports at Wesbaden and Dagastan. Then you drift out of civilization and into the Ba Ran Archipelago, and no one goes there, not even pirates."

"And you're sure this here is the horn?"

"Yep, every sailor who's ever been in the Sharon knows it. It'd be impossible to miss old Drumindor."

Though the coast was still many leagues off, the ancient dwarven edifice was clearly visible now. It stood taller than anything Hadrian had ever seen, and he smiled at the irony, knowing dwarves built it. It was close to eight hundred feet from the raw rocky base, where waves crashed, to the top of the dome. It appeared to be equal parts fortification and monument. In some respects, it resembled two massive gears laid on their sides, huge cylinders with teeth jutting seaward. From the tops of each tower, smoke rose skyward. Midway up were fins—arced openings like gigantic teapot spouts that pointed seaward. Between the twin towers was a single-span stone bridge connecting them like a lintel over the entrance of the harbor.

"Can't even miss her at night, the way she lights up. You should see her during a full moon when they blow the vents. It puts on quite a show. She's built on a volcano, and the venting prevents too much pressure from building up. Ships in the area often arrange to pass the point at the full moon just for the entertainment. But they also keep their distance. The dwarves that built that fortress sure knew what they were doin'. No ship can enter Terlando Bay if the masters of Drumindor don't want them to. They can spew molten rock for hundreds of feet and burn a fleet of ships to drifting ash in minutes."

"We're familiar with how that works," Royce said, coldly.

Wyatt cocked an eyebrow. "Bad experience?"

"We had a job there once," Hadrian replied. "A dwarf named Gravis was angry about humans desecrating what he considered a dwarven masterpiece. We had to get in to stop him from sabotaging it."

"You broke into Drumindor?" Wyatt looked impressed. "I thought that was impossible."

"Just about," Royce answered, "and we didn't get paid enough for the trouble it gave me."

Hadrian snorted, "*You?* I was the one who nearly died making that leap. You just hung there and laughed."

"How'd you get in? I heard that place is kept tighter than Cornelius DeLur's purse," Wyatt pressed.

"It wasn't easy," Royce grumbled. "I learned to hate dwarves on that job. Well there and…" he trailed off rubbing his left shoulder absently.

"It will be the harvest moon in a few weeks. Maybe we we'll catch the show on the way back," Wyatt said.

The lookout announced the sighting of sails. Several ships clustered under the safety of the fort, but they were so far out that only their topsails showed.

"I would have expected the captain to have ordered a course change by now. He's letting us get awfully close."

"Drumindor can't shoot this far, can she?" Hadrian asked.

"No, but the fortress isn't the only danger," Wyatt pointed out. "It isn't safe for an Imperial vessel to linger in these waters. Delgos isn't officially at war with us, but everyone knows the DeLurs support the Nationalists and—well—accidents can happen."

They continued sailing due south. It was not until the point was well astern and nearly out of sight that the captain appeared on the quarterdeck. Now they would discover which direction the *Emerald Storm* would go.

"Heave-to, Mister Bishop!" he ordered.

"Back the mains'l!" the lieutenant shouted, and the men sprang into action.

This was the first time Hadrian had heard these particular orders and he was glad that, as ship's cook, he was not required to carry them out. It did not take long for him to see what was happening. Backing the mainsail caused it to catch the wind on its forward side. If the fore and mizzenmasts were also backed, the ship would sail in reverse. Since they remained trimmed as they were, the force of the wind lay balanced between them, leaving the ship stationary on the water.

Once the ship was heaved-to, the captain ordered a reading on the ship's position, then disappeared once more into his cabin, leaving Lieutenant Bishop on the quarterdeck.

"So much for picking a direction," Hadrian muttered to himself.

THE HORN

They remained stationary for the rest of that day. At sunset, Captain Seward ordered lights hauled aloft, but nothing further slipped his lips.

Hadrian served supper, boiled salt pork stew again. Even he was tired of his menu, but the only complaints came from the recently pressed, who were not yet hardened to the conformities of life at sea. Hadrian suspected most of the veterans on board would demand salt pork and biscuits even on land, rather than break the routine.

"He ez a murderer, dat ez why!"

Hadrian heard Staul shout as he entered the below deck with the last of the evening meals. The Tenkin was standing slightly crouched in the center of the crews' quarters. His dark tattooed body and rippling muscles were revealed as he removed his shirt. In his right hand he held a knife. A cloth wrapped his left fist. His chest heaved with excitement, a mad grin on his face, and a sinister glare in his eyes.

In front of Staul stood Royce.

"He keeled Edgar Drew. Everyone knows et. Now, he'll be dee one to die, eh?"

Royce stood casually, his hands loosely clasped before him as if he were just one of the bystanders—except—his eyes never left the knife. Royce followed it as a cat might watch the movement of a string. It only took Hadrian a second to see why. Staul was holding the knife by the blade. On a hunch, Hadrian scanned the room and found Defoe standing behind and to Royce's left, a hand hidden behind his back.

Staul took his attention off Royce for a moment, but Hadrian noticed his weight shift to his rear foot and hoped his friend noticed as well. An instant later Staul threw the knife. The blade flew with perfect accuracy, only when it arrived the thief was not there and the tip buried itself in a deck post.

All eyes were on Staul as he bristled with rage, shouting curses. Hadrian forced himself to ignore the Tenkin and searched for Defoe. He had moved. Spotting the glint of a blade in the crowd, he found him again. Defoe had slipped up behind Royce and lunged. Royce spun. Not taken in by the plot, he faced his old guild mate with the blade Staul had provided. Defoe halted mid-step, hesitated, and then backed away, melting into the crowd. Hadrian doubted anyone else noticed his involvement.

"Ah! You dance well!" Staul shouted and laughed. "Dat ez good. Perhaps next time you trip, eh?"

The excitement over, the crowd broke up. As they did, Jacob Derning muttered loud enough for everyone to hear, "Good to see I'm not the only one who thinks he killed poor Drew."

"Royce," Hadrian called, keeping his eyes focused on Jacob. "Perhaps you should take your meal up on the deck, where it's cooler."

"That was pleasant," Hadrian said, after the two had safely reached the galley and closed the door behind them.

"What was?" Poe asked, dishing out the last of the stew for the midshipmen.

"Oh, nothing really. A few crewmen just tried to murder Royce."

"What?" Poe almost dropped the whole kettle.

"Now can I kill people?" Royce asked, stepping into the corner and putting his back against the wall. He had an evil look on his face.

"Who tried to murder him?"

"Defoe," Royce replied. "So, what am I supposed to do now? Lie awake at night waiting for him and his buddies—I'm sorry, his *mates*—to knife me?"

"Who's Defoe?"

"Poe, would it be possible for Royce and me to sleep in here at night?"

"In the galley? I suppose. Won't be too comfortable, but if Royce is always on time for his watch, and if you tell Mister Bishop you want him to help with the nighttime boils, he might allow it."

"Great, I'll do that. While I'm gone, Poe, can you go below and get us a couple of hammocks that we can hang in here. Royce, maybe you can rig a lock for the door?"

"It's better than being bait."

"Who's Defoe?"

Royce worked both the second dogwatch and the first watch, which kept him aloft from sunset until midnight. By the time he returned, Hadrian had obtained permission for Royce to sleep in the galley. Poe had moved up what little gear they had and strung two hammocks between the walls of the narrow room.

"How is it?" the thief asked, entering the darkened galley and finding Hadrian hanging in the netting.

"Hmm?" he asked waking up. "Oh, okay I guess. The room is too narrow for me. I feel like I'm being bent in half, but it should be fine for you. How was your watch? Did you see Defoe?"

"Never took my eyes off old *Bernie*," he said, grinning and dodging a pot that hung from the overhead beam. Hadrian knew Royce must have enjoyed a bit of revenge on Defoe. If there was ever a place where Royce held an advantage, it was a hundred feet in the air, dangling from beams and ropes in the dark of night.

Hadrian shifted his weight, causing his hammock to swing. "What did you do?"

"Actually, I didn't do anything, but that was what drove him crazy. He's still sweating."

"So he did recognize you."

"Oh, yeah, and it was like there were two moons out tonight, his face was so pale."

Royce checked the lines and the mountings of the hammock Poe had installed for him and looked generally pleased with the work.

"To be honest, I'm surprised Defoe didn't suffer an accidental fall."

Royce shook his head. "Two accidents off my mast is just bad planning. Besides, Defoe wasn't trying to kill me."

"Sure looked that way from where I was standing. And it seemed pretty organized too."

"You think so?" he asked, sitting on the crate of biscuits Poe had brought up for the morning's breakfast. "It's not how I would do it. First, why stage the fight in a room full of witnesses? If they had killed me, they would hang. Second, why attack me below? Like I said, the sea is the perfect place to dispose of a body, and the closer to the tail you get your victim, the easier it is."

"Then what do you think they were up to?"

Royce pursed his lips and shook his head. "I have no idea. If it was a diversion to rifle our belongings, why not hold it topside? For that matter, why bother with a diversion at all? There have been plenty of times while we were on deck to go through our stuff."

"You think it was just to intimidate us?"

"If it was, it wasn't Defoe's idea. Threatening to kill me but not finishing the job is famously fatal. He would know that."

"So, Derning put them up to it?"

"Maybe, but…I don't know. Derning doesn't seem like someone Defoe would take orders from—especially not such stupid orders."

"Makes sense, so then—"

The muffled thump, like another body hitting the deck, brought them to their feet. Hadrian threw open the door of the galley and cautiously looked about the deck.

The larboard watch was on duty, but rather than the typical watch-and-snooze routine, they were hard at work running a boat drill. They hoisted the longboat from the yard and had it over the side, where it bumped the gunwale once more before being lowered into the sea.

"Odd time for a lifeboat drill," Wyatt said, walking toward them from the shelter of the forecastle.

"Trouble sleeping?" Royce asked.

Wyatt beamed a grin. "Look who else is on duty," he told them, pointing at the quarterdeck where Sentinel Thranic, Mister Beryl, Doctor Levy, and Defoe stood talking.

They slipped around the forecastle, moving quickly to the bow. Looking over the rail, Hadrian saw six men rowing toward a nearby light.

"Another ship," Royce muttered.

"Really?"

"A small, single-mast schooner. No flag."

"Is there anything in the longboat?" Hadrian asked. "If that's payment going to—"

Royce shook his head. "Just the crew."

They watched as the sound of the oars faded, then waited. Hadrian strained, peering into the darkness, but all he could see was the bobbing light of the little boat and the one marking its destination.

"Boat's coming back," Royce announced, "and there's an extra head now."

Wyatt squinted. "Who would they be picking up in the middle of the night from Delgos?"

They watched as the longboat returned. Just as Royce said, there was an additional man—a passenger. Wrapped in ship's blankets, he was small and thin, with a long pasty face and white hair. He looked to be very old, far too old to be of any use as a sailor. He came aboard and spoke to Thranic and Doctor Levy at length. The old man's things were gathered and deposited beside him. One of the bags came loose and two weighty, leather-bound books spilled onto the bleached deck. "Careful, my boy," the old man cautioned the sailor. "Those are one of a kind and, like me, are very old and sadly fragile."

"Gather his things and take them to Dr. Levy's quarters," Thranic ordered. Glancing toward the bow, he stopped abruptly. He glared at them, licking his thin lips in thought, then slowly approached. As he did, he held his dark cloak tight, his shoulders raised to protect his neck from the cold wind. Between this and his stooped back, he resembled a scavenger bird.

"What are all of you doing on deck? None of you are part of the larboard watch."

"Off duty, sir," Wyatt answered for them. "Just getting a bit of fresh air."

Thranic peered at Hadrian and took a step toward him. "You're the cook, aren't you?"

Without thinking, Hadrian felt at his side for the hilt of his absent sword. Something about the sentinel made him flinch. Sentinels were always scary, but this one was absolutely chilling. Returning his gaze was like staring into the eyes of restrained madness.

"You joined this voyage along with..." Thranic's eyes shifted to Royce. "This one—yes, the nimble fellow—the one so good at climbing. What's your name? Melborn isn't it? Royce Melborn? I heard you were seasick. How odd."

Royce remained silent.

"Very odd, indeed."

"Sentinel Thranic?" the old man called, his weak voice barely making the trip across the deck. "I would rather like to get out of the damp wind, if I could." He coughed.

Thranic stared a moment longer at Royce then pivoted sharply and left them.

"Not exactly the kind of guy you want taking an interest in you, is he?" Wyatt offered.

With the longboat back aboard, the captain appeared on the quarterdeck and ordered a new course—due east, into the wind.

Chapter 9

ELLA

Another dispatch from Sir Breckton, sir," the clerk announced, handing a small scroll to the Imperial chancellor. The elderly man returned to the desk in his little office and read the note. A scowl grew across his face.

"The man is incorrigible!" The chancellor burst out to no one, then pulled a fresh sheet of parchment and dipped his quill.

The door opened unexpectedly and the chancellor jumped. "Can't you knock?"

"Sorry, Biddings, did I startle you?" the Earl of Chadwick asked, entering with his exquisite floor-length cape trailing behind him. He had a pair of white gloves draped over one forearm as he bit into a bright red apple.

"You're always startling me. I think you get a sadistic pleasure from it."

Archibald smiled. "I saw the dispatch arrive. Is there any word from the *Emerald Storm*?"

"No, this is from Breckton."

ELLA

"Breckton? What does he want?" Archibald sat in the armchair opposite the chancellor and rested his booted feet on a footstool.

"No matter how many times I tell him to wait and be patient, he refuses to grasp that we know more than he does. He wants permission to attack Ratibor."

Archibald sighed. "Again? I suppose you see now what I've had to put up with all these years. He and Enden are so headstrong I—"

"Were," the chancellor corrected, "Sir Enden died in Dahlgren."

Ballentyne nodded. "And wasn't that a waste of a good man." He took another bite and, with his mouth still full, went on. "Do you need me to write him personally? He is my knight after all."

"What would help is to be able to tell him *why* he doesn't need to attack."

Archibald shook his head. "Saldur and Ethelred are still insisting on secrecy regarding the—"

The chancellor raised a hand, stopping him. Archibald looked confused and the chancellor pointed at the chambermaid on her knees, scrubbing the floor near the windows of his office.

Ballentyne rolled his eyes. "Oh, please. Do you really think the scrub girl is a spy?"

"I have always found it best to err on the side of caution. She doesn't have to be a spy to get you hanged for treason."

"She doesn't even know what we are talking about. Besides, look at her. It isn't likely she'll be bragging in some pub. You don't go out at night boasting in bars, do you, lass?"

Ella shook her head and refused to look up so that her brown, sweat-snarled hair continued to hang in her face.

"See!" Archibald said in a vindicated tone. "It is like censoring yourself because there is a couch or a chair in the room."

"I was referring to a more subtle kind of danger," Biddings told him. "Should something happen. Something unfortunate with the plan such that it fails—someone always has to be blamed. How fortunate it would be to discover a loquacious earl who had boasted details to even a mindless chambermaid."

Archibald's smirk faded immediately.

"The third son of a dishonored baron doesn't rise to the rank of Imperial chancellor by being stupid," Biddings said.

"Point taken." Archibald glanced back at the scrub girl with a new expression of loathing. "I had best return to Saldur's office or he'll be looking for me. Honestly, Biddings, I'm really starting to detest staying in this palace."

"She still won't see you?"

"No, I can't get past her secretary. That Lady Amilia is a sly one. Plays all innocent and doe-eyed, but she guards the empress with ruthless determination. And Saldur and Ethelred are no help at all. They insist she plans to marry Ethelred. It has to be a lie. I simply can't imagine Modina wanting that old moose."

"Particularly when she could choose a young buck like yourself?"

"Exactly."

"And your desire is true love, of course, with absolutely no thought about how marrying Modina would make you emperor."

"For a man who went from third baron's son to chancellor, I am surprised you can even ask me that."

"Archie!" bellowed the voice of Regent Saldur, echoing down the hall outside the office.

"I'm in with Biddings!" Archibald shouted back through the open door. "And don't call me—" He was interrupted by the sudden rush of the scrub girl running, bucket in hand, from the office. "Looks like she doesn't like Saldur any more than I do."

ELLA

❧

Arista spilled scrub water onto her skirt, causing it to plaster the rough material to her legs. Her thin cloth shoes made a disagreeable slapping noise as she ran down the corridor. The sound of Saldur's voice made her run faster.

That was close yet she wondered if even Saldur, who had known her since birth, would recognize her now. There was nothing magical about her transformation, but that did not make it any less impenetrable. She wore dirty rags, lacked makeup, and her once lustrous hair was now a tangled mess. It had lightened, bleached by the same sun that tanned her skin. Still, it was more than just her appearance. Arista had changed. At times, when she caught her own reflection it took a moment to register that she was seeing herself and not some poor peasant woman. The bright-eyed girl was gone, and a dark brooding spirit possessed her battered body.

More than anything else, the sheer absurdity of the situation provided the greatest protection. No one would believe that a sheltered, self-indulgent princess would willingly scrub floors in the palace of her enemy. She doubted even Saldur's mind would grant enough latitude to penetrate the illusion. Even if some thought she looked familiar—and several seemed to—their minds simply could not bend that far. They could no more accept that she was Arista Essendon than the notion of talking pigs or that Maribor was not god. To entertain such an idea would require a mind open to new possibilities, and no one at the palace fit that description.

The only one she worried about, beside Saldur, was the empress's secretary. She was not like the others—she noticed Arista. Amilia saw through her veneer with suspicious eyes. Saldur clearly surrounded the empress with his best and brightest, and Arista did all she could to avoid her.

THE EMERALD STORM

On the road north from Ratibor, Arista fell in with a band of refugees fleeing to Aquesta and arrived nearly a month ago. The spell led her to the palace itself. Things grew more complicated after that. If she was more confident in the magic and her ability to use it, she might have returned to Melengar right away with the news that Gaunt was a prisoner in the Imperial palace. As it was, she felt the need to see him for herself. She managed to obtain a job as a chamber maid, hoping to repeat the location spell inside the castle walls at various locations, only this turned out to be impossible. Closely watched by the headmistress, Edith Mon, she rarely found enough free time and privacy to cast the spell. On the few occasions she succeeded, the smoke indicated a direction, but the maze of corridors blocked any attempt to follow. Magically stymied, Arista sought to determine Gaunt's whereabouts by eavesdropping while at the same time learning her way around the grounds.

"What have ya done now?" Edith Mon shouted at Arista as she entered the scullery.

Arista had no idea what a hobgoblin looked like, but she guessed it probably resembled Edith Mon. She was stocky and strong. Her huge head sat on her shoulders like a boulder, crushing whatever neck she might have once had. Her face, pockmarked and spotted, provided the perfect foundation for her broad nose with its flaring nostrils through which she breathed loudly, particularly when angry, as she was now.

Edith yanked the bucket from her hands. "Ya clumsy little wench! Ya best pray you spilled it only on yerself. If I hear ya left a dirty puddle in a hallway…"

Edith had threatened to cane her on three occasions, but was interrupted each time—twice by the head cook. Arista was not sure what she would do if it came to that. Scrubbing floors was one thing, but allowing herself to be beaten by an old hag was something else. If it came to that, Edith might discover there was more to her new chambermaid than she thought. Arista often amused herself by contemplating which curse might be best for old Edith. At that moment, she was considering the virtues of skin worms, but all she said was, "Is there anything else today?"

The older woman glared. "Oh! You think yer sumptin', don't ya? You think yer better than the rest o' us, that yer arse shines o' silver. Well it don't! Ya don't even have a family. I know you live in that alley with the rest o' them runners. Yer one dodgy smile away from makin' yer meals whorin', so I'd be careful sweetie!"

There were several snickers from the other kitchen workers. Some risked Edith's wrath by pausing in their work to watch. The scullery maids, charwomen, and chambermaids all reported to Edith. The others, like the cook, butcher, baker, and cupbearer reported to Ibis Thinly, but sided with Edith—after all, Ella was the *new* girl. In the lives of those who lived in the scullery, this was what passed for entertainment.

"Is that a yes or a no?" Arista asked calmly.

Edith's eyes narrowed menacingly. "No, but tomorrow ya start by cleanin' every chamber pot in the palace. Not just emptin' them, mind ya. I want them scrubbed clean."

Arista nodded and started to walk past her. As she did, cold water rained down as Edith emptied the bucket on her.

The room burst into laughter. "A shame it wasn't clean water. Ya could use a bath." Edith cackled.

The uproar died abruptly as Ibis appeared from out of the cellar.

"What's going on here?" The chief cook's booming voice drew everyone's attention.

"Nothing, Ibis," Edith answered. "Just training one o' my girls is all."

The cook spotted Arista standing in a puddle, drenched from head to foot. Her hair hung down her face, dripping filthy water. Her entire smock soaked through, the thin material clung indecently to her skin, causing her to fold her arms across her breasts.

Ibis scowled at Edith.

"What is it, Ibis?" Edith grinned at him. "Don't like my training methods?"

"No, I can't say I do. Why do you always have to treat them like this?"

"What are you gonna do? You gonna take Ella under your wing like that tramp Amilia? Maybe this one will become archbishop!"

There was another round of laughter.

"Cora!" Ibis barked. "Get Ella a table cloth to wrap around her."

"Careful, Ibis. If she ruins it, the chamberlain will have at you."

"And if Amilia hears you called her a tramp, you might lose your head."

"That little pretender doesn't have the piss to do anything against me."

"Maybe," the chief cook said, "but she's one of *them* now, and I'll bet that any noble who heard that you insulted one of their own—well, they might take it personally."

Edith's grin disappeared and the laughter vanished with it.

Cora returned with a tablecloth, which Ibis folded twice before wrapping around Arista's shoulders. "I hope you have another kirtle at home, Ella, it's gonna be cold tonight."

Arista thanked him before heading out the scullery door. It was already dark and, just as Ibis had predicted, cold. Autumn was in full swing, and the night air shocked her wet body. The castle courtyard was nearly empty with only a few late carters dragging their wagons out through the main gate. A page raced between the stables and the keep hauling armloads of wood, but most of the daily throng of activity that usually defined the yard was absent. She passed through the great gates, where the guards ignored her grateful that the rules restricting servants to remain within the palace had been rescinded shortly after the empress's acclaimed speech. She could not imagine spending all night under the same roof as Edith Mon. The moment she reached the bridge and stepped beyond the protection of the keep's walls, the full force of the wind struck her. She clenched her jaw to stifle a cry, hugged her body with fingers turning red, and shivered so badly it was hard to walk.

Not skin worms. No. Not nearly bad enough.

"Oh, dear!" Mrs. Barker exclaimed, rushing over as Arista entered Brisbane Alley. "What happened, child? Not that Edith Mon again?"

Arista nodded.

"What was it this time?"

"I spilled some wash water."

Mrs. Barker shook her head and sighed. "Well, come over to the fire and try and dry off before you catch your death."

She coaxed Arista to the communal fire pit. Brisbane Alley was literally the end of the road in Aquesta, a wretched little dirt patch behind Brickton's Tannery where the stench from the curing hides kept away any except the most desperate. Newcomers without money, relatives, or connections settled here. The lucky ones lived huddled under canvas sheets, carts, and the wagons they arrived in. The rest, like Arista, simply huddled against the tannery wall, trying to block the wind as they slept. That is, until the Barkers adopted her.

Brice Barker worked shouting advertisements through the city streets for seven coppers a day. All of that went to buy food to feed six children and his wife. Lynnette Barker took in what sewing work she could find. When the weather turned colder, they offered Arista a place under their wagon. She had only known them for a few weeks, but already she loved them like her own family.

"Here, Ella," Lynnette said, bringing an old kirtle for her to put on. The dress was little more than a rag, worn thin and frayed along the hem. Lynette also brought Esrahaddon's robe. Arista went around the corner and slipped out of her wet things. Lynnette's dress did nothing to keep out the cold, but the robe vanquished the wet chill instantly in uncompromising warmth.

"That's really a wonderful robe, Ella," Lynnette told her, marveling at how the firelight made it shimmer and reflect colors. "Where did you get it?"

"A...friend left it to me when he died."

"Oh, I'm sorry," she said, sadly. Her expression changed then from sadness to concern. "That reminds me, a man was looking for you."

"A man?" Arista asked as she folded the tablecloth. If anything happened to it, Edith would make Ibis pay.

"Yes, earlier today. He spoke to Brice while he was working on the street and mentioned he was looking for a young woman. He described you perfectly, although oddly enough, he didn't know your name."

"What did he look like?" Arista hoped her concern was not reflected in her voice.

"Well," Lynnette faltered, "that's the thing. He wore a dark hood and a scarf wrapped about his face, so Brice didn't get a good look at him."

Arista pulled the robe tightly about her. *Was he here? Had the assassin managed to track her down?* Lynnette noticed the change in her and asked, "Are you in trouble, Ella?"

"Did Brice say I lived here?"

"No, of course not. Brice is many things, but he's no fool."

"Did he give a name?"

ELLA

Lynnette shook her head. "You can ask Brice about him when he returns. He and Wery went to buy flour. They should be back soon."

"Speaking of that," Arista said, fishing coins out of her wet dress, "here's three copper tenents. They paid me this morning."

"Oh, no. We couldn't—"

"Of course, you can! You let me sleep under your wagon, and you watch my things when I'm at work. You even let me eat with you."

"But three! That's your whole pay, Ella, you won't have anything left."

"I'll get by. They feed me at the palace sometimes, and my needs are pretty simple."

"But you'll want a new set of clothes, and you'll need shoes come winter."

"So will your children, and you won't be able to afford them without an extra three coppers a week."

"No, no—we can't. It is very nice of you, but—"

"Ma! Ma! Come quick! It's Wery!" Finis, the Barkers' eldest son, raced down the street shouting as he came. He looked frightened, his eyes filled with tears.

Lynnette lifted her skirt and Arista chased after. They rushed to Coswall Avenue, where a crowd formed outside the bakery. Pushing past them, a boy lay unconscious on the cobblestone.

"Oh, sweet Maribor!" Lynnette cried, falling to her knees beside her son.

Brice knelt on the stone, holding Wery in his arms. Blood soaked his hands and tunic. The boy's eyes were closed, his matted hair slick as if dipped in red ink.

"He fell from the baker's loft," Finis answered their unasked question, his voice quavering. "He was pulling one of them heavy flour bags down 'cause the baker said he'd sell us two cups for the price of one if he did. Pa and I told him to wait fer us, but he ran up, like he's always doin'. He was pulling *real* hard. As hard as he could, and then his hands slipped. He stumbled backward and..." Finis was talking fast, his voice rising as he did until it cracked and he stopped.

"Hit his head on the cobblestones," declared a stranger in a white apron holding a lantern. Arista thought he might be the baker. "I'm real sorry. I didn't think the boy would hurt himself like this."

Lynnette ignored the man and pried her child from her husband, pulling Wery to her breast. She rocked him as if he were a newborn. "Wake up, honey," she whispered, softly. Tears fell on Wery's blood-soaked cheeks. "Please baby, oh for the love of Maribor please wake up! Please, oh please..."

"Lynn, honey..." Brice started.

"NO!" she shouted at him, and tightened her grip on the boy.

Arista stared at the scene, her throat was tight, and her eyes were filling so quickly that she could not see clearly. Wery was a wonderful boy, playful, friendly. He reminded her of Fanen Pickering, which only made matters worse. But Fanen died with a sword in his hand, and Wery was only eight and likely never touched a weapon in his short life. She could not understand why such things happened to good people. Tears slipped down her cheeks as she watched the small figure of the boy dying in his mother's arms.

Arista closed her eyes, wiping the tears. When she opened them again she noticed several people in the crowd backing away.

Her robe was glowing.

Giving off a pale light, the shimmering material illuminated those around her in an eerie white radiance. Lynnette saw the glow and hope filled her face. She looked up at Arista, her eyes pleading. "Ella, can...can you save him?" she asked with trembling lips and desperate eyes. Arista began to form the word *no*, but Lynnette quickly spoke again. "You can!" she insisted. "I know you can! I've always known there was something different about you. The way you talk, the way you act. The way you forget your own name, and that—*that robe!* You can save him. I know you can. Oh, please, Ella," she paused and swallowed, shaking so hard it made Wery's head rock. "Oh, Ella I know—I know it's so much more than three coppers, but he's my baby! You will help him, won't you? Please, oh please, Ella."

Arista could not breathe. She felt her heart pounding in her ears and her body trembled. Everyone silently watched her. Even Lynette stopped her pleading. Arista found herself saying through quivering lips, "Lay him down."

Lynnette gently lowered Wery's body, his limbs lifeless, his head tilted awkwardly to one side. Blood continued to seep from the boy's wound.

Arista knelt beside him and placed a hand on the boy's chest. He was still breathing, but so shallow, so weak. She closed her eyes and began to hum softly. She heard the soft concerned mutterings of those in the crowd, and one by one, she tuned them out. She heard the heartbeats of the men and women surrounding her and forced them out as well. Then she heard the wind. Soft and gentle, it was there, moving, swirling between the buildings, across the street, skipping over stones. Above her she felt the twinkle of the stars and the smile of the moon. Her hand was on the body of the boy, but her fingers felt the strings of the instrument that she longed to play.

The gentle wind grew stronger. The swirl became an eddy, the eddy, a whirlwind, and the whirlwind, a vortex. Her hair whipped madly, but she hardly noticed. Before her lay a void, and beyond that a distant light. She could see him in the darkness, a dull silhouette before the brilliance, growing smaller as he traveled away. She shouted to him. He paused. She strummed the chords and the silhouette turned. Then, with all her strength, she clapped her hands together and the sound was thunder.

When she opened her eyes, the light from the robe had faded and the crowd was cheering.

Chapter 10

FALLEN STAR

"Sail ho!" the lookout shouted from the masthead.

The *Emerald Storm* was now two weeks out of Aquesta, slipping across the placid waters of the Ghazel Sea. The wind remained blowing from the southwest. Since rounding the Horn of Delgos, they made slow progress. The ship was close-hauled, struggling to gain headway into the wind. Mister Temple kept the top crews busy tacking the ship round, wearing windward, and keeping their course by crossing back and forth, but Hadrian guessed that a quickly walking man could make faster progress.

It was mid-morning, and seamen who were not in the rigging or otherwise engaged in the ship's navigation were busy scrubbing the deck with sandstone blocks or flogging it dry. All the midshipmen were on the quarterdeck taking instruction in navigation from Lieutenant Bishop. Hadrian heard the lookout's call as he returned to the galley after delivering the previous evening's pork grease. Making his way to the port side, he spotted a small white square on the horizon. Bishop immediately suspended class and took an eyeglass to see for himself, then sent a midshipman to the captain's cabin. The captain came so quickly he was still adjusting his hat as he appeared on the quarterdeck. He paused for a moment, tugged on his uniform, and sniffed the air with a wrinkle of his nose.

"Lookout report!" he called to the masthead.

"Two ships, off the port bow, sir!"

Hadrian looked again and just as the lookout reported, he spotted a second sail now visible above the line of the water.

"The foremost is showing two squares—appears to be a lugger. The farther ship...I'm seeing two red lateen sails, single-decked, possibly a tartane. They're running with the wind and closing fast, sir."

"What flag are they flying?"

"Can't say sir, the wind has them blowing straight at us."

Hadrian watched the ships approach, amazed at their speed. Already he could see them clearly.

"This could be trouble," Poe said.

Hadrian had been so intent on the ships that he failed to notice his assistant appear beside him. The thin rail of a boy was busy tying the black ribbon in his ponytail as he stared out at the vessels.

"How's that?"

"Those red sails."

Hadrian showed he didn't understand the significance.

"Only the Dacca use them."

"Beat to quarters, Mister Bishop," the captain ordered.

"All hands on station!" the lieutenant shouted. "Beat to quarters!"

Hadrian heard a drum roll as the boatswain and his mates cleared the deck. The midshipmen, dispersed to their stations, shouted orders to their crews.

"Come on!" Poe told him.

There was a pile of briquettes at the protected center of the forecastle, which Hadrian ignited with hot coals from the galley stove as soon as the surrounding deck had been soaked. Around it, archers prepped their arrows with oil. Seamen brought dozens of buckets of seawater, along with buckets of sand, and positioned them around the ship. It took only minutes to secure for battle, and then they waited.

The ships were closer and larger now, but still the flags they flew were invisible. The *Storm* remained deathly silent, the only sound coming from the wind, waves, and the creaking hull. A random gust fluttered the lugger's flag.

"They're flying the Gribbon of Calis, sir!" the lookout shouted.

"Mister Wesley," the captain addressed the midshipman stationed on the quarterdeck. "You've studied signals?"

"Aye, sir."

"Take a glass and get aloft. Mister Temple, run up our name and request theirs."

"Aye, aye, sir."

Still no one moved or spoke. All eyes were on the approaching vessels.

"Lead vessel is the *Bright Star*, aft vessel is…" Wesley hesitated. "Aft vessel isn't responding, sir."

"Two points 'a port!" the captain shouted abruptly, and Wyatt spun the wheel, weathering the ship as close to the wind as possible, heading them directly toward the lugger. The topmen went into action like a hundred spiders crawling along the shrouds, working to grab every bit of wind possible.

"New signal from the *Bright Star*," Wesley shouted. "Hostile ship astern!"

. Small streaks of smoke flew through the otherwise clear sky. The tartane was firing arrows at the *Bright Star*, but the shots fell short, falling into the sea a good two hundred yards astern.

"Ready the forward ballista!" the captain ordered. A squad of men on the forecastle began to crank a small capstan, which ratcheted the massive bowstring into firing position. They lighted another brazier in advance of the stanchion as an incendiary bolt was loaded. Then they waited, once more watching the ships sail closer.

Everything about the Dacca ship was exotic. Made of dark wood, the vessel glittered with gold swirls artfully painted along the hull. She bore long decorative pendants of garish, bright colors. A stylized image of a black dragon in flight adorned the scarlet mainsail, and on the bowsprit was the head of a ghoulish beast with bright emerald eyes. The sailors appeared as foreign as the ship. They were dark-skinned, powerful brutes wearing only bits of red cloth wrapped around their waists.

Poorly handled, the *Bright Star* lost the wind and her momentum. Behind her, the tartane descended. Another volley of arrows from the Dacca smoked through the air. This time several struck the *Bright Star* in the stern, but one lucky shot made it to the mainsail, setting it aflame.

Although victorious over the lugger, the tartane chose to flee before the approaching *Emerald Storm*. It came about and Hadrian watched Captain Seward ticking off the distance as the *Storm* inched toward it. Even after the time lost during the turn, the Dacca ship was still out of ballista range.

"Helm-a-lee. Bring her over!" the captain shouted. "Tacks and sheets!"

The *Emerald Storm* swung round to the same tack as the tartane, but the *Storm* did not have the momentum under her, nor the nimbleness of the smaller ship. The tartane was the faster vessel, and all that the crew of the *Emerald Storm* could do was watch as the Dacca sailed out of reach.

Seeing the opportunity lost, Captain Seward ordered the *Storm* heaved-to and the long boats launched. The *Bright Star's* mainsail and mast burned like a giant torch. Stays and braces snapped and the screams of men announced the fall of the flaming canvas to the deck. Still, the ship's momentum carried it astern of them. As it passed, they could see the terrified sailors struggling hopelessly to put out the flames that enveloped the deck. Before the long boats were in the water, the *Bright Star* was an inferno with most of the crew already in the sea.

The boats returned laden with frantic men. Nearly all were tawny-skinned, dark-eyed sailors dressed in whites and grays. They lay across the deck coughing, spitting water, and thanking Maribor as well as any nearby crew member.

The *Bright Star* was an independent Wesbaden trader from Dagastan heading home to western Calis with a load of coffee, cane, and indigo. Despite the *Storm's* timely intervention, more than a third of the small crew perished. Some passed out in the smoke while fighting the flames, and others remained trapped below deck. The captain of the *Bright Star* perished, struck by one of the fiery arrows the Dacca had rained on his vessel. This left only twelve men, five of whom lay in Doctor Levy's care with burns.

Mister Temple sized up the able-bodied survivors and added them to the ship's complement. Royce was back at work aloft as Hadrian finished serving dinner to the crew. Hadrian's easy going attitude and generosity with the galley grease had won several friends. There had been no more attempts on Royce's life, but they still did not know why Royce had been targeted, or by whom. For the moment, it was enough that Defoe, Derning, and Staul remained at a safe distance.

"Aye, this is Calis, not Avryn." Hadrian heard one of the new seamen saying in a harsh gravelly voice as he brought down the last messkid. "The light of civilization grows weak like a candle in a high easterly wind. The farther east you go, the stronger the wind blows till out she goes, and in the darkness ye stand!"

A large number of the off-watch clustered around an aft table, where three of the new sailors sat.

"Then there you are in the world of the savage," the Calian sailor went on. "A strange place, me lads, a strange place indeed. Harsh violent seas and jagged inlets of black-toothed rock, gripped tight by dense jungle. The netherworld of the Ba Ran Ghazel, the heart o' darkness is a place of misery and despair, the prison where Novron drove the beasties to their eternal punishment. They can't help but try to get out. They look at the coasts of Calis with hungry eyes and they find footholds. Like lichen, they slip in and grow everywhere. The Calians try to push them back, but it be like trying to swat a sky of flies or hold water in yer hands." He cupped his palms pretending to lose something between his fingers.

"Goblin and man living so close together tain't natural," another said.

The first sailor nodded gravely. "But nothin' in them jungles be natural. They have been linked for too long. The Sons of Maribor and the Spawn of Uberlin be warring one moment, then trading the next. Just to survive, the Calian warlords took to the ways of the goblins, and in so doing, spread the cursed practices of the Ba Ran to their kin. Some of these warlords are more goblin now than men. They even worship the dark god, burning tulan leaves and making sacrifices. They live like beasts. At night, the moon makes them wild, and in the darkness their eyes glow red!"

Several of the men made sounds of disbelief.

"It's the truth, me lads! Centuries ago, when the first empire fell, the eastern lords were abandoned to their fate. Left alone in the deep dark of the Calian jungles, they lost their humanity. Now the great stone fortresses along the Goblin Sea that once guarded the land from invasion be the home of Tenkin warlords—half human, half goblin monsters. They've turned their backs on the face of Maribor and embraced the ways of the Ghazel. Aye, me fellows, the state of Calis is a fearful one. So, thankful we be for your daring act of kindness, for we'd be at the mercy of fate if ya hadn't pulled us from the sea. If it wasn't for your bravery, we'd surely be dead now...or worse."

"Wasn't much bravery needed," Daniels said. "The *Storm* could have whipped those buggers in a dead calm with half the crew drunk and the other half sick with the fever."

"Is that what you think?" Wyatt asked. Hadrian did not notice him sitting silently in the gloom beyond the circle of the candle's light. "Is that what you *all* think?" His tone was oddly harsh—challenging. Wyatt sighed, and with an exasperated shake of his head, got up and climbed the ladder to the deck.

Having finished with the messkids, Hadrian followed. He found the helmsman on the forecastle. His hands gripped the rail as he stared at the shimmer of the new moon rolling on the back of the black sea.

"What's that all about?"

"We're in trouble and—" he paused, angrily motioning at the quarterdeck. Catching himself, he clenched his teeth as if by doing so he could trap the words inside his mouth.

"What kind of trouble?" Hadrian glanced at the quarterdeck.

"The captain doesn't want me to say anything. He's a damn fool who won't listen to reason. I should disobey him and alter the ship's course right now. I could relieve Bliden on the wheel early and take us off course. No one would know until the reckoning is taken tomorrow at noon."

"Wesley would know." Hadrian pointed to the young man climbing to the quarterdeck on his nightly round as officer of the first watch. "He'd have you hauled to Mister Bishop before you could blink."

"I could deal with Wesley if I had to. The deck is slippery, you know?"

"Now you're starting to sound like Royce. What's going on?"

"I suppose if I am contemplating killing a midshipman it hardly matters if I break captain's orders to keep quiet." Wyatt looked once again at the sea. "They're coming back."

"Who?"

"The Dacca. They didn't run; they're regrouping." He looked at Hadrian. "They dye their sails with the blood of their enemies. Did you know that? Hundreds of small ruddy-red boats line the coves and ports of their island. They know we're hugging the coast and sailing against the wind. They'll chase us down like wolves. Ten, twenty lateen-rigged tartanes will catch the wind that we can't. The *Storm* won't stand a chance."

"What makes you so sure? You could be wrong. The captain must have a good reason to stay on course."

"I'm not wrong."

Chapter 11

THE HOODED MAN

The hooded man walked away again.

Arista cowered deeper into the shadows under the tavern steps. She wanted to disappear, to become invisible. Her robe had turned a dingy brown, blending with the dirty wood. Drawing up the hood, she waited. It was *him*—the same man Lynette described. He was looking for her. She heard the sound of his boots on the cobblestone. They slowed, hesitated, and then grew louder.

He was coming back again!

The tall, dark figure appeared at the end of the alley for the third time. He paused. She held her breath. The streetlamps revealed a frightening figure dressed in a black, hooded cloak with a thick scarf hiding his face. He wore an unseen sword—she could hear the telltale clap.

He took a tentative step toward her hiding place, then another, and then paused. The light's glare exposed white puffs issuing from his scarf. His head turned from side to side. He stood for several seconds, then pivoted so sharply his boot heel dug a tiny depression in the gravel, and walked away. After several tense minutes, Arista carefully crept out.

He was gone.

The first light of dawn rose in the east. If only she could make it back to the palace. At least there she would be safe from the assassin and away from the inevitable questions: "Who is she? How did she do it? Is she a witch?"

She had left Brisbane Alley before anyone thought to ask, but what about after? She had drawn too much attention, and—although she doubted anyone would connect the dots—the unabashed use of magic would cause a stir.

Removing the robe, she carefully tucked it under the tavern steps and set off toward the palace. The guards ignored her as usual, and she went about her tasks without incident. Throughout the day she had the good fortune to work relatively unnoticed, but by midday news of her actions the night before had reached the palace. Everyone buzzed about the disturbance on Coswell Street. A boy had been brought back to life. By evening, rumors named the Witch of Melengar as the culprit. Luckily, no one suspected the scrub girl Ella of any more wrongdoing than failing to return the borrowed tablecloth.

She was exhausted. It was not merely losing a night's sleep while avoiding the assassin. Saving Wery had drained her. After leaving the palace, she returned to the alley and retrieved the wizard's robe. She did not dare put it on for fear someone might recognize it. She rolled it up and, clutching it to her chest, stood on the edge of the broad avenue, unable to decide what to do next. Staying would be sheer stupidity. Looking down the broad length of Grand Avenue she could see the front gates of the city. It felt like a lifetime since she was home. It would be so good to see a familiar face, to hear her brother's voice—to rest.

She knew she should leave. She should go that very minute, but she was so tired. The idea of setting out into the cold dark, alone and hungry, was too much. She desperately needed a safe place to sleep, a hot meal, and a friendly face—which meant just one thing—the Barkers. Besides, she could not leave without retrieving her pearl-handled hairbrush, the last remaining keepsake from her father.

Nothing had changed at the end of Brisbane Alley. The length was still dotted with small campfires and littered with bulky shadows of makeshift tents, carts, wagons, and barrels. People moved about in the growing dark. Some glanced at her as she passed, but no one spoke or approached her. She found the Barkers' wagon and, as always, a great tarp stretched out from it like a porch awning. One of the boys spotted her, and a moment later Lynette rushed out. Without a word, she threw her arms around Arista and squeezed tightly.

"Come, have something to eat," she said, wiping her cheeks and leading Arista by the hand. Lynette laid a pot on the fire. "I saved some just in case. I had to hide it, of course, or the vultures would have gobbled it all down. I wasn't sure you'd be back…"

The rest of the Barkers gathered around the fire. The boys, Finis and Hingus, sat on the far side. Brice Barker, dressed in his usual white shirt and gray trousers, sat on an upturned crate whittling a bit of wood. No one spoke. Arista took a seat on a wooden box, feeling awkward.

Is that apprehension in their eyes, or outright fear?

"Ella?" Lynette finally asked in a small, tentative voice. "Who are you?"

"I can't tell you that," she said after a long pause. She expected them to balk or argue. Instead, they all nodded silently as if expecting her answer, just as she had expected their question.

"I don't care who you are, you're always welcome at this fire," Brice said. He kept his eyes on the flames, but his words betrayed an emotion she did not expect. Brice, who made his living shouting in the streets all day, hardly ever spoke.

Lynette dished out the bit of stew she had warmed up. "I wish there was more. If I had only known you'd be back."

"How is Wery?" Arista asked.

"He slept all night, but was up most of the day running around causing a nuisance as usual. Everyone who's seen him is saying the same thing—it was a miracle."

"Everyone?" Arista asked with concern.

"Folks been stopping by all day to see him and asking about you. Many said they had sick children or loved ones who are dying. One got so angry he knocked down the canvas and nearly upset the wagon before Finis brought Brice home to clear him out."

"I'm sorry."

"Oh, don't be! Please—no—don't ever be sorry," Lynette pleaded. She paused, her eyes tearing again. "You won't be able to stay with us anymore, will you?"

Arista shook her head.

"The hooded man?"

"And others."

"I wish I could help," Lynette said.

Arista leaned over and hugged her. "You have…more than you'll ever know. If I could just get a good night's sleep, then I—"

"Of course you can. Sleep in the wagon, it's the least we can do."

Arista was too exhausted to argue. She climbed up and, in the privacy of the cart, put the robe on to fight away the night's cold. She crawled across a lumpy bedding of coarse cloth that smelled of potatoes and onions and laid her head down at last. It felt so good to close her eyes and let her muscles and mind go. She could hear them whispering outside, trying not to disturb her.

"She's a servant of Maribor," one of the boys said. She could not tell which. "That's why she can't say. The gods never let them say."

"Or she could be Kile—a god disguised and doing good deeds," the other added. "I heard he gets feathers from Muriel's cloak for each one he does."

"Hush! She'll hear you," Lynette scolded. "Go clean that pot."

Arista fell asleep to their whispers and woke to loud voices.

"I tell you I don't know what you're talking about! I don't know anything about a witch." It was Brice's voice, and he sounded frightened.

Arista peered out from the wagon. An Imperial soldier stood holding a torch, his way blocked by Brice. Behind him, farther up the alley, other soldiers pounded on the door to the tannery and forced their way into the other tents.

"Sergeant," the man in front of Brice called, "over here!"

Three soldiers walked fast, their armor jangling, hard boots hammering the cobblestone.

"Tear down this hovel and search it," the sergeant ordered. "Continue to do the same for all these places. They're an eyesore and should be removed anyway."

"Leave them alone," Arista said, stepping out of the wagon. "They haven't done anything."

"Ella!" Brice snapped. "Stay out of this."

The sergeant moved briskly toward Arista but Brice stepped in the way.

"Leave my daughter alone," he threatened.

"Brice, no," Arista whispered.

THE HOODED MAN

"I am only here for the witch," the soldier told them. "But if you insist, I will be happy to torch every tent in this alley."

"She's no witch!" Lynette cried, clutching Wery to her side. "She saved my baby. She's a servant of Maribor!"

The sergeant studied Arista briefly, sucking on his front teeth. "Bind her!" he ordered.

Two of his men stepped forward with a length of rope and grabbed hold of Arista by her arms. They immediately cried out in pain, let go, and stumbled backward. Esrahaddon's robe glowed a deep pulsating red. The guards glared at her in fear, shaking their injured hands.

Seeing her chance, Arista closed her eyes and began to concentrate. She focused on blocking out the sounds of the street and on—

Pain exploded across her face.

She fell backward to the ground where she lay dazed. Her eyesight darkened at the edges, a ringing wailed in her ears.

"We'll have none of that!" the sergeant declared.

She looked up through watery eyes, seeing him standing over her rubbing his knuckles. He drew his sword and pointed it at Brice.

"I know better than to let you cast your spells, witch. Don't make another sound, and remove that robe. Do it now! I'll strip you naked if needed. Make no sudden moves or sounds, or I'll cleave off this man's head here and now."

Lynette was somewhere to her right, and Arista heard her gasp in horror.

"The robe. Take it off!"

Arista wiggled out of the robe, leaving her clothed only in Lynette's thin kirtle. The sergeant sucked on his teeth again and stepped closer. "Are my men going to have any more trouble with you?" He lifted the point of his sword toward Brice once again.

Arista shook her head.

"Good. Bind her tightly. Wrap her wrists and fingers and find something to gag her with." The guards approached again and jerked her arms so roughly behind her back that she cried out.

"Please don't hurt her," Lynette begged. "She didn't do anything wrong!"

They tied her wrists, wrapping the rope around her fingers, pulling until the skin pinched painfully. As they did, the sergeant ordered Lynette to pick up the robe and hand it to him. One of the soldiers grabbed Arista by the hair, dragging her to her feet. Another took hold of one of her sleeves and ripped it off.

"Open yer mouth," he ordered, pulling Arista's head back. When she hesitated, the soldier slapped her across the face. Again she staggered, and might have fallen if not for the other guard still holding her hair. The slap was not nearly as painful as the blow the sergeant gave, but it watered her eyes again. "Now open!"

He stuffed the material into her mouth, jamming it in so far Arista thought she would choke. He tied it in place by wrapping more rope around her head and wedging it between her lips. When they tied one final length around her neck, Arista feared they might hang her right there.

"Now, that should keep us safe," declared the sergeant. "We'll cut those hands off when we get to the palace, and after you've answered questions I expect we'll take that tongue out as well."

A crowd gathered as they dragged her away, and Arista could hear Lynette weeping. As they reached Coswell, the patrons of The Bailey turned out to watch. The men stood on the porch, holding mugs. She heard the word *witch* muttered more than once as she passed by.

By the time they reached the square she was out of breath and choking on the gag. When she lagged behind, the guard holding the leash jerked hard and she fell. Her left knee struck the cobblestone of Bingham Square and she screamed, but the sound came out as a muffled grunt. Twisting, she landed on her shoulder to avoid hitting her face. Lying on her side, Arista cried in agony from the pain shooting up her leg.

"Up!" the soldier ordered. The rope tightened on her throat, the rough cord cutting her skin. The guard growled, "Get up, you lazy ass!" He pulled harder, dragging her a few inches across the stones. The rope constricted. She heard the pounding of blood in her ears.

"Up, damn you!"

She felt the rope cut into her neck. She could barely breathe. The pounding in her ears hammered like drums, pressure building.

"Bruce?" one of the guards called. "Get her up!"

"I'm trying!"

There was another tug and Arista managed to sit up, but she was light-headed now. The street tilted and wobbled. It was becoming hard to see as darkness grew at the edges of her vision. She tried to tell them she was choking. All that came out was a pitiful moan.

She struggled to reach her knees, but the dizziness worsened, the ground shifted and dipped. She fell, hitting her shoulder again, and rolled to her back. She looked up at the soldier holding the leash and pleaded with her eyes, but all she saw in reply was anger and disgust.

"Get up or—" He stopped. The soldier looked abruptly to his right. His face appeared puzzled. He let go of the rope and took a step backward.

The cord loosened, the pounding eased, and she could breathe again. She laid in the street, her eyes closed, happy to be alive. The clang of metal and the scuffle of feet caught her attention. Arista looked up to see the would-be strangler collapse to the street beside her.

Standing an arm's length away, the hooded man loomed with a blood-coated sword. From his belt he drew a dagger and threw it.

Somewhere behind her there was a grunt and a sound like a sack of flour hitting the ground.

The hooded man bolted past her. She heard a cry of pain. Metal struck metal, then another grunt, this one followed by a gurgled voice speaking garbled words. Another clash, another cry. She twisted around, rolling to her knees. She found him again. He stood in the center of Bingham Square, holding his sword in one hand and a dagger in the other. Three bodies lay on the ground. Two soldiers remained.

"Who are you?" the sergeant shouted at him. "We are Imperial soldiers acting on official orders."

The hooded man said nothing. He rushed forward, swinging his blade. He dodged to the right, and catching the sergeant's sword high, he stabbed the man in the neck with his dagger. As he did, the remaining soldier swung at him. The hooded man cried out then whirled in rage. He charged the last soldier, striking at him, his overwhelming fury driving the guard back.

The soldier turned and ran. The hooded man gave chase. The guard nearly made it to the end of the street before he was cleaved in the back. Once the soldier collapsed, the man continued attacking his screaming victim, stabbing him until he fell silent.

Arista sat bound in the middle of the square, helpless as the hooded man turned and, with his sword and cloak dripping blood, came for her. He pulled Arista to her feet and into a narrow alley.

He was breathing hard, sucking wetly through the scarf. No longer having the strength, physical or mental, Arista did not resist. The world was spinning and the night slipped into the unreal. She did not know what was happening or why, and she gave up trying to understand.

He dragged her into a stable, pushing her against the rough-hewn wall. A pair of horses shifted fearfully, spooked by the smell of blood. He held her tightly and brought his knife to her throat.

THE HOODED MAN

Arista closed her eyes and held her breath. She felt the cold steel press against her skin as he drew it, cutting the cord away. He spun her around and cut her wrists loose, then the cord holding the gag fell free.

"Follow me, quickly," he whispered, pulling her along by the hand. Confused, she staggered after him. Something was familiar in that voice.

He led her through a dizzying array of alleys, around dark buildings and over wooden fences. Soon she had no idea where they were. He paused in a darkened corner, holding a finger to his scarf-covered lips. They waited briefly then moved on. The wind picked up, carrying an odor of fish, and Arista heard the sound of surf. Ahead she could see the naked masts of ships bobbing at anchor along the wharf. When he reached a particularly dilapidated building, he led her up a back stair into a small room and closed the door behind them.

She stood rigid near the door, watching him as he started a fire in an iron stove. Seeing his hands, his arms, and the tilt of his head—something was so familiar. With the fire stoked, he turned and took a step toward her. Arista shrank until her back was against the door. He hesitated and then nodded. She recognized something in his eyes.

Reaching up, he drew back his hood and unwrapped the scarf. The face before her was painful to look at. Deformed and horribly scarred, it appeared to have melted into a patchwork of red blotches. One ear was missing, along with his eyebrows and much of his hair. His mouth lacked the pale pink of lips. His appearance was at once horrid and yet so welcomed she could find no words to express herself. She broke into tears of joy and threw her arms around him, hugging as tightly as her strength allowed.

"I hope this will teach you not to run off without me, Your Highness," Hilfred told her.

She continued to cry and squeeze, her head buried in his chest. Slowly his arms crept up, returning her embrace. She looked up and he brushed strands of tear-soaked hair from her face. In more than a decade as her protector, he had never touched her so intimately. As if realizing this, Hilfred straightened up and gently escorted her to a chair before reaching for his scarf.

"You're not going back out?" she asked fearfully.

"No," he replied, his voice dropped a tone. "The city will be filled with guards. It won't be safe for either of us to venture in public for some time. We'll be all right here. There are no occupied buildings around, and I rented this flat from a blind man."

"Then why are you covering up?"

He paused a moment, looking at the scarf. "The sight of my face—it makes people—uneasy, and it is important that you feel safe and comfortable. That's my job, remember?"

"And you do it very well, but your face doesn't make me uncomfortable."

"You don't find me...unpleasant to look at?"

Arista smiled warmly. "Hilfred, your face is the most beautiful thing I've ever seen."

The flat Hilfred stayed in was very small, just a single room and a closet. The floor and walls were rough pine planks weathered gray and scuffed smooth from wear. There was a rickety table, three chairs, and a ship's hammock. The single window was hazy from the buildup of ocean salt, admitting only a muted gray light. Hilfred refused to burn a single candle after dark for fear of attracting attention. The small stove kept the drafty shack tolerably warm at night, but before dawn it was extinguished for fear of someone seeing the smoke.

THE HOODED MAN

For two days they stayed in the shack, listening to the wind buffet the roof shingles and howl over the stovepipe. Hilfred made soup from clams and fish he bought from the old blind man. Other than that, neither of them left the little room. Arista slept a lot. It seemed like years since she had felt safe, and her body surrendered to exhaustion.

Hilfred kept her covered and crept around the flat cursing to himself whenever he made a noise. On the night of the second day, she woke when he dropped a spoon. He looked at her sheepishly and cringed at the sight of her open eyes.

"Sorry, I was just warming up some soup. I thought you might be hungry."

"Thank you," she told him.

"Thank you?"

"Yes, isn't that what you say when someone does something for you?"

He raised what would have been his eyebrows. "I've been your servant for more than ten years, you've never once said *thank you.*"

It was the truth, and it hurt to hear it. What a monster she had been. "Well overdue then, don't you think? Let me check your bandage."

"After you eat, Your Highness."

She looked at him and smiled. "I have missed you so," she said. Surprise crossed his face. "You know, there were times growing up that I hated you. Mostly after the fire—for not saving my mother, but later I hated the way you always followed me. I knew you reported my every move. It's a terrible thing for a teenage girl to have an older boy silently following her every step, watching her eat, watching her sleep, knowing her most intimate secrets. You were always silent, always watchful. Did you know I had a crush on you when I was fourteen?"

"No," he said, curtly.

"You were what, a dashing seventeen? I tried everything to make you jealous. I chased after all the squires at court, pretending they wanted me, but none of them did. And you…you were such the loathingly perfect gentleman. You stood by stoically, and it infuriated me. I would go to bed humiliated, knowing that you were standing just outside the door.

"When I was older, I treated you like furniture—still, you treated me as you always did. During the trial—" she noticed Hilfred flinch, and decided not to finish the thought. "And afterward, I thought you believed what they said and hated me."

Hilfred put down the spoon and sighed.

"What?" she asked, suddenly fearful.

He shook his head and a small, sad laugh escaped his lips. "It's nothing, Your Highness."

"Hilfred, call me Arista."

He raised his brow once more. "I can't. You're my princess, and I am your servant. That is how it has always been."

"Hilfred, you've known me since I was ten. You've followed me day and night. You've seen me early in the morning. You've seen me drenched in sweat from fevers. I think you can call me by my first name."

He looked almost frightened, and resumed stirring the pot.

"Hilfred?"

"I am sorry, Your Highness. I cannot call you by your given name."

"What if I command you to?"

"Do you?"

"No." Arista sighed. "What is it with men who won't use my name?"

Hilfred glanced at her.

"I only knew him briefly," she explained, not knowing why. She had never spoken about Emery to anyone before. "I've lived so much of my life alone. It never used to bother me and there's never been anyone—until recently."

Hilfred looked down and stirred the soup.

"He was killed. Since then, I have felt this hole. The other night I was so scared. I thought—no, I was certain—I was going to my death. I lost hope and then you appeared. I could really use a friend—and if you called me by—"

"I can't be your friend, Your Highness," Hilfred told her coldly.

"Why not?"

There was a long pause. "I can't tell you that."

A loud silence filled the room.

Arista stood, clutching the blanket around her shoulders. She stared at Hilfred's back until it seemed her stare caused him to turn and face her. When he did, he avoided looking in her eyes. He set out bowls on the table. She stood before him, blocking his way.

"Hilfred, look at me."

"The soup is done."

"I'm not hungry. Look at me."

"I don't want it to burn."

"Hilfred."

He said nothing and kept his eyes focused on the floor.

"What have you done that you can't face me?"

He did not answer.

The realization dawned on her and devastated Arista. He was not there to save her. He was not her friend. The betrayal was almost too much to bear.

"It's true," her voice quivered. "You do believe the stories they say about me: that I am a witch, that I am evil, that I killed my father over my lust for the throne. Are you working for Saldur, or someone else? Did you steal me from the palace guards for some political advantage? Or is this all some plan to—to control me, to get me to trust you and lure me into revealing something?"

Her words had a profound effect on him. He looked pained, as if rained by blows. His face strained, his jaw stiff.

"You could at least tell me the truth," she said. "I should think you owe that much to my father, if not to me. He trusted you. He picked you to be my bodyguard. He gave you a chance to make something of yourself. You've enjoyed the privilege of court life because of his faith in you."

Hilfred was having trouble breathing. He turned away from her and, grabbing his scarf, moved toward the door.

"Yes, go—go on!" She shouted. "Tell them it didn't work. Tell them I didn't fall for it. Tell Sauly and the rest of those bastards that—that I'm not the stupid little girl they thought I was! You should have kept me tied and gagged, Hilfred. You're going to find it harder to haul me off to the stake than you think!"

Hilfred slammed his hand against the doorframe, making Arista jump. He spun on her, his eyes fierce and wild in a way she had never seen before, and she stepped back.

"DO YOU KNOW WHY I SAVED YOU?" he shouted, his voice broken and shaking. "Do you? Do you?"

"To—to hand me over and get—"

"No! No! Not now. Back *then*," he cried, waving his arm. "Years ago, when the castle was burning. Do you know why I saved you then?"

She did not speak. She did not move.

"I wasn't the only one there, you know. There were others. Soldiers, priests, servants, they all just stood watching. They knew you were inside, but not a single person did anything. They just watched the place burn. Bishop Saldur saw me running for the castle and actually ordered me to stop. He said it was too late, that I would die. I believed him. I truly did, but I went in anyway. Do you know why? DO YOU?" He shouted at her.

She shook her head.

THE HOODED MAN

"Because I didn't care! I didn't want to live...not if you died."
Tears streamed down his scarred face. "But don't ask me to be your
friend. That is far too cruel a torture. As long as I can maintain a safe
distance, as long as...as long as there is a wall between us—even if
it is only one of words, I can tolerate—I can *bear* it." Hilfred wiped
his eyes with his scarf. "Your father knew what he was doing—oh
yes, he knew *exactly* what he was doing when he appointed me your
bodyguard. I would die a thousand times over to protect you. But
don't ask me to be grateful to him for the life he's given me, for it has
been one of pain. I wish I had died that night so many years ago, or
at least in Dahlgren. Then it would be over. I wouldn't have to look
at you. I wouldn't have to wake up every day wishing I had been born
the son of a great knight, or you the daughter of a poor shepherd."

He turned away, covering his eyes and laying his head against the
threshold. Arista did not recall doing it, but somehow she crossed
the room. She took Hilfred's face in her hands and, rising up on her
toes, she kissed his mouth. He did not move, but he trembled. He
did not breathe, but he gasped.

"Look at me," she said extending her arms to display her stained
and torn kirtle. "A shepherd's daughter would pity me, don't you
think? She took his hand and kissed it. "Can you ever forgive me?"

He looked at her, confused. "For what?"

"For being so blind."

Chapter 12

SEA WOLVES

As it had for days, the *Emerald Storm* remained on its easterly course, making slow progress against a headwind that refused to shift. Maintaining direction required frequent tacking, which caused the top crews to work all night. Royce, as usual, had drawn the late shift. It was not Dime's fault. Royce had concluded that the mainmast captain was a fair man, but Royce was the newest member of a crew that rewarded seniority. He did not mind the shift. He enjoyed the nights he spent aloft. The air was fresh, and in the dark among the ropes, he was as comfortable as a spider in his web. This afforded Royce the opportunity to relax, think, and occasionally amuse himself by tormenting Defoe, who panicked any time his old guild mate lost track of Royce.

Royce hung in the netting of the futtock shroud, his feet dangling over the open space—a drop of nearly a hundred feet. Above lay the dust of stars, while on the horizon the moon rose as a sliver—a cat's eye peering across the water at him. Below, lanterns flickered on the bow, quarterdeck, and the stern outlining the *Emerald Storm*. To his left, he could just make out the dark coast of Calis. Its thick vegetation was occasionally punctuated by a cliff or the brilliant white plume of a waterfall catching moonlight.

The seasickness was gone. He could not recall a more miserable time than his first week on board. The nausea and dizziness reminded him of being drunk—a sensation he hated. He spent most of the first night hugging the ship's figurehead and vomiting off the bow. After four days, his stomach settled but he remained drained and tired easily. It took weeks, but he forgot all that as he nested in the rigging looking out at the dark sea. It surprised him just how beautiful the black waves could be, the graceful undulating swells kissed by the barefaced moon, all below a scattering of stars. Only one sight could surpass it.

What is she doing right now? Is she looking at the same moon and thinking of me?

Royce reached inside his tunic, pulled out the scarf, and rubbed the material between his fingers. He held it to his face and breathed deep. It smelled like her. Soft and warm, he kept it hidden—his tiny treasure. On the nights of his sickness, he had lain in the hammock clutching it to his cheek as if it was a magic talisman to ward off misery. It was how he fell asleep.

The officers' deck hatch opened, and Royce spotted Beryl stepping out into the night air. Beryl liked his sleep, and being senior midshipman, rarely held the late watch. He stood glancing around, taking in the lay of the deck. He cast an eye up at the maintop, but Royce knew he was invisible in the dark tangles. Beryl spotted Wesley making his rounds on the forecastle and made his way across the waist and up the stair. Wesley looked concerned at his approach but held his ground. Perhaps the boy would get another beating tonight. Whatever torments Beryl planned for Wesley were no concern of Royce, and he thought it might be time to scare Defoe again.

"I won't do it," Wesley declared, drawing Royce's attention. Once more Royce noticed Beryl nervously looking upward.

Who are you looking for, Mister Beryl?

He unhooked himself from the shrouds and rolled over for his own glance upward. As usual, Defoe was keeping his distance.

No threat there.

Royce climbed to the yard, walked to the end and, just as he had done during the race with Derning, slid down the rope so he could hear them.

"I can make life on this ship very difficult for you," Beryl threatened Wesley. "Or have you forgotten your two days without sleep? There is talk that I will be made acting lieutenant, and if you think your life is hard with my current rank, as a lieutenant it will be a nightmare. And I'll see to it that any transfer is refused."

"I don't understand."

"You don't have to. In fact, it's better if you don't. That way you can sound sincere if the captain questions you. Just find him guilty of something. Misconduct, disrespect, I don't care. You put his buddy the cook on report for not saluting, do something like that. Only this time it needs to be a flogging offense."

"But why me? Why can't *you* invent this charge?"

"Because if the accusation comes from you, the captain and Mister Bishop will not question it." He grinned. "And if they do— it's your ass, not mine."

"And that's supposed to entice me?"

"No, but I'll get off your back. If you don't—you won't eat, you won't sleep, and you'll become very accident-prone. The sea can be dangerous. Midshipmen Jenkins lost both thumbs on our last voyage when he slipped with a rope, which is strange 'cause he didn't handle ropes that day. Invent a charge, make it stick, and get him flogged."

"And why do you want him whipped?"

"I told you. My friends want blood. Now do we have a deal?"

Wesley stared at Beryl and took a deep breath. "I can't misrepresent a man, and certainly not one under my command, simply to avoid personal discomfort."

"It will be a great deal more than discomfort, you little git!"

"The best I can do is to forget we had this conversation. Of course, should some unusual or circumstantial accusation be leveled against Seaman Melborn, I might find it necessary to report this incident to the captain. I suspect he will take a dim view of your efforts to advance insubordination on his vessel. It could be viewed as the seeds of mutiny, and we both know the penalty for that."

"You don't know who you're playing with, boy. As much as you'd like to think it, you're no Breckton. If I can't use you, I'll lose you."

"Is that all, Mister Beryl? I must tack the ship now."

Beryl spit at the younger man's feet and stalked away. Wesley remained standing rigidly, watching him go. Once Beryl disappeared below, he gripped the rail and took off his hat to wipe the sweat from his forehead. Wesley took a deep breath, replaced his hat, straightened his jacket, and then shouted in a clear voice, "Hands to the braces!"

Royce had dealt with many people in his life, from serfs to kings, and few shocked him. He knew he could always depend on their greed and weakness, and he was rarely disappointed. Wesley was the first person in years to surprise him. While the young midshipman could not see it, the thief offered him the only sincere salute bestowed since Royce stepped aboard.

Royce ascended to the topsail to loose the yard brace in anticipation of Wesley's next order when his eye caught an irregularity on the horizon. At night, with only the suggestion of a moon, it was hard for anyone to tell where the sky ended and the sea began. Royce however, could discern the difference. At that moment, he noticed a break in the line. Out to sea, ahead of the *Storm*, a black silhouette broke the dusty star field.

"Sail ho!" he shouted.

"What was that?" Wesley asked.

"Sail off the starboard bow," he shouted, pointing to the southeast.

"Is there a light?"

"No, sir, a triangle-shaped sail."

Wesley moved to the starboard rail. "I don't see anything, how far out?"

"On the horizon, sir."

"The horizon?" Wesley picked up the eyeglass and panned the sea. The rest of the ship was silent except for the creaking of the oak timbers as they waited. "I'll be buggered," Wesley muttered as he slapped the glass closed and ran to the quarterdeck to pound on the captain's cabin. He paused and then pounded again.

The door opened to reveal the captain, barefoot in his nightshirt. "Mister Wesley, have we run aground? Is there a mutiny?" The captain's steward rushed to him with his robe.

"No, sir. There's a sail on the horizon, sir."

"A what?"

"A triangular sail, sir. Over there." Wesley pointed while handing him the glass.

"On the horizon you say? But how—" Seward crossed to the rail and looked out. "By Mar! But you've got keen eyes, lad!"

"Actually, the maintop crew spotted it first, sir. Sounded like Seaman Melborn, sir."

"Looks like *three* ships, Mister Wesley. Call all hands."

"Aye, aye, sir!"

Wesley roused Bristol, who woke the rest of the crew. In a matter of minutes men ran to their stations. Lieutenant Bishop was still buttoning his coat when he reached the quarterdeck, followed by Mister Temple.

"What is it, sir?"

"The Dacca have returned."

Wyatt, who was taking the helm, glanced over. "Orders, sir?" he asked coldly.

"Watch your tone, helmsman!" Temple snapped.

"Just asking, sir."

"Asking for a caning!" Mister Temple roared. "And you'll get one if you don't keep a civil tongue."

"Shut up the both of you. I need to think." Seward began to pace the quarterdeck, his head down, and one hand playing with the tie to his robe, the other stroking his lips.

"Sir, we only have one chance and it's a thin one at that," Wyatt said.

Mister Temple took hold of his cane and moved toward him.

"Belay, Mister Temple!" The captain ordered, before turning his attention back to Wyatt. "Explain yourself, helmsman."

"At that range, with the land behind us, the Dacca can't possibly see the *Storm*. All they can see are the lanterns."

"Good god! You're right, put out those—"

"No, wait, sir!" Wyatt stopped him. "We *want* them to see the lanterns. Lower the long boat, rig it with a pole fore and aft, and hang two lanterns on the ends. Put ours out as you light those then cast off. The Dacca will focus on it all night. We'll be able to bring the *Storm* about, catch the wind, and reach the safety of Wesbaden Bay."

"But that's not our destination."

"Damn our orders, sir! If we don't catch the wind, the Dacca will be on us by tomorrow night."

"*I'm* the captain of this ship!" Seward roared. "Another outburst and I'll not hold Mister Temple's hand."

The captain looked at the waiting crew; every eye was on him. He returned to pacing with his head down.

"Sir?" Bishop inquired. "Orders?"

"Can't you see I'm thinking, man?"

"Yes, sir."

The wind fluttered the sails overhead as the ship began to lose the angle on the wind.

"Lower the long boat," Seward ordered at last. "Rig it with poles and lanterns."

"And our heading?"

Seward tapped his lips.

"I shouldn't need to remind you, Captain Seward," Thranic said as he climbed the ladder to the quarterdeck, "that it is imperative we reach the port of Dagastan without delay."

Seward tapped his lips once more. "Send the long boat aft with a crew of four, have them stroke for their lives toward Wesbaden. The Dacca will think we've seen them and will expect us to head that way, but the *Storm* will maintain its present course. There is to be no light on this ship without my order, and I want absolute silence. Do you hear me? Not a sound."

"Aye, sir."

Seward glanced at Wyatt, who shook his head with a look of disgust. The captain ignored him and turned his lieutenant. "See to it, Mister Bishop."

"Aye, aye, sir."

"You should have tried for the long boat's crew," Wyatt whispered to Hadrian. "We all should have."

It was still dark, but the crescent moon had long since fallen into the sea. As per the captain's orders, the ship was quiet. The only sound came from the whispers of some of the men who had not returned to their hammocks after the long boat launched. Even the wind had died, and the ship rocked motionless and silent in the darkness.

"You don't have a lot of faith in Seward's decision?"

"The Dacca are smarter than he is."

"You've got to at least give him the benefit of the doubt. They might think we turned and ran."

Wyatt muffled a laugh. "If you were captain and decided to make a run for it against faster ships in the dead of night, would you have left the lanterns burning? The lantern ruse only works if they think we *haven't* seen them."

"I hadn't thought of that," Hadrian admitted. "We'll know soon enough if they took the bait. It's getting lighter."

"Where's Royce and his eagle eyes?" Wyatt asked.

"He went to sleep after his shift. Sleep and eat when you can so you don't regret it later—something we've learned over the years."

They peered out across the water as the light increased. "Maybe the captain was right," Hadrian said.

"How do you mean?"

"I don't see them."

Wyatt laughed. "You don't see them because you can't see anything, not even a horizon. There's fog on the water. It happens this time of year."

It grew lighter, and Hadrian could see Wyatt was right. A thick gray blanket of clouds surrounded them.

Lieutenant Bishop climbed to the quarterdeck and rapped softly on the captain's door. "You asked to be awakened at first light, sir," he whispered

The captain came out, fully dressed this time, and proudly strode to the bridge.

"Fog, sir."

The captain scowled at him. "I can see that, Mister Bishop. I'm not blind."

"No, sir."

"Send a lad with a glass up the main mast."

"Mister Wesley," Bishop called softly. The midshipman came running. "Take this glass to the masthead and report."

"Aye, sir."

Captain Seward stood with his hand fidgeting behind his back, rocking on his heels and staring out at the fog. "It looks promising so far, doesn't it, Mister Bishop?"

"It does indeed, sir. The fog will help hide us all the more."

"What do you think now, helmsman?" the captain asked Wyatt.

"I think I'll wait for Mister Wesley's report. If you don't mind, sir."

Seward folded his arms in irritation and began to pace, his short legs and plump belly doing little to impart the vision of a commanding figure.

Wesley reached the masthead and extended the glass.

"Well?" Seward called aloud, his impatience getting the better of him.

"I can't tell, sir. The fog is too thick."

"They say the Dacca can use magic to raise a fog when they want," Poe whispered to Hadrian as they watched. "They're likely using it to sneak up on us."

"Or maybe it's just because the air is cooler this morning," Hadrian replied.

Poe shrugged.

The crew stood around, silent and idle, for an hour before Mister Temple ordered Hadrian to serve the morning meal. The men ate then wandered the deck in silence, like ghosts in a misty world of white. The midday meal came and went as well, with no break in the mist that continued to envelop them.

Hadrian had just finished cleaning up when he heard Wesley's voice from the masthead shout, "Sail!"

Emerging from the hold, Hadrian felt a cool breeze as a wind moved the fog, parting the hazy white curtains veil after veil.

The single word left everyone on edge.

"Good Maribor, man!" Seward shouted up. "What kind of sail?"

"Red lateen sails, sir!"

"Damn!" Seward cursed. "How many?"

"Five!"

"Five? Five! How could there be five?"

"No, wait!" Wesley shouted. "Six to windward! And three more coming off the port bow."

The captain's face drained of color. "Good Maribor!"

Even as he spoke, Hadrian spotted the sails clustered on the water.

"Orders, Captain?" Wyatt asked.

Seward glanced around him desperately. "Mister Bishop, lay the ship on the port tack."

Wyatt shook his head defiantly. "We need to grab the wind."

"Damn you!" Seward hesitated only a moment than shouted, "So be it! Hard a port, helmsman. Bring her around, hard over!"

Wyatt spun the wheel, the chains cranking the rudder so that the ship started to turn. Mister Temple barked orders to the crew. The *Emerald Storm* was sluggish, stalling in the futile wind. The ship slowed to a mere drift. Then the foresail fluttered, billowed, and started to draw. She was coming around slowly. The yards turned as the men ran aft with the lee-braces. The mainsail caught the breeze and blew full. The ship creaked loudly as the masts took up the strain.

The *Storm* picked up speed and was halfway round and pointed toward the coast. Still, Wyatt held the wheel hard over. The wind pressed the sails and leaned the ship, dipping the beam dangerously low. Spray broke over the rail as men grabbed hold of whatever they could to remain standing as the deck tilted steadily upward. The captain glared at Wyatt as he too grabbed hold of the mizzen shroud, yet he held his tongue. Letting the wind take the ship full on with all sails set, Wyatt pressed the wheel, raising the ship on its edge. Bishop and Temple glanced from Wyatt to the captain and back again, but no one dared give an order in the captain's presence.

Hadrian also grabbed hold of a rail to keep from slipping down the deck. Holding tight, he worried that Wyatt might capsize her. The hull groaned from the strain, the masts creaked with the pressure, but the ship picked up speed. At first the ship bucked through the waves, sending bursts of spray over the deck, then faster she went until the *Storm* skipped the waves, flying off the crests with the wind squarely on her aft quarter. The ship made its tight circle and at last Wyatt let up, leveling the deck. The ship fell in direct line with the wind and the bow rose as she ran with it.

"Trim the sails" the lieutenant ordered. The men set to work once more, periodically glancing astern to watch the approach of the ships.

"Mister Bishop," Seward called. "Disburse weapons to the men and issue an extra ration of grog."

Royce was on his way aloft as the larboard crew came off duty. "How long do you think before they catch us?" he asked Hadrian, looking aft at the tiny armada of red sails chasing their wake.

"I don't know. I've never done this before. What do you think?"

Royce shrugged, "A few hours maybe."

"It's not looking good, is it?"

"And you wanted to be a sailor."

~

Hadrian went about the business of preparing for the evening meal, mindful that it might be the last the men would have. Poe, conspicuously absent, hastily entered the galley.

"Where you been?"

Poe looked sheepish. "Talking to Wyatt. Those Dacca ships are gaining fast. They'll be on us tonight for sure."

Hadrian nodded grimly.

Poe moved to help cut the salted pork, then added. "Wyatt has a plan. It won't save everyone, only a handful really, and it might not work at all, but it's something. He wants to know if you're in."

"What about Royce?"

"Him, too."

"What's the plan?"

"Sail!" they heard Mister Wesley cry even from the galley, "Two more tartanes dead ahead!"

Poe and Hadrian, like everyone else aboard, scrambled to the deck to see Mister Wesley pointing off the starboard bow. Two red sails were slipping out from hidden coves along the shore to block their retreat. Sailing nimbly against the wind, they moved to intercept.

"Clear the deck for action!" Seward shouted from the quarterdeck, wiping the sweat from his head.

Men scrambled across the ship, once more hauling buckets of sand and water. Archers took their positions on the forecastle, stringing their bows. Oil and hot coals were placed at the ready.

"We need to steer clear," the captain said. "Helm bring her—"

"We need speed, *sir*," Wyatt interrupted.

The captain winced at the interruption. "Be mindful, Deminthal, or I'll skip the flogging I owe you and have you hanged!"

"With all due respect, you abdicated that privilege to the Dacca last night. All the sooner if I alter course now."

"By Maribor! Mister Temple, take—" The captain stopped as he spotted the tartanes begin to turn.

"See! They expected us to break," Wyatt told him.

Realizing their mistake, the Dacca fought to swing back, but it was too late. A hole had been created.

Seward grumbled and scowled at Wyatt.

"Sir?" Temple asked.

"Never mind. Steady as she goes, Mister Bishop. Order the archers to take aim at the port side ship! Perhaps we can slow them down if we can manage to set one afire."

"Aye, aye, sir!"

Hadrian rushed to the forecastle. Having proved himself one of the best archers on the ship, his station was at the center of the port side. He picked a strong, solid bow and tested the string's strength.

"The wind will set the arrows off a bit toward the bow," Poe mentioned, readying a bucket of glowing hot coals. "Might want to lead the target a bit, eh?"

"You're my squire now as well?"

Poe smiled, and shook his head. "I've seen you in practice. I figure the safest place on this ship right now is here. I'll hand you the oiled arrows. You just keep firing."

The Dacca tartanes slipped through the waves, their red triangular sails billowing out sideways as they struggled on a tight tack to make the best use of the head wind. Dark figures scurried like ants across the decks and rigging of the smaller ships.

"Ready arrows!" Lieutenant Bishop shouted.

Hadrian fitted his first shaft in the string.

As the Dacca closed in on the *Storm*, they began to turn. Their yards swept round and their tillers cranked, pivoting much as Wyatt had, the action all the more impressive as both ships moved in perfect unison, like dancers performing simultaneous pirouettes.

"Light arrows!"

Hadrian touched the oil-soaked wad at the tip of the shaft to the pot of coals and it burst into flame. A row of men on the port side stood ready, a trail of soot-black smoke wafting aft.

"Take aim!" Bishop ordered as the Dacca ships came into range. On the deck of the tartanes, a line of flaming arrows mirrored their own. "Fire!"

Into the blue sky flew a staggered arc of fire trailing black smoke. At the same time, the Dacca launched their volley and the two passed each other in midair. All around him, Hadrian heard the pattering of arrows. The bucket brigade was running to douse the flames, and above Royce dropped along a line to kick free one lodged in the masthead before it could ignite the mainsail.

Poe had another arrow ready. Hadrian fitted it, lit it with the pot, took aim, and sent it into the lower yard of their mainsail. To his right, he heard the loud *thwack* of the massive ballista that sent forth a huge flaming missile. It struck the side of the tartane, splintering the hull and lodging there.

Hadrian heard a hissing fly past his ear. Behind him, the oil bucket splashed and the liquid ignited. Poe jumped backward as his trousers flamed. Grabbing a nearby bucket Hadrian smothered the burning oil with sand.

Another volley rained, peppering the deck. Boatswain Bristol, in the process of cranking the ballista for a second shot, fell dead with an arrow in his throat, his hair catching fire. Basil, the officers' cook, took one in the chest, and Seaman Bliden screamed as two arrows hit him, one in the thigh, and the other through his hand. Looking up, Hadrian saw this second volley came from the other ship.

Shaken but not seriously harmed, Poe found another oil bucket and brought it to Hadrian. As the two ships came closer, Hadrian found what he was looking for—a bucket at the feet of the archers. Leading his target, he held his breath, took aim, and released. The tartane's bucket exploded. Hadrian spotted a young Dacca attempt to douse the flames with water. Instantly the fire washed the deck. At that moment, the *Storm's* ballista crew, having loaded the weapon with multiple bolts this time, released a cruel hail on the passing Dacca. Screams bridged the gap between the ships as the *Storm* sailed on, leaving the burning ships in their wake.

Once more, the crew cheered their victory, but it was hollow. Amid the blackened scorch marks left by scores of arrows, a dozen men lay dead on the deck. They had not slipped through the trap unscathed, and the red sails behind them were closer now.

When night fell, the captain ordered the off-crew, including Hadrian and Royce, below deck to rest. They went to their quarters and took the opportunity to change into their cloaks and tunics. Hadrian strapped on his swords. It brought a few curious looks, but no one said a word.

Not a single man slept, and few even sat. Most paced with their heads bowed to avoid the short ceiling, but perhaps this time they were also praying. Many of the crew had appeared superstitious, but none religious—until now.

"Why don't we put inland?" Seaman Davis asked his fellow sailors. "The coast's only a few miles off. We could put in and escape into the jungle."

"Coral shoals ring the shores of Calis," Banner said, scraping the surface of the table with a knife. "We'd rip the bottom of the *Storm* a mile out, and the Dacca would have it. Besides, the captain ain't gonna abandon his ship and run."

"Captain Seward is an arse!"

"Watch yer mouth, lad!"

"Why? What's he gonna do that can be worse than the Dacca?"

To that, Banner had no answer. No one did. Fear spread through the crew, fear of certain death and the poison that comes from waiting idly for it. Hadrian knew from countless battles the folly of leaving men to stagnate with nothing else to occupy their thoughts.

The hatch opened and everyone looked up. It was Wyatt and Poe.

"What's the word?" Davis asked.

"It won't be long now, men. Make ready what you need to. The captain will call general quarters soon, I expect."

Wyatt paused at the bottom of the ladder and spoke quietly with Grady and Derning. They nodded then went aft. Wyatt motioned with his eyes for Hadrian and Royce to follow him forward. Only empty hammocks filled the cramped space, leaving them enough privacy to speak.

"So, what's this plan?" Royce whispered.

"We can't win a fight," Wyatt told them. "All we can hope to do is run."

"You said the *Storm* can't outrun them," Hadrian reminded him.

"I wasn't planning on outrunning them in the *Storm*."

Hadrian and Royce exchanged glances.

"The Dacca will want her and the cargo. That's why we made it through the blockade so easily. They were trying to slow us, not stop us. If I had followed Seward's orders, we'd all be dead now. As it is, I only bought us a few hours, but they were needed."

"Needed for what, exactly?" Royce asked.

"For darkness. The Dacca can't see any better at night than we can, and while they take the *Storm*, we'll escape. They'll bring as many of their ships alongside as they can to overwhelm our decks by sheer numbers. When they board us, a party of men I've hand-picked will take one of the tartanes. We'll cut the ship free and, with luck, get clear of the *Storm* before they see us. In the darkness and the confusion of battle, it might work."

They both nodded.

Wyatt motioned to Hadrian. "I want you to lead the boarding party. I'll signal you from the quarterdeck."

"What are you going to be doing?" Royce asked.

"You mean what are *we* going to be doing? I didn't come all this way not to find Allie. You and I will use the distraction to break into the captain's quarters and steal any orders or parchments we find. Just watch me. You'll know when."

"What about the elves below?" Royce asked.

"Don't worry about them. They want the ship whole. In all likelihood, the Dacca will treat them better than the New Empire has."

"Who's in this team of yours?" Hadrian asked.

"Poe, of course, Banner, Grady—"

"All hands on deck!" Temple shouted from above as drums thundered.

"See you above, gentlemen," Wyatt said while heading for the hold.

The sky was black. Invisible clouds covered the stars and shrouded the sliver of moon. Darkness wrapped the sea, a shadowy abyss where only the froth at the bow revealed the presence of water. Behind them, Hadrian saw nothing.

"Archers to the aft deck!"

Hadrian joined the others at the railing, where they lined up, ilder to shoulder, looking out across the *Emerald Storm's* wake.

"Light arrows!" came the order.

From across the water they heard a sound, and a moment later en around Hadrian screamed as arrows pelted the stern.

"Fire!" Bishop ordered.

They raised their bows and fired as one, launching their burning shafts blindly into the darkness. A stream of flame flew in a long arch, some dying with a hiss as they fell into the sea, others struck wood, their light outlining a ship about three hundred yards behind them.

"There," Bishop shouted. "There's your target men!"

They exchanged volley after volley. Men fell dead on both ships, thinning the ranks of archers. Small fires broke out on the tartane, illuminating it and its crew. The Dacca were short, stocky, and lean with coarse long beards and wild hair. The firelight cast them with a demonic glow that glistened off their bare, sweat-soaked skin.

When the tartane lay less than fifty yards astern, its mainmast caught fire and burned like a dead tree. The brilliant light exposed the sea in all directions and stifled the cheers of the *Storm's* crew when it revealed the positions of the rest of the Dacca fleet. Four ships had already slipped alongside them.

"Stand by to repel boarders!" shouted Seward. He drew his sword and waved it over his head as he ran to the safety of the forecastle walls.

"Raise the nets!" ordered Bishop. The rigging crew drew up netting on either side of the deck, creating an entangling barrier of rope webbing. Under command of their officers, men took position at the waist deck, cutlasses raised.

"Cut the tethers!" Mister Wesley's voice cried as hooks caught the rail.

The deck shook as the tartanes slammed against the *Emerald Storm's* hull. A flood of stocky men wearing only leather armor and red paint stormed over the side. They screamed in fury as swords met.

"Now!" Hadrian heard Wyatt shout at him.

He turned and saw the helmsman pointing to the tartane tethered to the *Storm's* port side near the stern, the first of the Dacca's ships to reach them. Most of its crew had already boarded the *Storm.* Poe, Grady, and others in Wyatt's team held back, watching him.

"Go!" he shouted and, grabbing hold of the mizzen's port side brace, cut it free and swung out across the gulf landing on the stern of the tartane.

The stunned Dacca helmsman reached for his short blade as Hadrian cut his throat. Two more Dacca rushed him. Hadrian dodged, using the move to hide the thrust. His broadsword drove deep into the first Dacca's stomach. The second man, seeing his chance, attacked, but Hadrian's bastard sword was in his left hand. With it he deflected a wild swing. Drawing the broadsword from the first Dacca's stomach, Hadrian brought it across, severing the remaining man's head.

With three bodies on the aft deck, Hadrian looked up to see Poe and the rest already in possession of the ship and in the process of cutting the tethers free. With the last one cut, Poe used a pole and pushed away from the *Storm.*

"What about Royce and Wyatt?" Hadrian asked, climbing down to the waist deck.

"They'll swim for it and we'll pick them up on the far side," Poe explained, as he ran past him heading aft. "But we need to get into the shadows now!"

Poe climbed the short steps to the tartane's tiny quarterdeck and took hold of the tiller. "Swing the boom!" he shouted in a whisper. "Trim the sails!"

"We know our jobs a lot better than you, boy!" Derning hissed at im. He and Grady were already hauling on the mainsail sheet, trying o tame the canvas that snapped above like a serpent, jangling the igging rings against the mast. "Banner, Davis! Adjust the headsail or a starboard tack."

Hadrian had never learned the ropes and stood by uselessly while the others raced across the deck. Even if he had picked up anything about rigging, it would not have helped. The Dacca tartane was quite different in design. Besides being smaller, the hull was sloped like a fishing vessel, but with two decks. It had just two sails; a headsail supported on a forward-tilting mast and the mainsail. Both were triangular and hung from long curved yards that crossed the masts at angles so that the vessel's profile appeared like the heads of two axes cleaving through the air. The deck was dark wood. Glancing around, Hadrian wondered if the Dacca stained it with the same blood as the sails. It was an easy conclusion to make after seeing the rigging ornamented with human skulls.

On the *Storm,* the battle was going badly. At least half the crew lay dead or dying. No canvas was visible, as the boarding party made striking the sails a priority. The deck was awash in stocky, half-naked men who circled the forecastle with torches, dodging arrows as they struggled to breech the bulwark.

Poe pushed the tartane's tiller over, pointing the bow away from the *Storm.* The wind caught the canvas and the little ship glided gently away. With the sails on the *Emerald Storm* struck, she was dead in the water and it was easy for them to circle her. Equally small crews remained to operate the other Dacca boarding ships, but that hardly mattered, as all eyes were on the *Storm.* As far as Hadrian could tell, no one noticed them.

"I'm bringing her 'round," Poe said. "Hadrian, stand by with that rope there and everyone watch the water for Wyatt and Royce."

"Royce?" Derning questioned with distaste. "Why are we picking up the murderer? I can handle the rigging just fine."

"Because Wyatt said so," Poe replied.

"What if we can't find them? What if they die before they can get off the ship?" Davis asked.

"I'll decide that when it happens," Poe replied.

"You? You're barmy, boy. I'll be buggered if I'll take orders from a little sod like you! Bloody Davis here's got more years at sea than you and he's a git if there ever was one. If we don't find Deminthal after the first pass, you'll be taking orders from me."

"Like I said," Poe repeated, "I'll decide that when it happens."

Derning grinned menacingly, but Hadrian did not think Poe, being at the stern, could have seen it in the darkness.

Royce wasted no time hitting the deck at the signal.

"We haven't got long," Wyatt told him. "The captain's quarters will be a priority."

He kicked the door open, shattering the frame.

Fully carpeted, the whole rear of the ship was one luxurious suite. Silk patterns in hues of gold and brown covered the walls, with matching upholstered furniture and a silk bedcover. A painting hung on one wall, showing a man bathed in sunlight, his face filled with rapture as a single white feather floated into his upraised hands. Vast stern windows banked the far wall, above which silver lanterns swayed. The bed stood to one side with a large desk across from it.

Wyatt scanned the room quickly then moved to the desk. He rifled the drawers. "He'll have put the orders in a safe place."

"Like a safe?" Royce asked, pulling a window drape aside to reveal a small porthole-size compartment with a lock. "They always put them behind the drapes."

"Can you open it?"

Royce smirked. He pulled a tool from his belt and within seconds the little door swung open. Wyatt reached inside, grabbing the entire stack of parchments and stuffing them into a bag.

"Let's get out of here," he said, making for the door. "Jump off the starboard side. Poe will pick us up."

They came out of the cabin into a world of chaos. Stocky men painted in red poured over the sides of the vessel. Each wielded short broad blades or axes that cut down everything before them. Only a handful of men stood on the waist deck, the rest had fallen back to the perceived safety of the forecastle. Those that tried to hold their ground died. Royce stepped out on the deck just in time to see Dime, his topsail captain, nearly cut in half by a cleaving blow from a Dacca axe.

Lieutenant Bishop and the other officers were slow in reaching the castle but now, as the Dacca flooded the deck, they were running full out to reach its walls. Stabbed in the back, Lieutenant Green collapsed. As he fell, he reached out, grabbing at anything. His hands found Midshipman Beryl running past and dragged him down as well. Beryl cursed and kicked Green off, but got to his feet too late. The Dacca circled him.

"Help me!" he cried.

Royce watched as the crew ignored him and ran on—all but one. Midshipman Wesley ran back just in time to stab the nearest Dacca caught off guard by the sudden change in his fleeing prey. Wielding his sword with both hands, Wesley sliced horizontally across the chest of the next brute and kicked him aside.

"Beryl! This way, run!" he shouted.

Beryl lashed out at the Dacca then ran to Wesley. Quickly surrounded, the Dacca drove them farther and farther away from the forecastle. An arrow from the walls saved Wesley from decapitation as the two struggled to defend themselves. Pushed by the overwhelming numbers, they retreated until their backs hit the rail.

A Dacca blade slashed Beryl's arm and then across his hip. He screamed, dropping his sword. Wesley threw himself between Beryl and his attacker. The young midshipman slashed wildly, struggling to defend the older man. Then Wesley was hit. He stumbled backward, reached out for the netting chains, but missed and fell overboard. Alone and unarmed, the Dacca swarmed Beryl, who screamed until they sent his head from his body.

No one noticed Wyatt or Royce creeping in the shadows around the stern, seeking a clear place to jump. They crouched just above the captain's cabin windows. Royce was about to leap when he spotted Thranic step out from the hold. The sentinel exited, a torch in hand, as if he merely wondered what all the noise was about. He led the seret to the main deck, where they quickly formed a wall around the sentinel. Seeing reinforcements, the Dacca rallied to an attack. They charged, only to die upon the serets' swords. The Knights of Nyphron were neither sailors nor galley slaves. They knew the use of arms and how to hold formation.

Gripping his bag to his chest, Wyatt leapt from the ship.

"Royce!" Wyatt shouted from the sea below.

Royce watched, impressed by the knight's courage and skill as they battled the Dacca. It looked as if they might just turn the tide. Then Thranic threw his flaming brand into the ship's hold. A rush of air sounded as if the ship were inhaling a great breath. A roar followed. A deep, resonating growl shook the timber beneath Royce's feet. Tongues of flame licked out of every hatch and porthole, the air filling with screams and cries. And in the flicking glow of burning wood and flesh, Royce saw the sentinel smile.

Hadrian and the tiny crew of the stolen Dacca ship had only just reached the starboard side of the *Storm* when the area grew bright. The *Emerald Storm* was ablaze. Within little more than a minute the fire had enveloped the deck. Men in the rigging had no choice but to jump. From that height, their bodies hit the water with a cracking sound. The rigging ignited, ropes snapped, and yards broke free, falling like flaming tree trunks. The darkness of the starless sea fell away as the *Emerald Storm* became a floating bonfire. Those near the rail leapt into the sea. Screams, cries, and the crackle and hiss of fire filled the night.

Looking over the black water, whose surface was alive with wild reflections, Hadrian spied a bit of sandy hair and a dark uniform. "Mister Wesley, grab on!" Hadrian called, throwing a rope.

Like a man in a dream, Wesley turned at the sound of his name. He looked at the tartane with confusion in his eyes until he spotted Hadrian reaching out. He took the rope thrown and was reeled in like a fish and hoisted on deck.

"Nice to have you aboard, sir," Hadrian told him.

Wesley gasped for air and rolled over, vomiting seawater.

"From that, I assume you're happy to be here."

"Wyatt!" Poe shouted.

"Royce!" Hadrian called.

"Over there!" Derning said, pointing.

Poe turned the tiller and they sailed toward the sound of splashing.

"It's Bernie and Staul," Grady announced from where he stood on the bow.

The two wasted no time scrambling up the ship's ropes.

"More splashing over there!" Davis pointed.

Poe did not have to alter course as the swimmers made good progress to them. Davis was the first to lend a hand. He reached out to help and a blade stabbed him in the chest before he was pulled overboard.

Hadrian saw them now, swarthy, painted brutes with long daggers, their wet, glistening skin shimmering with the light of the flames. They grabbed at the netting, and scrambled like rats up the side of the tartane.

Hadrian drew his sword and lashed out at the nearest one, who dodged and stubbornly continued to climb. The Tenkin warrior, Staul, stabbed another in the face and the Dacca dropped backward with a cry and a splash. Defoe and Wesley joined in, thrashing wildly until the Dacca gave up and fell away into the darkness.

"Watch the other side!" Wesley shouted.

Staul and Defoe took positions on the starboard rail, but nothing moved.

"Any sign of Davis?" Hadrian asked.

"Dee man be dead now," Staul said. "Be more keerful who you sail to, eh?"

"Bulard!" Defoe said, pointing ahead to more swimmers.

"And three more over there," Wesley announced, picking out faces in the tumultuous water. "One is Greig, the carpenter, and that's Doctor Levy, and there is…"

Hadrian did not need Royce's eyes to identify the other man. The infernal light coming off the burning ship suited the face. It was Sentinel Thranic, his hood thrown back, his pale face gleaming. Derning, Defoe, and Staul were bad enough. Now they had Thranic, of all people.

Thranic needed no help as he climbed nimbly up the side of the little ship, his cloak soaked, his face angry. If he were a dog, Hadrian knew he would be growling, and for that he was pleased. Bulard, the man who came aboard in the middle of the night, looked even paler than before. The reason became obvious the moment he hit the deck and blood mingled with seawater. Levy went to him and applied pressure to the wound.

"Hadrian…Poe!" Wyatt's voice carried from the sea below.

Poe steered toward the sound as the rest stood on their guard. This time there was no need. Wyatt and Royce were alone swimming for the boat.

"Where were you?" Wyatt asked, climbing aboard.

"Sorry, boss, but it's a big ocean."

"Not big enough," Derning said, looking over at what remained of the *Storm*, his face bright with the glow. "The Dacca are finally taking notice of us."

The main mast of the *Emerald Storm*, burning like a tree-sized torch, finally cracked and fell. The forecastle walls blazed. Seward, Bishop, and the rest were either lost to blades or burned alive. The *Storm* had blackened and cracked, allowing the ship to take on water. The hull listed to one side, sinking from the bow. As it did, the fire was still bright enough to see several of the Dacca on the nearest vessel pointing in their direction and shouting.

"Wheel hard over!" Wyatt shouted, running for the tiller. "Derning, Royce, get aloft! Hadrian, Banner—the mainsail braces. Grady to the headsail braces! Who else do we have here? Bernie, join Derning and Royce. Staul help with the mainsail. Mister Wesley, if it wouldn't be too much trouble, perhaps you could assist Grady on the forward braces. Bring her round east, nor'east!"

"That will put us into the wind again!" Grady said, even as Wyatt brought the ship round.

"Aye, starboard tack. With fewer crew and the same ship, we'll be lighter and faster."

They got the ship around and caught what wind they could.

"Here, Banner, take the tiller," Wyatt said as he scanned the deck. "We can dump some gear and lighten the load further. Who's that next to you?"

Wyatt stopped abruptly when he saw Thranic's face look up.

"What's he doing on board?" Wyatt asked.

"Is there a problem, helmsman?" Thranic addressed him.

"You fired the ship!" Wyatt accused. "Royce told me he saw you throw a torch in the hold. How many oil kegs did you break to get it to go up like that?"

"Five, I think. Maybe six."

"There were elves—they were locked in the hold—trapped down there."

"Precisely," Thranic replied.

"You bastard!" Wyatt rushed the sentinel, drawing his cutlass. Thranic moved with surprising speed and dodged Wyatt's attack, throwing his cloak around Wyatt's head and shoving the helmsman to the deck as he drew a long dagger.

Hadrian pulled his swords and Staul immediately moved to intercept him. Poe drew his cutlass, as did Grady, followed quickly by Defoe and Derning.

From the rigging above, Royce dropped abruptly into the midst of the conflict, landing squarely between Thranic and Wyatt. The sentinel's eyes locked on the thief and smouldered.

"Mister Wesley!" Royce shouted, keeping his eyes fixed on Thranic. "What are your orders, sir?"

At this everyone stopped. The ship continued to sail with the wind, but the crew paused. Several glanced at Wesley. The midshipman stood frozen on the deck, watching the events unfold around him.

"*His* orders?" Thranic mocked.

"Captain Seward, Lieutenant Bishop, and the other midshipmen are dead," Royce explained. "Mister Wesley is senior officer. He is, by rights, in command of this vessel."

Thranic laughed.

Wesley began to nod. "He's right."

"Shut up, boy!" Staul snapped. "Et ez time vee took care of dis bidness 'ere."

Staul's words brought Wesley around. "I am no boy!" Turning to Thranic, he added. "What I am, *sir*, is the acting-captain of this ship and as such, you, and everyone else," he glanced at Staul, "*will* obey my orders!"

Staul laughed.

"I assure you this is no joke, seaman. I also assure you that I will not hesitate to see you cut down where you stand, and anyone else who fails to obey me."

"And 'ow do you plan to do dat?" Staul asked. "Dis ez not dee *Emerald Storm*. You command no one 'ere."

"I wouldn't say that," Hadrian commented, maintaining his familiar smile at Staul.

"Neither would I," Royce added.

"Me neither," Derning joined in, his words quickly echoed by Grady.

Wyatt got to his feet slowly. He glared at Thranic, but said, "Aye, Mister Wesley is captain now."

Poe, Banner and Greig acknowledged with communal "Ayes."

What followed was a tense silence. Staul and Defoe looked at Thranic, who never took his gaze off Royce. "Very well, *captain*," the sentinel said at length. "What are your orders?"

"I am hereby promoting Mister Deminthal to acting lieutenant. Everyone will follow his instructions to the letter. Mister Deminthal, you will confine your orders to saving this vessel from the Dacca and maintaining order and discipline. There are to be no executions and no disciplinary actions of any kind without my authorization. Is that clear?"

"Aye, sir."

"Petty Officer Blackwater, you are hereby appointed master-at-arms. Collect the weapons, but keep them at the ready. See to it Mister Deminthal's and my orders are carried out to the letter. Understood?"

"Aye, sir."

"Mister Grady, you are now boatswain. Mister Levy, please take Mister Bulard below so that he can be properly cared for. Let me know if there is anything you need. Mister Derning will be top captain, Seamen Bernie and Melborn report to him for duties. Mister Deminthal, carry on."

"Your sword," Hadrian addressed Staul. The Tenkin hesitated, but after a nod from Thranic, handed the blade over. As he did, he laughed and cursed in the Tenkin language.

"You'd have found that a bit harder than you think," Hadrian replied to Staul and was rewarded with the Tenkin's shocked expression.

Wyatt had everything nonessential and not attached to the ship thrown overboard. Then he ordered silence and whispered the order to change tack. The boom swung over, catching the wind and angling the little ship out to sea. Well behind them, the last light of the *Emerald Storm* disappeared, swallowed by the waves. Not quite so far away, they could see lanterns bobbing on the following ships. From the sound of shouts, they were displeased at losing their prize. All eyes faced astern, watching the progression of lanterns as the Dacca continued following their previous tack. After a while, two ships altered course, but guessed incorrectly and turned westward. Eventually all the lanterns disappeared.

"Are they gone?" Hadrian heard Wesley whisper to Wyatt.

He shook his head. "They just put out the lanterns, but with luck they will think we're running for ground. The nearest friendly port is Wesbaden back west."

"For a helmsman, you're an excellent commander," the young man observed.

"I was a captain once," Wyatt admitted. "I lost my ship."

"Really? In whose service, the Empire or the old Warric fleet?"

"No service. It was *my* ship."

Wesley looked astonished. "You were...a pirate?"

"Opportunist, sir. Opportunist."

Hadrian awoke to a misty dawn. A steady breeze pushed the tartane through undulating waves. All around them lay a vast and empty sea.

"They're gone," Wesley answered the unasked question. "We've lost them."

"Any idea where we are?"

"About three days sail from Dagastan," Wyatt answered.

"Dagastan?" Grady muttered, looking up. "We're not headed there, are we?"

"That was my intention," Wyatt replied.

"But Wesbaden is closer."

"Unfortunately, I confess no knowledge of these coasts," Wesley said. "Do you know them well, Mister Deminthal?"

"Intimately."

"Good. Then tell us, is Mister Grady correct?"

Wyatt nodded. "Wesbaden is closer, but the Dacca know this and will be waiting in that direction. However, since it is impossible for them to be ahead of us, our present course is the safest."

"Despite our earlier differences, I agree with Mister Deminthal," Thranic offered. "As it turns out, Dagastan was the *Storm's* original destination, so we must continue toward it."

"But Dagastan is much farther away from Avryn," Wesley said. "The *Storm's* mission was lost with her sinking. I have no way of knowing her original destination, and even if I did, I have no cargo to deliver. Going farther east only increases our difficulties. I need to be mindful of provisions."

"But you do have cargo," Thranic announced. "The *Storm's* orders were to deliver myself, Mister Bulard, Dr. Levy, Mister Bernie, and Staul to Dagastan. The main cargo is gone, but as an officer of the realm it is your duty to fulfill what portion you can of Captain Seward's mission."

"With all due respect, Your Excellency, I have no way to verify what you say."

"Actually, you do." Wyatt pulled a bent and battered scroll from his bag. "These are Captain Seward's orders."

Wesley took the damp scroll and asked, "But how did you come by this?"

"I knew we'd need charts to sail by. Before I left the *Storm*, I entered the captain's cabin and, being in a bit of a hurry, I just grabbed everything on his desk. Last night I discovered I had more than just charts."

Wesley nodded, accepting this and, Hadrian thought, perhaps choosing not to inquire further. He paused a second before reading. Most were awake now and, having heard the conversation, watched Wesley with anticipation. When he finished he looked over at Wyatt.

"Was there a letter?"

"Aye, sir," he said and handed over a sealed bit of parchment. This Wesley did not open, but slipped carefully into his coat.

"We will maintain course to Dagastan. Being bound by Imperial naval laws, I must do everything in my power to see the *Storm's* errand is fulfilled."

Chapter 13

THE WITCH OF MELENGAR

Modina stared out her window as usual, watching the world with no real interest. It was late and she feared sleep. It always brought the dreams, the nightmares of the past, of her father, and of the dark place. She sat up most nights, studying the shadows and the clouds as they passed over the stars. A line of moonlight crossed the courtyard below. She noted how it climbed the statues and the far gate wall, just like the creeping ivy. Once green, the plant was now a ruddy red. It would go dormant, appearing to die, but would still hang on to the wall. It would continue its desperate grip on the stone even as it withered. For it, at least, there would be a spring.

The hammering at her chamber door roused her. She turned, puzzled. No one ever knocked, except for Gerald, who always used a light tap. Amilia came and went frequently but never knocked. Whoever it was beat the door with a fury.

The pounding landed harder and with such violence that the door latch bounced with a distinct metallic clank as it threatened to break. It never occurred to her to ask who was there. It never crossed her mind to be fearful. She slid back the bolt, letting the door swing inward.

Standing outside was a man she vaguely recognized. His face was flushed, his eyes glassy, and the collar to his shirt lay open.

"There you are," the Earl of Chadwick exclaimed. "At long last I am rewarded with your presence. Permit me to introduce myself again, in case you've forgotten me, which I am sure you have not. I am Archibald Ballentyne, the twelfth Earl of Chadwick." He bowed low, taking an awkward step when he lost his balance. "May I come in?"

The empress said nothing, and the earl took this as an invitation. Pushing his way into the room, he held a finger to his lips. "Shh, we need to be quiet, lest someone discover I'm here." The earl stood wavering, his glazed eyes canvassing the full length of Modina's small body. His mouth hung partially open and his head moved up and down, as if trying to save his eyes the effort.

Modina was dressed in her thin nightgown, but did not think to cover herself.

"You're beautiful. I thought so from the first. I wanted to tell you before this, but they wouldn't let me see you." The earl pulled a bottle of liquor from his breast pocket and took a swallow. "After all, I am the hero of your army, and it isn't fair that Ethelred gets to have you. You should be mine. I earned you!" The earl shouted, raising his fist.

Pausing, he looked toward the open door. After a moment he continued. "What has Ethelred ever done? It was my army that saved Aquesta and would have crushed Melengar if they had let me. But they didn't want me to. Do you know why? They knew if I took Melengar, then I would be too great to hold back. They're jealous of me, you know. And now Ethelred is planning to take you, but you're mine. *Mine* I say!" He shouted this last bit, then cringed. Once more, he placed a finger to his lips. "Shh."

Modina watched the earl with mild curiosity.

"How can you want *him*?" He slammed his fist against his chest. "Am I not handsome? Am I not young?" He twirled around with his arms outstretched until he staggered. He steadied himself on the bedpost. "Ethelred is old, fat, and has pimples. Do you really want that? He doesn't care about you. He's only after the crown."

The earl took a moment to glance around the empty room. "Don't get me wrong," he said in a harsh whisper. He leaned in so close he had to put a hand on her shoulder to steady himself. "I want the crown, too—anyone saying different is a liar. Who wouldn't want to be emperor of the world, but..." he held up a wavering finger, "*I* would have loved you."

He paused, breathing hotly into her face. He licked his lips and caressed her skin through the thin nightgown. His hand left her shoulder and inched up her neck, his open fingers slipping into her hair. "Ethelred will never look at you like this." Archibald took her hand and placed it against his chest. "His heart will never pound like mine just by being near you. I want power. I want the throne, but I also want you." He looked into her eyes. "I love you, Modina. I love you and I want you for my own. You should be *my* wife."

He pulled her to him and kissed her mouth, pressing hard, pinching her lips to her teeth. She did not struggle—she did not care. He pulled back and searched her face. She did not respond except to blink.

"Modina?" Amilia called, entering the room. "What's going on?"

"Nothing," Ballentyne said, sadly. He looked at Modina. He searched her face again. "Absolutely nothing at all."

He turned and left the room.

"Are you all right?" Amilia rushed to the empress, brushing her hair back and looking her over. "Did he hurt you?"

"Am I to marry Lord Ethelred?"

Amilia held her breath and bit her lip.

"I see. When were you going to tell me? On my wedding night?"

"I—I just learned about it recently. You had that fainting spell and I didn't want to upset you."

"It doesn't upset me, Amilia, and thank you for stopping by."

"But, I—" Amilia hesitated.

"Is there something else?"

"Ah—no, I just—you're different suddenly. We should talk about this."

"What is there to talk about? I will marry Ethelred so he can be emperor."

"You'll still be empress."

"Yes, yes, there's no need to worry. I am fine."

"You're never *fine*."

"No? It must be the good news that I am to become a bride."

Amilia's expression looked terrified. "Modina, what's going on? What's happening in that head of yours?"

Modina smiled. "It's okay Amilia. Everything will be *fine*."

"Stop using that word! You're really frightening me," Amilia said, reaching toward her.

Modina pulled away, moving to the window.

"I'm sorry I didn't tell you myself. I'm sorry there was no guard at the door. I'm sorry you had to hear such a thing from the brandy-soaked breath of—"

"It's not your fault, Amilia. It's important to me that you know that. You're all that matters to me. It's amazing how worthless a life feels without someone to care for. My father understood that. At the time, I didn't, but now I do."

"Understand what?" Amilia asked, shaking.

"That living has no value—it is what you do with life that gives it worth."

"And what are you planning to do with your life Modina?"

Modina tried to force a smile. She took Amilia's head in her hands and kissed her gently. "It's late. Goodbye, Amilia."

Amilia's eyes went wide with fear. She began shaking her head faster and faster. "No, no, no! I'll stay here. I don't want you left alone tonight."

"As you wish."

Amilia looked pleased for a moment then fear crept back in. "Tomorrow I'll assign a guard to *watch* you."

"Of course you will," Modina replied.

True to her word, Amilia remained in Modina's chamber all night, but slipped out before dawn while the empress still slept. She went to the office of the master-at-arms and burst in on the soldier on duty, unannounced.

"Why wasn't there a guard outside the empress's door last night? Where was Gerald?"

"We couldn't spare him, milady. The Imperial guard is stretched thin. We are searching for the witch, the Princess of Melengar. Regent Saldur has commanded me to use every man I have to find her."

"I don't care. I want Gerald back watching her door. Do you understand?"

"But milady—"

"Last night the Earl of Chadwick forced his way into the empress's room. In her room! And has it occurred to you—to anyone—that the witch might be coming to kill the empress?"

A long pause.

"I didn't think so. Now, get Gerald back on his post at once."

Leaving the master-at-arms, Amilia roused Modina's chambermaid from her bunk in the dormitory. After the girl had dressed, she hurried her along to Modina's room.

"Anne, I want you to stay with the empress and watch her."

"Watch her, what for? I mean, what should I be watching for, milady?"

"Just make certain the empress doesn't hurt herself."

"How do you mean?"

"Just keep an eye on her. If she does anything odd or unusual, send for me at once."

Modina heard Anne enter the room quietly. She continued pretending to sleep. Near dawn she stretched, yawned, and walked over to the washbasin to splash water on her face. Anne was quick to hand her a towel and grinned broadly to have been of assistance.

"Anne, is it?" Modina asked.

The girl's face flushed, and her eyes lit up with joy. She nodded repeatedly.

"Anne, I am starved, would you please run to the kitchen and see if they can prepare me an early breakfast? Be a dear and bring it up when it's ready."

"I—I—"

Modina put on a pout, and turned her eyes downward. "I am sorry. I apologize for asking so much of you."

"Oh, no, Your Gloriousness, I will get it at once."

"Thank you, my dear."

"You are most welcome, Your Worship."

Modina wondered if she kept her longer how many elaborate forms of address she might come up with. As soon as Anne left the room Modina walked to the door, closed it, and slid the deadbolt. She walked toward the tall mirror that hung on the wall, picking up the pitcher from the water basin as she passed. Without hesitation, she struck the mirror, shattering both. She picked up a long shard of glass and went to her window.

"Your Eminence?" Gerald called from the other side of the door. "Are you all right?"

Outside the sun was just coming up. The autumn morning light angled in sharp, slanted shafts across the courtyard below. She loved the sun and thought its light and warmth would be the only thing, besides Amilia, that she would miss.

She wrapped her gown around the end of the long jagged piece of glass. It felt cold. Everything felt cold to her. She looked down at the courtyard and breathed in a long breath of air scented with the dying autumn leaves.

The guard continued to bang on the door. "Your Eminence? He repeated. "Are you all right?"

"Yes, Gerald," she said, "I am *fine*."

Arista entered the palace courtyard, walking past the gate guards, hoping they could not hear the pounding of her heart.

This must be how Royce and Hadrian feel all the time. I'm surprised they don't drink more.

While easy for Royce, for her it was literally death defying. She shook from both fear and the early morning chill. Esrahaddon's robe was lost the night of Hilfred's rescue, leaving her with only Lynette's kirtle.

Hilfred. He'll be furious if he reads the note.

The Emerald Storm

It hurt her heart just to think of him. He had stood in her shadow for years, serving her whims, taking her abuse, trapped in a prison of feelings he could never reveal. Twice he nearly died for her. He was a good man—a great man. She wanted to make him happy. He deserved to be happy. She wanted to give him what he never thought possible, to fix what she had broken.

For three nights they hid together, and every day Hilfred tried to convince her to return to Melengar. At last she agreed, telling him they would leave tomorrow. Arista slipped out when Hilfred left to get supplies. If all went well, she would be back before he was and they could leave as planned. If not—if something happened—the note would explain.

It had occurred to her, only the night before, that she never cast the location spell in the courtyard. From there, the smoke would certainly locate the wing and, if lucky enough, she might even pinpoint Gaunt's exact window. The information would be invaluable to Royce and Hadrian and could make the difference between a rescue and a suicide mission. And as much as she did not want to admit it, she owed Esrahaddon as well. If doing this small thing could save Degan Gaunt, a good man wrongly imprisoned, ease the wizard's passing, and vanquish her guilt, it was worth the risk.

The gate guards paid little attention when she entered. She took this as a good sign that no one had connected Ella the scrub girl to the Witch of Melengar. All she needed to do now was cast the spell and walk out again.

She crossed the inner ward to the vegetable garden. The harvest had come and gone, the plants were cleared, and the soil had been turned to await the spring. The soft earth would allow her to draw the circle and symbols required. She clutched the pouch of hair still in the pocket of her kirtle as she glanced around. Nothing looked amiss. The few guards on duty ignored her.

As casually as she could, she began drawing a circle by dragging her foot in the dirt. When she had finished, she moved on to the more tedious task of the runes, which was more time consuming to do with her toe than with her hand and a bit of chalk. All the while, she worried that her drawing would be obvious from any number of upper-story windows.

She was just finishing the second to last rune when a guard exited the palace and walked toward her. Immediately she crouched, pretending to dig. If he questioned her, she could say Ibis sent her to look for potatoes, or that she thought she might have dropped the pantry key when she was in the courtyard. She hoped he would just walk by; she needed to be the invisible servant this one last time. It quickly became apparent that he was specifically coming for her. As he closed the distance, her only thought was of Hilfred and how she wished she had kissed him goodbye.

Amilia was in her office quickly going over instructions with Nimbus. They had only ticked off a few items for the wedding preparations. If she could give him enough to keep busy, she could return to Modina. The urgency pulled at her every minute she was away.

"...if you get done with that, then come see me and I'll give you more to do," she told him curtly. "I have to get back to the empress. I think she might do something stupid."

Nimbus looked up. "The empress is a bit eccentric certainly, but, if I may, she has never struck me as stupid, milady."

Amilia narrowed her eyes at him suspiciously.

Nimbus had been a good and faithful servant, but she did not like the sound of that. "You notice too much, I think, Nimbus. That's not such a good trait when working in an Imperial palace. Ignorance is perhaps a better choice for survival."

"I'm just trying to cheer you up," he replied, sounding a little hurt.

Amilia frowned and collapsed in her chair. "I'm sorry. I am starting to sound a bit like Saldur, aren't I?"

"You still have to work on making your veiled threats sound more ominous. A deeper voice would help, or perhaps toying with a dagger or swishing a glass of wine as you say it."

"I wasn't threatening you, I was—"

He cut her off. "I'm joking, milady."

Amilia scowled then pulled a parchment off her desk, crumpled it into a ball, and threw it at him. "Honestly, I don't know why I hired you."

"Not for my comedy, I sense."

Amilia gathered a pile of parchments, a quill, and bottle of ink and headed for the door. "I'm going to be working from Modina's room today. Look there if you need me."

"Of course," he said as she left.

Not far down the hall, Amilia saw Anne walking by with a tray of food. "Anne," she called, rushing toward her. "I told you to stay with the empress!"

"Yes, milady, but…"

"But what?"

"The empress asked me to fetch her breakfast."

A cold chill shot up Amilia's spine. The empress *asked* her. "Has the empress ever spoken to you before?"

On the verge of tears, Anne shook her head. "No, milady, I was very honored. She even knew my name."

Amilia raced for the stairs, her heart pounding. Reaching the top and nearing the bedchamber she feared what she would find. Nimbus was right; perhaps more than he knew. Modina was not stupid, and her mind filled with the many terrible possibilities. Arriving at the door, she pushed Gerald aside and burst into the empress's room. She steeled herself, but what she saw was beyond her wildest imaginings.

Modina and Ella sat together on the empress's bed, hand-in-hand, chatting.

Amilia stood, shocked. Both glanced up as she entered. Ella's face was fearful, but Modina's expression was calm as usual, as if expecting her.

"Ella?" Amilia exclaimed. "What are you doing—"

"Gerald," Modina interrupted, "from now on, no one, and I mean *no one*, is to enter without my say so. Understood?"

"Of course, Your Eminence." Gerald looked down guiltily.

Modina waved her hand. "It's not your fault. I didn't tell you. Now please close the door."

He bowed and drew the door shut.

Amilia meanwhile stood silent, her mouth agape, but no words came out.

"Sit down before you fall down, Amilia. I want to introduce you to a friend of mine. This is Arista, the Princess of Melengar."

Amilia tried to make sense out of the senselessness. "No, Modina, this is Ella—a scullery maid. What's going on?" Amilia asked desperately. "I thought—I thought you might be—" her eyes went to the broken pitcher and shards of mirrored glass scattered across the corner of the room.

"I know what you thought." The empress said, looking toward the window. "That's another reason you should be welcoming Arista. If I hadn't seen her in the courtyard and realized—well—anyway, I want you two to be friends."

Amilia's mind was still whirling. Modina appeared more lucid than ever, yet she made no sense. Maybe she only sounded rational. Maybe the empress had cracked altogether. At any moment, she might introduce Red the elkhound from the kitchen as the Ambassador of Lanksteer.

"Modina, I know you think this girl is a princess, but just a week ago you also thought you were dead and buried, remember?"

"Are you saying you think I'm crazy?"

"No, no, I just…"

"Lady Amilia," Ella spoke for the first time, "my name is Arista Essendon, and I *am* the Princess of Melengar. Your empress isn't crazy. She and I are old friends."

Amilia stood staring at the two of them, confused. Were they both insane? How could—oh sweet Maribor. It's her! The long fingernails, the way she met Amilia's stare, the bold inquiries about the empress. Ella was the Witch of Melengar. "Get away from her!" Amilia yelled.

"Amilia, calm down."

"She's been posing as a maid to get to you."

"Arista's not here to harm me. You're not, are you?" she asked Ella, who shook her head. "There, you see. Now come here and join us. We have much to do."

"Thrace," Ella spoke, looking nervously at Modina. The empress raised a hand to stop her.

"The both of you need to trust me," Modina said.

Amilia shook her head. "But how can I? Why should I? This—this woman—"

"Because," the empress interrupted, "we have to help Arista."

Amilia would have laughed at the absurdity if Modina did not look so serious. In all the time she took care of her, Amilia never saw her so focused, so clear-eyed. She felt out of her element. The hazy Modina was gone, but she was still speaking nonsense. She had to make her understand, for her own good. "Modina, guards are looking for this woman. They've been combing the city for days."

"That's why she is going to stay here. It's the safest place. Not even the regents will look for her in my bedroom. And it will make helping her that much easier."

"Help her? Help her with what?" Amilia was nearly at the end of her own sanity just trying to follow this absurd conversation.

"We're going to help her find Degan Gaunt, the true Heir of Novron."

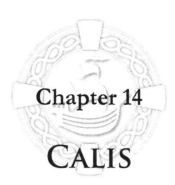

Chapter 14

CALIS

The port of Dagastan surprised first-time visitors from Avryn, who thought of everywhere else as less civilized or uncultured. Calis was generally held, by those who had never been there, to be a crude, ramshackle collection of tribal bands living in mud or wooden huts within a dense and mysterious jungle. It shocked most when they first laid eyes on the massive domes and elegant spires rising along the coast. The city was astonishingly large and well developed. Stone and gray brick buildings sat densely packed on a graduated hillside rising from the elegant harbor that put Aquesta's wooden docks to shame. Here, four long, carved stone piers stretched into the bay, along which stately towers rose at regular intervals, facilitating the needs of the bustling trade center. Masts of more than a hundred ships lined the harbor, nearly all of them exotic merchant vessels.

Hadrian remembered the city the moment it came into view. The heat of the ancient stones, the spice-scented streets, the exotic women—all memories of an impetuous youth that he preferred to forget. He had left the east behind without regret, and it was not without reservations that he found himself returning.

CALIS

No bells rang in the towers along the harbor as they entered, no alarm signaled as the blood-red sails of their Dacca-built tartane entered port. A pilot boat merely issued out and hailed them at their approach.

"En dil dual lon duclim?" the pilot called to them.

"I can't understand you," Wesley replied.

"Vaat ez dee name of your vessel? And dee name of dee captain?" the pilot repeated.

"Oh, ah—it doesn't have a name, I'm afraid, but my name is Wesley Belstrad."

The pilot jotted something on a hand-held tablet, frowning. "Vere ez you outing from?"

"We are the remaining crew of the *Emerald Storm*, Her Imperial Majesty's vessel out from the capital city of Aquesta."

"Vaat ez your bidness 'ere and 'ow long staying vill you be?"

"We are making a delivery. I am not certain how long it will take."

The pilot finished asking questions and indicated they should follow him to a berth. Another official was waiting on the dock and asked Wesley to sign several forms before allowing anyone to set foot on land.

"According to Seward's orders, we are to contact a Mister Dilladrum. I will go ashore and try to locate him," Wesley announced. "Mister Deminthal, you and Seaman Staul will accompany me. Seaman Blackwater, you will be in charge here until my return. See to it that the stores are secured and the ship buttoned down."

"Aye, sir." Hadrian saluted. The three disembarked and disappeared into the maze of streets.

"Wonderful luck we've had in picking up survivors, eh?" Hadrian mentioned to Royce as he met his partner on the raised aft deck of the ship.

The others remained at the waist or the bow, staring in fascination at the port around them. There was a lot to take in. Unusual sounds drifted from the urban landscape. The jangle of bells, the ringing of a gong, shouts of merchants in a strange musical language, and above it all the haunting voice of a man singing in the distance. Dockworkers moved cargo to and from ships. Most were dressed in robes with vertical stripes, their skin a tawny brown, their faces bearded. Bolts of shimmering silks and sheer cloth waited to be loaded, as did urns of incense and pots of fragrant oil, whose scents drifted on the harbor breeze. The stone masonry of the buildings was impressive. Intricate designs of flowers and geometric shapes adorned nearly all the constructions. Domes were the most prolific of the architectural styles, some inlaid in gold, others in silver or in colorful tiles. The larger buildings displayed multiple domes, all featuring a central spire pointing skyward.

It was the first time in three days that they had the opportunity to speak alone. "I thought you showed great restraint, and I was impressed with your diplomatic solution to our little civil war," Hadrian told Royce.

"I'm just watching your back, like Gwen asked." Royce took a seat on a thick pile of netted ropes.

"It was a stroke of brilliance, appointing Wesley," Hadrian remarked. "I wish I had thought of it. I like that boy. Did you see the way he picked Staul and Wyatt to go with him? Wyatt knows the docks, and Staul knows the language and possibly the city. Perfectly sensible choices, but they're also the two who would make the most trouble out of his sight. He's a lot more like his brother than he thinks. It's a shame they were born in Chadwick. Ballentyne doesn't deserve them."

"It's not looking good, you know that, right?" Royce asked. "What with the weapons and Merrick's payment going down with the *Storm*, and everyone in charge now dead. I don't see where we go from here."

Hadrian took a seat on the railing beside Royce. Water lapped against the wooden hull of the tartane and seagulls cried overhead. "But we still have Merrick's orders and that letter. What did it say?"

"I didn't read it."

"Weren't you the one who called me stupid because—"

"I never had a chance. Wyatt grabbed them first. Then there was this little incident with a burning ship and lots of swimming. Now Wesley has them and he's hardly slept. I've not had an opportunity."

"Then we'll have to stick to that letter until you either get a chance to take a peek or we solve this riddle. I mean, what is the Empire doing sending weapons to Calis when they need them to fight the Nationalists?"

"Maybe bribing Calis to join the fight on their side?"

Hadrian shook his head. "Rhenydd could beat them in a war all by itself. There's no organization down here, no central authority, just a bunch of competing warlords. The whole place is corrupt, and they constantly fight each other. There is no way Merrick could convince enough leaders to go fight for the New Empire—most of these warlords have never even heard of Avryn. And what's with the elves? What were they doing with them?"

"I have to admit, I'd like to know that myself," Royce said.

Hadrian's glance followed Thranic as he came topside and laid among the excess canvas at the bow, his hood pulled down to block the light, his arms folded across his chest. He almost looked like a corpse in need of a coffin.

Hadrian gestured toward the sentinel. "So, what's going on between you and Thranic anyway? He appears to *really* hate you— even more than most people."

Royce did not look in his direction. He sat nonchalantly, pretending to ignore the world as if they were the only two aboard. "Funny thing that. I never met him, never heard of him until this voyage, and yet I know him rather well, and he knows me."

"Thank you, Mister Esrahaddon. Can you provide me with perhaps a more cryptic answer?"

Royce smiled. "I see why he does it now. It's rather fun. I'm also surprised you haven't figured it out yet."

"Figured what out?"

"Our boy Thranic has a nasty little secret. It's what makes him so unpleasant and at the same time so dangerous. He would have killed Wyatt, might even given you a surprise or two. With Staul added to the mix and Defoe slinking about, it wasn't a battle I felt confident in winning, even if I didn't have Gwen's voice echoing in my head."

"You aren't going to tell me, are you?"

"What would be the fun in that? This will give you something to do. You can try to guess, and I can amuse myself by insulting your intelligence. I wouldn't take too long, though. Thranic is going to die soon."

Wesley returned and trotted up the gangway to address them. "I want volunteers to accompany me, Sentinel Thranic, Mister Bulard, Doctor Levy, and Seamen Staul and Bernie inland. We will be traveling deep into the Calian jungles. The journey will not be without significant risks, so I won't order anyone to follow me who doesn't want to go. Those who choose to stay behind will remain with the ship. Upon my return, we will sail for home where you will receive your pay."

CALIS

"Where in the jungle are you headed, Mister Wesley?" Banner asked.

"I must deliver a letter to Erandabon Gile, who I am informed is a warlord of some note in these parts. I have met with Mister Dilladrum, who has been awaiting our arrival and has a caravan prepared and ready to escort us. Gile's fortress, however, is deep in the jungles, and contact with the Ba Ran Ghazel is likely. Now, who is with me?"

Hadrian, who was one of the first to raise his hand, found it strange that he was among the majority. Wyatt and Poe did not surprise him, but even Jacob and Grady joined in after seeing the others. Only Greig and Banner abstained.

"I see," Wesley said with a note of surprise as well. "All right then, Banner, I'll leave you in charge of the ship."

"What are we to do while yer gone, sir?" Banner asked.

"Nothing," he told them. "Just stay with the ship and out of the city. Don't cause any trouble."

Banner smiled gleefully at Greig. "So, we can just sleep all day if we want?"

"I don't care what you do, as long as you protect the ship and don't embarrass the Empire."

Both of them could hardly contain their delight. "I'll bet the rest o' you are wishing you hadn't raised your hands now."

"You realize there's only about a week's worth of rations below, right?" Wyatt mentioned. "You might want to eat sparingly."

A worried look crossed Banner's face. "You're gonna hurry back, right?"

THE EMERALD STORM

Wesley led them off the ship and into the city, setting a brisk pace and keeping a sharp eye on the line of men. The old man, Antun Bulard, was the only straggler, but this had more to do with his age than his wounds, which had turned out to be only superficial cuts.

Loud-colored tents and awnings lined the roads of Dagastan from the harbor to the square. Throngs filled the paved pathways as merchants shouted to the crowds, waving banners with unrecognizable symbols. Old men smoked pipes beneath the shelter of striped canopies as scantily dressed women with veiled faces stood provocatively on raised platforms, gyrating slowly to the beat of a dozen drummers, bell ringers, and cymbal players. There was too much happening to focus on any single thing. Everywhere one looked there was dazzling color, tantalizing movement, intoxicating scents, and exciting music. Overwhelmed, the little parade of sailors marched in step with Mister Wesley as he led them to their promised guide. He and his team were waiting along a paved avenue not far from the city's Grand Bazaar.

Dilladrum looked like an overweight beggar. His coat and dark britches were faded and poorly patched. Long, dirty hair burst out from under a formless felt hat as if in protest. His beard, equally mismanaged, showed bits of grass nested in its folds. His face was dusky and his teeth yellow, but his eyes sparkled in the afternoon sun. He stood on the roadside before a train of curious beasts. They appeared to be shrunken, shaggy horses. The animals were loaded with bundles and linked together by leads from one to the next. Six short, half-naked men helped Dilladrum keep the train under control. They wore only breechcloths of loose linen, and clattering necklaces of colored stones. Like Dilladrum, they grinned brightly at the sailors' approach.

"Welcome, welcome, gentlemen," he warmly addressed them. "I am Dilladrum, your guide. Before we leave our fair city, perhaps you would like some time to peruse our fine shops? As per previous arrangements, I and my Vintu friends will be providing you with food, water, and shelter, but we will be many days afield and as such, some comforts as could be obtained in the bazaar might make your trek more pleasant. Consider our fine wines, liquors, or perhaps an attractive slave girl to make the camps more enjoyable."

A few eyes turned appraisingly toward the shops where dozens of colorful signboards advertised in a foreign tongue. Music played—strange twanging strings and warbling pipes. Hadrian could smell lamb spiced with curry, a popular dish as he recalled.

"We will leave immediately," Wesley replied, louder than was necessary for merely Dilladrum to hear him.

"Suit yourself, good sir." The guide shrugged sadly. He made a gesture to his Vintu workers and the little men used long switches and yelping cries to urge the animals of the caravan forward.

As they did, one spotted Hadrian and paused in his work. His brows furrowed as he stared intently until a shout from Dilladrum sent him back to herding.

"What was that all about?" Royce asked. Hadrian shrugged, but Royce looked unconvinced. "You were here for what—five years? Anything happen? Anything you want to share?"

"Sure," he replied, with a sarcastic grin. "Right after you fill me in on how you escaped from Manzant Prison and why you never killed Ambrose Moor."

"Sorry I asked."

"I was young and stupid," Hadrian offered. "But I can tell you that Wesley is right about the jungle being dangerous. We will want to watch ourselves around Gile."

"You met him?"

Hadrian nodded. "I've met most of the warlords of the Gur Em, but I'm sure everyone's forgotten me by now."

As if overhearing, the train worker glanced over his shoulder at Hadrian once more.

"Everywhere landward from Dagastan is uphill," Dilladrum was saying as the troop walked along the narrow dirt path through farmlands dotted by domed grass huts. "That is the way of the world everywhere, is it not? From the sea, we always need to go up. It makes the leaving that much harder, but the returning that much more welcome."

They walked two abreast, with Wesley and Dilladrum, Wyatt and Poe, Royce and Hadrian, in front, while Thranic's group followed behind the Vintu and the beasts. It was disconcerting to have Thranic and his crew behind them, but it was better than having to walk with them. Dilladrum set a brisk pace for a portly little man, stepping lively and thrusting his bleached walking stick out with practiced skill. He bent the brim down on his otherwise shapeless hat to block the sun, making him look comical even while Hadrian wished he had a silly-looking hat of his own.

"Mister Dilladrum, what exactly are your instructions concerning us?" Wesley inquired.

"I am contracted to safely deliver officers, cargo, and crew of the *Emerald Storm* to the Palace of the Four Winds in Dur Guron."

"Is that the residence of Erandabon Gile?"

"Ah, yes, the fortress of The Panther of Dur Guron."

"Panther?" Wyatt asked.

Dilladrum chuckled. "It is what the Vintu call the warlord. They are a very simple folk, but very hard workers, as you can see. The Panther is a legend among them."

"A hero?" Wesley offered.

"A panther is not a hero to anyone. A panther is a great cat that hides himself in the jungle. He is a ghost to those who seek him, deadly to those he hunts, but to those he doesn't, he is merely a creature deserving of respect. The Panther does not concern himself with the Vintu, but stories of his valor, cruelty, and cunning reach them."

"You are not Vintu?"

"No. I am Erbonese. It is a region to the northwest, not far from Mandalin."

"And the Tenkin?" Wesley asked. "Is the warlord one of them?"

Dilladrum's expression turned dark. "Yes, yes. The Tenkin are everywhere in these jungles." He pointed to the horizon ahead of them. "Some tribes are more welcoming than others. Not to worry, my Vintu and I know a good route. We will pass through one Tenkin village, but they are friendly and familiar to us, like the one you call Staul, yes? We will make it safely."

As they climbed higher, they entered a great plain of tall grass that swayed enchantingly with the breeze. Climbing a large rock, they could see for miles in all directions except ahead, where a tall, forested ridge rose up several hundred feet. They made camp just before sundown. Hardly a word passed between Dilladrum and the Vintu, but they immediately went to work setting up decorative tents embroidered with geometric designs and neatly bordered canopies. Cots and small stools were put out for each, along with sheets and pillows.

Cooked in large pots over an open fire, the evening meal was strong and spicy enough to make Hadrian's eyes water. It was tasty and satisfying after weeks eating the same tired pork stew. The Vintu took turns entertaining. Some played stringed instruments similar to a lute, others danced, and a few sang lilting ballads. The words Hadrian could not understand, but the melody was beautiful. Animal calls filled the night. Screeches, cries, and growls threatened in the darkness, always too loud and too close.

On their third day out, the landscape began to change. The level plains tilted upward and trees appeared more frequently. The forests that had lined the distance were upon them, and soon they were trudging under a canopy of tall trees whose massive roots spread out across the forest floor like the fingers of old men. At first it was good to be out of the sun, but then the path became rocky, steep, and hard to navigate. It did not last long, as they soon crested a ridge and began a sharp descent. On the far side of the ridge, they could see a distinct change in the flora. The undergrowth thickened, turning a deeper green. Larger leaves, vines, thickets of creepers, and needle-shaped blades encroached on the track, causing the Vintu to occasionally move ahead to chop a path.

The next day it began to rain, and while at times it poured and at others it would only mist, it never ceased.

"They always seem content, don't they?" Hadrian mentioned to Royce as they sat under the canopy of their tent watching the Vintu preparing the evening meal. "It could be blazingly hot or raining like now, and they don't seem to care one way or the other."

"Are you now saying we should become Vintu?" Royce asked. "I don't think you can just apply for membership into their tribe. I think you need to be born into it."

"What's that?" Wyatt asked, coming out of the tent the three shared, wiping his freshly shaved face with a cloth.

"Just thinking about the Vintu and living a simple existence of quiet pleasures," Hadrian explained.

"What makes you think they're content?" Royce asked. "I've found that when people smile all the time they're hiding something. These Vintu are probably miserable—economically forced into relative slavery, catering to wealthy foreigners. I'm sure they would smile just as much while slitting our throats to save themselves another day of hauling Dilladrum's packs."

"I think you've been away from Gwen too long. You're starting to sound like the *old Royce* again."

Across the camp they spotted Staul, Thranic, and Defoe. Staul waved in their direction and grinned.

"See, big grin," Royce mentioned.

"Fun group, eh?" Hadrian muttered.

"Yeah, they are a group aren't they," Royce nodded thoughtfully. "Why would a sentinel, a Tenkin warrior, a physician, a thief, and… whatever the heck Bulard is go into the jungles of Calis to visit a Tenkin warlord? And what is Bulard's deal?"

Wyatt and Hadrian shrugged in unison.

"Isn't that a bit odd? We were all on the same ship together for weeks, and we don't know anything about the man beyond the fact that he doesn't look like he's seen the sun in a decade. Perhaps if we found out, it would provide the common connection between the others and this Erandabon fellow."

"Defoe and Bulard share a tent," Hadrian pointed out.

"Who's Defoe?" Wyatt asked.

"That's Royce's pet name for Bernie," Hadrian quipped.

"Hadrian, why don't you go chat with Bulard," Royce said. "I'll distract Defoe."

"What about me?" Wyatt asked.

"Talk with Derning and Grady. They don't seem as connected to the others as I first thought. Find out why they volunteered."

The Vintu handed out dinner, which the *Storm's* crew ate sitting on stools the Vintu provided. Dinner consisted mostly of what appeared to be shredded pork and an array of unusual vegetables in a thick, hot sauce that needled the tongue.

After the meal, darkness descended on the camp and most retired to their tents. Antun Bulard was already in his, just like he always stayed in his cabin aboard ship. The light in Bulard and Defoe's tent flickered and the silhouettes of their heads bobbed about, magnified on the canvas walls. A few hours after dark, Defoe stepped out. An instant later, Royce swooped in.

"How you been, *Bernie*," Royce greeted Defoe, who flinched noticeably. "Going for a walk?"

"Actually, I was about to find a place to relieve myself."

"Good, I'll go with you."

"Go with me?" he asked nervously.

"I've been known to help people relieve themselves of a great many things." Royce put an arm around Defoe's shoulder as he urged him away from the tents. Once more, Defoe flinched. "A little jumpy, aren't we?"

"Don't you think I have good reason?"

Royce smiled and nodded, "You have me there. I honestly still can't figure out what you were thinking."

The two were outside the circle of tents, well beyond the glow of the campfire, and still Royce urged him farther away.

"It wasn't my idea. I was just following orders. Don't you think I'd know better than to—"

CALIS

"Whose idea was it?"

Defoe only hesitated a moment, "Thranic," he said, then hastily added, "but he just wanted you bloodied. Not dead, just cut."

"Why?"

"Honestly, I don't know."

They stopped in a dark circle of trees. Night frogs croaked hesitantly, concerned by their presence. The camp was only a distant glow.

"Care to tell me what all of you are doing here?"

Defoe frowned. "You know I won't, even to save my life. It wouldn't be worth it."

"But you told me about Thranic."

"I don't like Thranic."

"So, he's not the one you're afraid of. Is it Merrick?"

"Merrick?" Defoe looked genuinely puzzled. "Listen, I never faulted you for Jade's death or the war you waged on the Diamond. Merrick should have never betrayed you like that, not without first hearing your side of it."

Royce took a step forward. In the darkness of the canopy, he was certain Defoe could barely see him. Royce, on the other hand, could make out every line on Defoe's face. "What's Merrick's plan?"

"I haven't seen Merrick in years."

Royce drew out his dagger and purposely allowed it to make a metal scraping sound as it came free of its scabbard. "So, you haven't seen him. Fine. But you're working for him, or someone else who's working for him. I want to know where he is and what he's up to, and you're going to tell me."

Defoe shook his head. "I—I really don't know anything about Marius or what he's doing nowadays."

Royce paused. Every line of Defoe's face revealed he was telling the truth.

"What have we here?" Thranic asked. "A private meeting? You've strayed a bit far from camp, dear boys."

Royce turned to see Thranic and Staul. Staul held a torch, and Thranic carried a crossbow.

"It's not safe to venture too far away from your friends, or didn't you think about that, Royce?" Thranic told him, then fired the crossbow at Royce's heart.

"Antun Bulard, isn't it?" Hadrian asked, sticking his head in the tent.

"Hmm?" Antun looked up. He was lying on his stomach, writing with a featherless quill worn to only a few inches in length. He had on a pair of spectacles, the top of which he peered over. "Why, yes, I am."

The old man was more than just pale—he was white. His hair was the color of alabaster while his skin was little more than wrinkled quartz. He reminded Hadrian of an egg, colorless and fragile.

"I wanted to introduce myself." Hadrian slipped fully inside. "All this time at sea, and we never had the opportunity to properly meet. I thought that was unfortunate, don't you?"

"Why, I—who are you again?"

"Hadrian, I was the cook on the *Emerald Storm*."

"Ah, well, I hate to say it Hadrian, but I was not impressed with your cooking. Perhaps a little less salt and some wine would have helped. Not that this is any great feast," he said, gesturing toward his half-eaten meal. "I am too old for such rich foods. It upsets my stomach."

"What are you writing?"

"Oh, this? Just notes, really. My mind isn't what it once was, you see. I'll forget everything soon, and then where will I be? A historian who can't remember his own name. It really could come to that, you know. Assuming I live that long. Bernie keeps reassuring me I won't live out this trip. He's probably right. He's the expert on such things, after all."

"Really? What kind of things?"

"Oh, spelunking, of course. I'm told Bernie is an old hand at it. We make a good team, he and I. He digs up the past and I put it down, so to speak." Antun chuckled to himself until he coughed. Hadrian poured the man a glass of water, which he gratefully accepted.

After he had recovered, Hadrian asked, "Have you ever heard of a man called Merrick Marius?"

Bulard shook his head. "Not unless I have and then forgotten. Was he a king or a hero, perhaps?"

"No, I actually thought he might have been the man who sent you here."

"Oh, no. Our mandate is from the Patriarch himself, though Sentinel Thranic doesn't tell me much. I'm not complaining, mind you. How often does a priest of Maribor have the opportunity to serve the Patriarch? I can tell you precisely—twice. Once when I was so much younger, and now that I am nearly dead."

"I thought you were a historian? You are also a priest?"

"I know I don't look much like one, do I? My calling was the pen, not the flock."

"You've written books, then?"

"Oh, yes, my best is still the *History of Apeladorn*, which I am constantly having to append, of course."

"I know a monk at Windermere Abbey who'd love to meet you."

"Is that up north near Melengar? I passed through there once about twenty years ago." Antun nodded thoughtfully. "They were very helpful, saved my life if I recall correctly."

"So, you're on this trip to record what you see?"

"Oh, no, that's only what I've been doing so far. As you can imagine, I don't get out much. I do most of my work in libraries and stuffy cellars, reading old books. I was in Tur Del Fur before setting off on this wonderful trip. This has been an excellent opportunity to record what I see firsthand. The Patriarch knows about my research on ancient Imperial history, and that's why I am here. Sort of a living, breathing version of my books, you see. I suppose they think that if they put in the right questions, out will pop the correct answers, like an oracle."

Hadrian was about to ask another question when Grady and Poe poked their heads in.

"Hadrian," Poe caught his attention.

"Well, isn't my tent the social center tonight," Antun remarked.

"I'm kinda busy at the moment, can this wait?" Hadrian asked.

"I don't think so. Thranic and Staul just followed Royce and Bernie into the jungle."

Royce heard the click of the release and began to move even before the hiss of the string indicated the missile's launch. Still, his reflexes could not move faster than a flying bolt. The metal shaft pierced his side below the ribcage. The impact thrust him backward, where he collapsed in pain.

"Lucky we found you, Bernie," Thranic told the startled thief as he moved away from Royce's body. "He would have killed you. Isn't that what you said bucketmen do? Now, don't you feel foolish for saying I couldn't protect you?"

"You could have hit me!" Defoe snapped.

"Stop being so dramatic. You're alive, aren't you? Besides, I heard the conversation. It didn't take much for you to give me up. In my profession, lack of faith is a terrible sin."

"In mine, it is all too often justified," Defoe snarled back.

"Get back to the camp before you're missed."

Defoe grumbled as he trotted back up the path. Thranic watched his retreat.

"We might have to do something about him," the sentinel told the Tenkin. "Funny that you, my heathen friend, should be my stalwart ally in all this."

"Bernie, 'e dinks too much. Me? I am just greedy, and derefore trustworzy. We going to just leave dee body?"

"No, it's too close to the path we'll be taking tomorrow, and I can't count on the animals eating him before we break camp. Drag him away. A few yards should be enough."

"Royce?" Hadrian shouted from behind them on the trail.

"Quickly, you idiot. They're coming!"

Staul rushed forward and, planting his torch in the ground, lifted Royce and ran with him into the jungle. He only traveled a few dozen yards when he cursed.

Royce was still breathing.

"*Izuto!*" the Tenkin hissed, drawing his dagger.

"Too late," Royce whispered.

Hadrian led them into the trees the way Royce went earlier. Ahead he spotted the glow of a torch and ran toward it. Behind him Wyatt, Poe, Grady, and Derning followed.

"There's blood here," Hadrian announced when he got to the burning torch thrust in the ground. "Royce!"

"Spread out!" Wyatt ordered. "Sweep the grass and look for more blood."

"Over here!" Derning shouted, moving into the ferns. "There, up ahead. Two of them, Staul and Royce!"

Hadrian cut his way through the thick undergrowth to where they lay. Royce was breathing hard, holding his blood-soaked side. His face was pale, but his eyes remained focused.

"How ya doing, buddy?" Hadrian asked, dropping to his knees and carefully slipping an arm under Royce.

Royce didn't say anything. He kept his teeth clenched, blowing his cheeks out with each breath.

"Get his feet, Wyatt," Hadrian ordered. "Now lift him gently. Poe, get out front with the torch."

"What about Staul?" Derning asked.

"What about him?" Hadrian glanced down at the big Tenkin whose throat lay open, slit from ear to ear.

When they returned to camp, Wesley ordered Royce taken to his tent, which was the largest and originally reserved for Captain Seward. He sent Poe for Doctor Levy, but Hadrian intervened. Wesley appeared confused but, as Royce was Hadrian's best friend, he did not press the issue. The Vintu were surprisingly adept at first aid, and under Hadrian's watchful eye they cleaned and dressed the wound.

CALIS

The bolt aimed at Royce's heart had entered and exited cleanly. He suffered significant blood loss, but no organ damage, nor broken bones. The Vintu sealed the tiny entry hole without a problem. The larger tearing of his flesh at the exit was another matter. It took a dozen bandages and many basins of water before they got the bleeding under control and Royce lay calmly sleeping.

"Why wasn't I notified about this? I'm a physician, for Maribor's sake!"

Hadrian stepped outside the tent flap to find Levy arguing with Wyatt, Poe, Grady, and Derning who, at Hadrian's request, guarded the entrance.

"Ah, Doctor Levy, just the man I wanted to see," Hadrian addressed him. "Where's your boss? Where's Thranic?"

Levy did not need to answer, as across the camp Thranic walked toward them alongside Wesley and Defoe.

Hadrian drew his sword at their approach.

"Put away your weapon!" Wesley ordered.

"This man nearly killed Royce tonight," Hadrian declared, pointing at Thranic.

"That's not the way he tells it," Wesley replied. "He said Royce attacked and murdered Staul over accusations the Tenkin made about Royce killing Drew aboard the *Storm*. Thranic and Seaman Bernie claim they were witnesses."

"We don't *claim* anything, we saw it," Thranic said, coolly.

"And how do you *claim* this took place?" Hadrian asked.

"Staul confronted Royce, telling him he was going to Wesley with evidence. Royce warned him that he would never live to see the dawn. Then when Staul turned to walk back to camp, Royce grabbed him from behind and slit his throat. Bernie and I expected such treachery from him, but we couldn't convince Staul not to confront the blackguard. So we followed. I brought a crossbow, borrowed from Mister Dilladrum's supplies, for protection. I fired in self-defense."

"He's lying," Hadrian declared.

"Oh, were you there?" Thranic asked. "Did you see it happen as we did? Funny, I didn't notice your presence."

"Royce left the camp with Bernie, not Staul," Hadrian said.

Thranic laughed. "Is that the best you can come up with to save your friend from a noose? Why not say you saw Staul attack him unprovoked, or me for that matter?"

"I saw Royce leave with Bernie, too, and Thranic and Staul followed after them," Wyatt put in.

"That's a lie!" Defoe responded, convincingly offended. "I watched Royce leave with Staul. Thranic and I followed. I worked the topmast with Royce. I was there the night Edgar Drew died. Royce was the only one near him. They were having an argument. You all saw how agile he is. Drew never had a chance."

"Why didn't you report it to the captain?" Derning asked.

"I did," Defoe declared. "But because I didn't actually see him push poor Drew off, he refused to do anything."

"How convenient that Captain Seward is too dead to ask about that," Wyatt pointed out.

Thranic shook his head with a pitiful smile, "Now, Wesley, will you actually take the word of a pirate and a cook over the word of a Sentinel of the Nyphron Church?"

"Your Excellency," Wesley said, turning to face Thranic. "You will address me as *Mister* Wesley or *sir*, is that understood?" Thranic's expression soured. "And *I* will decide whose word I will accept. As it happens, I am well aware of your personal vendetta against Royce Melborn. Midshipman Beryl tried to convince me to bring false charges. Well, sir, I did not buckle to Beryl's threats, and I'll be damned if I will be intimidated by your title."

"Damned is a very good choice of words, *Mister* Wesley."

CALIS

"Sentinel Thranic," Wesley barked at him. "Be forewarned that if any further harm befalls Seaman Melborn that is even remotely suspicious, I will hold you responsible and have you executed by whatever means are at hand. Do I make myself clear?"

"You wouldn't dare touch an ordained officer of the Patriarch. Every king in Avryn—why the regents themselves would not oppose me. It is you who should be concerned about execution."

Wyatt, Grady, and Derning drew their blades and Hadrian took a step closer to Thranic.

"Stand down, gentlemen!" Wesley shouted. At his order, they paused. "You are quite correct, Sentinel Thranic, that your office influences how I treat you. Were you an ordinary seaman, I would order you flogged for your disrespect. I am well aware that upon our return to Aquesta you could ruin my career, or perhaps have me imprisoned or hanged. But let me point out, sir, that Aquesta is a long way from here, and a dead man has difficulty requesting anything. It would be in my best interest, therefore, to see you executed here and now. It would be a simple matter to report you and Seaman Bernie lost to the dangers of the jungle."

Defoe looked worried and took a subtle step away from Thranic's side.

"I would have thought I could rely on your family's famous code of honor," Thranic said in a sarcastic tone.

"You can, sir, and you are, as indeed that is all that keeps you alive at this moment. It is also what you can count on to have you executed should you threaten Seaman Melborn again. Do I make myself clear?"

Thranic fumed but said nothing. He simply turned and walked away with Defoe following after.

Wesley exhaled loudly and straightened his vest. "How is he doing?" he asked Hadrian.

"Sleeping at the moment, sir. He's weak, but should recover. And thank you, sir."

"For what?" Wesley replied. "I have a mission to accomplish, Blackwater. I can't have my crew killing one another. Derning, Grady, take a few others and bring Staul's body back to camp. Let's not leave him to the beasts of this foul jungle."

Chapter 15

THE SEARCH

I think I saw him."

Arista woke at the sound. Disoriented, she did not know where she was at first. Turning over, she found Thrace in a small streak of moonlight. The empress was dressed in her wispy, thin nightgown that fluttered in the draft. She stood straight, hair loose, eyes lost to a vision beyond the window's frame.

It had been nearly a week since Gerald invited Arista to the empress's bedroom, and she wondered if this was a sign she was on the right path. If fate could speak, surely this is how it would sound.

Thrace saw to her safety, guarding her like the mother of a newborn. Soldiers stood outside her door at all times, now in pairs with strict orders to prevent the entry of anyone without permission. Only Amilia and Nimbus ever entered the chamber, and even they knocked. At her urging, Thrace ordered Nimbus to carry messages to Hilfred.

In her nightgown, Thrace looked almost like the girl from Dahlgren, but there was something different about her—akin to sadness, yet lacking even the passion for that. Often she would sit and stare at nothing for hours, and when she spoke her words were dull and emotionless. She never laughed, cried, or smiled. In this way, she appeared to have successfully transformed from a lively peasant girl into a true empress—serene and unflappable. Yet at what cost?

"It was late like this," Thrace said, looking out the window. Her voice sounded disconnected, as if in a trance. "I was having a dream, but a squeaking noise woke me. I came to the window and I saw them. They were in the courtyard below. Men with torches, as many as a dozen and they wheeled a sealed wagon. The men were knights, dressed in black and scarlet armor like those we saw in Dahlgren. They spoke of the man inside the box as if he was a monster, and even though he was hooded and chained, they were afraid. After taking him away, the wagon rolled back out of the courtyard." Thrace turned to face her. "I thought it was a dream until just now. I have a lot of unpleasant dreams."

"How long ago did this happen?"

"Three months, perhaps more."

Shivering, Arista sat up. The fire had long since died and the stone walls did nothing to keep the chill out. The window was open again. Regardless of the time of day, or how cold the temperature, Thrace insisted. Not with words—she rarely spoke—but each time Arista closed the window, the girl opened it again.

"That would coincide with Gaunt's disappearance. You never heard anything else about this prisoner?"

"No, and you would be surprised how much you hear when you are very quiet."

"Thrace, come—"

The empress halted her by the sudden tilt of her head and the curious look on her face. "No one calls me that anymore."

"A shame. I've always liked the name."

"Me, too."

THE SEARCH

"Come back to bed. You'll catch a cold."

Thrace walked toward her, looking at where the mirror once hung. "I will need to get a new mirror before Wintertide."

Dawn brought breakfast and morning reports from Amilia and Thrace's tutor. Nimbus was bright-eyed and cheery, bowing to both—a courtesy Amilia refused to extend to Arista. The Imperial secretary looked haggard. The dark circles under her eyes grew deeper each day. Holding her jaw stiff and her fists clenched, she glared at Arista eating breakfast in Thrace's bed. Despite Amilia's obvious contempt, Arista could not help but like her. It was not hard to recognize the same fierce protectiveness that Hilfred exhibited.

"They've stopped the search for the Witch of Melengar," Amilia reported, looking coldly at Arista. "They think she's either headed to Melengar or Ratibor. Patrols are still out, but no one really expects to find her."

"What about where Degan Gaunt might be held?" Arista asked.

Amilia glanced at Nimbus, who stepped up. "Well, my research at the Hall of Records is inconclusive. In ancient Imperial times, Aquesta was a city called Rionillion, and a building of some significance stood on this site. Ironically, several parchments refer to it as a prison, but it was destroyed during the early part of the civil wars that followed the death of the last emperor. Later, in 2453, Glenmorgan the First built a fortress here as a defense against rebellions. That fortress is the very palace in which we now stand.

"None of the histories mention anything about a dungeon—odd given the unrest. I've made a detailed search of nearly every section of the palace, interviewed chambermaids, studied old maps and plans, but I haven't uncovered a single mention of any kind."

"What does Aquesta do with criminals?" Arista asked.

"There are three jails in the city that deal with minor offenses and the Warric prison in Whitehead for harsher cases that don't result in execution. And then there is the infamous Manzant Prison and Salt Mine in Maranon for the most severe crimes."

"Perhaps it's not a dungeon or prison at all," Arista said. "Maybe it's merely a secret room."

"I suppose I could make some inquiries along those lines."

"What is it, Amilia?" Thrace asked, catching a thoughtful look on her secretary's face.

"What? Oh, nothing…" Amilia's expression switched to annoyance. "This is very dangerous. Asking all these questions and nosing about. It's risky enough ordering extra food with each meal. Someone will notice. Saldur is not a fool."

"But what were you thinking just now, Amilia?" Thrace repeated.

"Nothing."

"Amilia?"

The secretary frowned. "I just—well, a few weeks ago you talked about a dark hole…"

"You think I was there—in this dungeon?"

"Don't, Modina. Don't think about it," Amilia begged. "You're too fragile."

"I have to try. If I can remember—"

"You don't *have* to do anything. This woman—she comes here—she doesn't care about you—or what might happen. All she cares about is herself. You've done more than enough. If you won't turn her in, at least let me get her out of here and away from you. Nimbus and I—"

"No," Thrace said softly. "She needs us…and I need her."

THE SEARCH

v

"Dirt," Thrace said and shivered.

Arista looked over. She was in the midst of trying to determine how to finish her latest letter to Hilfred when she heard the word. The empress had knelt before the open window since Amilia and Nimbus left, but this was the first she had spoken.

"Damp, cold—terrible cold, and voices, I remember them—cries and weeping, men and women, screams and prayers. Everything was dark." Thrace wrapped her arms around herself and began to rock. "Splashing, I remember splashing, a hollow sound, creaking, a whirl, and the splash. Sometimes there were distant, echoing voices coming from above, falling out of a tunnel. The walls were stone, the door wood. A bowl—yes, every day a bowl—soup that smelled bad. There was so little to eat."

Thrace rocked harder, her voice trembling, her breath hitching.

"I could hear the blows and cries, men and women, day and night, screaming for mercy. Then I heard a new voice added to the wailing, and realized it was my own. I killed my family. I killed my mother, my brother, and little Hickory. I destroyed my whole village. I killed my father. I was being punished."

Thrace began to cry.

Arista moved to her, but the girl jumped at her touch and cowered away. Crawling against the wall and sobbing, she rubbed the stone with her hands, wetting it with her tears.

Fragile? Arista thought. Thrace took a blow that would kill most people. No matter what Amilia believed, Thrace was not fragile. Yet even granite will crack if you hit it with a big enough hammer.

"Are you all right?" Arista asked.

"No, I keep searching but I can't find it. I can't understand the sounds. It is so familiar and yet..." she trailed off and shook her head. "I'm sorry, I wanted to help. I wanted—"

"It's okay, Thrace. It's okay."

The empress frowned. "You have to stop calling me that." She looked up at her. "Thrace is dead."

Chapter 16

THE VILLAGE

It was perpetually twilight. The jungle's canopy blocked what little sunlight managed to penetrate the rain clouds. A hazy mist shrouded their surroundings and intensified the deeper they pressed into the jungle. Exotic plants with stalks the size of men's legs towered overhead. Huge leaves adorned with intricate patterns and vibrant flowers of purple, yellow, and red surrounded the party. It left Hadrian feeling small, shrunken to the size of an insect, crawling across the floor of a giant's forest.

Rain constantly plagued them. The sound of water danced on a million leaves, sounding like thunder. When actual thunder cracked, it was the voice of a god. Everything was wet. Clothes stuck to their skin and hung like weights. Boots squished audibly with every step. Their hands were wrinkled like those of old men.

Royce rode on the back of a Gunguan, what the Vintu called the pack ponies. He was awake but weak. A day had passed since the attack, because Wesley had insisted on burying Staul. Their new captain proclaimed he would not allow the beasts to have a taste of any of his crew and insisted on a deep grave. No one complained at the strenuous work of cutting through the thick mat of roots. Hadrian doubted Wesley really cared about the fate of Staul's carcass, but the work granted Royce time to rest, kept the crew busy, and affirmed Wesley's commitment to them. Hadrian thought once again about the similarities between the ex-midshipman and his famous brother.

Royce traveled wrapped in his cloak with the weight of the rain collapsing the hood around his head. It was not a good sign for Thranic and Defoe. Until now, Royce had played the part of the good little sailor, but with the re-emergence of the hood and the loss of his white kerchief, Hadrian knew that role had ended. They had spoken little since the attack. Not surprisingly, Royce was in no mood for idle discussion. By now, Hadrian guessed his friend had imagined killing Thranic a dozen times, with a few Defoes thrown in here and there for variety. Hadrian had seen Royce wounded before and was familiar with the cocooning—only what would emerge from that cloak and hood would not be a butterfly.

Thranic, Defoe, and Levy traveled at the end of the train and Hadrian often caught them whispering. They wisely kept their distance, avoiding attention. Wesley led the party along with Dilladrum, who made a point of not taking sides or venturing anything remotely resembling an opinion. Dilladrum remained jolly as always and focused his attention on the Vintu.

Hadrian was most surprised with Derning. When Royce was most vulnerable, his shipboard nemesis had come to his aid rather than taking advantage. Hadrian would have bet money that, on the subject of Royce's guilt, Derning would have sided with Thranic. Wyatt never had the chance to find out his reason for volunteering, but now more than ever Hadrian was convinced Derning was not part of Thranic's band. Antun Bulard was part of Thranic's troop— of that he had no doubt—but the old man lacked the ruthlessness of the others. He was merely a resource and, having shown an interest, Hadrian became Bulard's new best friend.

"Look! Look there." Bulard pointed to a brilliant flower blooming overhead. The old man took to walking beside Hadrian, sharing his sense of discovery along the way. "Gorgeous, simply gorgeous. Have you ever seen the like? I dare say I haven't. Still, that isn't saying much, now is it?"

Bulard reminded Hadrian of a long-haired cat; his usually billowing robe and fluffy, white hair deflated in the rain leaving a remarkably thin body. He held up a withered hand to protect his eyes as he searched the trees.

"Another one of those wonderful long-beaked birds," the historian said. "I love the way they hover."

Hadrian smiled at him. "It's not that you don't mind the rain that amazes me, it's that you don't seem to notice it at all."

Bulard frowned. "My parchments are a disaster. They stick together, the ink runs, I haven't been able to write anything down, and as I mentioned at our first meeting, my head is no place to store memories of such wonderful things. It makes me feel I have wasted my life locked in dusty libraries and scriptoriums. Don't do what I did, Hadrian. You're still a young man. Take my advice, live your life to the fullest. Breathe the air, taste the wine, kiss the girls and always remember that the tales of another are never as wondrous as your own. I'll admit I was, well, concerned about this trip. No, I will say it truthfully—I was scared. What does a man my age have to be afraid of, you wonder? Everything. Life becomes more precious when you have less to spare. I'm not ready to die. Why, look at all that I have never seen."

"You have seen horses before, and known women, right?" Hadrian asked, with a wry grin.

Bulard looked at him curiously, "I'm a historian, not a monk."

Hadrian nearly tripped.

"I realize I don't look it now, but I was quite handsome once. I was married three times, in fact. Outlived all of them, poor darlings. I still miss them, you know—each one. My silly, little mind hasn't misplaced their faces, and I can't imagine it ever will. Have you ever been in love, Hadrian?"

"I'm not sure. How do you tell?"

"Love? Why, it's like coming home."

Hadrian considered the comment.

"What are you thinking?" Bulard asked.

Hadrian shook his head. "Nothing."

"Yes you were. What? You can tell me. I am an excellent repository for secrets. I will likely forget, but if I don't, well, I'm an old man in a remote jungle. I'm sure to die before I can repeat anything."

Hadrian smiled then shrugged. "I was just thinking about the rain."

The trail widened, revealing a great, cascading waterfall and a dozen grass-thatched buildings clustered at the center of a small clearing. The domed-roof huts rested on high wooden stilts accessed by short stairs or ladders, depending on the size and apparent prestige of the structure. A fire pit occupied the very center of the clearing, surrounded by a ring of colorfully painted stones and wooden poles decorated in animal skins, skulls, and strings of bones, beads, and long vibrant feathers. The inhabitants were dark-haired, dark-eyed, umber-skinned men and women dressed in beautifully painted cloths and silks. They paused as Dilladrum advanced respectfully. Elder men met him before the fire ring, where they exchanged bows.

"Who are these people, do you suppose?" Bulard asked.

THE VILLAGE

"Tenkins," Hadrian replied.

Bulard raised his eyebrows.

The village was familiar to Hadrian, though he had never been there. Hundreds of similar ones were scattered across the peninsula, mirror images of each other. The rubble of Eastern Calis was the last standing residue of the first empire. After civil wars tore apart the west, Calis still flew the old Imperial banners, and for centuries formed the bulwark against the advancing Ghazel horde. Time, however, was on the Ghazel's side. The last of the old world died when the ancient eastern capital of Urlineus fell to the goblin hordes sweeping through the jungles. They might have overrun all of Avryn, if not for Glenmorgan III.

Glenmorgan III had rallied the nobles and defeated the goblins at the Battle of Vilan Hills. The Ghazel fell back, but were never driven off the mainland. Betrayed shortly after his victory, Glenmorgan III never finished his work of re-establishing the kingdom's borders. This task fell to lesser men who squabbled over the spoils of war and were too distracted to stop the Ghazel from digging in. Urlineus, the last great city of the Old Empire, remained in the hands of the Ghazel, and Calis had never been the same.

Fractured and isolated, the eastern half of the country struggled against the growing pressure of the Ghazel nation in a maelstrom of chaos and confusion. Self-appointed warrior-kings fought against each other. Out of desperation, some enlisted the aid of the Ghazel to help vanquish a rival. Ties formed, lines blurred, and out of this tenuous alliance the Tenkins were born—humans who had adopted the Ghazel's ways, traditions, and beliefs. For this, Calians ostracized the Tenkin, forcing their kind deeper into the jungles, where they lived on the borderlands between the anvil and the hammer.

Dilladrum returned. "This is the village of Oudorro. I've been here many times. Although Tenkin, they are a friendly and generous people. I have asked them to let us rest here for the night. Tomorrow morning we will push on toward the Palace of the Four Winds. Beyond this point, travel will be much harder and unpleasant, so we will need a good night's rest. I must caution you, however, please do nothing to offend or provoke these people. They are courteous but can be fierce if roused."

The physical appearance of the Tenkin always impressed Hadrian. Staul was a crude example of his kin, and these men were more what he remembered. Lean, bronzed muscles and strong facial features that looked hewn from blocks of stone were the hallmarks of the Tenkin warrior. Like the great cats of the jungle, their bodies were graceful in their strength and simplicity. The women were breathtaking. Long, dark hair wreathed sharp cheekbones and almond eyes. Their satin-smooth skin enveloped willowy curves. The *civilized* world never saw Tenkin women. A closely guarded treasure, they never left their villages.

The inhabitants showed neither fear nor concern at the procession of the foreigners. Most observed their arrival with silent curiosity. The women showed more interest, pressing forward to peer and talking amongst themselves.

"I thought Tenkins were grotesque," Bulard said with the casual manner and volume of a man commenting on animals. "I had heard they were abominations of nature, but these people are beautiful."

"A common misconception," Hadrian explained. "People tell tales that Tenkin are the result of interbreeding between Calians and Ghazel but if you ever saw a goblin, you'd understand why that's not possible."

"I guess you can't believe everything you read in books. But don't spread that around, or I'll be out of a job."

When they reached the village center, the Vintu went about their work and began unpacking. They moved with stoic familiarity. The party waited, listening to the hiss of rain on the fire and the mummer of the crowd gathering around them. With an expectant expression,

THE VILLAGE

Dilladrum struggled to see over their heads. He exchanged looks with Wesley but said nothing. Soon a small elderly Tenkin entered the circle dressed in a leopard wrap. His skin was like wrinkled leather and his hair gray steel. He walked with a slow dignity and an upturned chin. Dilladrum smiled and the two spoke rapidly. Then the elderly Tenkin clapped his hands and shouted. The crowd fell back and he led the crew of the *Emerald Storm* into the largest of the buildings. It had four, tree-sized pillars holding up a latticework of intertwined branches overlaid with thatch. The interior lacked partitions and stood as an open hall lined with tanned skins and pillows made from animal hides.

Waiting inside were four Tenkins. Three men and a woman sat upon a raised mound covered in luxurious cushions. Their leopard-clad guide bowed deeply to the four then left. Outside, the rain increased and poured off the thatched roof.

Dilladrum stepped forward, bowed with his hands clasped before him, and spoke in Tenkin, which was a mix of the old Imperial tongue and Ghazel. Hadrian had mastered a working knowledge of the language, but the isolation between villages caused each to develop a slightly different dialect. While Hadrian missed a number of Dilladrum's words, he recognized that formal introductions were being made.

"This is Burandu," Dilladrum explained to the *Emerald Storm's* crew in Apelanese. "He is Elder." Dilladrum paused to think then added, "Similar to the lord of a manor, but not quite. Beside him is Joqdan, his warlord—chief knight, if you will. Zulron is Oudorro's oberdaza." He gestured at a stunted, misshapen Tenkin, the only one Hadrian had ever seen. "The closest thing to his office in Avryn might be a chief priest as well as doctor, and next to him is Fan Irlanu. You have no equivalent position for her. She is a seer, a visionary."

"Velcome peoples of Great Avryn," Burandu spoke haltingly in Apelanese. Despite his age, betrayed only by a head of startling white hair, he looked as strong and handsome as any man in the village. He sat adorned in a silk waistcloth and kilt, a broad necklace of gold, and wore a headdress formed from long, brightly colored feathers. "Vee are pleazed to 'ave you in our 'ome."

"Thank you, sir, for granting us an invitation," Wesley replied.

"Vee enjoy company of doze Dilladrum brings. Once brothers, in ancient days past—ez good to sit, to listen, to find each other. Come, drink, and remember."

Zulron cast a fine powder over a brazier of coals. Flames burst forth, illuminating the lodge.

They all sat amid the pillows and hides. Royce found a place within the shadows against the rear wall. As always, Thranic and Defoe kept their distance from the rest of the party. They sat close to the four Tenkins, where the sentinel watched Zulron with great interest. Bulard invited Hadrian to sit beside him.

"This explains a great deal," said the old man, pointing to the decorations in the hut. "These are people lost in time. Do you see those decorated shields hanging from the rafter with the oil lamps? They used to do that in the ancient Imperial throne room, and the leaders mirror the Imperial body, represented by a king and his two councilors; always a wizard and a warrior. Although the seer is probably an addition of the Ghazel influences. She is lovely."

Hadrian had to agree, Fan Irlanu was stunning, even by Tenkin standards. Her thin silk gown embraced her body with the intimacy of liquid.

Food and wine circulated as men carried in jugs and platters. "After eating," Burandu said to Wesley, "I ask you, Dilladrum, and your second to meet at my *durbo*. I discuss recent news on dee road ahead. I fear dee beasts are loose and you must be careful. You tell me of road just traveled."

THE VILLAGE

Wesley nodded with a mouthful of food, then after swallowing added, "Of course, Your, ah…" He hesitated before simply adding, "sir."

Bulard looked at the sliced meat set before him with suspicion. Hadrian chuckled, watching the old man push it around his plate. "It's pork. Wild pigs thrive in these jungles and the Tenkin hunt them. You'll find it a little tougher and gamier than what you're used to back home, but it's good—you'll like it."

"How do you know so much about them?" the old man asked.

"I lived in Calis for several years."

"Doing what?"

"You know, I still ask myself that." Hadrian stuffed a hunk of pork in his mouth and chewed, but Bulard's expression showed he did not understand. At last Hadrian gave in. "I was a mercenary. I fought for the highest bidder."

"You seem ashamed." Bulard tried a bit of fruit and grimaced. "The mercenary profession has a long and illustrious history. I should know."

"My father never approved of me using my training for profit. In a way, you might say he thought it sacrilegious. I didn't understand then, but I do now."

"So, you were good?"

"A lot of men died."

"Battles are sometimes necessary and men die in war—it happens. You have nothing to be ashamed of. To be a warrior and alive is a reward Maribor bestows on the virtuous. You should be proud."

"Except there was no war, just battles. No cause, just money. No virtue, just killing."

Bulard wrinkled his brows as if trying to decipher this and Hadrian got up before he could think of anything else to ask.

When the meal was over, three Tenkin boys held large palm branches over the heads of Burandu, Wesley, Dilladrum, and Wyatt as they ventured out into the rain. With the Elder gone, formalities relaxed. The Vintu headed out to resume camp preparations before all daylight was lost. Across the hall, Thranic and Levy spoke quietly with the oberdaza, Zulron, and all three left together. Poe, Derning, and Grady helped themselves to a jug of wine and reclined casually on the pillows.

Hadrian sat beside Royce. "Wanna try the wine?"

"It's not time for drinking yet," the hood replied.

"How you feeling?"

"Not good enough."

"You need to get the dressing on your wound changed?"

"It can wait."

"Wait too long and it will fester."

"Leave me alone."

"You should at least eat. The pork is good. Best meal you'll have for a while, I think. It'll help you heal."

There was no reply. They sat listening to the wind and rain on the grassy roof and low conversations punctuated by the occasional laugh and clink of ceramic cups.

"Are you aware you're being watched?" Royce asked. "The Tenkin on the dais, the one Dilladrum called Joqdan, the warlord. He's been staring at you since we entered. Do you know him?"

Hadrian looked at the bald, muscular man wreathed in a dozen bone necklaces. "Never seen him before. The woman next to him—she looks oddly familiar."

"She looks like Gwen."

"That's it. You're right. She does look just like her. Is Gwen from—"

"I don't know."

"I just assumed she was from Wesbaden. Everyone in Avryn who's from Calis is from there, but she could be from a village like this, huh?" Hadrian chuckled. "What an odd pairing you two make. Maybe Gwen's from this very village. That could be her sister up there, or cousin. You might be meeting the bride's family before the wedding, just like a proper suitor. You should brush your hair and take a bath. Make a good enough impression, and the two of you could settle down here. You'd look good bare-chested in one of those kilts."

Hadrian expected a cutting retort. All he heard from his friend was a harsh series of breaths. Looking over he noticed the hood was drooping.

"Hey, you're really not doing too good, are you?"

The hood shook.

Hadrian placed a hand on Royce's back. His cloak was soaked and hot. "Damn it. I'll convince Wesley to extend our stay. In the meantime, let's get you dry and in a bed."

With a flaming brand the oberdaza led Thranic and Levy toward a cliff wall at the edge of the village, where the great waterfall thundered. Somehow even the plunging water felt foul as it splattered against rocks, casting a damp mist. Thranic continually wiped the tainted wet from his face. Everything about the village was evil. Everywhere stood signs that these humans had turned their backs on Novron and embraced his enemy—the hideous feathers they wore, the symbolic designs in the pillows, the tattoos on their bodies. They did not whisper, but rather shouted their allegiance to Uberlin. Thranic could not imagine a greater blasphemy, and yet the others were blind to their transgressions. Given the opportunity, Thranic would burn the whole village to ash and scatter the remains. He had tried to prepare himself for what to expect even before the *Emerald Storm* set sail, but now, surrounded by their poison, he longed to strike a blow for Novron. While he could not safely put a torch to this nest of vipers, there was another profanation he could rectify, one that these worshipers of Uberlin might even assist him with.

The powder the oberdaza used to ignite the braziers had caught his attention. The Tenkin witch doctor was also an alchemist. Zulron was not like the rest of the heathens. He lacked their illusionary facade, their glimmer of false beauty. One leg was shorter than its partner, causing Zulron to shuffle with a noticeable limp. One shoulder rode up, hugging his chin, while the other slipped low, dangling a weak and withered arm. Singular in his wretched appearance, this honest display of his evil made him more trustworthy than the rest.

As they reached the waterfall, Zulron led them along a narrow path around the frothing pool to a crack in the cliff face. Within the fissure was a cave, its ceiling teamed with chattering bats and its floor was laden with guano.

"This is my store room and workshop," Zulron explained as he pushed deeper into the cavern. "It stays cooler here and is well protected from wind and rain."

"And what prying eyes can't see…" Thranic added, guessing at the truth of the matter. Years of dealing with tainted souls left him with an understanding of evil's true nature.

Zulron paused only briefly, to cast a glance over his low-slung shoulder at the sentinel. "You see more clearly than the rest of your brethren."

"And you speak Apelanese better than yours."

"I'm not built for hunting. I rely on study and have learned much about your world."

"This is disgusting." Levy grimaced, carefully picking his path.

"Yes," the oberdaza agreed. He walked through the guano as if it were a field of spring grass. "But these bats are my gatekeepers, and their soil, my moat."

Soon the cave grew wide and the floor cleared of filth. In the center of the cavern, was a domed oven built of carefully piled stones. Surrounding it were dozens of huge clay pots, bundles of browned leaves, and a vast pile of poorly stacked wood. On shelves carved from the stone walls rested hundreds of smaller ceramic jars and a variety of stones, crystals, and bowls.

Zulron reached into one of the pots and threw a handful of dust into the mouth of the oven. Thrusting his torch at the base, fire roared to life, which he fed with wood. When the oven was sated and he had finished lighting a number of oil lamps, he turned to Levy. "Let me see it."

The doctor set his pack on the floor and withdrew the bundle of bloody rags. He took the bandages and studied each, even holding them to his nose and sniffing. "And you say these belong to the hooded one among you? It is his blood?"

"Yes."

"How was he wounded?"

"I shot him with a crossbow."

Zulron showed no surprise. "Did you not wish him dead? Or are you a poor hunter?"

"He moved."

Zulron raised a dark brow. "He is quick?"

"Yes."

"Sees in the dark?"

"Yes."

"And you came by ship, yes? How did he fare on the water?"

"Poorly—very sick for the first four days I hear."

"And his ears, are they pointed?"

"No. He has no elven features. This is why we need you to test the blood. You know the method?"

The oberdaza nodded.

Thranic felt a twinge of regret that this creature was so unworthy to Novron. He sensed a kinship of minds. "How long?"

Zulron rubbed the crusted bandages between his fingers. "Days with this. It is too old. If we had a fresh sample—it could be quick."

"Getting blood from him is nearly impossible," Levy grumbled.

"I will start the test with these, but I'll also see what I can do to get fresh blood. He will need treatment soon."

"Treatment?"

"The jungle does not abide the weak or the wounded for long. He will summon me or die."

"How much gold will you want?" Thranic asked.

Zulron shook his head. "I have no need for gold."

"What payment then?"

"My reward will not come from you. I will reap my own reward, and it is no concern of yours."

The Tenkin granted them the use of three sizable huts and Wesley divided his crew accordingly. The accommodations were surprisingly luxurious, subdivided by walls of wide woven ribbons that gave the impression of being inside a basket. Carpets of tight-threaded fibers inlaid with beautiful designs covered the floor. Peanut-shaped gourds hung from the rafters, burning oil that provided more than enough light.

THE VILLAGE

Having convinced Wesley to linger in the village, Hadrian watched over Royce, who looked worse with each passing hour. Royce's skin burned and sweat poured down his forehead even as he shivered beneath two layers of blankets.

"You need to get better, pal," Hadrian told him. "Think of Gwen. Better yet, think what she'll do to me if I come back without you."

There was no reaction. Royce continued to shiver, his eyes closed.

"May I enter?" a soft voice asked. Hadrian could only see the outline in the doorway, and for an instant he thought it was Gwen. "It 'as been said 'e grows worse, but you 'ave refused Zulron to see 'im."

"Your oberdaza has been keeping close company with the man who nearly killed my friend. I do not feel comfortable letting Zulron treat him."

"Vill you allow me? I am not as skilled as Zulron, but know some dings."

Hadrian nodded and waved her in.

"I am Fan Irlanu," she said, dipping her head into the hut while outside two other women waited in the rain, holding covered baskets.

"Hadrian Blackwater, and this is Royce."

She nodded, then knelt beside Royce and placed a hand to his forehead. "'E 'as fever."

She motioned for the oil lamp and Hadrian pulled it down, then helped her open Royce's cloak and pull back his tunic to reveal the stained bandage that she carefully removed. Irlanu grimaced as she peeled back the cloth and studied the wound.

She shook her head. "Et ez dee *shirlum-kath*," she said, pressing lightly on the skin around the wound, causing Royce to flinch in his sleep. "See 'ere?" she scraped a long nail along the edge of the bloody wound and drew away a squirming parasite the size of a coarse hair that twisted and curled on her fingertip. "Dey are eating 'im."

Fan Irlanu waved to the women outside who entered and deposited their baskets beside her. She spoke briefly in Tenkin, ordering them to fetch other items that Hadrian was unfamiliar with, and the two dashed from the hut.

"Can you help him?"

The woman nodded as she took out a stone mortar and began crushing bits of what looked to be dirt, leaves, and nuts with a pestle. "Dey are common 'ere vis open vounds. Left alone, dee *shirlum-kath* vill devour 'im. 'E die soon vis out help, so I make a poison for dee *shirlum-kath.*"

One of the women returned with a gourd and an earthen pot in which Fan Irlanu mixed the contents of her mortar with oil, beating it until she had a thick, dark paste that she spread over Royce's wound, packing it into the puncture. They turned him over and did the same to the exit wound. Then she placed a single large, foul-smelling leaf over each and together they wrapped him in fresh cloth. Royce barely woke during the procedure. Groggy and confused, he soon passed out once more.

Fan Irlanu covered Royce back up with the blankets and nodded approvingly. "'E vill get better now, I dink. I brew drinks—more poison for dee *shirlum-kath* and a tea for strength. When 'e wakes up, make 'im drink both, eh? Den 'e feel better much faster."

Hadrian thanked her. As she left, he wondered what was it about Royce being near death that always summoned beautiful women.

When Royce woke the next morning the fever was gone and he was strong enough to curse. According to him, the draught Fan

Irlanu provided tasted worse than fermented cow dung. The tea, he actually liked. By the following day he was sitting up and eating, by the third he was able to walk unassisted to the communal *ostrium* for his meals.

No one complained about the delay as the rain continued. Seeing Royce in the *ostrium* that morning, Grady winked and asked Hadrian if it might be possible for Royce to have a relapse.

"'E ez good?" Fan Irlanu asked, coming to them after the evening meal concluded. Her movement was entrancingly graceful, her dress glistened like oil in the lamplight. All eyes followed her.

"No—but he's feeling a lot better," Hadrian replied. His mischievous grin left a puzzled expression on her face.

"My language is perhaps not—"

"I am very good, thank you," Royce told her. "Apparently I owe you my life."

She shook her head. "Repay me by getting strong—ah, but I do 'ave a favor to ask of your friend, Hay-dree-on. Joqdan, varlord of dee village asks dat 'e speak vis you at dee *sarap*."

"Me?" Hadrian asked, looking across to where the man in the bone necklaces sat. "Is it all right if Royce joins us? I'd like to keep an eye on him."

"But of course, if 'e ez up to et."

Hadrian helped Royce to his feet and, as the rest watched with envious stares, the two followed Fan Irlanu out of the *ostrium*. The sun had not yet set, but for what little light the jungle permitted it might just as well have. Oil lamps hung from branches, illuminating the path, decorating the village like a Summersrule festival. The rain still poured, so they left the lodge under the protection of palm branches. Hadrian knew *sarap* translated to, "meeting place," or "talking place." In this case, it was a giant Oudorro tree from which, he recently learned, the village took its name.

THE EMERALD STORM

The tree was not as tall as it was round. Great, green leaves thrived on many of its branches, despite the fact that the center of the trunk was completely hollow. The space within provided shelter from the rain and was large enough for the four of them. A small, ornately decorated fire pit dominated the center of the floor and glowed with red coals. Around this they took seats on luxurious pillows of silk and satin. The interior walls were painted with various ocher and umber dyes smeared into the wood, apparently by stained fingers. The images depicted men and animals—twisted shapes of strange visions. There were also mysterious symbols and swirling designs. Illuminated by the glowing coals, the interior of the tree felt eerily talismanic, creating a sensation that left Hadrian on edge.

Joqdan was already there. He had not waited for a boy with the palms, and his bare head and chest were slick with rain. They all exchanged bows respectfully.

"Pleezed am I," Joqdan greeted them. "Mine speech…ez, ah… not good as dee learned. I varrior—do not speak to out-side-erz. You are…" he paused for a moment thinking hard, "Special. Am honored. Velcome you to Oudorro, Galenti. I…" he paused, thinking again, and quickly became frustrated and turned to Fan Irlanu.

"Dee Varlord Joqdan regrets dat language skills are not good enough to honor you, and 'e asks dat I speak words," Fan Irlanu told them as she removed her wet wrap. "'E says dat 'e saw you fight in dee arena at Drogbon. 'E 'as never forgotten et. To 'ave such a legend 'ere ez great honor. As you do not wear dee laurel, 'e dinks you do not vish be recognized. 'E 'as asked you 'ere to pay proper respect in private."

Hadrian glanced briefly at Royce, who remained silent but attentive. "Thank you," he told Joqdan. "And he is right—I would prefer not to be recognized."

"Joqdan begs permission to ask a question of dee great Galenti. 'E would like to know vie you left."

THE VILLAGE

Hadrian paused only a moment then replied. "It was time to seek new battles."

The Warlord of Oudorro nodded as Fan Irlanu translated his words.

At that moment, something about Fan Irlanu caught Royce's attention and he rapidly approached her. She did not move, although given the ominous manner of his advance, Hadrian guessed that most anyone else would have taken a step back.

"Where did you get that mark on your shoulder?" Royce asked, indicating a small swirling tattoo.

"That is the mark of a seer," Zulron declared, startling all of them as he entered.

Unlike the other men of the village, Zulron wore a full robe. Made from a shimmering cloth, it was open enough for them to see his misshapen body covered in strange tattoos. The one that spread across his face resembled the web of a spider.

"Fan Irlanu is a vision-walker," he explained, staring admiringly at her. "It is a talent and a gift bestowed by Uberlin upon those endowed with the hot blood of the Ghazel. Few are born each age, and she is very powerful. She can see the depths of a heart and the future of a nation." He paused to run his fingers gingerly down the side of her cheek. "She can see all things except her own destiny."

"You don't suffer from a language barrier, I see," Hadrian said.

Zulron smiled. "I am the oberdaza. I know the movement of the stars in the Ba Ran and the books of your world. All mysteries are revealed to me."

"Is it true that you are a visionary?" Royce asked Fan Irlanu.

She nodded. "Vis dee burning of dee tulan leaves I—"

"Give him a demonstration," Zulron interrupted, causing her to look sharply at him. "Read this one's future," he said, gesturing toward Royce.

A puzzled look crossed her face, but she nodded.

Joqdan put a firm hand to Zulron's shoulder and spun him around, but spoke too quickly for Hadrian to understand. The two argued briefly, but all he caught was one word of Zulron's reply, *"Important."*

When he turned back, Zulron's eyes fell on Hadrian, who he openly studied. "So, you are the legendary Galenti." He raised an eyebrow. "Looking at you, I would say Joqdan is mistaken, but I know Joqdan is never mistaken. Still, you don't look like the Tiger of Mandalin. I'd thought you would be much bigger." He turned abruptly back to Fan Irlanu. "The leaves, burn them."

As Fan Irlanu moved to a stone box, Zulron asked them to take seats around the glowing coals of the fire ring.

Hadrian took Royce aside. "Perhaps we should go. I can't say I like Mister Witch doctor's attitude much, seems like he's up to something. The fact that he's been spending time with Thranic doesn't help."

Royce glanced at Fan Irlanu. "No, I want to stay."

"What's all this about?"

"The tattoo—Gwen has the same one."

Reluctantly, Hadrian sat.

Fan Irlanu returned with several large, dry leaves. Even withered and brittle, they were a brilliant shade of red. She held them over the coals and muttered something while crushing the leaves and letting them fall onto the embers. Instantly a thick, white smoke billowed. It did not rise, but pooled and drifted. Fan Irlanu used her hands to contain the smoke, wafting it, scooping it, swirling it into a cloud before her. Then she bent and breathed in the ashen mist. Repeatedly, she swept the smoke and inhaled deeply.

The last of the leaves burned away and the smoke faded. Fan Irlanu's eyes closed and she began swaying on her knees, humming softly. After a few minutes, she reached out her hands.

"Touch her," Zulron instructed Royce.

THE VILLAGE

Royce hesitated briefly. He looked at her the way Hadrian had seen him eye an elaborate lock. The greater the potential treasure behind the door, the more tension showed in Royce's eyes, and at that moment he looked as if Fan Irlanu might hold the secret to a fortune. He reached out his fingers. At his touch, she took hold of him.

There was a pause, then Fan Irlanu began to moan and finally shake her head, slowly at first but faster and faster the longer she held on. Her mouth opened and she groaned the way one might in a nightmare, struggling to speak but unable to form words. She jerked, her eyes shifting wildly under closed lids, her voice louder but saying nothing distinguishable.

Joqdan's face was awash with concern, making Hadrian wonder if something was wrong. Fan Irlanu continued to struggle. Joqdan started to move, but a quick glare from Zulron held him back. At last, the woman screamed and collapsed on the pillows.

"Leave her alone!" Zulron shouted in Tenkin.

Joqdan ignored him, rushing to her side. Fan Irlanu laid on the ground thrashing. She cried out and then became still.

Joqdan clutched her, whispering in her ear. He held her head and placed a hand near her mouth to feel for breath. *"You've killed her!"* he shouted at Zulron. Without another word, he lifted the seer in his arms and ran out into the rain.

"What's going on? What's happening?" Hadrian asked.

"Your friend is not human," the oberdaza declared. Zulron stepped up to face Royce. "Why are you here?"

"We're part of the crew of the *Emerald Storm* on our way to deliver a message to the Palace of the Four Winds," Hadrian answered for him.

Zulron did not take his eyes off Royce. "For three thousand years the ancient legends have told of the Day of Reckoning, when the shadow from the north will descend to wash over our lands."

Derning, Grady, Poe, and Bulard entered. "What's going on?" Derning asked. "We heard a woman scream and saw the big guy carrying her away."

"There was an accident," Hadrian explained.

Both Derning and Grady immediately looked at Royce.

"We don't know what happened to her," Hadrian continued. "She was doing a kind of spiritual demonstration—reading Royce's fortune or something, and she collapsed."

"She collapsed?" Derning said.

"She was breathing tulan leaf smoke. Maybe it was a bad batch."

Zulron ignored their conversation and continued to glare at Royce, "The Ghazel legend, preserved by oral memory from the time of the first Ghazel-Da-Ra, tells of death and destruction, revenge unleashed, the Old Ones coming again. I have seen the signs myself. I watch the stars and know. To the north, there have been rumblings. Estramnadon is active, and Avempartha has been opened. Now here is an elf in my village, where one has never walked before."

"An elf?" Derning asked, puzzled.

"That is what killed Fan Irlanu," Zulron told them. "Or at the very least has driven her insane."

"What?" Hadrian exclaimed.

"It's not possible to use the sight on an elf. The lack of a soul offers up only infinity. For her it was like walking off a bottomless cliff. If she lives, she will never be the same."

"You're the village healer. Shouldn't you be trying to help her?"

"He wants her dead," Royce finally spoke. Then looking at Zulron added, "You knew."

"What did he know?" Bulard asked, tense but fascinated. Grady and Derning also leaned forward.

"You knew I was elven, didn't you? But you told her—no—coerced her to do a reading," Royce said.

THE VILLAGE

Outside there were sounds of commotion, running feet and raised voices. Hadrian heard Wesley saying something over the heated shouts of Tenkins.

"Why did you want her dead?"

"I did nothing. You are the one that killed her. And killing a member of the village, especially a seer, is an unpardonable crime. The punishment is death." Zulron gave a smile before stepping outside.

The rest of them followed to find a gathering crowd.

"There he is!" Thranic shouted the moment Royce stepped out of the tree. He pointed and said, "There's your *elf!* I warned you about him."

"He has slain our seer, Fan Irlanu!" Zulron announced, and repeated it in Tenkin.

Burandu, Wesley, and Wyatt pushed their way through the mob.

"Is this true?" Wesley asked quickly, his voice nervous.

"Which?" Royce asked.

"Are you an elf, and did you just kill Fan Irlanu?"

"Yes, and I'm not sure."

The crowd grew and Hadrian could pick out words such as *justice*, *revenge*, and *kill* among the many Tenkin shouts.

"By Mar, man!" Wesley said fiercely but quietly to Royce. "What is it with you? I should let you hang just for the amount of trouble you've caused." He took a breath. The crowd pressed in. Lightning flashed overhead while thunder boomed. "What do you mean when you say you're not sure?" Wesley asked. He was speaking quickly, wiping the rain from his face.

"The murderer must pay for his crime, Burandu," Zulron declared in Tenkin. *"His soullessness has killed our beloved Fan Irlanu. The law demands justice!"*

"Where is Joqdan?" Burandu asked.

"Paying his last respects to his dead would-be wife. If he was here, he would agree."

"He lies! Zulron is to blame," Hadrian spoke in Tenkin, which drew a surprised look from everyone.

"What are they saying?" Wesley asked Hadrian.

"The oberdaza is pushing for our deaths and Burandu is buying it."

"Bring them all!" Burandu shouted.

The warriors of the village descended. Hadrian considered for a moment whether he should draw his swords, but decided against it. He shot a look at Royce to indicate he should not resist.

They were driven to the village center, where Dilladrum was shouting, "Let go of me! What are you doing?" When he saw Wesley he asked, "What did you do? I told you not to offend them!"

"We didn't offend them," Hadrian explained. "We killed their beloved seer."

"What!" Dilladrum looked as if he was about to faint.

"Actually, it is a misunderstanding, but I'm not sure we'll get the chance to explain," Wesley put in.

"At least Thranic will die with us," Royce said loud enough for the sentinel to hear.

"A martyr's death is a fair price to rid the world of you and your kind."

Lightning flashed again, revealing the pallid faces of the crew in its stark light.

Grady was shoved to the ground and reached for his sword.

"Grady, don't!" Hadrian said.

"That's right," Wesley shouted. "No one draw weapons. They'll slaughter us."

"They will anyway," Derning replied.

Poe and Hadrian pulled Grady back to his feet. All around them the ring of warriors formed a wall, behind which churned a crowd of shouting faces and raised fists. The rain-drenched mob pushed and cried, its words lost in a roar of hatred. Lightning flashed once more, and a single voice rang out, *"You knew!"*

Instantly the crowd fell silent and parted. Only the pour of rain disturbed the stillness as Fan Irlanu entered the circle. Joqdan at her side carried a deadly-looking spear, his eyes grim and focused on Zulron.

"Burandu, it is not the strangers fault. It was Zulron who asked that I do the reading. He knew this one had elven blood. But I am still alive!"

"But—no…how could you…" Zulron stammered.

"He is not an Old One," Fan Irlanu said. *"He is a kaz! There is humanity in him—footholds, Zulron, footholds!"*

"What's going on?" Wesley asked Hadrian. "Isn't she the one Royce killed? What's she saying?"

"She seems a might upset," Grady said.

"But not at Royce," Poe remarked.

"Who then?" Grady asked.

"Zulron has tried to kill me. I have known for some time his ambitions were great. I saw the treachery in his heart, but I never expected he would go so far."

"Joqdan, what say you? Is what Fan Irlanu says true?" Burandu addressed his warlord.

Joqdan thrust his spear into the chest of Zulron.

The long blade passed fully through the oberdaza's body. Those nearby jostled backward, everyone moving away. Joqdan advanced the length of his spear's shaft and gripped Zulron by the throat. Holding him with strong arms, he spat in the witch doctor's face. The light faded from the oberdaza's eyes, and Joqdan withdrew his spear as Zulron fell dead.

"I think that answers your question," Poe remarked.

Burandu looked down at the body, then up at Joqdan, and nodded. *"Joqdan is never wrong. I am pleased you are safe, Fan Irlanu,"* he said to her. Then the Elder addressed Wesley and the others. "Forgive dee dishonor of evil Zulron. Judge us not by 'is actions. You too 'ave such men in your vorld, eh?"

Wesley glanced at Thranic and Royce.

Burandu shouted to his warriors and they dispersed the crowd. Many paused to kiss Fan Irlanu, who stood weakly, leaning against Joqdan. She offered a strained smile, but Hadrian could see the paleness of her face and the effort in her breathing.

The Elder spoke briefly with Joqdan and Fan Irlanu, then Joqdan lifted the seer once more and carried her to one of the smaller dwellings. Zulron's body was dragged away and with him went most of the Tenkins.

"That's it?" Grady asked.

"Wait," Dilladrum said as the leopard-skinned man approached. They spoke for a moment then Dilladrum returned. "The village of Oudorro asks our forgiveness for the misunderstanding and begs the honor to continue as our host."

They looked at one another skeptically.

"They are sincere."

Wesley sighed and nodded. "Thank them for their kindness, but we will be leaving in the morning."

"Kindness?" Derning muttered. "They nearly skinned us alive. We should get out now while we can."

"I see no advantage in venturing into these jungles at night," Wesley affirmed. "We will leave at first light."

"And what about Melborn?" Thranic hissed.

"You, Doctor Levy, and Seamen Blackwater and Melborn will come with me. The rest I order to quarters to get as much sleep as possible."

A young Tenkin trotted up to them and spoke to Dilladrum, his eyes watching Royce.

"What is it?" Wesley asked.

THE VILLAGE

"Fan Irlanu has requested Royce and Hadrian."

Wesley nodded at them, but added, "Try not to start a war this time. You are to report to me directly after—by your honor, gentlemen."

Before Thranic could object, they both nodded and offered an "Aye, aye, sir."

Fan Irlanu lay on a bed beneath a thin white sheet as a young girl patted her forehead with a damp cloth, rinsed repeatedly in a shallow basin. Joqdan remained at her side. His great spear, still covered in Zulron's blood, stood by the door.

"Is she really all right?" Hadrian asked.

"I vill be fine," Fan Irlanu replied. "Et vas a terrible shock. Et vill take time."

"I'm sorry," Royce offered.

"I know," she told him. Her face was sympathetic to the point of sadness. "I *know* you are."

"You saw something?"

"Vere I to touch Joqdan's 'and vis dee tulan smoke in me, I could tell us vaat 'e ate for dee midday meal yesterday and vaat 'e vill eat tomorrow. If I touched Galenti's 'and, I could name dee woman 'e vill marry and ou vill outlive dee other. I could also tell dee precise events dat vill surround 'is death. So clear ez my sight dat I can see a life in detail, but not you. You are a mystery, a cloud. Looking into you ez like seeing a mountain range in a thick fog—I can only see dee 'igh points vis no means of connecting dem. You are *kaz* in dee Ghazel tongue—in your language a *mir*, yes?—a mix of 'uman and elven blood. This gives you a long life." She paused to gather some strength. Joqdan's brow furrowed further.

"Imagine looking down a road, you see most dings clearly, dee trees, dee rocks, dee leaves. But vis you, et ez as if I am standing 'igh in dee air staring out at dee 'orizon—very few details. My sight can only span so far, and dat does not include dee lifespan of a *kaz*. Dere ez too much."

"But you saw something."

"I saw many dings. Too many," she told him. Her eyes were soft and comforting.

"Tell me," Royce said. "Please, I know a woman. She is very much like you, but something troubles her. She won't speak of it, and I think she has seen things like you have—things that trouble her."

"She ez Tenkin?"

"I'm not sure, but she bears the same mark as you."

Fan Irlanu nodded. "I sent for you because of vaat I saw. I vill tell you vaat I know and den I must rest. I may sleep for a long time, and Joqdan vill not allow any to disturb me. So I must speak now. I am certain I vill not see you again. As I said, I saw much, but understood little—too much distance, too much time. Most are vague feelings dat are 'ard to put in vords, but vaat I sensed vas powerful."

Royce nodded.

She paused a moment, thinking, then said, "Darkness surrounds you, death ez everywhere, et stalks you, hunts you and you feed upon et—blood begets blood—dee darkness consumes you. In dis darkness, I saw two lights beside you. One vill blow out and in dat same breeze, dee other flickers, but et must not go out. You must protect dee flame against dee storm.

"I saw a secret—et ez ah…et ez 'idden. Et ez covered, dis great treasure. A man 'ides et, but a woman knows—she alone knows and so she prepares. She speaks in riddles dat vill be revealed—profound truths disguised for now. You vill remember veen dee time comes, dee path laid out for you—in dee dark."

THE VILLAGE

Joqdan spoke something in Tenkin, but Fan Irlanu shook her head and pushed on.

"I saw a great journey. Ten upon dee road, she ou vears dee light vill lead dee vay. Dee road goes deep into dee earth, and into despair. Dee voices of dee dead guide your steps. You walk back in time. Dee three 'zousand-year battle begins again. Cold grips dee vorld, death comes to all and a choice ez before you. You alone stand in dee balance, your veight vill tilt dee scales, but to vich side is unclear. You must choose between darkness and light, and your choice vill affect many." She paused, shaking her head slowly. "Like trees in a forest, like blades of grass—too many to count. And I fear dat in dee end you vill choose dee darkness and turn your back to dee light."

"You said *she*," Royce questioned. "Who did you mean? Is it Gwen?"

"I do not know names. Dey are mere feelings, glimpses of a dream."

"What is this secret?"

"I do not know, it ez 'idden."

"When you say there are two lights and one blows out, does that mean someone will die?"

She nodded. "I dink so—yes, et felt dat vay. I sensed a loss, so great I still feel et." She reached out and touched Royce's hand and a tear slipped down her cheek. "Your road ez one of great anguish."

Royce said nothing for a moment, and then asked, "What is this great journey?"

She shook her head. "I vish I knew more. Your life—your 'ole life 'as been pain and so much more lies ahead. I am sorry, but I cannot tell you more dan dat."

"She rests now," Joqdan told them. From his firm tone they knew it was time to go.

They walked out of the hut and found Wyatt watching out for them.

"Waiting up?" Hadrian asked.

"Didn't want you to step into the wrong hut by accident." He gave a wink.

"The rest bunked down?"

He nodded. "So, you're an elf," Wyatt said to Royce. "That explains a lot. What did the lady want?"

"To tell me my future."

"Good news?"

"It nearly killed her. What do you think?"

Chapter 17

THE PALACE OF THE FOUR WINDS

Thranic was furious. Wesley refused to take any action against Royce, and the sentinel railed that under Imperial law all elves were subject to arrest. Wesley had little choice but to acknowledge this, but added that, given their circumstances, he had neither a prison nor chains. He also pointed out that they were not within the bounds of the New Empire, and until they were he was the sole judge of the law.

"It is my duty to see this mission to completion," Wesley told the sentinel. "A bound man will only be a hindrance to this effort, particularly when he is injured and exhibits no desire to flee."

Royce watched all this with an expression of mild amusement. Thranic went on relentlessly, until finally Wesley gave in and approached Royce. "Will you give me your word you will not attempt to escape me or Sentinel Thranic before this mission is over?"

"On my word, sir," Royce replied. "There is nothing that could make me willingly leave Sentinel Thranic's side."

"There you have it," Wesley concluded, satisfied.

"He is an elf! What good is the word of an elf?" As Thranic straightened and rose above Wesley, the look on the sentinel's face caused him to take a step back. "As Secretary of Erivan Affairs, appointed by the Patriarch, it is my duty to purge the Empire of their foul influence. I demand you place the elf under my authority at once!"

Wesley hesitated. The challenge of a sentinel broke the nerve of many kings, and Thranic was more intimidating than any Hadrian had encountered. His hunched vulture demeanor and piercing glare were more than daunting.

Hadrian was tense. He knew the sentinel was already dead, but would prefer his partner got to pick his own time and place. If Wesley agreed to surrender Royce, there would be a battle here and now that would see one of them dead. Hadrian let his fingers slip slowly to the pommels of his swords and he marked the position of Defoe in anticipation.

Wesley locked his jaw and returned Thranic's glare. "He might be an elf, sir, but he is also one of *my* crew."

"Your crew? You no longer have a ship. You're nothing but a boy playing pretend captain!" the sentinel bellowed angrily.

Wesley stiffened.

"And what were you playing at in the hold of the ship, sir? Was that what you call administering your authority?"

This took Thranic by surprise.

"Oh, yes, the officers knew of your nightly visits to the *cargo*. It's a small ship, sir, and the officers' bunks were just above. We heard you every night torturing them, and I fear a good deal more than that. I am no great fan of elves but, by Maribor, there are limits to the abuses conscience permits! No, sir, I don't think I will be turning Seaman Melborn over to your authority anytime soon. Even should I trust you to treat him honorably, I need all the hands I can get and, as we both know, you are not an honorable man."

THE PALACE OF THE FOUR WINDS

"It is a pity to see such a young, promising lad throw his life away." Thranic fumed. "I'll see that you are executed for this."

"To do so, we must return to Avryn. Let's hope we both live to see that day."

❧

At dawn the crew of the *Emerald Storm* left the village and once more plunged into the jungle, traveling northeast of the Oudorro valley by a narrow, barely visible path. The rain left the ground swamped, but it had stopped at last. On the third day, cliffs and chasms barred their path. They followed ridgelines where a stumble could send a man falling hundreds of feet, walked perilous rope bridges that spanned raging rivers, and followed rocky clefts down into dark valleys. In the lower ravines it was dark, even at midday. Trees created phantom images. Rocks looked like crouching animals and stunted, gnarled bushes appeared like monsters in the mist.

Royce's health steadily improved, though his disposition remained unchanged. He was able to walk on his own most of the day and, thanks to Fan Irlanu's balm, his wounds no longer required a bandage.

They found the bodies on the fourth day out of Oudorro. Corpses laid on the path, dressed in clothes similar to those of Dilladrum and the Vintu. Flies hovered, and the stench of decay lingered in the air. They had been dead for some time, and many were missing limbs or showed evidence of bites.

"Animals?" Wesley asked.

"Maybe." Dilladrum looked off toward the east. "But perhaps the Panther is not able to contain his beasts, just as Burandu told us."

"You're saying the Ghazel did this?"

Dilladrum paused to study the jungle around them. "Impossible to say, yet these bodies are weeks old and it is not like the jungle to let them rot. Animals don't like Ghazel and will avoid an area with their smell, even if it means passing up a free meal.

"This man is Hingara." Dilladrum pointed to the body of a swarthy little man in a red cap. "He is a guide, like me. He set out for the Palace of the Four Winds with a party like ours weeks ago. He was a good man. He knew the jungle well and, as you can see, his group was large—as many as thirty men in all. What kind of animal do you think would attack so large a company? A pack of wolves, perhaps? A pride of lions? No, they would never attack a party this large. And what animal could kill without leaving a single body of their own behind? Ghazel, on the other hand…"

"What about them?" Wesley asked.

"They are like ghosts. Hingara could not have seen them coming. Imagine beings as nimble and at ease in these jungles as monkeys, but possessing the strength and ferocity of tigers. They have the instinct of beasts but the intelligence of men. On a rainy day they can smell a human three leagues away. This was a safe path, but I fear things have changed."

"There are only about eighteen bodies here," Wesley observed. "If he set out with thirty men, where are the rest?"

Dilladrum let his sight settle on the naval officer. "Where indeed."

Wesley grimaced as he looked at the dead. "Are you saying they took them to eat?"

"That's what they do." Dilladrum pointed to the torn and mutilated bodies. "They ate some on the spot in the fever following the battle, but I think they carried the rest back to their den, where I can only guess they feasted by barbequing them on spits and drinking warmed blood from the men's skulls."

"You don't know that!" Wesley challenged.

The Palace of the Four Winds

Dilladrum shook his head. "As I said, I am guessing. No one truly knows what goes on in their camps any more than a deer knows what goes on in the dining halls of a king."

"You make it sound as if they are our betters."

"In these jungles, they are. Here they are the hunters and we are the prey. I told you the trip would be harder from now on. We will burn no fire, cook no food, and pitch no tent. Our only hope of survival lies in slipping though unnoticed."

"Should we bury them?" Wesley asked.

"What the animals do not touch neither should we. It would announce our presence to the whole jungle. It is also not wise to linger. We should press on with all haste."

They traveled steadily downward now, following a rapidly flowing river through a cleft in the mountains. The lower they went, the higher the canopy rose, and the darker their world became. They camped along a bank where the river swirled around a break of boulders. With no fire or tent, it was not much of a camp. They huddled on a bare sandy patch exposed by a shift in the river's bend, eating cold, salted meat. Royce sat at the edge of the camp and watched Thranic watching him.

They had played this game each night since the village. Royce was certain Defoe had filled Thranic's head with numerous stories about his reign of terror against the Diamond. Thranic appeared aloof, but Royce was certain Defoe's words wormed in nonetheless. Without Staul, and with Defoe no longer a trusted ally, Thranic was dramatically weakened. The sentinel's confrontation with Wesley revealed Thranic's growing desperation—his failure another setback.

The balance was shifting, he was slipping from the hunter to the hunted, and with each day Royce grew stronger.

Royce enjoyed the game. He liked watching the shadows growing under Thranic's eyes as he got less and less sleep. He savored the way Thranic spun whenever an animal rustled branches behind him on the trail, his eyes searching rapidly for Royce. Mental torture was never something Royce aimed for, but in Thranic's case he was making an exception.

Royce's quick turn had saved his life. Although he might have bled to death if Hadrian and the others had not found him, or died from fever if the Tenkin woman had not helped. The wound itself was relatively superficial. For several days he had portrayed being weaker than he was. He had pain when pressing on his side and was still experiencing some lack of movement, but for the most part he was his old self again.

Royce might have continued the game longer, but it was becoming too dangerous. Wesley's defiance changed the playing field. The sentinel's options were diminishing. That ploy to force Wesley's hand was his last civil gambit. As long as Wesley remained a legitimate leader, those like Wyatt, Grady, Derning, and Poe would side with him. It would be obvious to Thranic that Wesley was a pawn blocking his forward movement, one that would need to be removed. It was time to deal with Thranic.

Royce curled up to sleep with the rest of them, but selected a place hidden by a small thicket of plants. In the darkness he laid there only briefly before leaving his blanket filled with brush and melted into the jungle.

Thranic had chosen to bed down near the river, which Royce thought considerate since he intended to dispose of his body in the strong current. Royce slipped around the outside of the camp until he came to where Defoe and Levy slept, only Thranic was missing.

THE PALACE OF THE FOUR WINDS

❧

Thwack! A narrow tree trunk splintered.

At the last moment, Royce had moved. A crossbow bolt lodged itself in the wood where a second before he had been crouching.

Thranic struggled desperately to crank back the string on his weapon. "Did you think to find me in my bed?" he hissed. "Did you really think killing me would be that easy—*elf?*"

He cranked back on the gear.

"You shouldn't fear me as much as you do. I am here to help you. It is my burden to help all of you. I will cleanse the darkness in your hearts. I will free you of the burden of your disgusting, offensive life. You no longer need to be an affront to Maribor. I will save you!"

"And who will save you?" Royce replied.

He was just a few feet from where he had been. Thranic glanced down to set the bolt in the track. He lifted the bow, but when he looked up Royce was gone.

"What do you mean?" Thranic asked, hoping Royce would reveal his position.

"You see awfully well in the dark, Thranic," Royce said from his right.

Thranic turned and fired, but the bolt merely ripped through an empty thicket.

"Well, but not perfectly," Royce observed, appearing once more, but much closer. Thranic immediately began ratcheting back his bow.

He had two more bolts.

"You also managed to slip into the trees without me seeing you. And you crept up behind me. That's remarkable, indeed. How old are you, Thranic? I'll bet you're older than you look."

The sentinel loaded the bolt, looked up, but once more Royce was gone.

"What are you driving at, elf?" Thranic asked, crossbow at his hip. Backing against a tree, he peered around the jungle.

"We're alike, you and I," Royce said from behind him.

Thranic spun around. He saw movement slipping through the brush and fired. The shot went wide and he cursed. Thranic began cranking back the string once more.

"Is that why you do it?" Royce asked. "Is that why you torture elves? Tell me, are you purging them—or yourself?"

"Shut up!" Thranic's hand slipped on the gear and the string snapped back, slashing his fingers. He was shaking now.

"You can't kill the elf inside, so you torture and murder all those you find."

He was closer.

"I said shut up!"

"How much elven blood does it take to wash away the sin of *being* one yourself?"

Closer still.

"Damn you!" he screamed, fighting with the bow that refused to cooperate with his shaking fingers.

He drew the string back again only to have it jump the track and snap free. He put a foot through the loop at the bow's nose and pulled. Now it was stuck. He pressed desperately on the ratchet handle. It refused to move. *Crack!* The winch snapped.

In horror, Thranic stopped breathing as he looked down. He struggled to pull the bowstring back with just the strength of his arms. He pulled with all his might, but he could not get it to the catch. He was giving Melborn too much time. He let the bow fall to the grass and drew his dagger.

He waited. He listened. He spun. He looked.

He was alone.

THE PALACE OF THE FOUR WINDS

∾

"Get up." Hadrian woke to Royce's voice as his friend moved through the camp. He knew the tone and instantly got to his feet.

"What is it?"

"Company," Royce told him, "Wake everyone."

"What's happening?" Wesley asked groggily as the camp slowly came alive.

"Quiet," Royce whispered. He crouched with his dagger drawn, staring out into the darkness.

"Ghazel?" Grady asked.

"Something," Royce replied. "A lot of somethings."

The rest of them heard it now, twigs snapping and leaves rustling. They were all on their feet with weapons drawn.

"Backs to the river!" Wesley shouted.

Ahead of them a light appeared, then disappeared, then another blinked. Two more flickered off to the right and left and sounds of movement grew louder and closer. Dovin Thranic stumbled back into camp, causing a brief alarm. Several people looked at him oddly but said nothing.

Everyone's attention remained on sounds from the trees.

Shadowy figures carried torches within the thick weave of the jungle. Slowly they climbed out of the brush and into the clearing, around the riverbank. Twenty approached from all sides at once. At first they appeared to be strange, monstrous beasts, until they fully entered the clearing, revealing themselves as men; stocky, bull-necked brutes with white painted faces, bone armor, and headdresses of long feathers. They moved with ease through the dense brush. In their hands were crude clubs, axes, and spears. They circled in silence, creeping forward.

"We come in peace!" Hadrian heard Dilladrum shout in Tenkin, his voice sounding weak. "We have come to see Warlord Erandabon. We bear a message for him."

As they grew nearer, they began hooting and howling, shaking their weapons. Some brandished teeth, while others beat their chests or stomped naked feet.

Dilladrum repeated his statement.

One of the larger men, who carried a decorated war axe, stepped forward and approached Dilladrum. *"What message?"* the Tenkin asked in a harsh, shallow voice.

"It is a sealed letter," Dilladrum replied. *"To be given only to the warlord."*

The man eyed each of them carefully. He grinned and then nodded. *"Follow."*

It was clearly the best they could expect, although Dilladrum mopped his forehead with his sleeve as he explained the situation.

The Tenkin howled orders. Torches went out and the rest melted back into the jungle. The leader remained as they quickly broke camp. Then, with a motion for them to follow, he ran back into the trees, his torch lighting the way. He led them at a brisk pace that had everyone panting for breath—and Bulard near collapse. Dilladrum shouted forward for a rest, or at least a slower pace. The only response was laughter.

"Our new friends aren't terribly considerate of an old man." Bulard panted in between wheezing inhales.

"That's enough!" Wesley shouted, and raised a hand for them to stop. The crew of the *Emerald Storm* needed little persuasion to take a break. The Tenkin and his torch continued forward, disappearing into the trees. "If he wants to keep jogging on without us, let him!"

"He's not," Royce commented. "He's hiding in the trees up ahead with his torch out. There are also several on either side of us with more than a few to our rear."

Wesley looked around then said, "I don't see anything at all."

Royce smiled. "What good is it having an elf in your crew if you can't make use of him?"

Wesley raised an eyebrow, looked back out into the trees, then gave up altogether. He pulled the cork from his water bag, took a swig, and passed it around. Turning his attention to the historian, who sat in the dirt doubled over, he asked, "How you doing, Mister Bulard?"

Bulard's red face came up. He was sweating badly, his thin hair matted to his head. He said nothing, his mouth preoccupied with the effort of sucking in air, but he managed to offer a smile and a reassuring nod.

"Good," Wesley said, "let's proceed, but *we* will set the pace. Let's not have them exhausting us."

"Aye," Derning agreed, wiping his mouth after his turn at the water. "It would be just the thing for them to run us in circles until we collapse, then fall on us and slit our throats before we can catch our breaths."

"Maybe that's what happened to the others we spotted. Perhaps it was these blokes," Grady speculated.

"We're going somewhere," Royce replied. "I can smell the sea."

It was true. Hadrian had not noticed it until that moment, but he could taste the salt in the air. What he assumed was wind in the trees he now realized was the voice of the ocean.

"Let's continue, shall we, gentlemen?" Wesley said and moved them out. As they did, the Tenkin's torch appeared once more and moved on ahead. Wesley refused to chase it, keeping them at a comfortable pace. The torch returned and after a few more tries to coax them, gave up and matched their stride.

Travel progressed sharply downward. The route soon became a rocky trail that plummeted to the face of a cliff. Below they could hear the crashing of waves. As dawn approached, they could see their destination. A stone fortress rose high on a rocky promontory that jutted into the ocean and guarded a natural harbor hundreds of feet below the rocky edge. The Palace of the Four Winds looked ancient, weathered by wind and rain until it matched the stained and pitted face of the dark granite upon which it sat. Built of massive blocks, it was inconceivable that men could have placed such large stones. Displaying the same austerity as the Tenkins, it lacked ornamentation. Ships filled the large sheltered bay on the lee side of the point. There were hundreds, all with reefed black sails.

When they approached the great gate, their guide stopped. *"Weapons are not allowed past this point."*

Wesley scowled as Dilladrum translated, but was not surprised. This was the custom even in Avryn. One did not expect to walk armed into a lord's castle. They presented their weapons and Hadrian noted that neither Thranic nor Royce surrendered any.

Thranic had been acting oddly ever since stumbling into camp. He had not said a word and his eyes never left Royce.

They entered the fortress, where a dozen well-equipped guards looked down from ramparts while another dozen lined their route. The exterior looked nearly ruined. Stone blocks had fallen and were left broken on the ground.

Inside the castle the decor was no more cheerful. Here, too, the withering decay of centuries of neglect left the once-great edifice little more than a primordial cave. Roots and fungi grew along the corridor crevices, dead leaves clustered in corners where the swirl of drafts deposited them. Dust, dirt, and cobwebs obscured the ancient decorative carvings, sculptures, and chiseled writings.

The Tenkins had strung crude banners over the walls, long pennants that depicted a white Tenkin-style axe on a black field. Just as in Oudorro, row upon row of shields hung from the ceiling like bats in a cavern. A massive fireplace occupied one whole side of the great chamber, a massive gaping maw of a hearth in which an entire

THE PALACE OF THE FOUR WINDS

tree trunk smoldered. Upon the floor lay the skin of a tiger whose head stared with gleaming emerald eyes and yellowing fangs. A stone throne stood at the far end of the hall. The base of the chair had cracked where a vine intertwined the legs, making it list to one side, its seat was draped in a thick piling of animal skins and on it sat a wild-eyed man.

His head sported a tempest of hair jutting in all directions, long and black with streaks of white. Deep cuts and burns scarred his face. Thick brows overshadowed bright, explosive eyes that darted about rapidly, rolling in his skull like marbles struggling to free themselves from the confines of his head. He was bare-chested except for an elaborate vest of small-laced bones. His long fingers absently toyed with a large, bloodstained axe lying across his lap.

"Who is this?" the warlord asked in Tenkin, his loud disturbing voice echoed from the walls. *"Who is this that enters the hall of Erandabon unannounced and unheralded? Who treads Erandabon's forest like sheep to be gathered? Who dare seek Erandabon in his den, his holy place?"*

A strange assortment of people surrounded him, and all eyes were on the party as they entered. Toothless, tattooed men spilled drinks while women with matted hair and painted eyes swayed back and forth to unheard rhythms. One lounged naked upon a silk cushion, with a massive snake coiled about her body as she whispered to it. Beside her an old hairless man with yellow nails as long as his fingers painted curious designs on the floor, and everywhere the hall was choked with the smoke of burning tulan leaves that smoldered in a central brazier.

In the darkest shadows were others. Hadrian could barely make them out through the fog of smoke and the flickering firelight. They clustered in the dark, making faint staccato chattering sounds like the whine of cicadas. Hadrian knew that sound well. He could not see them, merely the suggestion of movement cast in shadows upon stone. They shifted nervously, anxiously, like a pack of hungry dogs, their motions jittery and too fast to be human.

Dilladrum shooed Wesley forward. Wesley took a breath and said, "I am Midshipman Wesley Belstrad, acting captain of what remains of the crew of Her Imperial Majesty's ship the *Emerald Storm,* out of Aquesta. I have a message for you, Your Lordship." He bowed deeply. It looked comical to Hadrian that a lad of such noble bearing should bow before the likes of Erandabon Gile, who was just shy of a madman.

"Long Erandabon 'as waited for vord," the man upon the throne spoke in Apelanese. "Long Erandabon 'as counted dee moons and dee stars. Dee vaves crash nightly, dee ships approach and gather, dee darkness grows, and Erandabon vaits. Sits and vaits. Vaits and sits. Dee great shadow is growing in dee north. Dee gods come once more, bringing death and horror to all. Dee undying will crush dee vorld beneath deir step, and Erandabon ez made to vait. Vere ez dis message? Speak! Speak!"

Wesley took a step forward as he pulled the letter from his coat, but paused, noticing the broken seal. As he hesitated, an overly thin man dressed in feathers and paint snatched the letter away. He growled at Wesley like a dog showing his teeth. "Not approach dee great Erandabon vis unclean 'ands!"

The feathered man handed the message to the warlord who studied it for a moment, his eyes racing madly back and forth. A terrible grin grew across his face, and he tore the note into pieces and began eating it. It did not take long, and while he ate no one said a word. With his final swallow, the warlord raised his hand and said, *"Lock them away."*

Wesley stood, stunned, as Tenkin guards, approached and grabbed him. "What's happening?" he protested. "We are officials of the Empire of Avryn! You can't—"

Gile laughed as the guard dragged them down the hall.

"Wait!" another voice bellowed. "It was arranged!" Thranic deftly dodged the guards, advancing angrily on the warlord. "My team and I are to be given safe passage. I am here to pick up a Ghazel guide who will take us safely through Grandanz Og!"

Erandabon rose to his feet and raised his axe, halting Thranic mid-step. "Veapons did you bring? Food for dee Many did you deliver to Erandabon?" the warlord shouted at him.

"It sank!" Thranic yelled back. "And the deal wasn't based on the weapons or the elves."

The chattering sounds from the darkness grew louder. The noise appeared to disturb even the Tenkin. The hairless man stopped drawing his designs and shuddered. The woman with the snake gasped.

Erandabon remained oblivious to the rise in their tenor as he gibbered in glee. "No! Based on dee open gates of Delgos! Vaat proof of dis? Vaat proof does Erandabon 'ave? You vait 'ere. You stay sealed and if Drumindor does not fall, *you* vill be food for dee Many! Erandabon decrees it! Ou are you to defy Erandabon?"

"Who are you to defy Erandabon?" chanted the crowd. The warlord waved his hand in the air and the chattering grew loud again. The guards moved in with spears.

"Now we know what the Empire has been doing with the elves they've been rounding up," Royce muttered as he ran his fingers lightly along the length of the doorjamb. Hadrian noticed Wyatt turning away sharply.

The Tenkin locked them in cells buried in the foundation of the fortress. There were no windows. The only light came from the small, barred opening of the door beyond which torches mounted in iron sconces flickered intermittently. Hadrian and Royce were fortunate enough to share a cell with Wyatt and Wesley, while the others were in similar cells within the same block. The sounds of their independent conversations echoed as indiscernible whispers.

"It's ghastly," Wesley said, collapsing on the stone floor and dropping his head in his hands. "Admittedly, I've never held any love for those of elven blood," he gave Royce and apologetic glance, "but this—this is loathsome beyond human imagining. That the Empire could sanction such a vile and dishonourable act is...is..."

"And now we also know what that fleet of ships in the bay is for," Hadrian said. "They're planning to invade Delgos, and it would appear we delivered the orders for them to attack."

"But Drumindor is impregnable from the sea," Wesley said. "Do you think this Erandabon fellow knows that? All those ships will be burned to cinders the moment they enter the bay."

"No, they won't," Royce said. "Drumindor has been sabotaged. When they vent at the next full moon there will be an explosion, destroying it, and I suspect Tur Del Fur as well. After that, the armada can sail in unopposed."

"What?" Wesley asked. "You can't possibly know that."

Royce said nothing.

"Yes, he does," Hadrian said.

Realization crossed Wesley's face. "The seal was broken. You read the letter?"

Royce continued exploring the door.

"How is it going to explode?" Hadrian asked.

"The vents have been blocked."

"No..." Hadrian shook his head. "Only Gravis knew how to do that, and he's dead."

"Merrick found out somehow. He's doing the same thing Gravis tried. He's blocked the portals. When they try to vent during the harvest moon, the gas and molten rock will have nowhere to go.

THE PALACE OF THE FOUR WINDS

The whole mountain will blow. And that's what Merrick meant about turning the tide of war for the Empire. Delgos supports the Nationalists, funded largely by Cornelius DeLur. When they eliminated Gaunt, they cut off the rebellion's head. Now they will cut out its legs. Destroying Delgos will mean the New Empire will only need to deal with Melengar."

"But those ships we saw in the harbor were not just Tenkin. The vast majority were Ghazel," Hadrian pointed out. "Gile thinks he can use them as muscle, as his attack dogs, but goblins can't be tamed. He can't control them. The Empire is handing Delgos over to the Ba Ran Ghazel. Once they entrench themselves, the goblins will become a greater threat to the Empire than the Nationalists ever were."

"I doubt Merrick cares," Royce opined.

"You stole the letter from me and read it?" Wesley asked Royce. "And you had us deliver it to the warlord knowing it would launch an invasion?"

"Are you saying you wouldn't have? Those were your orders, sanctioned by the regents themselves."

"But giving Delgos to that…that…insane man and the Ghazel, it's…it's…"

"It's your sworn duty as an officer of the Empire."

Wesley stared, aghast. "My father used to say, 'A knight draws his sword for three reasons: to defend himself, to defend the weak, and to defend his lord,' but he always added, 'Never defend yourself against the truth, never defend the weakness in others, and never defend a lord without honor.' I don't see how anyone can find honor in feeding a child to goblins or handing over a nation of men to the Ghazel horde."

"Why did you let him deliver the letter?" Hadrian asked.

THE EMERALD STORM

"I just read it tonight during the water break. It was my last chance to get a look. I figured if we showed up completely empty-handed we'd be killed right away."

"I won't be party to this...this...atrocity! We must prevent Drumindor's destruction," Wesley announced.

"You realize interfering with this would be treason?" Royce told Wesley.

"By ordering the delivery of every man, woman, and child in Tur Del Fur into the bloodthirsty hands of the Ba Ran Ghazel, the empress has committed treason to her people. It is I who remain loyal...loyal to the cause of honor."

"It might comfort you to know that it is highly unlikely that Empress Modina gave this order," Hadrian told him. "We know her—met her before she became empress. She would never sanction anything like this. I was in the palace the day before we sailed from Aquesta, and she is not in charge. The regents are the ones behind this."

"One thing's for sure, if we foil Merrick's plan we won't have to look for him anymore. He'll find us," Royce added.

"This is all my fault." Wesley sighed. "My first command, and look where it has led."

"Don't beat yourself up. You did fine." Hadrian patted him on the shoulder. "But your duty is done now. You completed the task your lord set for you. Everything after this is of your own choosing."

"Not much of a choice, I'm afraid," he said, looking around their cell.

"How long before the harvest moon?" Royce asked.

"About two weeks, I would guess," Hadrian replied.

"It would take us too long to travel back by land. How long would it take us to get there by sea, Wyatt?"

The Palace of the Four Winds

"With the wind at our backs, we'd make the trip in a fraction of the time it took us to come out. Week and a half, maybe two."

"Then we still have time."

"Time for what?" Wesley asked. "We're locked in the dungeon of a madman at the edge of the world. Merely surviving will be a feat."

"You are far too pessimistic for one so young," Royce told him.

Wesley let out a small laugh. "All right, Seaman Melborn, how do you propose we sneak down to the harbor, capture a ship loaded with Ghazel warriors, and sail it out of a bay past an armada, when we can't even get out of this locked cell?"

Royce gave the door a gentle push and it swung open. "I unlocked it while you were ranting," he said.

Wesley's face showed his astonishment. "You're not just a seaman, are you?"

"Wait here," said Royce, slipping out.

He was gone for several minutes. They heard no sound. When he returned Poe, Derning, Grady, Dilladrum, and the Vintu followed. Royce had blood on his dagger and a ring of keys in his hand.

"What about the others?" Wesley asked.

"Don't worry, I won't forget about them," Royce said with a devilish grin. When he left, the others followed. A guard lay dead in a pool of blood and Royce was already at the door of the last cell.

"We don't need to be released," Defoe said from behind the door. "I could open it myself if I wanted to get out."

"I'm not here to let you out," Royce said, opening the door.

Defoe backed up and drew his dagger.

"Stay out of this, Defoe," Royce told him. "So far you've just been doing a job. I get that, but stand between me and Thranic and it gets personal."

"Mister Melborn!" Wesley snapped. "I can't let you kill Thranic."

Royce ignored him and Wesley appealed to Hadrian, who shrugged in response. "It's a policy of mine not to get in his way, especially when the other guy deserves it."

Wesley turned to Wyatt, whose expression showed no compassion. "He burned a shipload of elves and, for all I know, was responsible for taking my daughter. Let him die."

Doctor Levy stepped aside, leaving Thranic alone at the back of the cell with only his dagger for protection. By his grip and stance, Hadrian knew the sentinel was not a knife fighter. The sentinel was sweating, his eyes tense as Royce moved in.

"Might I ask why you're killing Mister Thranic?" Bulard asked suddenly, stepping between them. "Those of you intent on fleeing could make better use of your time than butchering a man in his cell, don't you think?"

"Won't take but a second," Royce assured him.

"Perhaps, perhaps, but I ask you not to. I am not saying he does not deserve death, but who are you to grant it? Thranic will die, and quite soon, I suspect, given where we are headed. Regardless, our mission is vital not just to the Empire, but to all of mankind, and we will need Thranic if we are to have any hope to complete it."

"Shut up, you old fool," the sentinel growled.

This caught Royce's attention, though he kept his eyes on Thranic. "What mission?"

"To find a very old and very important relic called the Horn of Gylindora that will be needed very soon, I'm afraid."

"The horn?" Hadrian repeated.

"Yes, given our precarious situation, I don't think it wise to give you a history lesson just now, but suffice to say it is in all of our best interest to leave Thranic alive—for now."

"Sorry," Royce replied, "but you'll just have to make do without—"

THE PALACE OF THE FOUR WINDS

The door to the cellblock opened and a pair of soldiers with meal plates stepped in. A quick glance at the dead guard and they ran.

Royce sprinted after them. Defoe quickly closed his cell door again.

"Go, all of you!" Bulard urged.

The party ran out of the cellblock and up the stairs. By the time they reached the top, the hallway was filled with loud voices.

"They got away," Royce grumbled.

"We gathered that from the shouting," Hadrian said.

They faced a four-way intersection of identical narrow stone corridors. Wall-mounted flames burned from iron cradles staggered at long intervals, leaving large sections of shifting shadows.

Royce glanced back toward the cellblock and cursed under his breath. "That's what I get for hesitating."

"Any idea which way now?" Wyatt asked.

"This way," Royce said.

He led them, trotting rapidly then stopped, abruptly motioning everyone into a doorway. Moments later a troop of guards rushed by. Wesley started forward and Royce hauled him back. Two more guards passed.

"*Now*, we go," he told them, "but stay *behind* me."

Royce continued along the multitude of corridors and turns, pausing from time to time. They climbed two more sets of stairs and dodged another group of soldiers. Hadrian saw the wonderment reflected in the party's faces at Royce's skill. It was as if he could see through walls, or knew the location of every guard. For Hadrian it was nothing new, but even he was impressed at their progress given that Royce was towing a parade.

A door unexpectedly opened and several Tenkins literally bumped into Dilladrum and one of the Vintu. Terrified, Dilladrum fled down a corridor, the Vintu following. The stunned Tenkins were not warriors, and were as scared as Dilladrum and retreated inside. Royce shouted for Dilladrum to stop, but it was no use.

"Damn it!" Royce cursed, chasing after them. The rest of the crew raced to keep up as they ran blindly through corridor after corridor. Rounding a corner Hadrian nearly ran into Royce, whose way was blocked by Tenkin warriors. The dead bodies of Dilladrum and the Vintu lay on the floor, blood pooling across the stone. Behind them, a small army cut off their retreat.

"Who are you to defy Erandabon?" chanted the crowd of Tenkin warriors.

"Get back!" Hadrian ordered, pushing Wesley and the others into a niche that afforded a small amount of defense. He pulled a torch from the wall and together with Royce formed a forward defense.

The Tenkin soldiers charged, screaming as they attacked.

Royce appeared to dodge the advance, but the foremost warrior fell dead. Hadrian drove the flame of his torch into the second Tenkin's face. Using his feet, Royce flipped the dead man's sword to Hadrian, who caught it in time to decapitate the next challenger.

Two Tenkins charged Royce, who simply was not where they expected him to be when they arrived. His movements were a blur, and two more collapsed. Hadrian advanced as Royce kicked the dead men's weapons behind to where Wyatt, Derning, and Wesley picked them up. Hadrian stood at the center now.

Three attacked. Three fell dead.

The rest retreated, bewildered, and Hadrian picked up a second blade.

Clap! Clap! Clap!

The warlord walked toward them, applauding and grinning. "Galenti, et ez you. So good to 'ave you back!"

Chapter 18

THE POT OF SOUP

A milia sulked in the kitchen, head in her hands, elbows resting on the baker's table. This was where it all started, when Modina's former secretary brought her to the kitchen for a lesson in table manners. Remembering the terror of those early days, it was staggering to realize those were better times.

Now a witch hid in Modina's room, filling the empress's head with nonsense. She was a foreigner, and the princess of an enemy kingdom, who spent more time with Modina than Amilia. She could be manipulating the empress in any number of ways. She tried to reason with Modina, but no matter what Amilia said the girl remained adamant about helping the witch find Degan Gaunt.

Amilia preferred the old days, when Modina left everything to her. Sitting there, she wondered what she should do. She wanted to go to Saldur and report the woman, but knew that would hurt Modina. The empress might never recover from a betrayal, especially from Amilia, whom she trusted implicitly. The loss would surely crush her fragile spirit, and Amilia saw disaster at the end of every path. She felt as if she were in a runaway carriage racing toward a cliff, with no way to reach the reins.

"How about I make you some soup?" Ibis Thinly asked her. The big man stood in his stained apron stirring a large, steaming pot into which he threw bits of celery.

"I'm too miserable to eat," she replied.

"It can't be as bad as all that, can it?"

"You have no idea. She's become a handful and then some. I'm actually afraid to leave her alone. Every time I walk out of her room, I'm frightened something terrible will happen."

It was late and they were the only two in the scullery. Long shadows traced up the far wall cast by the flames of the cook's hearth. The kitchen was warm and pleasant, except for a foul smell coming from the bubbling broth Ibis cooked on the stove.

"Oh, it can't be as bad as all that. Come on, can't I interest you in some soup? I make a pretty mean vegetable barley, if I do say so myself."

"You know I love your food. It's just that my stomach is in knots. I noticed a gray hair in the mirror the other day."

"Oh please, you're still just a girl," Ibis laughed, catching himself. "I guess I shouldn't speak to you that way, you being noble and all. I should be saying, 'Yes, Your Ladyship,' or in this case, 'no, no, Your Ladyship! If you will allow me to be so bold as to speak plainly in your presence. I beg to differ, for I think you are purty as a pot!' That would be a more proper response."

Amilia smiled. "You know, I never have understood that saying of yours."

Ibis drew himself up in feigned offense. "I'm a cook. I like pots." He chuckled. "Have some soup. Something warm in your belly will help untie some of those knots, eh?"

She glanced at the pot he was stirring and grimaced. "I don't think so."

"Oh, no, not this. Great Maribor, no! I'll make you something good."

Amilia looked relieved. "What is that you're making? It smells like rotten eggs."

"Soup, but it's barely fit for animals, made with all the worst parts of old leftovers. The smell comes from this horrid yellow powder I have to use. I try to dress it up as best I can. I throw some celery and spices in, just to ease my conscience."

"Who's it for?"

"I have no idea but in a little while a couple of guards will come by and take it. To be honest...I'm afraid to ask where it goes." He paused. "Amilia, what's wrong."

Amilia stared at the big pot, her mouth partially open. Noise on the stairs caught her attention. Two men entered the kitchen. She knew them by sight. They were guards normally assigned to the east wing's fourth-floor hall—the administration corridor, where she and Saldur worked. They recognized her as well and took a moment to bow. Amilia graciously inclined her head in response. Their looks revealed they found this courtesy odd but appreciated. Then they turned to Ibis.

"All done?"

"Just a sec, just a sec," he muttered. "You're early."

"We've been on duty since dawn," one of the guards complained. "This is the last job of the night. Honestly, I don't know why you put such effort into it, Thinly."

"It's what I do, and I want it done right."

"Trust me, no one is going to complain. Nobody cares."

"*I* care," Ibis remarked, his voice sharp enough to end the subject.

The guard shrugged his shoulders and waited.

"Who's the soup for?" Amilia asked.

The guard hesitated. "Not really supposed to talk about that, milady."

The other guard gave him a rough nudge. "She's the bloody Secretary to the Empress."

The first one blushed. "Forgive me, milady. It's just that Regent Saldur can be a little scary sometimes."

Amilia agreed in her head but externally remained aloof.

His friend slapped himself in the forehead rolling his eyes. "Blimey, James, you're a fool. Forgive him, milady."

"What?" James looked puzzled. "What'd I say?"

The guard shook his head sadly. "You just insulted the regent and admitted you don't respect Her Ladyship all in one breath."

James' face drained of color.

"What's your name?" she asked him.

"Higgles, milady." He swallowed hard and bowed again.

"Why don't *you* answer my question then?"

"We takes the soup to the north tower. You know, the one 'tween the well and the stables."

"How many prisoners are there?"

The two guards looked at each other. "None that we know of, milady."

"So, who is the soup for?"

He shrugged. "We just leave it with the Seret Knight."

"Soup's done," Ibis declared.

"Is that all, milady?" Higgles asked.

She nodded and the two disappeared out the door to the courtyard, each holding one of the pot's handles.

"Now, let me make *you* something." Ibis said, wiping his big hands on his apron.

"Huh?" Amilia asked, still thinking about the two guards. "No thanks, Ibis," she said, getting up. "There's something I need to do, I think."

THE POT OF SOUP

❧

The lack of a cloak became painfully uncomfortable when Amilia was halfway across the inner ward. The weather had jumped from a friendly autumn of brightly colored leaves, clear blue skies, and crisp nights to the gray, icy cold of pre-winter. A half moon glimmered through hazy clouds as she stepped through the vegetable garden, now no more than a graveyard of brown dirt. She approached the chicken coop carefully, trying to avoid disturbing the hens. There was nothing wrong with being out, no rules against wandering the ward at night, but at that moment she felt sinister.

She ducked into the woodshed just as James and Higgles passed by on their return journey. After several minutes, Amilia crept forward, slipped around the well and entered the northeast tower—the *prison tower* as she now dubbed it.

Just as described, a Seret Knight stood at attention dressed in black armor with the red symbol of a broken crown on his chest. Decorated with a red feather plume, the helm he wore covered his face. He appeared not to notice her, which was odd, as all guards bowed to Amilia now. The seret said nothing as she stepped around him toward the stairs. She was shocked when he made no move to stop her.

Up she went, periodically passing cells. None of the doors were locked, and she pushed some open and stepped inside. Each room was small. Old, rotted straw lay scattered across the ground. Tiny windows allowed only a fraction of moonlight to enter. There were heavy chains mounted to the walls and the floor. Some had a stool or bucket, but most were bare of any furniture. Amilia felt uncomfortable while in the rooms. It was not just the cold, it was the thought that she might end up in just such a place.

James and Higgles were correct; the tower was empty.

She returned down the steps to the seret. "Excuse me, but what are you guarding? There is no one here."

He did not respond.

"Where did the soup go?"

Again, the seret stood mute. Unable to see his eyes through the helm, and thinking perhaps he was asleep while standing up, she took a step closer. The seret moved and, as fast as a snake, his hand grabbed hold of his sword and drew it partway from its scabbard, allowing the metal to hiss, a sound that echoed ominously in the stone tower.

Amilia fled.

"Are you going to tell her?" Nimbus asked.

The two were in Amilia's office finishing the last of the invitation lists for the scribes to begin working on. Parchments were everywhere. On the wall hung a layout of the Great Hall, perforated with countless pinholes from the shifting of guest positions.

"No, I will not add to that witch's arsenal of insanity with tales of mysterious disappearing pots of soup! I've worked for months to put Modina back together. I won't allow her to be broken again."

"But what if—"

"Drop it, Nimbus." Amilia shuffled through her scrolls. "I should never have told you. I went. I looked. I saw nothing. I can't believe I even did that much. Maribor help me. The witch even had me out in the dark chasing her phantoms. What are you grinning at?"

"Nothing," Nimbus said. "I just have this impression of you slinking around the courtyard."

"Oh, stop it!"

"Stop what?" Saldur asked as he entered unannounced.

THE POT OF SOUP

The regent swept into her office and looked at each of them with a disarming smile.

"Nothing, Your Grace, Nimbus was merely having a little joke."

"Nimbus? Nimbus?" Saldur repeated while eyeing the man, trying to recall something.

"He's my assistant, and Modina's tutor, a refugee from Vernes," Amilia explained.

Saldur looked annoyed. "I'm not an idiot, Amilia, I know who Nimbus is. I was thinking about the name. The word is from the old Imperial tongue. Nimbus, unless I am mistaken, it means mist or cloud, isn't that right?" He looked at Nimbus for acknowledgement, but he merely shrugged apologetically. "Well, anyway," Saldur addressed Amilia. "I wanted to know how things were proceeding for the wedding. It is only a few months away."

"I was just sending these invitations to the scribes. I have them ordered by distance so those living the farthest away should have couriers leaving as early as next week."

"Excellent, and the dress?"

"I finally got the design decided. We're just waiting for material to be delivered from Colnora."

"And how is Modina coming along?"

"Fine, fine," she lied, smiling as best she could.

"She took the news of her wedded bliss well then?"

"Modina receives all news pretty much the same way."

Saldur nodded at her pleasantly. "Yes, true...true." He appeared so grandfatherly, so kind and gentle. It would be so easy to trust him if she had not seen first-hand the volcano that lurked beneath that warm surface. He brought her back to reality when he asked, "What were you doing in the northeast tower last night, my dear?"

She bit her tongue just in time to stop herself from replying with total honesty. "I bumped into some guards delivering soup there in the middle of the night, which I thought odd, because..."

"Because what?" Saldur pressed.

"Because there's no one in the tower. Well, besides a seret who appears to be standing guard over nothing. Do you know what that's all about?" she asked, pleased with how she managed to reinforce her innocence by casually turning the tables on the old man. She even considered batting her eyes, but did not want to push it. Memories of Saldur ordering the guard to "take her out of my sight" still rang in her head. She did not know what that order really meant, but she remembered the regret in the guard's eyes as he approached her.

"Of course I do. I am regent—I know *everything* that goes on."

"The thing is…that was quite a lot of soup for one knight. And it vanished, pot and all, in just a few minutes. But since you already know, I suppose it doesn't matter."

Saldur studied her silently for a moment. His expression was no longer the familiar one of condescension. She detected a faint hint of respect forming beneath his wrinkled brows.

"I see," he replied at length. He glanced over his shoulder at Nimbus, who was smiling back as innocent as a puppy. To her chagrin, Amilia noticed that he did bat his eyes. Saldur took no apparent notice of his antics, then reminded her not to seat the Duke and Lady Rochelle next to the Prince of Alburn before withdrawing from her office.

"That was creepy," Nimbus mentioned after Saldur left. "You poke your head in the tower and the next morning Saldur knows about it?"

Amilia paced the length of her office, which only allowed her a few steps each way before having to turn, but it was better than standing still. Nimbus was right. Something strange was going on with the tower, something that Saldur himself kept careful watch over. She struggled to think of alternatives, but her mind kept coming back to one name—Degan Gaunt.

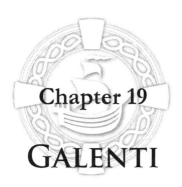

Chapter 19

GALENTI

The corridor outside the Great Hall in the Palace of the Four Winds was deathly silent as the small band remained huddled in the niche. All of the *Emerald Storm's* party now held swords salvaged from slain Tenkins, each one made from Avryn steel. Warriors took strategic positions, armed with Imperial-crafted crossbows, while the bulk of the Tenkin fighters moved back to allow them clear lines of sight. Clustered in a tight group, Hadrian's party made an easy target.

Erandabon stepped forward, but not so far as to block the path of the archers. "Erandabon did not recognize you, Galenti! Et 'as been many years, but you 'ave not lost your skill," he said, looking down at the bodies of his fallen warriors. "Vie travel vis such creatures as deez, Galenti? Vie suffer dee 'umiliation? It voud be dee same for Erandabon to slizzer on dee forest floor vis dee snakes, or vallow vis dee pigs. Vie do you do dis? Vie?"

"I came to see you, Gile," Hadrian replied. Instantly there was a gasp in the hall.

"Ha-ha!" The warlord laughed. "You use my Calian name, a crime for vich dee punishment ez death, but I pardon you, Galenti!

For you are not like deez." He waved his hand, gesturing vaguely. "You are in dee cosmos vis Erandabon. You are a star in dee 'eavens shining nearly as bright as Erandabon. You are a brother and I vill not kill you. You must come and feast vis me."

"And my friends?"

Erandabon's face soured. "Dey 'ave no place at dee table of Erandabon, dey are dogs."

"I will not eat with you if they are ill-treated."

Erandabon's eyes moved about wildly in random circles, then stopped. "Erandabon vill 'ave dem locked up again—safely dis time—for deir own good. And you vill eat vis Erandabon?"

"I will."

He clapped his hands and warriors tentatively moved forward.

Hadrian nodded and Royce and the others laid down their weapons.

The balcony looked out over the bay from a dizzying height. Moonlight revealed the vast fleet of Ghazel and Tenkin ships anchored in the harbor. Dotted with lights, the vessels bobbed on soft swells. Distant shouts rose with the cool breeze and arrived as faint whispers. Like the rest of the castle, the balcony was a relic of a forgotten time. While perhaps beautiful long ago, the stone railing had weathered over centuries to a dull, vague reminder of its previous glory. A lush covering of vines blanketed it with blooming white flowers the way a cloth might disguise a marred table. Beneath their feet, once-stunning mosaic tiles lay dirty, chipped, and broken. Several oil lanterns circled the balcony but appeared to be more for decoration than illumination. On a stone table lay a massive feast of wild animals, fruits, and drink.

GALENTI

"Sit! Sit and eat!" Erandabon told Hadrian as several Tenkin women and young boys hurried about, seeing to their every need. Aside from the servants, the two were alone. Erandabon tore a leg from a large roasted bird and gestured with it toward the bay. "A beautiful sight, eh, Galenti? Five 'undred ships, fifty 'zousand soldiers, and all of dem under Erandabon's command."

"There are not fifty thousand Tenkin in all of Calis," Hadrian replied. He looked at the food on the table dubiously, wondering if elf was somewhere on the menu. He selected a bit of sliced fruit.

"No," the warlord said, regretfully. "Erandabon must make do vis dee Ghazel. Dey are like ants spilling out of deir island holes. Erandabon cannot trust dem any more dan Erandabon can trust a tiger, even if Erandabon raised it from a cub. Dey are vild beasts, but Erandabon needs dem to reach dee goal."

"And what is that?"

"Drumindor," he said simply, and followed the word with a swallow of wine, much of which spilled unnoticed down the front of his chin. "Erandabon needs a shelter from dee storm, Galenti, a strong place to veather it. For centuries dee Ghazel 'ave known dat only Drumindor can stand against dee vinds about to blow. Dis ez vie dey 'ave struggled so 'ard to take et. Time ez running out, dee sand spills from dee glass and dey are desperate to flee dee islands. Erandabon could 'ave fifty 'zousand, perhaps 'undred 'zousand. Ants, Galenti, dey are everywhere in deez isles. Erandabon vill make do vis deez, too many ants spoil a picnic, eh, Galenti?" he laughed.

A servant refilled the wine glass that Hadrian had barely touched.

"What do you know about Merrick Marius?" Hadrian asked.

Erandabon spat, "'E is dirt, or pig, or pig in dirt. 'E promise weapons…dere is none. 'E promise food for dee Many…and dere is none. 'E vill make it 'ard for Erandabon to control dee ants. I vish 'e vas dead."

"I might be able to help you with that, if you tell me where he is."

The warlord laughed. "Oh, Galenti, you voud do dis for you I dink, not for Erandabon. But Erandabon does not know vere 'e ez."

"Do you expect him to visit again?" Hadrian pressed.

"No, dere be no need. Erandabon vill not be 'ere long. Dis place ez old. Et ez not good." He rolled a fallen block of granite from the balcony. "Erandabon and 'is ants vill go to dee great fortress vere even dee Old Ones cannot reach us. Erandabon vill vatch dee return of dee gods and dee burning of dee vorld. You could 'ave a seat beside Erandabon. You could lead dee ants."

Hadrian shook his head. "Drumindor will be destroyed. There will be no fortress for you and your ants. If you release me and my friends we can stop this from happening."

Erandabon roared a great laugh. "Galenti, you make big joke. You dink Erandabon is dumb like dee ants? Vie do you try to tell me such lies? You vill say anything to leave 'ere vis your dog friends."

He finished off the leg by ripping the meat from the bone and chewed it with an open mouth, spitting out bits of gristle.

"Galenti, you offer Erandabon so much 'elp. You must see 'ow great Erandabon ez and vish to please me. Erandabon likes dis. I know of someting you can do to please Erandabon."

"What is that?"

"Dere is a Ghazel chieftain, called Uzla Bar." He spat on the ground. "'E defies Erandabon. 'As even challenged Erandabon for control of dee ants. Now vis no food for dee Many, 'e be big problem for Erandabon. Uzla Bar attacks caravans from Avryn, stealing dee veapons and the Many's food to veaken Erandabon in dee eyes of dee ants. Uzla Bar challenge Erandabon to fight. But Erandabon ez no fool. Erandabon knows none of 'is varriors can vin against dee speed and strength of dee Ba Ran Ghazel. But den dee stars shine on Erandabon and bring you 'ere."

"You want me to fight him?"

"Dee challenge ez by Ghazel tradition. Dey are clan, not single fighters. Dey do not fight one to one. For dem single combat ez not known. Dee battle will be five against five in dee arena."

"Who will I be fighting with? You?"

He shook his head and laughed. "Erandabon does not dirty 'is 'ands so."

"Your warriors?"

"Vie should Erandabon use Tenkin Varriors. Erandabon need dem to control dee ants. I saw dose dogs dat you lead. Dey fight good. Ven backed in a corner, Erandabon saw dee bravery in deir eyes. Dey vill do vell vis you to lead dem. Erandabon knows you 'ave succeeded in dee arena vis lesser men. And if you lose—Erandabon ez same as before."

"And why would I do this?"

"Did you not offer to 'elp Erandabon, twice already?" he paused. "I can see you like your dogs. But you and dem keel many of my men. For dat you must die. But…if you do dis…Erandabon vill let you live. Do dis, Galenti, dee 'eavens voud be less bright vis out all etz stars."

Hadrian pretended to consider the proposal in silence. He waited so long that Erandabon became agitated. It was obvious the warlord had nearly as much riding on this fight as Hadrian did.

"You answer Erandabon now!"

Hadrian remained quiet for a few moments longer and then said, "If we win, I want our immediate release. You will not hold us until the full moon. I want a ship, a small, fast ship, fully provisioned and waiting the moment the battle is won."

"Done."

"I also want you to look into finding an elven girl who is called Allie. She may have been brought with the last shipment from Avryn. If she is alive, I want her brought here."

Erandabon looked doubtful, but nodded.

"I want my companions freed, treated well, and all of our weapons and gear returned to us immediately."

"I vill 'ave dee dogs you fought vis brought 'ere so you can feast vis dem veen I am gone. Along vis vaat other veapons you might need."

"And the others?"

"Dey did not keel my men, but I 'ave deal vis dem. I 'old dem until deal ez done. All goes vell—I send dem on deir vey. Deal no good, dey go to dee Ghazel. Do vee have a deal?"

"Yes. I agree."

"Excellent, Erandabon ez very 'appy. I get to see Galenti fight in my arena once more." Erandabon clapped twice and warriors appeared on the balcony each reverently carrying one of Hadrian's three swords. More approached with the rest of their gear. Erandabon took Hadrian's spadone and lifted it.

"Erandabon 'as 'eard of your famous sword. Et ez an old veapon of dee ancient style."

"It's a family heirloom."

The warlord gave it to Hadrian. "Dis," the warlord said, picking up Royce's dagger, "Dis Erandabon 'as never seen dee like. Does it belong to dee small one? Dee one ou fought next to you?"

"Yes." Hadrian saw the greed in Erandabon's eyes. "That's Alverstone. You don't even want to think of keeping *that* weapon."

"You vill not fight if Erandabon does?"

"That too," Hadrian told him.

"Dat one ez a *kaz*?"

"Yes, and as you saw he is a good fighter. I need him and his weapon." Hadrian strapped his swords back on, feeling more like himself again.

"So, dee Tiger of Mandalin vill fight for Erandabon."

"It looks that way," Hadrian said, then sighed.

"So, two sit the battle out?" Royce asked, checking over his dagger.

The sun had risen on a gray day. The seven of them ate together on the balcony. The food—leftovers from the warlord—was now suitable for the dogs.

Hadrian nodded. "I was thinking Wesley and Poe ought to be the ones, they're the youngest—"

"We'll draw lots," Wesley declared firmly.

"Wesley, you've never fought the Ba Ran Ghazel before. They are extremely dangerous. They're stronger than men, faster, too. To disarm them you literally have to, well, disarm them."

"We'll draw lots," Wesley repeated, and finding a dead branch snapped seven twigs—two shorter than the others.

"I have to fight, it's part of the deal," Hadrian said.

Wesley nodded and tossed one of the long twigs away.

"I'm fighting too," Royce told him.

"We need to do this fairly," Wesley protested.

"If Hadrian fights, so do I," the thief declared.

Hadrian nodded. "So, it will be between you five."

Wesley hesitated then threw aside another twig and held his fist out. Wyatt pulled the first stick, a long one. Poe drew next and got the first short twig. He showed no emotion and simply stepped back.

Grady drew—a long one. Derning drew last, receiving the other short stick and leaving the last long twig in Wesley's fist.

"When do we fight?"

"Tomorrow at sunset," Hadrian explained. "Ghazel prefer to fight in the dark. That gives us the day to plan, practice a few things, and take a quick nap before facing them."

"I don't think I can sleep," Wesley told them.

"Best give it a try anyway."

"I've never even seen a Ghazel," Grady admitted. "What are we talking about here?"

"Well," Hadrian began, "they have deadly fangs, and if given the chance will hold you down and rip with their teeth and claws. The Ghazel have no qualms about eating you alive. In fact, they relish it."

"So they're animals?" Wyatt asked. "Like bears or something?"

"Not really. They're also intelligent and proficient with weapons." He let this sink in a moment before continuing, "They're usually short-looking, but that's misleading. They walk hunched over and can stand up to our height, or taller. They are strong and fast and can see well in the dark. The biggest problem—"

"There's a bigger problem?" Royce asked.

"Yeah, funny that, but you see the Ghazel are clan fighters, so they're organized. A clan is a group of five made up of a chief, a warrior, an oberdaza, a finisher, and a range. The chief is usually not as good a fighter as the warrior. And don't confuse a Ghazel oberdaza with a Tenkin. The Ghazel version wields real magic, dark magic, and he should be the first one we target to kill. They won't know we are aware of his importance, so that might give us an edge."

"Leave him to me," Royce announced.

"The finisher is the fastest of the group, and it will be his job to kill us while the warriors and oberdaza keep us busy. The range will be armed with a trilon, the Ghazel version of a bow, and maybe throwing knives as well. He will likely stay near the oberdaza. The trilon isn't terribly accurate, but it's fast. His job won't be so much to kill us as to distract. You will want to keep your shield arm facing him."

"Will we have shields?" Grady asked.

"Good point." Hadrian looked over the weapons provided. "No, I don't see any. Well look at it this way, that's one less thing to worry about, right? The clan is well organized and experienced. They will communicate through clicks and chattering that will be gibberish to us, but they can understand everything we say. We'll use that to our advantage."

"How do we win?" Wyatt asked.

"By killing all of them before they kill all of us."

They spent the morning hours sparring and practicing. Luckily, they were all adept with basic combat. Wesley had trained with his brother, and as a result was a far better swordsman than Hadrian expected. Grady was tough and surprisingly fast. Wyatt was the most impressive. His ability with a cutlass showed real skill, the kind Hadrian recognized instantly as something he called *killing experience*.

Hadrian demonstrated some basic moves to counter likely scenarios. Most dealt with parrying multiple attacks, like those from both mouths and claws, something none of them had any training in. He also showed them how to use the trilon Erandabon provided, and each took their turn, with Grady showing the most promise.

Hungry after the morning's practice, they sat to eat once more.

"So, what's our battle plan?" Wyatt asked.

"Wesley and Grady will stay to the rear. Grady, you're on the trilon."

He looked nervous, "I'll do the best I can."

"That's fine, just don't aim anywhere near the rest of us. Ignore the battle in the center of the arena and concentrate your arrows on the oberdaza and the range. Keep them off balance as much as possible. You don't have to hit them, just keep them ducking.

"Wesley, you protect Grady. Wyatt, you and I will form the front and engage the warrior and chief. Just remember your line and stay away from him. Questions?"

If there were any, no one spoke up, so they all bedded down for a nap. After the workout even Wesley managed to fall asleep.

The arena was a large oval open-air pit surrounded by a stone wall, behind which tiers of spectators rose. Two gates at opposite ends provided entrance to opposing teams. Giant braziers mounted on poles illuminated the area. The dirt killing field, like everything else at the Palace of the Four Winds, had suffered from neglect. Large blocks of stone had fallen and small trees grew around them. Near the center a shallow, muddy pool formed. A partially hidden ribcage glimmered eerily in the firelight, and a skull hung from a pike that protruded from the earth.

Walking out, Hadrian's mind reeled with memories. The scent of blood and the cheering crowd opened a door he had thought locked forever. He was only seventeen the first time he entered an arena, yet his training made victory a certainty. He was the more knowledgeable, the more skilled, and the crowds loved him. He defeated opponent after opponent with ease. Larger, stronger men challenged him and died. When he fought teams of two and three, the results were always the same. The crowds began to chant his new name, Galenti—*killer*.

He traveled throughout Calis meeting with royalty, eating at banquets held in his honor, and sleeping with women given in tribute. He entertained his hosts with displays of skill and prowess. Eventually the battles became macabre. Multiple strong men were not enough. They tested him on Ghazel and wild animals. He fought boars, a pair of leopards, and finally the tiger.

He had killed scores of men in the arena without a thought, but the tiger in Mandalin was the last. Perhaps the blood he spilled finally soaked in, or he had grown older and matured beyond his desire for fame. Even now he was unsure what was the truth and what he merely wanted to believe. Regardless, everything changed when the tiger died.

Each man he fought had a choice, but not the cat. As he watched the regal beast die, for the first time he felt like a murderer. In the stands above, the crowd shouted *Galenti!* The meaning never sank in until that moment. His father's words reached him at last, but Danbury would die before Hadrian could apologize. Like the tiger, his father deserved better.

Now, as he entered the arena, the crowd once again shouted the name—*Galenti!* They cheered and stomped their feet like thunder. "Remember, Mister Wesley, stay back and guard Grady," Hadrian said, as they gathered not far from where the skull hung.

The far gate opened and into the arena came the Ba Ran Ghazel. Hadrian could tell from his friends' shocked expressions that even after his description they never expected what now came toward them. Everyone had heard tall tales of hideous goblins, but no one really expected to see one, much less five, scurrying in full battle regalia illuminated by the flickering red glow of giant torch fires.

They were not human, not animal, nor anything at all familiar. They did not appear to be of the same world. Movements defied eyesight, muscles flexed unnaturally. They drifted across the ground on all fours. Rather than walk, they skittered, their claws clicking on the stones in the dirt. Their eyes flashed in the darkness, lit from within, a sickly yellow glow rising behind an oval pupil. Muscles rippled along hunched backs and arms as thick as a man's thigh. Their mouths were filled with row upon row of needle-sharp teeth that spilled out each side as if there was not enough room to contain them.

The warrior and the chief advanced to the center. They were large, and even hunched over they still towered above Hadrian and Wyatt. Behind them the smaller oberdaza, decorated in dozens of multicolored feathers, danced and hummed.

"I thought they were supposed to be smaller," Wyatt whispered to Hadrian.

"Ignore it, they're puffing themselves up like frogs—trying to intimidate you—make you think you can't win."

"They're doing a good job."

"The warrior is on the left, the chief is on the right," Hadrian told him. "Let me take the warrior, you have the chief. Try to stay on his left side, swing low, and don't get too close. He'll likely kill you if you do, and watch for arrows from the range."

From the walls a flaming arrow struck the center of the field, and the moment it did, drums began to beat.

"That's our cue," Hadrian said, and walked forward along with Royce and Wyatt.

The Ghazel chief and warrior waited for them at the center. Each held a short, curved blade and a small, round shield. They hissed at Hadrian and Wyatt as they approached. Wyatt had his cutlass drawn, but Hadrian purposely walked to meet them with his weapons sheathed. This brought a look from Wyatt.

"It's my way of puffing up."

Before they reached the center of the arena, Hadrian had lost track of Royce, who veered away into a shadow between the glow of bonfires.

"When do we start?" Wyatt asked.

"Listen for the sound of the horn."

This comment was overheard by the chief, causing him to smile. He chattered to the warrior, who chattered back.

"They can't understand us, right?" Wyatt recited his line.

"Of course not," Hadrian lied. "They're just dumb animals. Remember, we want to draw them forward so Royce can slip up behind the chief and kill him. He's the one we need to kill first. He's their leader. Without him, they will all fall apart. Just step back as you fight, and he will follow you right into the trap."

More chattering.

Two more flaming arrows whistled and struck the ground.

"Get ready," Hadrian whispered, then very slowly drew both swords.

A horn sounded from the stands.

Wesley watched as Hadrian and the warrior slammed into one another, metal hissing. Wyatt, however, shuffled back like a dancer, his cutlass held up and ready. The chief stood still. Instead, he turned and sniffed the air.

Grady promptly let loose the first of his arrows. He aimed at the distant pile of dancing feathers, but greatly overshot. "Damn," he cursed, working to fit another in the string.

"Lower your aim," Wesley snapped.

"I never said I was a marksman, did I?"

Something hissed unseen by Wesley's ear. Grady fired a second shot. It landed too short, coming close to where Wyatt feinted trying to persuade the chief to follow him.

Hissing whistled by again.

"I think they're shooting their arrows at us," Wesley said, turning just in time to see Grady collapse with a black shaft buried in his chest. He hit the ground coughing and kicking. His hands struggled to reach the arrow. His fingers went limp, his hands flapped on the ends of his wrists. He flailed on the dirt, spitting blood, struggling to breathe. A third arrow hissed and struck Grady in the boot. His leg struggled to recoil, but his foot was pinned to the ground.

Wesley stared at him in horror as Grady shuddered, then fell still.

Royce was already close to the oberdaza when the horn sounded. The clash of steel let him know the fight was on. He had slipped around one of the shattered stone blocks trying to find a position behind the witch doctor, when the air felt wrong. It was no longer blowing, but bouncing—hitting something unseen. A quick glance at the field revealed only four Ghazel, the chief, the warrior, the oberdaza, and the range. Royce ducked just in time to avoid a slit throat. He spun, cutting air with Alverstone. Turning, he found himself alone. On instinct, he dodged right. Something cut through his cloak. He thrust back his elbow and was rewarded with a solid, meaty thump. Then it was gone again.

Royce spun completely around, but he could see nothing.

In the center of the arena Hadrian battled with the warrior while Wyatt taunted the chief, who was still reluctant to engage. The range fired arrow after arrow. Beside him, the oberdaza danced and sang.

GALENTI

Intuition told Royce to move again, only he was too late. Thick, heavy arms gripped him as the weight of a body drove him forward. His feet slipped and he fell, pulled down to the bloodstained earth. He turned his blade and stabbed, but it passed through thin air. He could feel clawed hands trying to pin him. Royce twisted like a snake, depriving his attacker of a firm grip. Royce repeatedly cut at the shadowy thing, but nothing connected. Then he felt the hot breath of the Ghazel finisher.

His stroke glanced off the Ghazel's shield. Hadrian thrust with his other sword, but found it blocked by an excellent parry. The warrior was good. Hadrian had not anticipated his skill. He was strong and fast, but more importantly, more frighteningly, the Ghazel anticipated Hadrian's moves perfectly. The warrior stabbed and Hadrian dodged back and to the left. The Ghazel bashed his face with his shield, having started his swing even before Hadrian turned. It was as if he was reading his mind. Hadrian staggered backward, putting distance between them to catch his breath.

Above, the crowd booed their displeasure with Galenti. Beside him, Wyatt was still playing with the chief. His ruse had bought the helmsman time. The chief was too afraid of Royce to engage, but it would not last long. Hadrian needed to finish his opponent quickly, only now he was not even certain he could win.

The warrior advanced and swung. Hadrian spun to the left. Once more, the Ghazel anticipated his move and cut Hadrian across the arm. He staggered back and dodged behind a large fallen block, keeping it between himself and his opponent.

The crowd booed and stomped their feet.

Something was very wrong. The warrior should not be this good. His form was bad, his strokes lacking expertise, yet he was beating him. The warrior attacked again. Hadrian took a step back and his foot caught on a rock and he stumbled. Once more, the Ghazel appeared to foresee this and was ready with a kick that sent Hadrian into the dirt.

He lay flat on his back. The warrior screamed a cry of victory and raised his sword for a downward, penetrating kill. Hadrian started to twist left to dodge the thrust, but at the last minute, while still concentrating his thoughts on turning left, he pulled back to center. The stroke of the warrior pierced the turf exactly where Hadrian would have been.

Grady was dead and the arrows were still coming.

Wesley was shaken. He already failed in his duty. Not knowing what else to do, he picked up the trilon, fitted an arrow, and let it loose. Wesley was no archer. The arrow did not even fly straight, but spun wildly, falling flat on the ground not more than five yards ahead of him.

In the center of the field, Hadrian was avoiding his opponent and the chief had finally decided to engage Wyatt. Royce was in the distance, on the ground and wrestling with something invisible not far from where the oberdaza danced and chanted.

This was not going as planned. Grady was dead and Hadrian... he saw the warrior raise his sword for the killing blow.

"No!" Wesley shouted. Just then, the sharp exploding pain from an arrow pierced his right shoulder and he fell to his knees.

GALENTI

The world spun. His eyes blurred. He gasped for air and gritted his teeth as darkness threatened at the edges of his eyesight. In his ears, a deafening silence grew, swallowing the sounds of the crowd.

The oberdaza! The memory of Hadrian's instructions surfaced. *The Ghazel version wields real magic, dark magic, and he should be the first one we target to kill.*

Wesley clutched the hilt of his sword, fighting back, willing himself not to pass out. He ordered his legs to lift him. Shaking, wobbling, they slowly obeyed. His heart calmed, his breathing grew deeper. The world came into focus once more and the roar of the crowd returned.

Wesley looked across the field at the witch doctor. He glanced at the trilon and knew he could never use it. He tried to raise the sword, but his right arm did not move. He shifted the pommel to the left. It felt awkward and clumsy, but it had strength. Listening to the sound of his heart pounding, he walked forward, slowly at first, but faster with each step. Another arrow hissed. He ignored it and began to jog. His feet pounded the moist, muddy ground. Wesley held his sword high like a banner. His hat flew off, his hair flowing in the breeze.

Another arrow landed just a step ahead of him and he snapped it as he ran. He felt a strange painful pulling and realized the wind was blowing against the feathers of the arrow that still protruded from his shoulder. He focused on the dancing witch doctor.

Out of the corner of his eye he saw the range put down his bow and run at him, drawing a blade. He was too late. Only a few more strides. The oberdaza danced and sang with his eyes closed. He could not see Wesley's charge.

Wesley never checked his pace. He never bothered to slow down. He merely lowered the point of his blade as if it were a lance and put on a last burst of speed—jousting like his famous brother—jousting on foot. Already the darkness was creeping in, tunneling his vision once more. His strength was running out, flowing away with his blood.

Wesley plowed into the oberdaza. The two collided with a loud *thrump!* They skidded together then rolled apart. Wesley's sword was gone from his hands. The arrow in his shoulder had snapped. The taste of blood was in his mouth as he laid face down, struggling to push himself up. A hot pain burst across his back, but it faded quickly as darkness swallowed him.

Royce twisted but could not break free of the claws that cut into his flesh, struggling to break his grip on Alverstone. He could not grab the shadow. Its body felt loose and slippery, as if it existed only where it wanted. Royce would get a partial grip and then it would dissolve.

Teeth grazed him as the Ghazel snapped, trying to rip his throat out. Each time, Royce knew to move. On the third attempt, he gambled and butted forward with his own head. There was a *thunk* and pain, but he was able to break free.

He looked around and once more the finisher was invisible.

Royce caught a glimpse of Wesley running across the field with his sword out in front of him, then dodged another attack. He avoided the blow, but fell to the ground. Weight hit him once more. This time the claws got a better grip. Rear claws scraped along Royce's legs, pinning him, stretching him out, holding him helpless. He felt the hot breath again.

There was a noise of impact not far away and a burst of feathers.

Suddenly Royce saw yellow eyes, bright glowing orbs inches away from his own. Fangs drenched with spit drooled on him.

"Ad haz urba!" the creature gibbered.

The Alverstone was still in Royce's hand. He just needed a little movement from his wrist. He spit in the Ghazel's eye and twisted. Like cutting through ripe fruit, the blade severed the hand of the Ghazel at the wrist. With a howl, the finisher lost support and fell forward. Royce rolled him over, using two hands to restrain his remaining claw, pinning the Ghazel with his knees. The finisher continued to snap, snarl, and rake. Royce severed the goblin's other hand, and the beast shrieked in pain until Royce removed its head.

The Ghazel warrior staggered suddenly, though Hadrian had not touched him. Trying to keep his distance, Hadrian was a good two sword lengths away, but the warrior clearly rocked as if struck. The Ghazel paused, confidence faded from his eyes, and he hesitated.

Hadrian looked over his shoulder to the hill and spotted Grady's body, but Wesley was gone. He looked over his opponent's shoulder and found Wesley on the ground. At his side, the oberdaza lay with the midshipman's cutlass buried in his chest. As Hadrian watched, the range stabbed Wesley in the back.

"Wesley! No!" he shouted.

Then Hadrian's eyes locked sharply on the warrior before him. "I only wish you could read my thoughts now," he said, sheathing both swords.

Confusion crossed the warrior's face until he saw Hadrian draw forth the large spadone from his back. Seizing the chance, the warrior swung. Hadrian blocked the stroke, which made the spadone sing. He followed this with a false swing, which the Ghazel nevertheless moved to dodge, setting it off balance. Hadrian continued to spin, carrying the stroke round in a full circle. He leveled the blade at waist height. There was nowhere for the Ghazel to go, and the great sword cut the warrior in half.

Wyatt was fighting the chief now, their swords ringing like an alarm bell as they repeatedly clashed. Blow after blow drove Wyatt farther and farther backward until Hadrian thrust the spadone through the Chief's shoulder blades.

With a roar like a violent wind, the crowd jumped to its feet cheering and applauding.

Turning, Hadrian saw Royce kneeling beside Wesley's dead body. The range lay beside him. Hadrian ran to them as Wyatt checked on Grady.

Royce shook his head in silent reply to Hadrian's look.

"Grady is dead, too," Wyatt reported when he reached them.

Neither said a word.

The gates opened and Erandabon entered with a bright smile. Poe and Derning followed him. Derning stared at Grady's body. Erandabon lifted his arms to the stands like a conquering hero as the crowd cheered even louder. He approached them, exuberant and delighted.

"Excellent! Excellent! Erandabon ez very pleazed!"

Hadrian strode forward. "Get us to that ship now. Give me time to think, and I swear I'll introduce you to Uberlin myself!"

Chapter 20

THE TOWER

Modina watched Arista as she sat within the chalk circle on the floor of her bedroom, burning the hair. Together they watched the smoke drift.

"What is that awful smell?" Amilia said, entering and waving a hand in front of her face while Nimbus trailed behind her.

"Arista was performing a spell to locate Gaunt," Modina explained.

"She's doing magic—in here?" Amilia looked aghast, then added, "Did it work?"

"Sort of," Arista said with a decidedly disappointed tone. "He's somewhere directly northeast of here, but I can't pinpoint the exact location. That's always been the problem."

Amilia stiffened, her eyes glancing at Nimbus accusingly.

"I didn't say a word," he told her.

Amilia asked Arista, "If you find Degan Gaunt, what are you planning to do?"

"Help him escape."

"He is the general of an army poised to attack us." She turned to Modina. "I don't see why you are helping her—"

"I'm not trying to return him to his army," Arista cut in. "I need him to help me find something—something only the Heir of Novron can locate."

"So, you...and Gaunt...will leave?"

"Yes," Arista told her.

"And what if you are caught? Will you betray the empress by revealing the aid she has provided you?"

"No, of course not. I would never do anything to harm her."

"Why are you asking this, Amilia?" Modina looked from her to Nimbus and back again. "What do you know?"

Amilia hesitated for only a moment then spoke. "There is a Seret Knight standing guard in the north tower."

"I am not familiar with your palace. Is that unusual?" Arista asked.

"There's nothing to guard there," Amilia explained. "It's a prison tower, but none of the cells hold prisoners. Yet last night I watched two fourth-floor guards deliver a pot of soup there."

"To the guard?"

"No," Amilia said, "they delivered the soup to the tower. Less than five minutes later, I arrived. The soup was gone, pot and all."

Arista stood. "They were feeding a prisoner, but you say there are no occupied cells in the tower? Are you sure?"

"Positive. Every door was open and every cell vacant, and looked to have been that way for some time."

"I need to get in that tower," Arista declared. "I could burn a hair in one of the empty cells. If he's nearby, that could really tell us something."

"There is no way you are getting in that tower," Amilia told her. "You'd have to walk right past the knight. While the Secretary to the Empress might get away with such a thing, I highly doubt the fugitive Witch of Melengar will."

"I bet Saldur could walk in and out of there without question, couldn't he?"

"Of course, but you aren't him."

Arista smiled.

She turned to the tutor. "Nimbus, I have a letter for Hilfred and another for my brother. I wrote them in the event something happened to me. I want to give them to you now, just in case. Don't deliver them unless you know I am not coming back."

"Of course," he bowed.

Amilia rolled her eyes.

Arista handed the letters to Nimbus, and for no particular reason gave him a kiss on the cheek.

"Just make certain when you are caught that you don't drag Modina into it," Amilia said, leaving with Nimbus.

"What are you planning to do?" Modina asked.

"Something I've never tried before, something I'm not even certain I can do. Modina, I don't know what will happen. I might do some strange things. Please ignore them and don't interfere, okay?"

Modina nodded.

Arista knelt and spread her gown out around her. She took a deep breath, closed her eyes, and tilted her head back. She took another deep breath then sat still. She did not move for a long time. She sat breathing very slowly, very rhythmically. Her hands opened. Her arms lifted, as if floating on their own—pulled by invisible strings or rising on currents of air. She began to sway gently from side to side, her hair flowing back and forth. Soon she began to hum. The humming took on a melody, and the melody produced words Modina did not understand.

Then Arista began to glow. The light grew brighter with each word. Her dress turned pure white, her skin luminous. It soon hurt Modina's eyes to look at her, so she turned away.

The light went out.

"Did it work?" Modina asked. She turned back to face Arista and gasped.

❧

When Arista opened the door, the guard stared at her, stunned. "Your Grace! I didn't see you come in."

"You should be more watchful then," Arista said, frightened at the sound of her own voice—so familiar and yet so different.

The guard bowed. "Yes, Your Grace. I will. Thank you, Your Grace."

Arista hurried down the stairs, self-conscious and fearful as she clutched three strands of hair in her left hand and a chunk of chalk in her right. She felt exposed, walking openly in the hallways after hiding for so long. She did not feel any different. Only by looking at her hands and clothing could she see evidence that the spell had worked. She was wearing Imperial robes and her hands were those of an old man, with thick gaudy rings. Each servant or guard she passed nodded respectfully, saying softly, "Good afternoon, Your Grace."

Growing up with Saldur practically as her uncle had one advantage—she knew every line of his face, his mannerisms, and his voice. She was certain she could not perform a similar illusion with Modina, Amilia, or Nimbus, even if she had them in front of her for reference. This took more—she *knew* Saldur.

By the time she reached the first floor of the palace she was gaining confidence. Only two concerns remained. What if she ran into the real Saldur, and how long would the spell last? Stumbling through what had to be an advanced magical technique, she worked solely by intuition. She knew what she wanted and had a general idea how to go about it, but the result was more serendipity than skill. So much of magic was guesswork and nuance. She was starting to understand that now and could not help but be pleased with herself.

Unlike what she had managed in the past, this was completely new. Something she did not even know was possible. Casting an enchantment on herself was a frightening prospect. What if there were rules against such things? What if the source of the Art forbade it and imposed harm to those who tried? She never would have attempted it under different circumstances, but she was desperate. Still, having done so, and succeeded, she felt thrilled. She had invented it. Perhaps no wizard had ever managed such a thing!

"Your Grace!" Edith Mon was caught by surprise, coming around a corner where they nearly collided. She carried a stack of sheets in her arms and nearly lost them. "Forgive me, Your Grace! I—I—"

"Think nothing of it, my dear." The, *my dear*, at the end of the sentence came out unconsciously—it just felt right. Hearing it sent a chill through her, which proved it was pitch perfect. This might be fun, if not for the mortal fear.

A thought came into her head. "I have heard reports that you've been treating your staff poorly."

"Your Grace?" Edith asked, looking nervous. "I—I don't know what you mean?"

Arista leaned toward her with a smile that she knew from experience would appear all the more frightening for its friendly, disarming quality. "You aren't going to lie to my face, are you Edith?"

"Ah—no, sir."

"I don't like it, Edith, I don't like it at all. It breeds discontent. If you don't stop, I will need to find a means of correcting your behavior. Do you understand me?"

Edith's eyes were wide. She nodded her head as if it were hinged too tight.

"I will be watching you. I will be watching *very* closely."

With that, Arista left Edith standing frozen in the middle of the corridor, clutching her bundle of sheets.

The guards at the front entrance bowed and opened the doors for her. Stepping outside, her senses were alert for any sign of trouble. She could smell the bread in the ovens of the bake house. To her left, a boy chopped wood, and ahead of her two lads shoveled out the stable, placing manure in a cart, no doubt for use in the garden. The afternoon air was cold and the manure steamed. She could see her breath puffing in steamy clouds as she marched between the brick chicken coop and the remnants of the garden.

She reached the north tower, opened the door, and entered. A Seret Knight with a deadly looking sword strapped to his belt stood at attention. He said nothing and she did the same while looking about.

The tower was cylindrical with arched windows that allowed light to stream in and gleam off the polished stone floor. A tall, arched frame formed the entrance to the spiral stair. Across from it, a small fireplace provided heat for the guard. Covered in cobwebs, a wooden bench stood beside a small, empty four-legged table. The only unusual thing was the stone of the walls. The rough-hewn rock of the upper portion of the tower was lighter in color than the more neatly laid, darker stone beneath.

The knight appeared uncomfortable at her silence.

"Is everything all right here?" Arista asked, going for the most neutral thing she could think of.

"Yes, Your Grace!" he replied enthusiastically.

"Very good," she said, and casually shuffled to the stairs and began to climb. She glanced behind her to see if the guard would follow, but he remained where he was without even looking in her direction.

She went up one flight and stopped at the first open cell. Just as Amilia reported, it appeared long abandoned. She checked to make certain the cell door would not lock and then carefully closed it. She got on her knees and quickly drew the circle and the runes.

She placed the blond hairs on the floor, lining them up in rows. Picking up several pieces of straw, she twisted them tightly into a rope-stalk. She repeated the phrase she had used for weeks and instantly the top of the straw caught fire, becoming a tiny torch. She recited the location spell and touched the flame to one of the hairs. It heated up like a red coil and turned to ash. Arista looked for the smoke, but there was none. She glanced around the room confused. She looked at the smoke coming off the straw; it drifted straight up. There was no wind, no draft of any kind in the cell.

She tried again with the second hair. This time putting out the straw, thinking its smoke might be interfering. Instead she cast the burn spell directly on the hair, followed by the location incantation. The hair turned to ash without a trace of the familiar light-gray smoke.

Was something about the tower blocking her spell? Could it be like the prison where they kept Esrahaddon? The Old Empire had placed complicated runes on the walls, blocking the use of magic. She looked around. The walls were bare. No, she thought, she would not have been able to cast the burn spell if that were the case. For that matter, she guessed her Saldur guise would have failed the moment she entered.

She had only one hair left. She considered moving to a different room, and then the answer dawned on her. She recited the spell once more. Picking up the last hair and holding it between her fingers, she burned it.

There it was! The smoke was pure white now and spilled straight down between her fingers like a trickle of water. It continued to fall until it met the floor, where it immediately disappeared.

She stood in the cell trying to figure it out. According to the smoke, Gaunt was very close and directly below her, but there was nothing down there. She considered that perhaps there might be a door in the fireplace. No, she concluded, the opening was too small. There simply was nothing else below her except—the guard!

Arista gasped.

She checked her hands, reassured to see the wrinkled skin and ugly rings, and went back down the stairs to the base of the tower. The guard remained standing statue-like with his helm covering every trace of his features.

"Remove your helm," she ordered.

The knight hesitated only briefly, then complied.

She knew exactly what Degan Gaunt looked like from his image in Avempartha. The moment he removed his helm, her hopes disappeared.

She forgot herself for a moment and sighed most un-Saldur-like.

"Is there something wrong, Your Grace?"

"Ah—no, no," she replied quickly and started to leave.

"I assure you, sir, I told her nothing of the prisoner. I refused to speak a single word."

Arista halted. She pivoted abruptly, causing her robes to sweep around her majestically. The dramatic motion had a visible impact on the guard and she finally understood why Saldur always did that.

"Are you certain?"

"Yes!" he declared, but doubt crossed his face. "Did she say differently? If she did, she's lying."

THE TOWER

Arista said nothing but merely continued to stare at him. It was not an intentional act; she was merely trying to determine what to say next. She was not sure how to form her statement to get the knight to talk without being obvious. As she stood there formulating her next words, the knight broke under her stare.

"Okay, I did threaten to unsheathe my sword, but didn't. I was very careful about that. I only pulled it partway out. The tip never cleared the sheath, I swear. I just wanted to scare her off. She did not see anything. Watch." The knight pulled his sword and gestured toward the floor. "See, nothing."

Arista's eye immediately focused on the large emerald in the pommel and she bit her tongue to restrain herself. It all made sense. There was only one thing still to learn. It was a gamble, but a good one she thought. She asked, "Did Gaunt like his soup?"

She held her breath as she waited for his answer.

"He ate it, but none of them have ever liked it."

"Very good," she said, and left.

When Arista returned, Modina did not speak a word. After admitting her the empress stood watching cautiously. Arista started to laugh, then rushed forward and gave her an unexpected hug. "We've found him!"

Chapter 21

DRUMINDOR

L ed by a fast-walking Tenkin warrior, the few remaining members of the *Emerald Storm's* crew made their way down from the Palace of the Four Winds through a series of damp caves to the base of the blackened cliffs where the surf attacked the rock. In a tiny cove, a little sloop waited for them. Smaller and narrower than the Dacca vessel, the ship sported two decks but only a single mast. Wyatt rapidly looked the ship over, declaring it sound, and Poe checked for provisions, finding it fully stocked for a month-long trip.

They quickly climbed aboard. Poe and Hadrian cast off while Wyatt grabbed the wheel. Derning and Royce ran up the mast and loosed the headsail, which billowed out handsomely. The power of the wind just off the point was so strong that the little sloop lurched forward, knocking Poe off his feet. He got up and wandered to the bow.

"Look at them. They're everywhere," he said, motioning out at the hundreds of black sails filling the harbor like a hive of bees.

"Let's just hope they let us through," Derning said.

"We'll get through," Hadrian told them. He was seated on a barrel holding Wesley's hat, turning it over and over. Hadrian had refused to leave Wesley and Grady in Erandabon's hands. Their bodies had been brought aboard for a proper burial at sea. He kept Wesley's hat. He was not sure why.

"He was a good man," Royce said.

"Yes, he was."

"They both were," Derning added.

The tiny sloop was a bit hard to manage with just the five of them, but it would be ideal once they picked up Banner and Grieg in Dagastan. She was a fast ship, and they were confident they could reach Tur Del Fur in time. The armada of Tenkin and Ghazel ships looked to be still gathering.

"Jacob, trim the foresail, I'm bringing her over two points," Wyatt snapped as he gripped the slick ship's wheel. "And everyone jump lively, we're in the Ba Ran Archipelago and this is no place for slow-witted sailors."

The moment they cleared the cove they understood Wyatt's warning. Here the sea was a torrent of wave-crashed cliffs and splintered islands of jagged rock. Towering crags rose from dense fog, and blind reefs of murderous coral lay in ambush. Currents coursed without reason, rogue waves crashed without warning, and everywhere the dark water teamed with sweeping triangles of black canvas—each emblazoned with white slashes that looked vaguely like a skull. The Ghazel ships spotted them the moment they cleared the point. Five abruptly changed course and swooped in.

The black ships of the Ba Ran Ghazel made the Dacca look like incompetent ferrymen as they channeled through the surf and flew across the waves.

"Run up the damn colors!" Wyatt shouted, but Royce was already hauling the black banner with white markings that stretched out long and thin.

The Emerald Storm

There was a brief moment as Hadrian watched the approaching sails that he cursed himself for trusting Erandabon Gile. But after the colors were hoisted, like a shiver of sharks the sails peeled off, swirling back around to resume their earlier paths.

Wyatt cranked the wheel until they were pointed for Dagastan and ordered Royce to the top of the masthead to watch for reefs. No one spoke after that, except for Royce who shouted out obstacles and Wyatt who barked orders. It only took a few hours before they cleared the last of the jagged little islands, leaving both the archipelago and the black sails behind. The little sloop rolled easily as it entered the open waters of the Ghazel Sea.

The crew relaxed. Wyatt set a steady course. He leaned back against the rail, caught the sea spray in his hand, and wiped his face as he looked out at the ocean. Hadrian sat beside him, head bowed while he turned Wesley's hat over in his hands

Erandabon had sent a messenger to Hadrian as they left the arena. The search for Allie had produced no results. All previous shipments had been delivered to the Ghazel weeks ago. He knew females, especially young ones, were considered a rare delicacy. She was dead, likely eaten alive by a high-ranking goblin who would have savored the feast by keeping the girl conscious as long as possible. For Ghazel, screams were a garnish.

Hadrian sighed. "Wyatt...I have something to tell you... Allie..."

Wyatt waited.

"Allie is dead. As part of the deal, I made Gile investigate. The results weren't good."

Wyatt turned to gaze once more at the ocean. "You—you made that part of the deal? Asking about my daughter?"

"Yeah, Gile was a little put out but—"

"What if he had said no?"

"I wasn't going to accept that answer."

"But he could have killed all of us."

Hadrian nodded. "She's your daughter. If I thought she was alive, trust me, Royce and I would be on it, even if that meant heading back into the Ba Ran Islands, but…well. I'm really sorry. I wish I could have done more." He looked down at the hat in his hands. "I wished I could have done a lot more."

Wyatt nodded.

"We can still save Tur Del Fur," Hadrian told him. "And we wouldn't have that chance without you. If we succeed, she won't have died in vain."

Wyatt turned to look at Hadrian. He opened his mouth then stopped and looked away again.

"I know," Hadrian said, once more fidgeting with Wesley's hat. "I know."

Greig and Banner were pleased to see them. Nights living on the little Dacca ship were getting cold and provisions dangerously low. They had already resorted to selling nets and sails to buy food in town. They made a hasty sale of the Dacca ship since the Tenkin vessel was far faster and already loaded.

Wyatt aimed the bow homeward, catching the strong autumn trade winds. The closer they came to home, the colder it got. The southern currents that helped warm Calis did not reach Delgos, and soon the wind turned biting. A brief rainstorm left a thin coat of ice on the sheets and deck rails.

Wyatt continued at the helm, refusing to sleep until he was near collapse. Hadrian concluded that, failing to save Allie, Wyatt placed his absolution in saving Delgos instead. In a way, he was certain that they all did. Many good people died along the trip—they each felt the need to make their sacrifice mean something. Even Royce, suffering once more from seasickness, managed to climb to the top of the mainsail where he replaced the Ghazel banner with Mister Wesley's hat.

They explained the events of the previous weeks to Grieg and Banner, as well as Merrick's plan and the need to reach Drumindor before the full moon. Each night they watched the moon rise larger on the face of the sea—the lunar god indifferent to their race against time. Fortune and the wind were with them. Wyatt captured every breath, granting them excellent speed. Royce spotted red sails off the port aft twice, but they remained on the horizon and each time vanished quietly in their wake.

Shorthanded, and with Royce seasick, Hadrian volunteered for mast work. Derning spent the days teaching him the ropes. He would never be very good at it. He was too big, yet he managed to grasp the basics. After a few days he was able to handle most of the maneuvers without instruction. At night, Poe cooked while Hadrian sat practicing knots and watching the stars.

Instead of hugging the coast up to Wesbaden, they took a risk and sailed due west off the tip of Calis directly across Dagastan Bay. The gamble almost proved to be a disaster, as they ran into a terrible storm producing mountainous waves. Wyatt expertly guided the little sloop, riding the raging swells with half canvas set, never leaving the wheel. Seeing the helmsman's rain-lashed face exposed in a flash of lightning, Hadrian seriously began to wonder if Wyatt had gone mad. By morning, the sky had cleared and they could all see Wesley's hat still blowing in the wind.

The gamble paid off. Two days ahead of the harvest moon they rounded the Horn of Delgos and entered Terlando Bay.

Drumindor

࿔

As they approached the harbor, the Port Authority stopped them. They did not care for the style of the ship or the black sails— Wesley's hat notwithstanding. Held directly under the terrifying smoking spouts of Drumindor, dock officers boarded and searched the vessel thoroughly before allowing them to pass below the bridge between the twin stone towers. Even then they were given an escort to berth fifty-eight, slip twenty-two of the West Harbor. Being familiar with the city and the Port Authority, Wyatt volunteered to notify the officials of the impending invasion and warn them to search for signs of sabotage.

"I'm off mates," Derning announced once they had the ship berthed. The topman had a small bundle over his shoulder.

"What about the ship and the stores?" Grieg asked. "We'll want to sell it—you'll get a share."

"Keep it—I have business to attend to."

"But what if we can't get…" Grieg gave up as Derning trotted away into the narrow streets. "That seemed a bit abrupt—man's in a hurry to go somewhere."

"Or just glad to be back in civilization," Banner mentioned.

Tur Del Fur welcomed sailors like no other port. Brightly painted buildings with exuberant decorations received them to a city filled with music and mirth. Most of the shops and taverns butted up against the docks, where loud signs fought for attention: *The Drunken Sailor—join the crew! Fresh beef & poultry! Pipes, Britches & Hats! Ladies of the Bay, (we wring the salt out!)*

For recently paid sailors who might have been at sea for two or more years, they screamed paradise. The only oddity remained the size and shapes of the buildings. Whimsical western decorations could not completely hide the underlying history of this once-dwarven city. Above every door and threshold was the sign: *"Watch your head."*

Seagulls cried above them as they crisscrossed a brilliant blue sky. Water lapped the sides of ships that creaked and moaned like living beasts stretching after a long run.

Hadrian stepped onto the dock alongside Royce. "Feels like you're gonna fall over, doesn't it?"

"To answer your question from before…No, I don't think we should be sailors. I'd be happy never to see a ship again."

"At least you don't have to worry about land sickness."

"Still feels like the ground is pitching beneath me."

The five of them bought fresh-cooked fish from dock vendors and ate on the pier. They listened to the shanty tunes spilling out of the taverns and smelled the pungent fishy reek of the harbor. By the time Wyatt returned to the ship, he was red-faced angry.

"They are going through with the venting! They refused to listen to anything I said," he shouted, trotting up the quay.

"What about the invasion?" Hadrian asked. "Didn't you tell them about that?"

"They didn't believe me! Even Livet Glim, the port controller—and we were once mates! I shared a bunk with him for two years and the bloody bastard refuses to, as he puts it, 'Turn the entire port on its ear because one person thinks there might be an attack.' He says they haven't heard anything from any other ships, and they won't do a thing unless the armada is confirmed by other captains."

"It will be too late by then."

"I tried to tell them that, but they went on about how they *had* to regulate the pressure on the full moon. I went to every official in the city, but no one would listen. After a while I think they became suspicious that *I* was up to something. I stopped when they threatened to lock me up. I'm sorry."

"Maybe if we all went?"

DRUMINDOR

Wyatt shook his head. "It won't do any good. Can you believe this? After all we've been through, we get here and it won't change a single thing. Unless..." He looked directly at Hadrian.

"Unless what?" Poe asked.

Hadrian sighed and looked at Royce, who nodded.

"What am I missing?" Poe asked.

"Drumindor was built by dwarves thousands of years ago," Hadrian explained. "Those huge towers are packed with stone gears and hundreds of switches and levers. The Tur Del Fur Port Authority only knows what a handful of them actually do. They know how to vent the pressure and blow the spouts, and that's about it."

"We know how to shut it off," Royce said.

"Shut it off?" Poe asked. "How do you shut off a volcano?"

"Not the volcano, the system," Hadrian went on. "There's a master switch that locks the whole gearing system. Once dropped, the fortress doesn't build pressure anymore. The volcano just vents itself. It won't be able to stop the invasion, but it won't explode either."

"How does that help?"

"If nothing else, it will prevent the instant destruction of this city. When the black sails appear, people might have time to evacuate, maybe even put up a defense. Once the system is shut down, Royce and I can crawl through the portals to find out what Merrick did. If we can get it fixed in time, we can raise the master switch and barbeque an armada of very surprised goblins."

"Can we help?" Banner asked.

"Not this time," Hadrian told him. "Can you four handle this ship alone?"

Wyatt nodded. "It will be tough with no topmen, but we'll work something out."

"Good, then you get out of here before the fleet comes in. You were a good assistant, Poe. Stick with Wyatt and you'll be a captain one day. This one we have to do alone."

Legend held that dwarves existed centuries before man walked the face of the world. Back in an age when they and the elves fought for supremacy of Elan, dwarves were a powerful and honorable nation governed by their own kings with their own laws and traditions. It was a golden age of great feats, wondrous achievements, and marvelous heroes. Then the elves won the war.

The strength of the dwarves was shattered forever, and the emergence of men destroyed what remained. Although never enslaved like the remnants of the elves, men distrusted and shunned the sons of Drome. Fearful of a unified dwarven kingdom, humans forced the dwarves out of their homeland of Delgos into a shadowy existence of nomadic persecution. Despite their skills in crafts, humans scattered them whenever they gathered in groups too large for comfort. For their own survival, dwarves learned to hide. Those that could adopted human ways and attempted to fit in. Their culture obliterated by centuries of careful erasure, little survived of their former glory except what stone could tell. Few dwarves, and even fewer humans, possessed the imagination to recall a day when they ruled half the world—unless, like Royce and Hadrian, they were staring up at Drumindor.

The light of the setting sun bathed the granite rock, making it shine like silver. Sheer walls towered hundreds of feet, rising out of the bedrock of the burning mountain's back. The twin towers stood joined by the thin line of what appeared from that distance to be a wafer-thin bridge. The tops of the towers smoldered quietly, leaking thin plumes of dark smoke out of every vent, creating a thin, gray cloud that hovered overhead. Up close, the scope and mammoth size were breathtaking.

They had one night and the following day to accomplish the same magic trick they had performed many years earlier. It was dark by the time they purchased the necessary supplies, slipped through the city of Tur Del Fur, and hiked up into the countryside, following goat paths into the foothills that eventually led to the base of the great fortress itself.

"Is this where it was?" Royce asked stopping and studying the base of the tower.

"How should I know?" Hadrian replied as his eyes coursed up the length of the south tower. Up close, it blocked everything else out, a solid wall of black rising against the light of the moon. "I can never understand why such small people build such gigantic things."

"Maybe they're compensating," Royce said, dropping several lengths of rope.

"Damn it, Royce. It's been eight years since we did this. I was in better shape then. I was younger and, if I recall, I vowed I would never do it again."

"That's why you shouldn't make vows. The moment you do, fate starts conspiring to shove them down your throat."

Hadrian sighed, staring upward. "That's one tall tower."

"And if the dwarves were still here maintaining it, it would be impregnable. Lucky for us, they've let it rot. You should be happy—the last eight years would only have eroded it further. It should be easier."

"It's granite, Royce. Granite doesn't erode much in eight years."

Royce said nothing as he continued to lay out coils of rope, checking the knots in the harnesses and slipping on his hand-claws.

"Do you recall that I nearly fell last time?" Hadrian asked.

"So don't step there this time."

"Do you remember what the nice lady in the jungle village told you? One light will go out?"

"We either climb this or let the place blow. We let the place blow and Merrick wins. Merrick wins, he gets away and you never find Degan Gaunt."

"I never thought you cared all that much if I ever found Gaunt." Hadrian looked up at the tower again. "At least not *that* much."

"Honestly? I don't care at all. This whole quest of yours is stupid. So you find Gaunt—then what? You follow him around being his bodyguard for the rest of your life? What if he's like Ballentyne? Wouldn't that be fun? Granted it will be exciting, as I'm sure anyone with a sword will want to kill him, but who cares? There's no reward, no point to it. You feel guilt—I kinda get that. You ran out on your father and you can't say you're sorry anymore. So for that, you'll spend your life following this guy around being his butler? You're better than that."

"I think there was a compliment in there somewhere—so thanks. But if you're not doing this to help me find Gaunt, why are you?"

Royce paused. From a bag he drew out Wesley's hat. He must have fetched it down before they left the ship. "He stuck his neck out for me three times. The last one got him killed. There's no way this fortress is blowing up."

Even in the dark, Royce found handholds and spots to place his feet that Hadrian could never have spotted in the full light of day. Like a spider, he scaled the side of the tower until he came to the base of the first niche. There, he set his first anchor and dropped a rope to Hadrian. By the time Hadrian reached the foothold of that niche, Royce was already nailing in the next pin and sending down another coil. They continued this way, finding minute edges where several thousand years of erosion revealed the maker's seams in the rock. Centuries-old crevices and cracks allowed Royce to climb what was once slick, smooth stone.

Two hours later, the trees below appeared like tiny bushes and the cold, wintry winds buffeted them like barn swallows. They were only a third of the way up.

"It's time," Royce shouted over the howl of the wind. He anchored a pin, tied a rope to it, and climbed back down.

Hadrian groaned. "I hate this part!"

"Sorry buddy, nothing I can do about it. The niches are all over that way." Royce gestured across to where the vertical grooves cut into the rock on the far side of a deep crevasse.

Royce tied the rope to his harness and linked himself to Hadrian.

"Now, just watch me," Royce told him and, taking hold of the rope, he sprinted across the stone face. Reaching the edge of the crevasse, he leapt, swinging out like a clock's pendulum. He cleared the gap by what looked like only a few inches. On the far side, he clung to the stone, dangling like a bug on a twig. He slowly pulled himself up and drove another pin. Then, after tying off the rope, waved to Hadrian.

If Hadrian missed the jump, he would slip into the crevasse where he would end up dangling helplessly, assuming the rope held him. The force of the fall could easily pop out the holding pin, or even snap the rope. He took a deep breath of cold air, steadied himself, and began to run. On the far side, Royce leaned out for him. He reached the edge and jumped. The wind whistled past his face, blurring his vision as tears streaked across his cheeks. He struck the far side just short of the landing, bashing his head hard enough to see stars. He tasted blood and wondered if he had lost his front teeth even as his fingertips lost their tenuous hold and he began to fall. Royce tried to grab him, but was too late. Hadrian fell.

He dropped about three inches.

Hadrian dangled from the rope Royce had the forethought to anchor the moment his partner had landed. Hadrian groaned in pain while wiping blood from his face.

"See," Royce shouted in his ear, "that went *much* better than last time!"

They continued scaling upward, working within the relative shelter of the vertical three-sided chimneys. They were too high now for Hadrian to see anything except the tiny lights of the port city. Everything else below was darkness. They rested for a time in the semi-sheltered niche and then climbed upward again.

Higher and higher, Royce led the way. Hadrian's hands were sore from gripping the rope and burned from the few times he slipped. His legs, exhausted and weak, quivered dangerously. The wind was brutal. Gusting in an eddy caused by the chimney they followed, it pushed outward like an invisible hand trying to knock them off. The sun came up and Hadrian was nearing the end of his endurance when they finally reached the bridge. They were slightly more than two-thirds of the way, but thankfully they did not need to reach the top.

What appeared from the ground to be a thin bridge was actually forty-feet thick. They scrambled over the edge, hauled up their ropes, ducked into a sheltered archway, and sat in the shadows catching their breath.

"I'd like to see Derning scale *that*," Royce said, looking down.

"I don't think anyone but you could manage it," Hadrian replied. "Nor is there anyone crazy enough to try."

Dozens of men guarded the great gates at the base of the tower, but no one was on the bridge. It was thought impossible for intruders to start at the top, and the cold wind kept the workers inside. Royce gave the tall slender stone doors a push.

"Locked?" Hadrian asked.

Royce nodded. "Let's hope they haven't changed the combination."

Hadrian chuckled. "Took you eighteen hours last time, right after you told me, 'this will only take a minute.'"

"Remind me again why I brought you?" Royce asked, fanning his hands out across the embossed face of the doors. "Ah, here it is."

Royce placed his fingers carefully and pushed. A hundred tons of solid stone glided inward as if on a cushion of air, rotating open without a sound. Inside, an enormous cathedral ceiling vaulted hundreds of feet above them. Shafts of morning sunshine entered through distant skylights built into the dome overhead, revealing a complex world of bridges, balconies, archways, and a labyrinth of gears. Some gears lay flat, while others stood upright. Some were as small as a copper coin, and then there were those that were several stories tall and thicker than a house. A few rotated constantly, driven by steam created from the volcanically superheated seawater. The majority of the gears, particularly the big ones, remained motionless, waiting. Aside from the mechanisms, nothing else moved. The only sound was the regular, ratcheting rhythm and the whirl of the great machine.

Royce scanned the interior. "Nobody home," he said at length.

"Wasn't last time either. I'm surprised they haven't tightened security up more."

"Oh, yeah, a single break-in after centuries is something to schedule your guards around."

"They'll be kicking themselves tomorrow."

They found the stairs—short shallow steps built for little feet that they took two and three at a time. Ducking under low archways,

Hadrian nearly had to crawl through the entrance to the Big Room. This was a name Hadrian gave it the last time they visited. The room itself was huge, but the name came from the master gear. It stood on edge and what they could see was as high as a castle tower, but most of its bulk sunk beneath the floor and through a wall, leaving only a quarter of the gear visible. Its edge was crenellated like the merlons on a castle battlement, only larger—much larger. It meshed with two other gears, which connected to a dozen more that joined the dwarven puzzle.

"The lock was at the top, right?" Royce asked.

"Think so—yeah, Gravis was up there when we found him."

"Okay, I'll handle this. Keep an eye out."

Royce leapt up to one of the smaller gears and walked up the teeth like a staircase. He jumped from one to the next until he reached the master gear. It was harder to climb, since the teeth were huge, but for Royce this was no problem. He was soon out of sight and a few minutes later a loud stone upon stone sound echoed as a giant post of rock descend from the ceiling, settling in the valley between two teeth, locking the great gear.

When Royce returned he was grinning happily.

"I'd love to see the look on Merrick's face when this place doesn't blow. Even if the Ghazel take the city, he'll be scratching his head for months. There's no way he can know about this master switch. Gravis only knew because it was his ancestor that designed the place."

"And we only know because we caught him in the act." Hadrian thought a moment. "Do you think Merrick might be nearby, waiting for the fireworks?"

Royce sighed. "Of course not. If it were me, I wouldn't be within a hundred miles of this explosion. I don't even want to be here now. Don't worry, I know him. The fact that this mountain doesn't explode will drive him nuts. All we have to do is drop the right hints to the wrong people and we won't have to look for him—he'll find us. Now come on, let's see if we can find what is blocking the vents so we can put this back in place and cook some goblins."

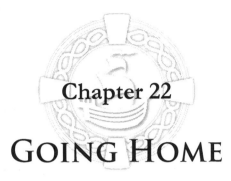

Chapter 22

GOING HOME

A rchibald Ballentyne stared out the window of the Great Hall. It looked cold. Brown grass, blowing dead leaves, clouds that looked heavy and full of snow, and geese that flew away before a veil of gray all reminded him the seasons had changed. Wintertide was less than two months away. He kicked the stone of the wall with his boot. It made a muffled thud and sent a pain up his leg, making him wince.

Why do I have to think of that? Why do I always have to think of that?

Behind him, Saldur, Ethelred, and Biddings debated something, but he was not listening. He did not care anymore. Maybe he should leave. Maybe he should take a small retinue and just go home to Chadwick and the sanctity of his Gray Tower. The place would be a wreck by now, and he could busy himself with repairing the damage the servants caused in his absence. Bruce was likely dipping into his brandy store and the tax collectors would be behind in their duties. It would feel nice to be home for the holiday. He could invite a few friends and his sister over for—he stopped and considered kicking the wall again, but it hurt enough last time.

GOING HOME

Sleeping in a tent this time of year would be miserable. Besides, what would the regents say? Moreover, what would they do in his absence? They treated him badly enough when he was here, how much worse would they conspire against him if he left?

He did not really want to be home. Ballentyne Castle was a lonely place, all the more horrid in winter. He used to dream of how all that would change when he married, when he had a beautiful wife and children. He used to fantasize about Alenda Lanaklin. She was a pretty thing. He also often imagined taking the hand of the King Armand's daughter, Princess Beatrice. She was certainly appealing. He even spent many a summer evening watching the milkmaids in the field and contemplating the possibility of snatching one from her lowly existence to be the new Lady Ballentyne. How grateful she would be, how dutiful, how easily controlled. That was all before he came to Aquesta—before he met her.

Even sleep gave him no solace as he dreamed about Modina now. He danced with her and it was their own wedding day. He despised waking up. Archibald did not even care about the title anymore. He would give up the idea of being emperor if he could have her. He even considered that he would give up being earl—but she was marrying—*Ethelred!*

He refused to look at the regent. The fool cared nothing for her. How could he be so cold as to force a girl to marry him just for the political benefit? The man was a blackguard.

"Archie…Archie!" Ethelred was calling him.

He cringed at the sound of the name he hated and turned from the window with a scowl.

"Archie, you need to talk to your man Breckton."

"What's wrong with him now?"

"He's refusing to take my orders. He insists he serves only you. You need to set him straight on the lay of things. We can't have knights whose allegiance is strictly to their lords. They have to recognize the supremacy of the Empire and the chain of command."

"Seems to me that's what he is doing, observing the chain of command."

"Yes, yes, but it is more than that. He's becoming obstinate. I'm going to be the emperor in a couple of months and I can't have my best general requiring that I get your permission to give him an order."

"I'll speak with him," Archibald said miserably, mostly just so he could stop listening to Ethelred's voice. If the old bastard was not such an accomplished soldier, he would seriously consider challenging him, but Ethelred had fought in dozens of battles, while Archibald had only engaged in practice duels with blunt-tipped swords. Even if he wanted to commit suicide, he certainly would not give Ethelred the satisfaction.

"What about Modina?" Ethelred asked.

At the sound of the name, Archibald focused back on the conversation.

"Will she be ready?"

"Yes, I think so," Saldur replied. "Amilia has been doing wonders with her."

"Amilia?" Ethelred tapped his forehead. "Isn't she the maid you promoted to Imperial secretary?"

"Yes," Saldur said, "and I've been thinking that after the wedding, I want to keep her on."

"We'll have no use for her *after* the wedding."

"I know, but I think I could use her elsewhere. She's proven herself to be both intelligent and resourceful."

"Do whatever you like with her, I certainly don't—"

"Queens always have need of secretaries, even when they have husbands," Archibald interrupted. "I understand you're going to assume total control of the Empire, but she'll still need an assistant."

Ethelred looked at Saldur with a puzzled expression. "He doesn't know?"

"Know what?" Archibald asked.

Saldur shook his head. "I felt the fewer that knew the better."

"After the wedding," Ethelred told Archibald, "once I am crowned emperor, I'm afraid Modina will have an unfortunate accident—a fatal accident."

◈

"It's all arranged," Nimbus reported. Arista paced the room and Modina sat alone on the bed. "I got the uniform to him, and tonight the farmer will smuggle Hilfred into the gate just before sunset in the hay cart."

"Will they check that?" Arista asked, pausing in her journey across the room.

"Not anymore, not since they called off the witch hunt. Things are business as usual again. They know the farmer. He's in and out every third day of the week."

Arista nodded and resumed her pacing.

"The same wagon will cart you all out at dawn. You will go out through the city gates. There will be three horses waiting at the crossroads for you with food, water, blankets, and extra clothing."

"Thank you, Nimbus." Arista hugged the beanpole of a man, bringing a blush to his cheeks.

"Are you sure this will work?" Modina asked.

"I don't see why not," Arista said. "I'll do just what I did last time. I'll become Saldur and Hilfred will be a fourth-floor guard. You're sure you took the right uniform?"

Nimbus nodded.

"I'll order the guard to open the entrance to the prison. We'll grab Gaunt and leave. I will instruct the seret to remain on duty and tell no one. Believing I'm Saldur, no one will know he's gone for hours, maybe even days."

"I still don't understand." Modina looked puzzled. "Amilia said there was no prison in the tower and that all the cells were empty."

"There is a secret door in the floor. A very cleverly hidden door, sealed with a gemlock."

"What's a gemlock?"

"A precious stone cut to produce a specific vibration that when held near the door trips the lock open. I used a magical variation on my tower door back home, and the church used a far more sophisticated version to seal the main entrance to Gutaria Prison. They are doing the same thing here, and the key is the emerald in the pommel of the sword the Seret Knight wears."

"So, you will make your escape tonight?" the empress asked.

Arista nodded. The empress looked down, a sadness creeping into her eyes. "What's wrong?" Arista asked.

"Nothing. I'm just going to miss you."

Arista's stomach twisted as she looked out the window and watched the sun set. *Am I being foolish?* Her plan had always been to merely locate Gaunt, not break him out. Now that she knew exactly where he was, she could return home and have Alric send Royce and Hadrian to rescue him. Only that was before—before she found Hilfred, before she was reunited with Thrace, and before she knew she could impersonate Saldur. It seemed like such an easy thing to do that leaving without Gaunt seemed an unnecessary risk. The smoke verified he still lived, but would he be alive several weeks from now?

She was alone with Modina. They had not said a word to each other for hours. Something was troubling the empress—something more than usual. Modina was stubborn, and no force could move her once she decided on a course. Apparently the course she decided on was to not talk.

The gate opened and the hay cart entered.

Arista watched intently. Nothing seemed amiss, no guards, no shouting, just a thick pile of hay and a slow-walking donkey pulling it. The farmer, an elderly man, parked the cart by the stables, unhitched his donkey, hitched it to a new cart, and led the animal out again. Staring at the cart, she could not help herself. The plan had been to wait until just before dawn, but she could not leave Hilfred lying there. She managed to restrain herself only until she saw the harvest moon begin to rise, then she stood.

"It's time," she said.

Modina lifted her head.

Arista walked to the middle of the room and knelt.

"Arista, I…" Modina began hesitantly.

"What is it?"

"Nothing…Good luck."

Arista got up and crossed the room to hug her tightly. "Good luck to you, too."

The empress shook her head. "You keep all of it—I'm not going to be needing any."

Arista traveled down the stairs, disguised as Regent Saldur, wondering what Modina had almost said. The excitement of the night, however, kept her thoughts jumping from one thing to the next. She discovered that she could remain in her disguise for a long time. It broke when she slept, but it would last beyond what she would need that night. This gave her greater confidence. Although she was still concerned about bumping into the real Saldur, the thought of seeing Hilfred again was overwhelming.

Her heart leapt just thinking about traveling home to Melengar with Hilfred once more at her side. It had been a long and tiring road, and she wanted to be home. She wanted to see Alric and Julian, and to sleep in her own bed. She vowed she would treat Melissa better and planned to give her maid a new dress for Wintertide. Arista was occupied in a long list of Wintertide presents for everyone when she stepped outside. The broad face of the harvest moon illuminated the inner ward, allowing her to see as clear as if it were a cloudy day. The courtyard was empty as she crept to the wagon.

"Hilfred!" she whispered. There was no response, no movement in the hay. "Hilfred." She shook the wagon. "It's me, Arista."

She waited.

Her heart skipped a beat when the hay moved. "Princess?" it said hesitantly.

"Yes, it's me. Just follow." She led him into the stables and to the last stall, which was vacant. "We need to wait here until it is nearly dawn."

Hilfred stared at her dubiously, keeping a distance.

"How...?" he began, but faltered.

"I thought Nimbus explained I would appear like this."

"He did."

Hilfred's eyes traveled up and down her figure, a look on his face as if he had just tasted something awful.

"The rumors are true," she admitted, "at least the ones about me using magic."

"I've known that, but your hair, your face, your voice." He shook his head. "It's perfect. How do I know you're not the real Saldur?"

Arista closed her eyes, and in an instant Saldur disappeared and the Princess of Melengar returned.

Hilfred stumbled backward until he hit the wall of the stall. His eyes wide and his mouth open.

"It *is* me," she assured him. Arista took a step forward and watched him flinch. It hurt her to see this, more than she would have expected. "You need to trust me," she told him.

"How can I? How can I be certain it's really you, when you trade skins so easily?"

"Ask me a question that will satisfy you."

Hilfred hesitated.

"Ask me, Hilfred."

"I have been with you daily since I was a very young man. Give me the names of the first three women I fell in love with and the name of the one I lost because of the scars on my face."

She smiled and felt her face blush. "Arista, Arista, Arista, and no one."

He smiled. She did not wait for him. She knew he would never presume upon her to take such a step on his own. She threw her arms around his neck and kissed him. She could feel the sudden shock in the tightening of his muscles, but he did not pull away. His body relaxed slowly and his arms surrounded her. He squeezed so that her cheek pressed against his, her chin resting on his shoulder.

"Maribor help me if you really are Saldur," Hilfred whispered in her ear.

She laughed softly and wondered if it was the first time she had done so since Emery died.

Chapter 23

THE HARVEST MOON

Royce and Hadrian began investigating the spouts, giant tunnels bored out of the rock through which molten lava would blast on its way to the sea. There were dozens, each one aiming in a different direction, their access to the mountain's core sealed off by gear-controlled portals. They climbed the interior until they reached the opening and the sky.

The sun was up and the sight below forced Hadrian's stomach into his mouth. They were well above the bridge level. The world looked very small and very far away. Tur Del Fur was a small cluster of petite buildings crouched in the elbow of a little cove. Beyond it rose mountains that looked like little hills. Directly below, the sea appeared like a puddle with tiny flashes of white that took Hadrian a moment to realize were the crests of waves. What he thought might be insects were gulls circling far below.

None of the spouts were blocked, none of the portals tampered with.

"Maybe it's in the other tower?" Hadrian asked after they climbed out of the last tunnel.

Royce shook his head. "Even if that one is blocked, the pressure will vent here. Both have to be closed. It's not the spouts or the portals, it's something else—something we've overlooked—something that can seal all the exits at once to make the mountain boil over. It has to be another master switch, one that locks all the portals closed."

"How are we going to find that? Do you see how many gears are in here? And it could be any one. We should have brought Magnus."

"Sure, with him it would be easy to find—in a year or two. Look at this place!" Royce gestured at the breadth of the tower, where the sun's light pierced through skylights spraying the tangled riddle of a million stone gears. Some spun, some whirled, some barely moved, and everywhere were levers. Like arrows peppering a battlefield, stone arms protruded. Just as the gears came in various sizes, so too did the levers—some tiny and others the size of tree trunks. "It's a wonder they ever learned how to vent the core."

"Exactly," Hadrian said. "No one knows what most of this stuff does anymore. The Port Authority leaves it alone for fear they might destroy the world or something, right? So whatever Merrick did, it's a sure bet the folks in charge here don't know anything about it. It has to be a lever that hasn't been moved in centuries, maybe even thousands of years. It might show signs of recent movement, right?"

"Maybe."

"So we just need to find it."

Royce stared at him.

"What?"

"We only have a few hours left, and you're talking about finding a displaced grain of sand on a beach."

"I know, and when you come up with something better we'll try it. Until then, let's keep looking."

Hours passed and still they found nothing. Adding to the dilemma was the interior of Drumindor itself, which was a maze of corridors, archways, and bridges. Often they could see where they wanted to go but did not know how to get there. When they arrived, they discovered it was not what they expected and had to backtrack. Luck remained on their side, however, as they saw precious few people. They spotted only a handful of workers and even fewer guards. All of them were easily avoided. The sunshine passing through the skylights shone with the brilliance of midday, then passed to evening, and they still had not found their goal.

Finally, they headed for the bottom of the tower.

It was their last resort, as the Drumindor defensive garrison fortified the first three floors. Approximately forty soldiers guarded the base, and they had a reputation for their harsh treatment of intruders. Still, whatever Merrick did, he most likely did to the mechanism that controlled the lava's release. Descending yet another winding staircase they paused in a sheltered alcove just outside a large chamber. Peering in, they saw it was similar to an interior courtyard, or a theater, with four gallery balconies ringing it with pillared archways stacked one upon another.

"There." Royce pointed to an opening in the room below that radiated a yellow glow. "It has to be in there."

They crept down the stairs to the bottom. Elaborate square-cut designs of inlaid bronze and quartz lined the tiled floor. It picked up the glow coming from the open doorway on the far side. The air warmed dramatically as hot gusts of sulfur-laced air blew in their faces.

"This has to be it," Royce whispered.

They looked up at the stacked galleries of arched openings circling the walls above them and slowly, carefully stepped forward together, crossing the shimmering tile, heading for the glowing doorway.

"Halt!" The command echoed through the chamber the moment they reached the center of the room. "Lie face down, arms and legs spread."

They hesitated.

Twenty archers appeared, moving out from behind the pillars of the galleries with stretched bows aimed down on Royce and Hadrian from three sides. Pikemen entered the hall in an orderly march, boot heels clicking on the tile. They spread out, forming two lines. A dozen more armored men issued down the side corridor from the second-story gallery and proceeded in two-by-two formation to the bottom of the stairs, fanning out to block any retreat back the way they had come.

"Now, lie on your bellies, or we will cut you down where you stand."

"We're not here to cause trouble, we're here—" Hadrian's words were cut short as an arrow hissed through the air and glinted off the stone less than a foot from them.

"Now!" the voice shouted.

They laid down.

The moment they did, troops from in front and behind entered, pinning them and stripping them of their weapons.

"You have to listen to us. There's an invasion coming—"

"We've heard all about your phantom armada, Mister Blackwater, and you can give up that charade."

"It's real! They will be here tonight, and if you don't fix the tower, all of Delgos will be taken!"

"Bind them!"

They brought forth chains, tongs, and a brazier. Smiths arrived and went to work hammering manacles onto their wrists and legs.

"Listen to me!" Hadrian shouted. "At least check the pressure-release controls, see if something is wrong."

There was no reply except the smith's hammer pounding the manacles closed.

"What is the harm in checking?" Hadrian went on. "If I am wrong, what does it matter? If I am right and you don't even look, you're sealing the fate of the Delgos Republic. Just humor me. If nothing else, it will shut me up."

"Slitting your throat will do that, too," the voice said. "But I will send a worker if you two come quietly without resistance."

Hadrian was not certain what kind of resistance he expected them to give as the smith finished attaching another chain to his legs, but nodded anyway.

He gave the order and the guards pulled them to their feet. It was hard navigating stairs with hobbled legs. Hadrian nearly fell more than once, but soon they reached the main gate at the bottom of the fortress.

The gigantic doors of stone soundlessly swept open. Outside, the late-afternoon sun revealed a contingent of port soldiers waiting. The commander of the fortress guard stepped forward and spoke quietly with the Port Authority Captain for some time.

"You don't think these guys are always waiting out here, do you?" Hadrian whispered to Royce. "We've been set up, haven't we?"

"It didn't tip you off when they called you by name?"

"Merrick?"

"Who else."

"That's a bit farfetched. How could he possibly expect us to be here? We didn't even know we would be here. He can't be that smart."

"He is."

A runner appeared, trotting up from the bottom of the tower and reported to the commander with a sharp salute.

"Well?" the fortress commander asked.

THE HARVEST MOON

The runner shook his head. "There is no problem with the pressure-release control—everything checked out fine."

"Take them away," the commander ordered.

The Tur Del Fur City Prison and Workhouse sat back, hidden on a hillside away from the dock, the shops, and the trades. It appeared as little more than a large, stone box at the end of Avan Boulevard with few windows and a spiked iron fence. Hadrian and Royce both knew it by reputation. Most offenders typically died within the first week due to execution, suicide, or brutality. The magistrate's role was merely to determine the manner of execution. Parole was not an option. Only those known to be serious threats came here. Petty thieves, drunks, and malcontents went to the more popular and lenient Portside Jail. For those in Tur Del Fur Prison, this was the end of the road, literally as well as figuratively.

Royce and Hadrian hung by their wrists with their ankles chained to the wall of cell number three, where they had spent the last few hours. The room was smaller than those in Calis. There was no window, stool, nor pot—not even straw. It was a small, stone closet with a single metal door. The only light came from the gap between the door and the frame.

"You're awfully quiet," Hadrian said to the darkness.

"I'm trying to figure this out," Royce replied.

"Figure it out?" Hadrian laughed even though his arms and wrists burned like fire from the metal cutting into his skin. "We're hanging chained to a wall waiting execution, Royce. There's not that much to it."

"Not *that*. I want to know why we didn't find anything wrong with the spouts."

"Because there's a million levers and switches in there and we were looking for just one?"

"I don't think so. When we got to the bridge what was it you said? You said you didn't think anyone except I could scale that fortress. I think you're right. I know Merrick couldn't. He's a genius, not an elf. I always outdid him when it came to anything physical."

"So?"

"So, a thought has been nagging me since they brought us here. How could Merrick get into Drumindor to sabotage it?"

"He figured another way in."

"We spent weeks trying to do that, remember?"

"Maybe he bribed someone on the inside, or maybe he paid someone to break in."

"Who?" Royce thought a minute. "This is too important to trust to someone who *might* be able to do it—he would need someone he *knew* could do it."

"But how do you know someone can do something until they've actually—" Hadrian stopped himself as the realization hit. "Oh, that's not good."

"Throughout this whole thing we've been following two letters, both written by Merrick. The first we thought was intercepted and delivered to Alric, but what if it was *intentionally* sent to him? Everyone knows we work for Melengar."

"Which led us to the *Emerald Storm*," Hadrian said.

"Right. Where we got the next letter—the one to be delivered to that crazy Tenkin in the jungle, and it just happened to mention that Drumindor was set to blow."

"I'm not liking where this is heading," Hadrian muttered.

"And what if Merrick knew about the master gear?"

"That's impossible. Gravis is dead. Crushed, as I recall, under one of those big gears."

"Yes. *He* is dead, but Lord Byron isn't. He probably boasted about how he saved Drumindor by hiring two no-account thieves."

"It still seems too perfect," Hadrian tried to convince himself. "In retrospect, sure, it sounds like the pieces fall into place, but there are too many things that could have gone wrong along the way."

"Right. That's why he had someone on board the *Storm* making sure it all worked—Derning. Did you see the way he took off the moment we hit dock? He knew what was coming and wanted to get away."

"I should have let you kill him."

Silence.

"You're nodding, aren't you?"

"I didn't say a word."

"Bastard," Hadrian grumbled.

"You know the worst thing?"

"I've got a pretty long list of *bad* things right now, and I'm not sure which one I would put on top. So I'll bite."

"We did exactly what Merrick *couldn't* do himself. He used us to disarm Drumindor."

"So he never sabotaged anything? That would explain why Gile laughed when I told him Drumindor was going to explode. He knew it wasn't. Merrick promised he would have it intact. Merrick's a bloody genius."

"I think I mentioned that once or twice."

"So now what?" Hadrian asked.

"Now nothing. He's beaten us. He's sitting somewhere with a warm cup of cider smiling smugly with his feet up on the pile of money he's just been paid."

"We have to warn them to re-engage the master gear."

"Go ahead."

Hadrian began shouting until the little observation door opened, flooding the cell with light.

"We need to speak to someone. It's important."

"What is it?"

"We realized the mistake we made. We were tricked. You need to tell the commander at Drumindor that we locked the master gear. We can show him where it is and how to release it.

"You two never stop, do you? I'm not sure if you're really saboteurs or just plain nuts. One thing's for certain, we're going to find out how you got in, and then we're going to kill you."

The observation door closed, casting them back into darkness.

"That worked out really well," Royce said. "Feel better now?"

"Bastard."

Chapter 24

THE ESCAPE

Arista stayed in the corner of the stable, wrapped in Hilfred's arms most of the night. He stroked her hair, and from time to time without any particular reason, kissed her passionately. It felt safe, and lying there Arista realized two things. First, she was certain she could be content remaining in his arms forever. And second, she was not in love with Hilfred.

He was a good friend, a piece of home she missed so dearly that she drank him in with a desert-born thirst, but something was missing. She thought it strange that she came to this conclusion while in his arms. Yet she knew it with perfect clarity. She did not love Hilfred and she had not loved Emery. Hilfred was the big brother she had grown up with, and Emery she had barely known. She was not even certain what love was, what it should feel like, or if it existed at all.

Noblewomen rarely knew the men they married before their wedding day. Perhaps they grew to love their husbands in time, or merely grew to believe they did. At least she knew Hilfred loved her. He loved enough for both of them. She could feel it radiating off him like warmth from smoldering coals. He deserved happiness after so long, after so much sacrifice; she would make it up to him. She would return to Melengar and marry him. She would make him Archduke Reuben Hilfred. She laughed softly at the thought.

"What?"

"I just remembered your first name is Reuben."

Hilfred laughed then pointed to his face. "I look like this, and you're making fun of my *name*?"

She took his face in her hands. "I wish you wouldn't do that. I think you're beautiful."

He kissed her again.

Periodically, Hilfred would peek out at the sky and check the position of the moon. Eventually he returned and said, "It's time."

She nodded and once more Arista transformed into the morose visage of the Regent Saldur.

"I still can't believe it," Hilfred told her.

"I know. I'm really starting to get the hang of this. Care to kiss me again?" she asked, and laughed at his expression. "Now remember, don't do anything. The idea is to just walk in and walk out. No fighting, understand?"

Hilfred nodded.

They stepped out of the stable. As they did, Arista looked up at Modina's window. It was dark, but she was certain she saw her figure sitting framed within it. Once again she recalled her final words, and regretted not asking her to come. Maybe she would have refused, but now it was too late. Arista wished she had at least asked.

Nipper came out of the kitchens, yawning and carrying two empty water buckets. He stopped short, surprised to see them.

She ignored him and headed directly to the tower.

Just as before, the Seret Knight stood at attention in the center of the room, his face hidden, his shoulders back, the jeweled sword at his side.

"I am going to see Degan Gaunt. Open up."

THE ESCAPE

The guard drew his sword.

There was a brief moment of terror when Arista's heart pounded so loudly she thought the seret might hear. She glanced at Hilfred and saw him flinch, his hand approaching his own weapon. Then the knight bent on one knee and lightly tapped the stone floor with the pommel. The stones immediately slid away, revealing a stair curving into the darkness.

"Shall I come with you, Your Grace?"

Arista considered this. She had no idea what was down there. It could be one cell or a maze of corridors. It might take her a long time to discover where Gaunt was. Just outside, she heard Nipper filling his buckets; the castle was already waking up.

"Yes, of course. Lead the way."

"As you wish, Your Grace." The knight pulled a torch from the wall and descended the steps.

It was dark inside. The stair was narrow and oppressive. Ahead, she could hear the sounds of faint weeping. The same heavy stones that made up the base of the tower formed the dungeon. Here, however, decorations adorned the walls. Nothing recognizable, merely abstract designs carved everywhere. Arista felt she had seen them before, not these exactly, but similar ones.

Then she felt it.

Like the snap of a twig or the crack of an egg, a tremor passed through her body—a sudden disconcerting break.

She looked down. The old man's hands were gone and she was seeing her own fingers and sleeves revealed in the flickering torchlight.

With his back turned, the knight continued to escort them. As he reached the bottom of the stairs he began to turn, saying, "Your Grace, I—"

Before he was fully around, Hilfred shoved her aside.

He drew his sword just as the knight's eyes widened. Driving his blade at the man's chest, the black armor turned the tip. It skipped off, penetrating the gap between the chest plate and the right pauldron, piercing the man's shoulder.

The knight cried out.

Hilfred withdrew his sword. The knight staggered backward, struggling to draw his own. Hilfred swung at the knight's neck. Blood exploded, spraying both of them. The seret made no further noise as he crumpled and fell.

"What happened?" Hilfred asked, picking up the torch.

"The walls," she said, touching the chiseled symbols, "They have runes on them like in Gutaria Prison. I can't do magic in here. Do you think anyone heard that?"

"I'm sure the kid fetching water did," he said. "Will he do anything?"

"I don't know. We should close the door," Arista said, picking up the sword with the emerald and looking up the long staircase at the patch of light at the top. What they covered so casually minutes ago now appeared so far—so dangerous. "I'll do it. You find Gaunt."

"No. I won't leave your side. There could be more guards. Forget the door, we'll find him together and get out of here." He took her left hand and pulled her along. Her right hand held onto the sword.

The hallways were narrow stone corridors without any light, except what came from the torch they held. The ceiling arched to a peak not more than a foot above Arista's head, forcing Hilfred to stoop. Wooden doors began appearing on either side, so short they looked more like livestock gates.

"Gaunt!" Hilfred yelled.

"Degan Gaunt!" Arista shouted.

They ran down the darkened passageways pounding on doors, calling his name, and peering inside. The hallway ended at a T-intersection. With only one torch, there was no option to spilt up, even if Hilfred could be convinced. They turned right and pressed on, finding more doors.

"Degan Gaunt!"

"Stop!" Arista stopped suddenly.

"Wha—"

"Shush!"

Very faintly—"Here!"

They trotted down the next corridor, but reached a dead end.

"This place is a maze," Arista said.

They ran back, and took another turn. They called again.

"Here! I'm here!" Came the reply, louder now.

Running once more they again met a solid wall. They retraced their steps, found another corridor that appeared to go in the right direction and followed it as far as the hallway allowed.

"Degan!" she cried.

"Over here!"

It was coming from the last door in the block.

When they reached it, Arista bent down and held up the torch. In the tiny grated window, she saw a pair of eyes. She grabbed the door handle and pulled—locked. She tried the gemstone but nothing happened.

"Damn it!" she cried. "The guard, he must have the key. Oh, how could I be so stupid? I should have searched him before we ran off."

Hilfred hammered the wooden door with his sword. The hard oak, nearly as solid as stone, gave up only sliver-size chips.

"We'll never get the door open this way. Your sword isn't doing anything! We have to go back for the keys."

Hilfred continued to strike the door.

"We'll be back, Degan!" Arista said before starting back down the hall carrying the torch.

"Arista!" Hilfred shouted as he chased after her.

They rounded the corridors, turning left then right and then—

"Arista, my dear! What a surprise," Saldur greeted her as they nearly ran into the regent. Around him were five Seret Knights with swords drawn and torches held high.

Hilfred pushed Arista back. "Run!" he told her.

Saldur laughed. "There is nowhere to run to, dear boy. You're both quite trapped."

Saldur, his hair loose and wild, wore a white linen nightgown over which he had pulled a red silk robe that he was still in the midst of tying about his waist. "You've been very clever, Arista, but you've always been a clever girl, haven't you? Always poking your nose into places you shouldn't.

"And you, Hilfred, reunited with your princess once more, I see. It is a wonderfully gallant gesture to defend her with your life, but it is also futile, and where is the honor in futility? There is no other exit from this dungeon. These men are Seret Knights, highly skilled, brutally trained soldiers who will kill you if you resist."

Saldur took the torch from the lead seret, who now also drew a dagger. "You have wasted half your life protecting this foolish girl, whose stupidity and rash choices have dragged you through torment and fire. Put down your sword and back away."

Hilfred checked his grip and planted his feet.

"When I was fifteen, you told me I would die if I tried to save her. That night I ran into an inferno of smoke and flame. If I didn't listen to you then, what makes you think I will now?"

Saldur sighed. "Don't make them kill you."

Hilfred stood his ground.

"Stop, please. I beg you!" Arista shouted. "Sauly, I'll do anything you ask. Please, just let him go."

"Persuade him to put down his sword and I will."

"Hilfred—"

"Not even if you order me to," his voice grave. "There is no power in Elan capable of making me walk away from you—not now, not ever again."

"Hilfred…" she whispered as tears fell.

He glanced at her. In that moment of inattention, the seret saw an opening and slashed. Hilfred dodged.

Swords clashed.

"NO!" Arista cried.

Hilfred swung for the throat again, but the knight ducked. Hilfred's blade struck the wall, kicking up sparks. The knight stabbed him in the side. Hilfred gasped and staggered but managed to lunge and thrust his sword at the knight's chest. Again the point of the blade deflected off the black armor, but this time he was not fortunate enough to connect.

Arista watched as a second knight lunged, driving his sword through Hilfred's stomach. The sword pierced his body, pushing out the back of his tunic.

"No! NO!" she screamed, falling against the wall as her knees threatened to buckle.

With blood spilling from his lips, Hilfred struggled to raise his sword again. The foremost knight brought his own blade down, severing Hilfred's arm at the elbow in a burst of warm blood that splashed across Arista's face.

Hilfred collapsed to his knees. His body hitched.

"A—Aris…" he sputtered.

"Oh, Hilfred…" Arista whispered as her eyes burned.

The knights stood over him. One raised his sword.

"ARISTA!" he cried.

The knight's sword came down.

Arista collapsed as if the blade pierced them both. She slumped to the floor. She could not speak. She could not breathe. Her eyes locked on the dead body of Hilfred as a warm wetness pooling across the stone floor crept between her fingers.

"Hilfred," she mouthed the word. She had no breath left to speak it.

Saldur sighed. "Get him out of here."

"What about her?"

"They went through so much trouble to get in, let's find her a nice permanent room."

Chapter 25

INVASION

Wy hat do you think is going to happen?" Hadrian asked Royce as they sat in the dark.

"The fleet will come in and there will be no pressure to fire the spouts. The Ghazel will land without opposition and slaughter everyone. Eventually they'll reach here, break in, and butcher us."

"No," Hadrian said, shaking his head. "See, that's where you're wrong. The Ghazel will eat us alive, and they'll take their time savoring every moment. Trust me."

They hung in silence.

"What time do you think it is?" Hadrian asked.

"Close to sunset. It was pretty late when they brought us in."

Silence.

They could hear the random movements of guards on the other side of the door, muffled conversation, the slide of a chair, occasional laughter.

"Why does this always happen?" Royce asked. "Why are we always hanging on a wall waiting to die by slow vivisection? I just want to point out that this was your idea—*again.*"

"I've been waiting for that. But, I believe I told you not to come." Hadrian shifted in his chains and sighed. "I don't suppose there's much chance of a beautiful princess coming in here and saving us again."

"That card's been dealt."

"I wish I had met Gaunt," Hadrian said at length. "It would have been nice to actually meet the man, you know? My whole life was fated to protect this guy and I never even saw him."

They were quiet for a time then Royce pursed his lips and made a *hmm* sound.

"What?"

"Huh? Oh—nothing."

"You're thinking something, what is it?"

"Just interesting that you thought Arista was beautiful."

"Don't you?"

"She's okay."

"You're blinded by Gwen."

Hadrian heard Royce sigh. There was a silence then he said, "She already named our children. Elias if we had a boy—or was it Sterling, I forget—and Mercedes if a girl. She even took up knitting and made me a scarf."

"For what it's worth, I'm sorry I dragged you into this."

"She wanted me to go, remember? She said I had to protect you. I had to save your life."

Hadrian looked over at him. "Good job."

Chairs moved in the outer office, footsteps, a door banged, agitated voices. Hadrian caught snippets of the conversation.

"…black sails…a dark cloud on the ocean…"

"No, someone else…"

A chair turned over and hit the floor. More hurried footsteps. Silence.

"Sounds like the fleet is in." Hadrian waited, watching the door to their cell. "They left us for dead, didn't they? We told them this would happen. We came all this way to try and save them. You'd think they'd have the decency to let us out when they saw we were right."

"Probably think we're behind it. We're lucky they didn't just kill us."

"Not sure that's lucky. A nice, quick decapitation is kind of appealing right now."

"How long do you think before the Ba Ran find us?" Royce asked.

"You in a hurry?"

"Yeah, actually. If I have to be eaten, I would sort of like to get it over with."

Hadrian heard the sound of breaking glass.

"Ah, well that didn't take long, did it?" Royce muttered miserably.

Footsteps shuffled in the outer room, a pause then the steps started again, coming closer. There were sounds of a struggle and a muffled cry. Hadrian braced himself and watched the door as it opened. What stood in the doorway shocked him.

"You boys ready to go?" Derning asked.

"What are *you* doing here?" They both said in unison.

"Would you prefer me to leave?" Derning smiled. Noticing the riveted manacles, he grimaced. "Thorough buggers, aren't they? Hang on. I saw some tools out here."

Royce and Hadrian looked at each other, bewildered.

"Okay, so he's not a beautiful princess. But it works for me."

There was some slamming and an "Ah-hah!" Then Derning returned with a hammer and a chisel.

"The Ghazel fleet arrived and Drumindor isn't working, but it didn't blow up either, so I guess we have you to thank for that," Derning told them as he went to work on the manacle pins.

"Don't mention it. And I'm not just saying that. I really mean... don't mention it," Hadrian said with a wince.

"Now, half the folks—the smart half—are running, the others are going to try to fight. That means we don't have much time to get out of here. I have horses and provisions waiting just outside town. We'll take the mountain road north. I'll ride with you as far as Maranon and then I'll be going my own way."

"But I still don't get why you're here." Royce said as Derning finished with one of the metal bracelets. "Don't you work for Merrick?"

"Merrick Marius?" Derning laughed. "That's funny. Grady and I were convinced you two worked for Marius." Derning finished cracking open the manacles on Royce then turned to Hadrian. "We work for Cornelius DeLur. Imagine my surprise yesterday when I checked in and found out you worked for Melengar. DeLur got a big kick out that. The old fat man has a sick sense of humor sometimes."

"I'm confused. Why were you on the *Storm*?"

"When the Diamond found that message from Merrick, Cosmos thought it important enough to relay to Daddy, and Cornelius sent us. Grady and I started as sailors and are still well-known on the Sharon. We were so sure Royce killed Drew, which is why we thought you two were mixed up with Merrick. We thought it had something to do with that horn comment that Drew made."

"Defoe—I mean Bernie killed him," Royce said simply.

"Yeah, we figured that out. And, of course, that horn thing had nothing to do with Merrick. That was all Thranic's group. When we heard you had been arrested, it wasn't too hard to find ya."

He finished freeing Hadrian, who rubbed his wrists.

INVASION

"Come on, most of your gear is out here." He pulled Alverstone out of his belt and handed it to Royce. "Took this off one of the guards. I think he thought it was pretty."

Outside their cell the tiny jail office was empty except for two guards. One looked dead but the other might have just been unconscious. They found their possessions in a series of boxes set aside in a room filled with all manner of impounded items.

Outside, dawn rose and people were running with bundles in their arms. Mothers held crying children to their breasts. Men struggled to push overfilled carts uphill. Down in the harbor they could see a forest of dark masts. Drumindor stood a mute witness to the sacking of the city.

Derning led them up refugee-choked streets. Fights broke out. Roads were blocked, and finally Derning resorted to the roofs. They scaled balconies and leapt alleys, trotting across the clay-tiled housetops until they cleared the congestion. They dropped back to the street and were soon at the city's eastern gate. Hundreds of people were rushing by with carts and donkeys, women and children mostly, traveling with boys and old men.

Derning stood just outside the gates looking worried. He whistled and a bird call answered in response. He led them off the road and up an embankment.

"Sorry, Jacob," said a spindly youth, emerging with four horses. "I figured it was best to wait out of sight. If anyone saw me with these, I wouldn't keep them for long."

From the crest of the hill they could see the bay far below. Smoke rose thickly from the buildings closest to the water.

"We weren't able to stop it," Derning said, looking at the refugees fleeing the city, "but, between you defusing the explosion and my reporting to Cornelius so he could raise the alarm, it looks like we saved a lot of lives."

The Emerald Storm

They mounted up and Hadrian took one last look at Tur Del Fur as the flames, fanned by the morning's sea breeze, swept through the streets below.

Chapter 26

PAYMENT

M errick entered the Great Hall of the Imperial Palace of Aquesta. Servants were hanging Wintertide decorations, which should have given the room a festive feel, but to Merrick it was still just a dreary chamber with too much stone and too little sunlight. He never cared for Aquesta, and regretted that it would be the capital of the New Empire—an empire whose security he had ensured. He would have preferred Colnora. At least it had glass streetlamps.

"Ah! Merrick," Ethelred greeted him. The regents, Earl Ballentyne, and the chancellor were all gathered around the great table. "Or should I call you Lord Marius?"

"You should indeed," Merrick replied.

"You bring good news then?"

"The best, Your Lordship—Delgos has fallen."

"Excellent!" Ethelred applauded.

Merrick reached the table and pulled off his gloves, one finger at a time. "The Ghazel invaded Tur Del Fur five days ago, meeting only a weak resistance. They took Drumindor and burned much of the port city."

"And the Nationalist Army?" Ethelred asked, sitting down comfortably in his chair with a smile stretching across his broad face.

"As expected, the army packed up and went south the moment they heard. Most have family in Delgos. You can retake Ratibor at will. You won't even need the army, a few hundred men will do. Breckton can turn his attention north to Melengar and begin plans for the spring invasion of Trent."

"Excellent! Excellent!" Ethelred cheered. Saldur and the chancellor joined in his applause, granting each other smiles of relief and pleasure.

"What happens when the Ghazel finish with Delgos and decide to march north?" the Earl of Chadwick asked. Seated at the far end of the table, he did not appear to share his companions' gaiety. "I'm told there's quite a lot of them and hear they're fearsome fighters. If they can destroy Delgos, what assurance do we have they won't attack us?"

"I am certain the Nationalists will halt their ambitions in the short term, milord," Merrick replied. "But even if not, we face no threat from the Ba Ran Ghazel. They are a superstitious lot and expect some sort of world-ending catastrophe to beset them shortly. They want Drumindor as a refuge, not as a base for launching attacks. This will buy the time you need to take Melengar, Trent, and possibly even western Calis. By then the Empire will be supreme and the Nationalists a memory. The remaining residents of Delgos, those once-independent merchant barons, will beg for Imperial intervention against the Ghazel and eagerly submit to your absolute rule. The empire of old will be reforged."

The earl scowled and sat back down.

"You are indeed a marvel and deserving of your new title and station, Lord Marius."

PAYMENT

"Because you already have Gaunt and Esrahaddon is dead, I believe that finishes my employment obligations."

"For now," Ethelred told him. "I won't let a man of your talents get away that easily. Now that I have found you, I want you in my court. I will make it worth your loyalty."

"Actually, I already spoke with His Grace about the position of Magistrate of Colnora."

"Magistrate, eh? Want your own city, do you? I like the idea. Think you can keep the Diamond under your thumb? I suppose you could—certainly, why not? Consider it done, Lord Magistrate, but I insist you do not take your post until after Wintertide. I want you here for the festivities."

"Ethelred is getting married and crowned emperor," Saldur explained. "The Patriarch will be coming to perform the ceremony himself and, if that's not enough, we will be burning a famous witch."

"I wouldn't miss it."

"Excellent!" Ethelred grinned. "I trust accommodations in the city are to your liking? If not, tell the chamberlain and he'll find a more suitable estate."

"The house is perfect. You are too kind, my lord."

"I still don't see why you don't simply stay in the palace."

"It is easier for me to do business if I am not seen here too frequently. And now, if you'll forgive me, I must—"

"You aren't leaving?" Ethelred asked, disappointed. "You just got here. With news like this we have to celebrate. Don't doom me to merrymaking with the likes of an old cleric and a melancholy earl. I'll call for wines and beef. We'll get some entertainment, music, dancers, and women. How do you like your women, Marius? Thin or plump, light or dark, saucy or docile? I assure you, the lord chamberlain can fill any order."

"Alas, my lord, I have some remaining business to which I must attend."

Ethelred frowned. "Very well, but you must show up for Wintertide. I insist."

"Of course, my lord."

Merrick left while the Imperial rulers exchanged congratulatory accolades. Outside a new carriage waited, complete with four white horses and a uniformed driver. On the seat rested the package from the city constable. Merrick had offered brandy in trade and the constable leapt at the opportunity. A bottle of fine liquor in return for the worthless remnants of the defunct witch-hunt was the sort of good fortune that the sheriff was unaccustomed to receiving. Unwrapping it, Merrick ran his fingers over the shimmering material of the robe.

The carriage traveled up The Hill and turned on Heath Street, one of the more affluent neighborhoods in the city. The homes, though not terribly large, were tasteful and elegant. A servant waited dutifully to remove his cloak and boots while another stood by with a warm cup of cider. Merrick never drank wine, ale, or spirits and was amused to see this accommodation taken into account. He sat in the drawing room surrounded by burgundy furnishings and dark wood paneling, sipping his drink and listening to the pop of the fireplace.

A knock sounded at the door. He nearly rose to answer when he spotted one of his new servants trotting to the foyer.

"Where is she, Merrick?" he heard an angry voice shout.

A moment later the valet led two men into the drawing room.

"Please have a seat, both of you." Merrick reclined in his soft chair, warming his hands with his cup. "Would either of you care for a drink before we conduct business? My servants can bring you whatever you like, but I must say the cider is especially good."

"I said, where is she?"

PAYMENT

"Relax, Mister Deminthal, your daughter is fine and I'll bring her down shortly. You fulfilled your end of the bargain brilliantly, and I always honor my commitments. I merely wish to go over a few details. Only a formality, I assure you. First, let me congratulate you, Wyatt. May I call you Wyatt? You've done an excellent job. Poe's report gave you extremely high marks.

"He tells me you were instrumental in getting Royce and Hadrian on board, and even after the unexpected sinking of the *Emerald Storm*, your quick thinking saved the ship's orders and the mission. I'm especially impressed by how you won over Royce's trust—no small feat, I might add. You must be a very convincing fellow, as demonstrated by how you persuaded the Port Authority that Royce and Hadrian were in Tur Del Fur to destroy Drumindor. I'm convinced it is only by your skill and intelligence that the operation was such a wonderful success."

Merrick took a sip from his cider and sat back with a grin. "I have just one question. Do you know where Royce and Hadrian are now?"

"Dead. By the Ghazel or the Tur Del Fur officials, whoever got them first."

"Hmm, I doubt that. Royce is not easy to kill. He has gotten out of much more difficult situations before. I would say he leads a charmed life, but I know all too well what kind of life he's lived. Still, I wouldn't even trust Death to bind him long."

"I want my daughter—now," Wyatt said quietly through clenched teeth.

"Of course, of course. Mister Poe, would you be so kind as to run up and bring her down, third door on the left." Merrick handed him a key. "Seriously, Wyatt, you are a very capable man. I could use you."

"Do you think I *liked* doing this? How many hundreds of people are dead because of me?"

"Don't think of it that way. Think of it as a job, an assignment, which you performed with panache. I don't see talent such as yours often, and I could find other use of your skills. Join with me and you'll be well compensated. I am working on another project now, for an even more lucrative employer, and I am in a position to make a great many good things happen for you. You and your daughter can live like landed gentry. How would you like your own estate?"

"You kidnapped my daughter. The only business I'm interested in doing with you is arranging your death."

"Don't be so dramatic. Ah, see, here she is now. Safe and sound."

Poe escorted a little girl down the steps. Around ten years old, her light-brown hair was tied in a bow and she wore an elegantly tailored blue dress with fine leather shoes.

"Daddy!" she shouted.

Wyatt rushed over, throwing his arms around her. "Did they hurt you, honey?"

"No, I'm okay. They bought me this pretty dress and got me these shoes! And we played games."

"That's good, honey." Turning to Merrick, Wyatt asked, "What about Elden?"

"He's fine, still in Colnora. Waiting for you, I presume. Wyatt, you really need to consider my offer, if for no other reason than your own safety."

Wyatt spun on him. "I did your job! You sat there and told me I did it *brilliantly!* Why are you still threatening us?"

Merrick looked at the girl. "Poe, take Allie in the kitchen. I think there are some cookies she might like."

Wyatt held her to him.

"Don't worry, she'll be right back."

"Do you like cookies?" Poe asked her. The little girl grinned, bobbing her head. She looked up at her father.

PAYMENT

Wyatt nodded. "It's okay, go ahead. Hurry back, honey."

Poe and Allie left the room hand in hand.

"I'm not threatening you. As I already said, I'm very pleased with your skills. I am merely trying to protect you. Consider for a moment, what if Royce is not dead? He'll put two and two together, if he hasn't already. You should be afraid of what he'll do to you—and your daughter. Royce will probably kill Allie first and make you watch."

"He's not like that."

Merrick released a small chuckle. "Oh, sir, you have no idea what Royce is like. I will grant you his association with Hadrian Blackwater has tempered him greatly. Twelve years with that idealistic dreamer has made him practically human, but I *know* him. I know what lurks beneath. I have seen things that make even my hardened heart shudder. Get his anger up, and you'll unleash a demon that no one can control. Believe me, he is *like that* and so much more. Nothing is beyond him."

Allie returned with a handful of sugar cookies. Taking her hand, Wyatt headed for the door. He paused at the threshold and looked back. "Merrick, if what you say about Royce is true, then shouldn't *you* be the one who's afraid?" Wyatt walked out, closing the door behind him.

Merrick sipped his cider again, but it had gone cold.

THE RIYRIA REVELATIONS

If you enjoyed this novel, you will be happy to learn that...

The Emerald Storm is the fourth in a six-book series entitled The Riyria Revelations. This saga is neither a string of sequels nor a lengthy work unnaturally divided. Instead, The Riyria Revelations was conceived as a single epic tale told through six individual episodes. While a book might hint at building mysteries or thickening plots, these threads are not essential to reach a satisfying conclusion to the current episode—which has its own beginning, middle, and end.

Eschewing the recent trends in fantasy toward the lengthy, gritty, and dark, The Riyria Revelations brings the genre back to its roots. Avoiding unnecessarily complicated language and world building for its own sake, this series is a distillation of the best elements of traditional fantasy—great characters, a complex plot, humor, and drama all in appropriate measures.

While written for an adult audience, The Riyria Revelations lacks sex, excessive violence, and profanity, making it appropriate for readers thirteen and older.

Books in the Riyria Revelations

The Crown Conspiracy

Avempartha

Nyphron Rising

The Emerald Storm

Wintertide

Percepliquis

About the Author

Born in Detroit, Michigan, Michael J. Sullivan was raised in Novi. He has also lived in Vermont, North Carolina, and Virginia. He worked as a commercial artist and illustrator, founding his own advertising agency in 1996, which he closed in 2005 to pursue writing fulltime. His first published novel, The Crown Conspiracy was released in October 2008 and sold out its first printing in December 2009. He currently resides in Fairfax, Virginia with his wife and three children.

Awards for Riyria Books

2010 Foreword Magazine Book of the Year Finalist (Avempartha)
2010 Foreword Magazine Book of the Year Finalist (Nyphron Rising)
2009 Book Spot Central Tournament of Books Finalist (Avempartha)
2009 Dark Wolf Award for Top 10 Fantasy Books (Riyria Revelations)
2009 National Indie Excellence Award Finalist (Crown Conspiracy)
2008 ReaderViews Literary Award Finalist (Crown Conspiracy)
2007 Foreword Magazine Book of the Year Finalist (Crown Conspiracy)

Fantasy Sites Recognition

Named Anticipated Releases of 2010—Fantasy Book Critic
Named one of the Notable Fantasy Books of 2009—Fantasy Book Critic
Named one of the top 5 Fantasy Books of 2009—Dark Wolf's Fantasy Reviews
Named a Notable Indie of 2008—Fantasy Book Critic

Websites

Author's Homepage: www.michaelsullivan-author.com
Author's Blog: www.riyria.blogspot.com

Contact

Twitter: twitter.com/author_sullivan
Email: michael.sullivan.dc@gmail.com

WITHDRAWN

8970359R0

Made in the USA
Lexington, KY
20 March 2011